W9-ARS-442

IAQ

3.00

More Praise for Barbara Riefe

"In the gifted hands of Barbara Riefe, the ancient nations
of the eastern forests come vividly to life. It will draw you
into a breathtaking world you never knew existed."
—Richard S. Wheeler,
award-winning author of *Badlands*

"SUPERB NOVEL and a classy example of the 'Eastern
Western.' I especially like Riefe's crackling dialogue, especially that between Margaret Addison and Two Eagles.
The Iroquois lore is wonderful stuff: patching the canoe
with the stomach fat from a slain trapper, making canoes,
wilderness Indian medicine, folkways of the Oneidas, and
making fire. *The Woman Who Fell From The Sky* is filled

"

his

$3.00

Forge books by Barbara Riefe
For Love of Two Eagles
Mohawk Woman
The Woman Who Fell from the Sky

BARBARA RIEFE

FOR LOVE OF TWO EAGLES

A TOM DOHERTY ASSOCIATES BOOK
NEW YORK

This book is fondly dedicated to
Sandy Conzen Stefany

NOTE: If you purchased this book without a cover you should be aware
that this book is stolen property. It was reported as "unsold and destroyed" to the publisher, and neither the author nor the publisher has received any payment for this "stripped book."

This is a work of fiction. All the characters and events portrayed in this
book are fictitious, and any resemblance to real people or events is purely
coincidental.

FOR LOVE OF TWO EAGLES

Copyright © 1995 by Barbara Riefe

All rights reserved, including the right to reproduce this book, or portions
thereof, in any form.

Cover art by Brad Schmehl
Map by Ellisa Mitchell

A Forge Book
Published by Tom Doherty Associates, Inc.
175 Fifth Avenue
New York, NY 10010

Forge® is a registered trademark of Tom Doherty Associates, Inc.

ISBN: 0-812-53660-6
Library of Congress Card Catalog Number: 94-46578

First edition: March 1995
First mass market edition: January 1996

Printed in the United States of America

0 9 8 7 6 5 4 3 2 1

Happy, happy happy pair!
   None but the brave,
   None but the brave,
   None but the brave deserves the fair.

—Chorus, *An Ode in Honor of St. Cecilia's Day*
   John Dryden

CONTENTS

PLACE NAMES

Onneyuttahage—*Oneida castle (village)*
Massowaganine—*Onondaga castle*
Kanawage—*St. Lawrence River*
O-jik'-ha-dä-gé-ga—*the Wide Water—Atlantic Ocean*
Ne-ah'-gä-te-car-ne-o-di—*Lake Ontario*
Onekahoncka—*Mohawk castle nearest the Hudson River*
Tenotoge—*Mohawk castle nearest Onneyuttahage*
Shaw-na-taw-ty—*Hudson River*
Te-ugé-ga—*Mohawk River*
Lake Oneida
Ganawagehas—*Catskill Mountains*
Hochelaga—*Montreal*
Stadacona—*Quebec*

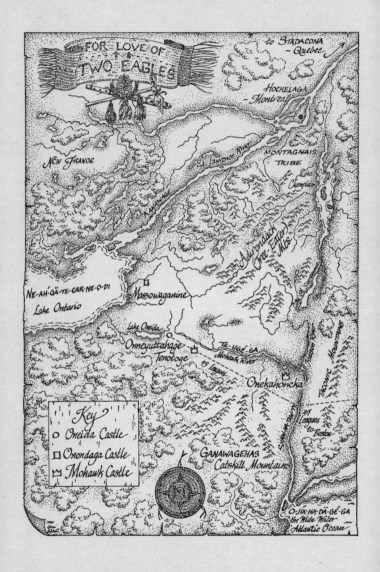

Cast of Characters

Oneidas

Margaret Addison—*wife of Two Eagles*

Tékni-ska-je-a-nah—*Two Eagles, a Pine Tree chief of the Oneidas*

Swift Doe—*Margaret's friend, Two Eagles' younger brother's widow*

Ossivendi Oÿoghi—*Blue Creek, Two Eagles' brother-in-law*

Karístatsi Sateeni—*Iron Dog, Blue Creek's longtime friend*

Ganōda—*Night Song, Blue Creek's onetime beloved who married an Onondagan*

Sa-ga-na-qua-de—*Anger Maker (He-who-makes-everyone-angry), Two Eagles' friend*

Tyagohuens—*Splitting Moon, Two Eagles' best friend*

Graywind—*Two Eagles' deceased wife*

Téklqʔ-èyo—*Eight Minks, who raised Two Eagles and his brothers from childhood*

Bone—*Mohican adoptee, Two Eagles' friend and Swift Doe's second husband*

Sho-non-ses—*His Longhouse, chief of the bear clan*

O-kwen-cha—*Red Paint, Two Eagles' friend*

Sku-nak-su—*Fox, Two Eagles' friend*

Tantanege—*Hare, Swift Doe's oldest son*

Moon Dancer—*go-ga-so-ho-nun-na-tase-ta, Keeper of the False Faces (False Face Society)*

Hat-ya-tone-nent-ha—*He-swallows-his-own-body-from-the-foot, chief of the turtle clan*

O-dat-she-dah—*Carries-a-quiver, chief of the wolf clan*

Sho-deg-wá•shon'—*White Moose, warrior*

Onondagas

Quana Gachga—*Tall Crow, Night Song's husband*
Gä-de-a-yo—*Lobster, Gordon Duncan, wartime white friend of Two Eagles and an Onondaga adoptee*

Mohawks

Joshú-we-agoochsa—*Hole Face, Mohawk sub-chief at Onekahoncka*

In Bedworth and Southampton

Benjamin Addison—*Margaret Addison's father*
Seth Wilson—*"Congregational missionary" employed by Addison*
Joshua Conklin—*first mate of the* Sea Robin

Aboard the *Dauntless*

Evan Box—*ship's master*
Abner Keaton—*emigrant bookseller*
Leonora Keaton—*his wife*
Hannah Keaton—*their daughter*
Reverend McCoy—*Baptist minister*
Enoch Taylor—*passenger*

Montagnais (Iron Axes)

Red Chin—*warrior*
Shot Sky—*chief*

In Boston

Reverend Timothy Allbright—*director of the Colonial Missionary Society*
Reverend Ernest Frame—*Allbright's associate*
Fisk Drummond—*missionary*
Dwight Hopkins—*missionary*

Jonathan Wilby—*missionary*
Sko-sko-wro-wa-neh—*Great Branch, Nipmuc guide*
De-hat-ka-dons—*He-looks-both-ways, Nipmuc guide*
Zachariah Judith—*farmer*
Jeremiah Hurley—*tavern owner*
Herbert Lansdowne—*constable*
Otis Macomber—*chief magistrate*
Dorcas Macomber—*his wife*
Hosea Ready—*master of the* Resolute

league—*three English statue miles*
nyoh—*yes*
neh—*no*

══ **PROLOGUE** ══

Sometime between the end of the Crusades in 1291 and the removal of the papacy from Rome to Avignon by Pope Clement V in 1309, a native tribe began a migration eastward, seeking land where there was good hunting and where they could grow corn, reaching the Mississippi somewhere south of St. Louis. En route they engaged in many battles with tribes already in possession of the land.

Crossing the Mississippi, leaving behind remnants of the tribe along the way, they continued eastward into Kentucky before heading north, until they reached the banks of the St. Lawrence.

In time they were driven from the St. Lawrence by hostile Adirondacks and migrated southward to settle in New York State, where they live to this day.

Their name was formed of two ceremonial words meaning "real adders," to which the French added *ois*.

They are the Iroquois.

I

BLUE CREEK

The last waves of vividly plumaged warblers, elegant tanagers, thrushes and vireos were returning home from beyond the Ganagawehas, the Catskill Mountains. Frogs and salamanders crowded the shallows at the edge of Lake Oneida for their annual mating. Pussy willows filled the headland and the south shore of the lake. On the near shore, fragrant, deep-lavendered orchis brightened the woodland. Maple flowers raised a hazy red canopy over the cove, shadowing the water out to where a man and a woman stood in sunlight.

She was tall, but he was more than a head taller. Her shoulders glowed golden in the sunlight. Her hair—not yet wet—was ash blond and her eyes were the striking blue of harebells. She was pregnant.

His shoulder-length hair was as black as obsidian, his dark brown eyes large and arresting as he gazed fondly at her. His skin was coppery and healed wounds showed on both shoulders and his upper left arm. He exuded extraordinary strength, almost as if its excess seeped from his pores.

His name was Tékni-ska-je-a-nah, Two Eagles; his blood made him an Oneida of the Iroquois, the Five Nations Confederacy. The great golden eagle was his óyaron that counseled and protected him, its tailfeather his medicine. At the moment it lay with his breechclout, leggins, moccasins and knife on a rock onshore.

Her name was Margaret Addison. English born and bred, she had come from her native land less than two years before to join her French husband-by-proxy, a captain of dragoons and aide-de-camp to then Governor-General Frontenac of New France in Quebec. Her ship, sailing from New York City up the Hudson River, had run onto a sandbar and while the crew worked frantically to free it it was attacked, plundered and burned by roving Mohawks. Margaret alone escaped, to be found the next day by Two Eagles and his friends. Eventually she married not her captain of dragoons but Two Eagles.

Now, looking up at her husband, she could tell herself that she loved him today more deeply than she'd ever dreamed she could love any man, even more than the night a year ago when they became husband and wife.

She splashed him. Pushing water with the heels of his hands, he drenched her. She squealed, dove and swam gracefully out of range. He dove, propelled himself underwater, caught her legs and pulled her deep beneath the surface. Wriggling free, she shot upward, gasping, laughing.

"You behave!" she shouted.

When he grabbed her, they rolled in embrace, her swollen belly pressed firmly to him. And in the clear water, girdled by a silver swath of minnows, they kissed, watched by a solitary blue warbler raising his melodic *zwee, zwee, zwee* to the sun. She touched his cheek.

"No one deserves to be this happy, this content."

He kissed her hand. "It is our share, we take it. These times are too few."

He led her toward shore, where she lay down in the shallow water. He set himself above her, nuzzling, kissing her hair and face lightly. Her flesh tingled under his touch, and she pulled him close, pressing her mouth to his.

For some time they lay on their backs, hands clasped, peering up through the foliage to the sun. Neither spoke.

The only sounds were the warbler's reprise and the gentle lapping of water.

They caressed each other, seen only by their serenader and a small red fox that paused to stare briefly, then moved on.

They sat up in the water. She pulled her knees up to her chin, resting her face on her crossed forearms. "My toes are cramped."

He massaged them. When they had relaxed he squeezed the water from her hair and combed it with his fingers. Then he massaged her nape and shoulders. She moaned appreciatively.

He glanced upward through the foliage. The sky descended in an enormous canopy from the high sun. She studied his profile as his eyes were upraised. He had so many praiseworthy qualities, so few bad ones, insignificant, actually. He had no sense of humor and seemed to see humor in others as a sign of weakness. His quick temper could be vicious. His literal-mindedness annoyed her. At times it was all she could do to keep from shaking him. The most trivial subject—whether a certain flower's fragrance was pleasing—could trigger argument. At times he could be as obstinate as a stump, as well as arrogant, smug, cynical.

All these quirks she overlooked. She had no choice; she adored him.

Water spilled from his lean, muscular body in gold threads as he arose and helped her up. They stood as close as her condition permitted, the water lapping their ankles. "Happy?" he asked. The question was unexpected; she could feel her expression say as much. He pointed. "With me?"

"Very. Need you ask?"

He did. He needed periodic reassurance. She thought back to how she had returned from Quebec to spend the rest of her life in the wilderness as his wife. Her adoption into the Oneida tribe had stirred doubt and apprehension. Renouncing civilization, she had tried to acclimate herself

to the primitive life. A daunting challenge. In time, it drew
on self-discipline and patience she never knew she had.
She'd observed life at Onneyuttahage, the Oneida castle,
before setting out for Quebec. But back then, certain that
her stay would be temporary, she'd made no effort to fit
in. The people's thinking, their beliefs, their customs were
of little interest to her. Back then.

Apart from Swift Doe—Two Eagles' brother's widow,
who had become her dearest friend—and his aunt, Eight
Minks, the matriarch of their longhouse—the women of
the tribe viewed her with suspicion, even disapproval.
Many had lost husbands, fathers and sons in the whiteskins' seven years of war; their resentment of her was understandable. The life was arduous, unrelievedly harsh.
The stink of human sweat mingled with the smells of
cooking, animal skins and rotten meat. Dogs yapped endlessly, eye-stinging smoke drifted through the longhouse,
there was the mud in spring, dust and burning heat in summer, bone-freezing cold in winter. Drudgery and boredom
marked daily life in the castle.

Aside from her love for Two Eagles just one other fac-
tor offset all the petty discomforts and inconveniences, the
cruelty and rampant superstition. The Oneida were a
happy people, happier, more content than were the English
or French. Mutual respect and consideration were all-
important in their relationships; they cared deeply about
their own, about each other. Many of their practices were
sound and practical. Children were disciplined solely by
their mothers, so there was no parental difference of opinion over wrong-doing or punishment. If a boy got into
mischief, his mother spoke quietly to him and told him to
mind his ways. If he continued to misbehave she might
throw a dipperful of water in his face. When an older boy
behaved badly, his mother threatened to put him out of the
longhouse, a very serious matter and a punishment seldom
necessary.

The people's diet, their clothing, their social conduct,
superstitions and taboos meant to Margaret, taking off the

dress of civilization and putting on that of a primitive tribe. Struggling, she attempted to make it hang right, look right, fit and feel comfortable.

The Oneida language was difficult, with so many jaw-breaking words and no written forms. Luckily many men who had fought in the war learned English and taught it to their women. As well, Oneida differed only slightly from Mohawk and Onondaga. The Seneca and Cayuga, the two other Iroquois tribes to the west, spoke a language somewhat difficult for the eastern tribes to understand, although that was no impediment to agreement and cooperation among the Five Nations of the confederacy.

Fitting in had been a gradual process. Margaret was still working toward it. In some ways, she was still an outsider, tolerated but not assimilated. By now, at the beginning of her second year, she had taught herself to ignore the hardships of her chosen lot. Still there were beliefs, teachings, ways of doing things she refused to accept. The strangling of the three dogs at the White Dog ceremony repelled her. She was the only one in the castle who refused to attend, after seeing it once.

The people's diet she often found off-putting. They ate almost all parts of every creature that walked, crawled or swam. They excepted the woodchuck because it dug in graves; the bat and porcupine with their special powers; and moles because they caused nosebleed. They avoided all snakes because they so hated and feared the rattlesnake and copperhead.

Margaret also drew the line at eating raw meat of any type, though uncooked organs were considered a delicacy by many in the tribe.

Oneida clothing was perfectly adapted to the climate of the area. The most comfortable footwear she had ever known were summer moccasins fashioned of twined corn husks. Babies were customarily tied to cradleboards, which seemed to keep them docile. The boards could be hung in the shade from a branch while the mother worked nearby.

"What are you thinking about?" Two Eagles interrupted her reverie.

"Nothing important."

"You have been quiet too long. For you." He grinned. "What is it?"

"Just thinking about the square peg in the round hole."

The puzzlement that shadowed his face reminded her that she shouldn't resort to metaphors.

"Me." She explained. "My fitting in."

"You fit. Eight Minks says you are as Oneida as any woman in the castle."

"Eight Minks is generous." She stood up, shading her eyes. "Do I . . . fit in? I try and try not to look too self-conscious."

"It is different for you."

" 'Different' is not the word." She went to the rock where they had left their clothing, dried herself with the edges of her hands and tossed her long hair, running her fingers through it. Two Eagles joined her. He stretched out his five-foot-long breechclout on the sand and put it on, arranging it so that it fell in equal lengths front and back before fastening his belt. His breechclout reached to within a hand's width of his knees.

She patted her stomach. "And now we are going to be parents."

"Our son."

"Maybe daughter."

"Son."

"If you say so."

"When?"

"Soon." She set his hand against the baby. It kicked. He jerked away his hand. She laughed.

Her dress was buckskin with a neatly fringed hem and long sleeves. The yoke was trimmed with white and purple beads, and had been woven for her by Swift Doe in the symbol of the bear clan. Her leggings, cut from a single buckskin, reached to just below the knee and were decorated along the seams with fine quillwork.

Two Eagles adjusted the bead-decorated band that held a single golden eagle feather, his óyaron. With handfuls of grass they wiped the sand from their feet before slipping into their moccasins and starting back up the path to the castle.

He took her hand. The air held the tang of fall even though the leaves had not yet begun changing their colors. Hatho, the spirit of the frost, would come tonight for the first time, she was certain. When the leaves fell in the heavens Orion would round Polaris. Orion the hunter, with his dogs would overtake the bear, slaying him. The hunting would begin for the men, and the women would roam the woodlands gathering hickory nuts and chestnuts, black walnuts, butternuts. In the evenings they would stuff moss in the cracks of the longhouses. The snowshoes would be taken out and repaired.

He stopped and held her and kissed her lingeringly. He placed both huge hands on her stomach. "Next year at this time I will take him hunting with me."

"He'll barely be walking." She laughed.

"On his cradleboard, on my back. My son, Canyewa Tawyne—Little Otter. Ben-ja-min."

Benjamin, after Margaret's father. Thoughts of her father, of mother, of England, Bedworth and home tugged at her heart.

2

In the little town of Bedworth in Warwickshire, across the puddle-strewn cobbled street from Hale and Grimshaw's Iron Works, stood the Runner and Horseshoe, its sign creaking rhythmically in the steady breeze off the Coventry canal. At a table inside set near the grimy front window sat two men, the older one in his fifties: expensively dressed, exuding wealth, successful in every visible respect, but looking careworn well beyond his years. Opposite him, sipping port, sat a man half his age: lean-faced, dark and good-looking. His eyes, set deep beneath the ridges of his brows, showed a mischievous twinkle, as if seriousness took conscious effort. At the moment he was making the effort; he listened to the older man and sympathized. At the same time he was eager to consummate the proposition being offered him. He badly needed the advance; he was near destitute, his business having gone bankrupt through no fault of his.

The tavern interior was gloomy in defiance of the bright sunshine outside, setting the gilt spear tips of the gate to the iron works gleaming. It was midafternoon, they were the only patrons, and their privacy was assured. The barkeeper was busy watering whiskey behind his bar at the far end of the room.

"We received one letter from her, which you've already seen," said the older man. "I've made a copy for you, in the event there's something in it that could be helpful in finding her. There's the name of the tribe, although no specific location."

Without opening it, his companion placed the letter in his inside pocket. The older man held another envelope up.

"This you must guard with your life; it's the key to your role, your disguise. It's your letter of introduction and recommendation to the Society in Boston."

"Wherever did you get it?"

"Oh, it's as fake as paste diamonds, and it grieves me to have to resort to such trickery, but desperate situations call for desperate measures."

He held out a third envelope. "Here is half the amount we agreed on for your services." The other man made no move to reach for it. "I trust you implicitly. I know we scarcely know one another but you come highly recommended as an honest man, a man of integrity and character."

"Indeed I am, Mr. Addison," the younger man assured him.

"I sincerely hope so. You're probably wondering why I don't go over there myself, if I'm so deeply committed to getting her back. It's this blasted sciatica."

"Painful?"

"At times excruciating. Three or four blocks is my limit walking—I can hardly wander around the wilds of North America."

"Sir, I'll do my best, but I can't promise success. A good deal of luck will have to fall to me...."

"Unquestionably. But please remember this"—the older man leaned forward—"you're our only hope. We're desperate. Her mother is beside herself."

"I understand."

"It'll be dangerous, enormously difficult, and when you get there she may refuse to come back with you. She can be alarmingly stubborn."

"So can I. I can also be very persuasive."

"She may even refuse to speak to you, avoid you like the pox, have them throw you out. But don't be deterred. Do your absolute utmost. Move every mountain to bring her back with you."

"I won't leave without her."

In his heart Seth sighed; whatever had prompted such windy assurance? He had made it sound like a guarantee!

"Who knows how it'll turn out," muttered the older man gloomily. Then he picked himself up. "Your stagecoach for London leaves at seven in the morning. It's only May, and the *Deliverance* isn't due in till August, but you did say something about spending the summer in London. Dear me, why anyone would want to spend summer in London—"

"I've friends there."

"I wish I could have gotten you an earlier passage. I tried my best but there wasn't a berth available on a single ship. There just aren't that many crossing. And August is a bit late in the year. If, God forbid, you miss the *Deliverance*—"

"I'll be on her."

"Keep a record of your expenses; whether you bring her back or not you'll be reimbursed to the farthing, as we agreed." He wound his watch. "I must get back to the office. I'll be there to see you off tomorrow. And please send word when you leave London in August. I'll rest easier knowing you're on your way. I can't think of anything else." He offered his hand. "Godspeed, Mr. Wilson, and may He be with your every step in the wilderness. We'll be praying nightly that you bring our only child back to us."

He put down money for the drinks and left. Wilson watched him cross the street and start up the other side, walking slowly, carrying the weight of his melancholy on his narrow shoulders. Opening the envelope, Wilson thumbed through the money. Even before this final meeting, he'd decided that finding Margaret Addison might not be his biggest challenge; it was winning her over and bringing her home. From all her father had told him, that threatened to be like trying to catch the fastest fish in the pond by hand.

He finished his drink, nodded to the barkeeper en route to the door and walked to the stagecoach office to purchase his ticket.

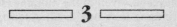

3

The Oneida castle, Onneyuttahage, stood on a flat rise, a timber palisade enclosing neatly laid-out long-houses. It was surrounded by open land that led to the main trail, woodlands and cornfields, in which squaws and small children were gathering the last of the crop. Behind the castle ran a stream that provided the tribe's water supply.

Within Onneyuttahage's twenty-foot-high walls were twenty-four longhouses separated by wide streets. Each longhouse consisted of a strong frame of upright poles that were strengthened with horizontal poles attached to withes, and surmounted with a rounded roof. Both sides and roof were covered with large strips of elm bark tied to the frame.

Every residence was eighty to one hundred feet long and twenty feet wide, with a six-foot-wide passageway running between the chambers. Smoke escaped from fires in the passageway through holes in the roof. A house with five fires contained twenty chambers, some of which were allocated to storage. Bunks built against the walls of the chambers were raised about a foot to avoid fleas and damp, and the bunks were covered with reed mats and bearskin robes.

The sun was starting down its afternoon path when into the castle came a ragged-looking warrior. He stood well over six foot, strong and muscular, but his body was brutally scarred, as if he'd run a gauntlet measured in hours, not distance. His scalp was covered by a dark red, healed wound. His nails had been pulled out, his fingertips healing into disfigured stumps. In his sunken face, in his eyes, lodged the suffering his flesh so vividly displayed. Men, women and children stopped what they were doing, paused in their conversations, and stared. Then one man rushed forward, seizing the arrival by the upper arms.

"Ossivenda Oÿoghi! Blue Creek!"

"Karístatsi Sateeni, Iron Dog."

"My friend! My friend!"

The others gathered around them, recognizing the newcomer and greeting him, many with shock and amazement.

"We thought you were dead," said Iron Dog, "killed in the war."

"I was captured by Huron snakes. Held prisoner for nearly three winters." Blue Creek looked through the crowd.

"Escaped?" a woman asked.

"Released. The French lace-cuffs made them let some of us go. We were kept near Napaee. They freed three of us at a time. My two companions and I made our way down to Cataraqui."

"Fort Frontenac," corrected a wizened elder.

"The two with me were Onondagas. We split up there." His eyes still traveled back and forth across the group. "Where is she?"

Karístatsi Sateeni, Iron Dog, averted his eyes. He stood more than a head shorter than Blue Creek. Although still a young man, his back was bowed, locking him in a permanent crouch. His deep-set eyes held an evil glint even when he smiled. He was distressingly homely, his nose much too large for his other features and bending in the middle of the bridge on its way down to enormous nostrils that glistened. Forever snuffling, he did so now and widened his smile, his misshapen, thin-lipped mouth revealing rotted and crooked teeth.

"Where?" Blue Creek repeated.

"Night Song?" asked Iron Dog.

"Who else?"

"Gone," said Eight Minks, pushing forward.

"Find her," said Blue Creek to Iron Dog. "Bring her to me."

"She has gone to Massowaganine," murmured Iron Dog. "To the Onondagas. She—"

"She married an Onondaga," Eight Minks went on.

Blue Creek stared long and hard at her. The crowd gazed fascinated at Blue Creek. His frightfully scarred flesh looked like parchment meticulously distressed with the point of a knife. Yet he stood as if unaware of his hideousness as the wind curled over the top of the palisade, catching the smoke from the cookfires.

"Married?" he murmured.

"She thought you were killed in the war," said Eight Minks. "We all did."

Word that Night Song had married another seemed to shrink Blue Creek. It was easy to see that she had dominated his thoughts for the years of his captivity, her image sustaining him. He paled slightly. His shoulders sank. His head tilted forward.

"She waited and waited even after word came that you were killed," added Iron Dog.

Blue Creek stiffened, grunted, shook off the blow. "Where is my sister? I must see my sister."

He pushed forward past Iron Dog through the circle of on-lookers, heading for Two Eagles' and Margaret's longhouse.

4

Two Eagles and Margaret drew closer to the open gate of the castle. Out came two familiar figures: Anger Maker and Splitting Moon—Two Eagles' close friends, and Margaret's, for they were among those who had accompanied her all the way to Quebec for her ill-fated reunion with Captain Pierre Lacroix, her husband-by-proxy. Anger Maker, Sa-ga-na-qua-de (He-who-makes-everyone-angry) was a huge-chested man with a voice all but incapable of any tone but a grumble. He took pains to irritate everyone within earshot, without preference or prejudice, and delighted in engaging someone in conversation, introducing a third party and then goading the two into arguing, while he backed away to enjoy the show. Because of his vexing personality, his wife had left their bed, and he could not find another woman to tolerate him. But he was a loyal friend and fearless in battle, so his quarrelsome nature was overlooked by Two Eagles and his other friends.

Tyagohuens, Splitting Moon, was built like an oak stump, with arms resembling tree trunks. His strength was prodigious, his outlook on life as bleak as the heart of winter. He wore his pessimism, like a badge of honor. With his old-fashioned tooth-ball tomahawk he fought like three men when aroused; like Anger Maker and Two Eagles he had done so with distinction against the lace-cuffs and their moccasin allies.

Two Eagles and Margaret greeted them.

"Guess who has shown up," murmured Anger Maker.

Splitting Moon grinned. "Blue Creek."

Two Eagles scoffed. "Blue Creek is dead, killed on the Kanawage in a skirmish with the Huron snakes."

"He is alive," said Anger Maker, and explained. Two Eagles listened, frowning, unable to hide his disbelief.

"Who is Blue Creek?" asked Margaret.

"Ossivenda Oÿoghi," Two Eagles replied.

"Graywind's brother," mumbled Splitting Moon, looking guiltily at Two Eagles.

Margaret gasped.

Two Eagles studied the ground, recalling the past. After he and the others found Margaret in the blasted tree and brought her to Onneyuttahage, he and Splitting Moon departed for the peace conference at Massowaganine in Onondaga Territory, leaving her with Aunt Eight Minks and Two Eagles' wife, Graywind. Graywind insisted that Margaret was to be her slave, despite his warning to leave her alone. With his departure, Eight Minks took up Margaret's protection. But while his aunt was asleep one night Graywind knocked Margaret unconscious and penned her in a bear cub cage outside, in a driving rainstorm, to teach her submission.

Eight Minks discovered Margaret early the next morning, freeing her and triggering a bitter argument with Graywind. The argument carried into the longhouse, into Eight Minks' chamber, where Graywind suddenly went wild, attempting to strangle Aunt Téklqʔ-eyo. In desperation, Margaret picked up the stone Graywind had used to knock her out and smashed Graywind in the head, killing her.

When Two Eagles returned, Eight Minks insisted that Graywind's death was an accident. If Margaret had not stopped her, Graywind would have strangled his beloved aunt. Though Two Eagles accepted Eight Minks' explanation, some of Graywind's close friends refused to and to this day kept their distance from Margaret, looking angry and disapproving whenever they saw her.

"I never knew Graywind had a brother," she murmured.

Two Eagles grunted. "It will be all right. He will be told the truth, that she caused her own death."

Anger Maker and Splitting Moon nodded. But their encouragement did little to reduce the unwelcome weight pressing Two Eagles' heart.

"He will do nothing," Two Eagles went on, "and say nothing. Otherwise he will have trouble to go with his grief."

"Oh dear . . ."

"Everyone knows Graywind's death was an accident," said Anger Maker.

"Not everyone saw it as such. Or wanted to." Margaret shook her head. "I must explain to him exactly what happened, the truth."

Two Eagles shook his head. "Better you keep away from him."

"He deserves to know the truth. Before the gossips fill his head with all sorts of nonsense. It's the least I can do. The story's become so mangled—"

Splitting Moon was scratching the side of his head, his face pinched in deep thought. "Two Eagles is right, you should let others tell him. Me, I will."

"Eight Minks will," said Two Eagles. "You were not there. She was. He will accept what she tells him. If he refuses to, if he wants to carry the stone of it around inside—that is up to him."

"I hate this," Margaret murmured.

"How does he look?" Two Eagles asked.

"How would anybody look who has been tortured day after day?" Splitting Moon made his favorite face. "It turned my stomach to look at him."

Anger Maker laughed. "Please, we all know how weak your stomach is."

"Ogechta," snarled Splitting Moon. "Two Eagles, he asked about Night Song as well as his sister." He shook his head. He has walked through a long fire and come back as hollow as an old hive. Better for him if the Huron snakes had killed him the day they captured him."

"The poor soul," murmured Margaret.

"He took everything they could do to him and survived," said Anger Maker. "He has heart and a spine, an *orochquine*, that one."

Two Eagles nodded. "That I give him, he always had both."

Anger Maker addressed Margaret. "He does not need your pity. He will start over, put his captivity, his suffering, the women he has lost out of his life behind him. He survived, now he will live."

Margaret eyed Two Eagles. "Help him, dear. Be friendly, take him hunting and fishing with you."

"I would, only he is like the red fox. He would rather be by himself."

"Not true," said Splitting Moon. "Iron Dog was always trailing around behind him. They were two trunks of the same tree."

"Karístatsi Sateeni?" asked Margaret. "That little sneak? He's always stirring up mischief."

"Now he's got his best friend back to help him stir," said Two Eagles.

"What is Blue Creek's clan?"

"The same as Graywind's, the turtle clan. Bone's clan before he married Swift Doe. Why do you ask? He will not be moving into our longhouse, if that is what worries you." He took her hand. "Come, let us go in. Maybe we will make it to the longhouse before he sees us."

"It's not funny!"

He smiled. "It will be all right, it will, you will see." The words came easily. But in his heart he wondered.

Iron Dog stood too close to Blue Creek, as if keeping his ear within reach of a whisper. Iron Dog's face glowed in anticipation, his eyes twinkling merrily. Margaret half expected him to rub his hands, so taken was he with the occasion. As Blue Creek regarded her, she noted that his scalp was grisly, his nailless fingers repulsive. He looked as if he'd stood surrounded by men and women with birch rods, beaten mercilessly, his wounds healing, beaten again, healing again and so on until not a square inch of flesh escaped scarring.

At sight of him Two Eagles changed his mind about avoiding contact, catching Margaret by surprise.

"This is my wife, Ossivenda Oÿoghi."

Blue Creek's eyes fell to her stomach. Margaret imagined she felt twin knives piercing it and she made a conscious effort to keep from clutching it protectively. Was he thinking that hers should be Graywind's stomach? That Two Eagles' seed was misplaced in this whiteskin stranger? That she had no business being there, let alone marrying Two Eagles? Didn't he remember that Graywind had been barren? Or was he deliberately overlooking that?

"Can we talk privately?" she asked.

Two Eagles moved slightly beside her, as if objecting. Blue Creek was continuing to stare at her stomach, making her increasingly uneasy.

But when she repeated the question, Blue Creek grunted. She took it as assent and walked off toward the open gate. She could hear him behind her. She turned to see Iron Dog tagging along.

"Not you," she said to him.

He looked at Blue Creek, who raised his chin sharply, gesturing Iron Dog back. Then Two Eagles stepped forward and stopped, the heel of his hand on his knife butt. She signaled him to stay back as Blue Creek followed her outside and into the woods.

"Téklqʔ-eyo told me about my sister," he said. "That Graywind tried to strangle her and you stopped it. You killed her."

"I did. But it was unintentional. You must believe that."

"Why must I?"

"She went wild. She would have killed Eight Minks."

He spoke to the ground, toeing it aimlessly with one ragged moccasin. He had yet to look her directly in the eye. "Did you have to strike her so hard?"

"The stone was heavy. I couldn't control it."

"Eight Minks says that Graywind struck you with the same stone earlier."

"She did. She knocked me out."

"It was not too heavy for her to control. And you look as strong as she."

"I did not try to kill her. Why would I do such a horrible thing? I, a white woman, a stranger, would I be so stupid as to deliberately commit murder?"

"Perhaps Two Eagles was in your eyes."

"He wasn't! I hardly knew him."

"You know him now. Now that Graywind sleeps with dirt in her mouth."

They walked on. The corn stood in orderly rows, its stalks twined with squash and bean vines.

"Please listen to me," she said, touching his arm. "Eight Minks was there, she saw it all."

"So she said."

"What she told you is exactly what happened. If you

can't believe her and refuse to believe me, there's nothing more I can do."

He met her eyes for the first time, staring. He'd refused to accept the truth. What now? Was he already planning his vengeance? His face shadowed.

"Nothing will bring my sister back from the Village of the Dead. If you schemed to murder her because you had Two Eagles in your eyes, or if it was an accident, does not matter. I only know that because of you, she sleeps with dirt in her mouth."

She sighed.

"Regardless, for what it's worth, I'm truly sorry it happened."

"You regret it?"

"Enormously."

"You should."

He eyed her with such malevolence that she shrank back slightly. She was tempted to say, Don't start anything. If you harm me Two Eagles will kill you. But if thoughts of vengeance were in his brain, her threats wouldn't stop them. She turned to go, then paused.

"One thing. I'm also sorry for what they put you through."

His grunt rejected her sympathy. "When you go back," he said, "do not let Iron Dog come. Tell him I want to be by myself."

She watched him walk off farther into the woods. From the back he looked like a tightened knot of suffering. Her heart went out to him, momentarily dispelling her mounting fears.

6

Benjamin Addison showed up at the coach office to see off Seth Wilson. Addison did not look like the same man Seth had talked to at the Runner and Horseshoe the previous afternoon. After little sleep, the older man's businesslike manner had changed to raw determination. While the through passengers stretched their legs, the two men talked in reasonable privacy on the street side of the coach.

"Hire help if you have to. Six men, ten, whatever it takes. Put it on your expense account. And you'll surely be carrying a weapon."

"I . . . hadn't thought about that. I mean, a missionary—"

"Think about it when you get to Boston. You'll be entering wild country, with a long way to go before you get to her, depend on it. Refer to her letter. There's a good deal between the lines."

Seth looked off at the chimney pots poking the sky. Then he aimlessly ran a finger along the coach door handle. The pleader now seemed to be baring his teeth. Addison took his arm, walking him across the street.

"Bring her home, Mr. Wilson. I don't care how, just do it. By fair means or foul."

"Sir . . ."

"Let's be clear on that. If it comes to deceiving her, don't hesitate."

"Sir, I'd still like to be on speaking terms with her when the ship leaves Boston."

Addison waggled a finger. "Fair means or foul," he repeated.

"Tie her up with a bag over her head?"

"If necessary."

"I was joking."

"I'm not. You'll have one shot in your gun, one chance to bring down the bird. Don't hesitate to lie until you're blue in the face, if need be. Dupe, deceive, cheat—"

"Sir—"

"All right, all right, maybe I am getting carried away, but you must have a number of plans ready. You must be creative, enterprising."

"Sir, the only plan that has a chance of working will be to win her friendship and with it her confidence, conduct myself in a straightforward manner—"

"Play on her heartstrings. Very important. *Very.* She can't help but be homesick. Tell her about Jesse, her mother. Make it sound as if she's pining away to within the shadow of the grave."

He sounded quite desperate.

"Another thought occurs to me. You're taking your half-pay with you—don't be afraid to spend it. I'm talking about bribery."

"You want me to *bribe* the red Indians?"

"They're human, aren't they? I'll wager they're as greedy as white men. Put it down as expenses."

"Whatever you say."

As the horn blared, the seven through passengers climbed into their seats, leaving five empty. The interior, completely lined with leather, smelled unpleasantly musty. Seth, the only passenger to board in Bedford, sat with his back to the boot, opposite an elderly man wearing a preposterous beard and a hat much too large for his small face. His hands were folded over a cane that stood upright between his knees. His cheeks were such a ripe red, Seth's first impression was of Father Christmas, although he wasn't certain Father Christmas was a drinker.

The coach swayed on its thoroughbraces as the driver and his assistant climbed up. The horn sounded and Addison lifted his hand in a weak wave and tried to smile. Seth

waved back and the coach lunged forward, nearly pitching
him into Father Christmas's lap.

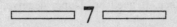

7

Swift Doe's sons were out of the longhouse, affording
their parents, as well as Two Eagles and Margaret, rare
privacy. The four adults sat under braided strings of corn,
dried fish and other foods suspended from the poles that
braced the roof. Bone, Swift Doe's husband and a Mohican adoptee, was curious about the liberated prisoner;
Bone had not joined the Oneida until long after Blue
Creek had gone to war. Margaret shared his curiosity.

Swift Doe sat fashioning a medicine mask for the False
Face Society of the tribe. Earlier, His Longhouse, Sho-
non-ses, chief of the bear clan, had burned tobacco at the
base of a healthy basswood tree and offered prayers. Then
he carved a face into the standing trunk. When it was almost finished he cut it out of the trunk and hollowed it
into a rough mask. Using a small adze and crook-knife,
Swift Doe was now in the midst of the more detailed carving. Watching her work, Margaret resolved to listen and
learn about the man from the past.

"Were you and Blue Creek friends before the seven
years of red days?" Bone asked.

Two Eagles shook his head. *"Neh."*

"Enemies," said Swift Doe. "Tell about when you and
Graywind were courting." Two Eagles' expression said
that he preferred not to, but Swift Doe went on. "Blue
Creek was always jealous of him; when Two Eagles and
Graywind started seeing each other, he caught fire."

"That is nonsense," rasped Two Eagles.

"He could not stand it." She turned to Bone. "Ask Eight

Minks if you think I stretch the fish." She turned back to
Two Eagles. "Blue Creek tried everything in his power to
discourage her from marrying you; tell them. Two Eagles
persisted, Graywind consented. Blue Creek never forgave
either of them. Oh, he did not care if she married, just as
long as she did not marry him. He and Two Eagles could
not stand the sight of each other."

"You chatter like a squirrel," snapped Two Eagles.
"Gossip out of your dreams! Blue Creek and I never had
words over Graywind."

"You did. When she warned Blue Creek to keep his
opinion out of her ear, that she had agreed to marry you,
had already baked the marriage bread, he threatened
you—"

"He said he disapproved, that is all. I told him Graywind and I did not care how he felt. That ended it, there
was no arguing."

"Blue Creek envied him back when they were small
boys even," Swift Doe went on.

"More gossip. You were peeing your cradleboard when
we were boys. You do not know what went on between
us."

Swift Doe continued with her carving. When completed,
the mask would be painted rēd or red and black, with
wisps of animal hair attached to the upper forehead and
holes drilled for thongs to fasten it to the wearer's head.
Medicine tobacco would then be tied to the part in the
hair.

Margaret eyed Two Eagles, who suddenly seemed more
eager to explain the story. "We did not like each other, that
does not mean we hated. In time he accepted our marriage.
He had to. But up to then we did not stalk each other with
knives." He frowned at Swift Doe, eliciting a smirk. "Neither of us raised a hand to the other."

"Not once?" Margaret persisted.

"Tell her about the buck," said Swift Doe. "It was when
they were boys."

"We were eighteen," growled Two Eagles. "Men. And it was nothing."

"They were out hunting," Swift Doe went on, "separately. Neither saw the other. Both shot at the same buck, both hit it, killed it. They came running in from opposite directions shouting, both claiming it. They argued, they fought."

"We did not fight!"

"Ok-kwen-cha and Sku-nak-su watched you."

"They watched nothing. Red Paint stretches the truth like wet sinew and Fox goes along with everything he says like an echo."

"They had to pull them apart or they would have killed each other."

"Ogechta!"

"Ask both of them," said Swift Doe to Margaret.

Margaret grinned at Two Eagles. "I can't wait."

Swift Doe dipped a finger into a clay pot filled with paint made from the fruit and root of the sumac mixed with red berries and bloodroot and began to paint. At the New Year's dance the members of the society would eat false face pudding and the mask, concealed behind a skin covering, would peer out and become friendly and potent. When worn in the ceremony it would be considered powerful. Following the dance, the society's members would care for it, protecting it and honoring it with tobacco incense.

"Did Blue Creek have other friends here?" Bone asked. "Or only Iron Dog?"

"He got along with everyone," said Two Eagles, "but not close. Only Iron Dog was close to him." Margaret sniffed in disapproval. "You despise Iron Dog."

"I don't, I just don't like two-faced sneaks."

"He licks the ground the chiefs walk on, that one," said Swift Doe, "but he does know how to *ga-sa-de-ga* Blue Creek."

"Manipulate," said Margaret. "That's him, all right."

"Never mind Iron Dog," said Two Eagles. "Blue Creek is the one to keep your eye on."

"Do you think he'd be foolish enough to try to avenge Graywind?" Margaret asked. "Hurt me?"

"Who can tell what an angry wasp will do? Just stay out of his way. You too, Bone. He is a brave warrior. Skilled in hand-to-hand combat. Careful, not reckless like Splitting Moon. A powerful wrestler, very strong in his upper body, quick like the copperhead and balanced like the gray squirrel. He could fight on a rope stretched over a gully and not be the one to fall."

"Is he good with weapons?" Bone asked.

"Very, especially his knife. He was back then. Maybe the Hurons have bled his courage. Some warriors survive torture and never pick up a weapon again."

"Maybe because fighting was what got them into trouble in the first place," said Margaret.

"I have never been tortured," said Bone.

Two Eagles grunted. "You have missed nothing. As for Blue Creek, he was a good warrior and a good man in many ways. But as bitter as the root bark of the black haw, even as a boy. Splitting Moon sees the black side of everything. Blue Creek lives his life down in the hole where the black comes from."

"He does not like you," said Swift Doe, dipping her finger and applying paint to the chin of the mask. "You make his spit bitter."

Two Eagles waved this away. "I do not ask anyone to like me."

"With Graywind dead—"

He glared. "Let us drop it."

"He is right," said Bone.

Swift Doe shrugged. "All I am saying is he disliked you even before you two married. Now he comes home to find her dead—"

"I get the feeling I'm his main target," said Margaret wearily.

"I think he is so battered and broken in body and in

spirit, he does not have the will to start anything," said Bone. "From the look of him he just about made it home."

Two Eagles nodded, but Swift Doe looked dubious. Margaret groaned silently and wondered why it was that when life was humming happily along—her first child expected, the tribes at peace and the future looking as rosy as a summer's dawn—a dragon had to come lumbering over the hill into view. The baby kicked. She grunted. Soon now.

Blue Creek and Iron Dog stood at the foot of Graywind's grave. The two-foot palisade enclosing it was weather-scarred and badly in need of fresh paint. Blue Creek gazed down, lost in thought. He had bathed in the stream and replaced his rags with clean, new buckskins, new leggins, corn husk moccasins. His crimson pate glowed in the sunlight.

"He neglects her grave," he said quietly.

"He has his whiteskin woman," said Iron Dog. "A flower dies, another takes its place."

"She carries my sister's *cian*."

"It will have yellow hair like her."

"Tell me about her."

"I can tell you this: she could have stopped Graywind from strangling old Eight Minks without killing her."

"*Nyoh*, when I suggested that, in her eyes I could see she agreed." The woodlands were alive with the droning of insects. Above the mountain ridge to the southeast, white lightning tore the heavens, vanishing, leaving the blue a shade darker. Thunder grumbled. "Rain is coming. Tell me about her, I said."

Iron Dog told him: Margaret's arrival at Onneyuttahage, Graywind's killing and Margaret's departure before Two Eagles and Splitting Moon returned from the peace conference at Massowaganine. Her capture by Burnt Eye, the sadistic Mohawk chief, her escape and reunion with Two Eagles and the journey to Quebec. Her return and their marriage.

"She is his wife." Iron Dog sneered the word. "An adoptee. But not one of us. She does not want to be. She disdains our sacred ceremonies; our ways and customs do not interest her. She is not popular. Graywind's friends avoid her. That white skin is like snake skin. Our people are repelled by the sight of it."

"Does he come here to Graywind's grave to pay his respects?"

"I have seen him."

"He brings his whiteskin?"

"*Neh*, she refuses to come. She is the one who should be tending the grave, *neh*? Keeping the pickets straight and freshly painted. She is one of those who has no respect for anything. I have even heard that she mocks Graywind."

Blue Creek tensed. He scowled. "How?"

"She jeers at her powers, at Agreskoue, the sun and our god of war, whom everyone knows was Graywind's confidante. Even worse, she implies that Graywind's brain was upside down in her head, giving as proof that she went wild the morning she met her death. You do not ask my opinion, but I give it to you anyway. She, the English, is not fit to step into Graywind's moccasins. Watch, when her *cian* is born she will flaunt it before you."

Blue Creek had bent to straighten some of the palisade pickets, bringing them into line with the others. "I will paint these and pull the weeds. But, my friend, you can do a great service for me."

"Name it," said Iron Dog.

"Keep an eye on the whiteskin. Listen. Everything you see and hear report to me at once."

"It will be my pleasure. What will you do, red-bib her white throat?"

"I would like that, before she bears the *cian*. That way Two Eagles' loss would be double."

Iron Dog thought. "Maybe. Or maybe it would be better to hold off, wait for the ideal opportunity. Meanwhile she will wait and wonder what you are scheming."

"You are right. I could see fear in her eyes but not enough. If I give her time it will grow and grow."

"Be careful with Two Eagles," Iron Dog advised. "He has a temper, that one."

"He is all wind, thunder with the sun out. If he gets in my way I will crush him like a bug. Her, too. They both must die, but as I say, not right away. Come, we need red paint for the palisade."

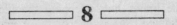

Not until three days later did Margaret go into labor. Instead of withdrawing into the woods, giving birth, biting the umbilical cord, washing the baby in stream water, wrapping it in a bear robe and staggering home—as was the Iroquoian custom—she resolved to have her baby in bed, "properly," as she described it. When the pains began, Eight Minks examined her and announced that the birth would be a breech delivery; Swift Doe looked worried.

Margaret stiffened and held her breath. "The pains are getting closer."

Earlier that morning Blue Creek had overheard Swift Doe's oldest son, Hare, tell a friend that the baby would be born before the sun reached the top of the sky. Even knowing the baby was due, the news struck Blue Creek like a hammer, triggering a seething rage. It was too soon, the whiteskin had not had time to worry herself to distraction over what he might do to her in revenge for Graywind's murder. Looking for Two Eagles, he found him sitting, wielding a bone tool, chipping flint into an arrowhead. The sky was darkening rapidly; thunder rumbled, as if to announce Blue Creek's frame of mind.

"Get up!" he ordered.

"Go away, I am busy." Two Eagles scowled.

"Up! We will have it out now."

"What?"

"Do not play stupid with me, Tékni-ska-je-a-nah."

He swatted the tool from Two Eagles' hand. Up he jumped into a half-crouch, to defend himself. Blue Creek swung his forearm horizontally, slamming him in the side of the neck, tilting his head sharply. In the same instant he crooked his left leg around Two Eagles' right leg and toppled him.

On him like a cat, Blue Creek drove his knee below Two Eagles' sternum. Two Eagles roared and rolled over onto all fours, scrambling to his feet with difficulty, pain still radiating from the point of contact. Dust rose, lightning flashed. As it began raining, a crowd quickly gathered.

"It's coming—" murmured Margaret between tightly clenched teeth. Rain drummed the longhouse roof. Eight Minks had spread a bear robe on the floor alongside Margaret's bunk. Swift Doe and she took hold to help the mother-to-be up into a sitting position. "Let go, what are you doing?" Margaret cried.

"You must get up," said Swift Doe.

"No! You give birth lying down."

"Up!" snapped Eight Minks. "You must kneel and push the baby out."

"That's ridiculous, let go of me!"

Rain splattered the two combatants, pocking the dust. Two Eagles went down again. Blue Creek kicked him savagely in the ribs, driving him onto his side. He scuttled clear, rose and came back at his attacker roaring, elbowing his throat, sending him staggering back choking, his cheeks filling with the color of his naked pate. He closed, seizing Two Eagles around the chest, tightening his grip, cutting off his wind. Two Eagles tilted his head back, his eyes swimming with pain. Up came his knee hammering the other's crotch. Blue Creek screamed and let go. Two Eagles ducked, ramming his chest, knocking him sprawling. The dust was turning to mud, threatening both men's footing, slowing them.

Together, Eight Minks and Swift Doe pulled Margaret bodily out of the bunk, forcing her to her knees on the robe.

"If I weren't helpless—" she protested.

"Spread your legs as far apart as you can." Impatiently, Eight Minks pulled back one leg, and Swift Doe the other. Margaret cried out. Eight Minks jammed a stick in her mouth. "Bite down hard! And push."

"Push!" echoed Swift Doe. Margaret fought back the pain, her mind whirling.

On his knees, Two Eagles straddled Blue Creek's chest, pushing his hands hard against his face, cutting off his wind. Blue Creek shook his head, kicked, arched his back, threw him off. Slipping and sliding, both regained their feet. Blue Creek flew at Two Eagles' back, crooking an arm at his throat, jamming his right elbow into his left palm, flattening his right hand against the back of Two Eagles' head, pressing forward to snap his neck. The rain battered them. Splitting Moon rushed out of the watching circle.

Margaret pushed with all her strength. The tiny feet emerged. The kneeling position combined with gravity to accelerate the birth. A boy, the women noted.

When the head appeared, Swift Doe caught and held up the baby, and Eight Minks retrieved the afterbirth, letting the blood drain into Margaret's son. Then Eight Minks cut the umbilical cord, murmuring gratefully that, for a breech birth, delivery had been unusually swift and uncomplicated.

Anger Maker joined Splitting Moon in breaking up the fight. The two antagonists were covered with mud. Two

Eagles staggered clear, his hand testing his windpipe gingerly. Splitting Moon and Anger Maker held Blue Creek. He shook free and leveled a finger at Two Eagles.

"Next time your friends will not save you!"

He started off. Two Eagles roared, leaped, grabbed his shoulders from the back, only to be pulled off by his friends.

He whirled on them. "Stay out of this!"

"They saved your life," said a grizzled elder, leaning on his stick. Others nodded. Blue Creek threw Two Eagles one last glare and stalked off. "With that hold he would have snapped your neck like a dry stick," the old man went on.

"What got into him?" Red Paint asked, coming up to Two Eagles with Fox.

Two Eagles rubbed his throat lightly. The *ochtaha* leaning on the stick was right. Splitting Moon and Anger Maker *had* saved his life. His cheeks burned in embarrassment. "It is about Graywind, and between us," he snarled, looking from one to the other. "If you two or any of you interfere again, I will break your heads!"

Margaret, now in bed, held her baby proudly. "Find Two Eagles. Tell him he has a son."

"Tell him yourself," said Eight Minks.

Margaret glanced toward the chamber entrance, at Two Eagles, dripping wet, holding up the flap, his free hand continuing to stroke his throat. His scowl slowly gave way to a broad smile.

9

When the rabbit thrust its head through the deer leg–sinew noose to get at the bait, the spring pole released, and the creature hanged itself. Its twitching slowed then, stopped, and it swung lightly in the breeze. Blue Creek knelt beside it.

"Next time I will kill him," he growled. Grasping the rabbit by its hindquarters, he lifted it upside down, severed the noose holding it and slit its throat in one swipe, letting the blood pour downward to avoid staining its fur. "Him and his whiteskin bitch murderer."

"You have been saying that for a week, since the *cian* was born," said Iron Dog, infolding his arms as Blue Creek shoved the rabbit at him. "But I have been thinking, it is too easy."

"It is right!"

"*Neh*, a quick death is too merciful. How much better if both be made to suffer for many moons. Two Eagles knows you want him with dirt in his mouth. Let that chew his stomach. And hers. Give their *cian* time to grow, until next year at this time." Iron Dog leaned forward his eyes gleaming evilly. "Then kidnap it."

Blue Creek stared. What an idea! His hateful expression softened and he nodded.

"And leave Onneyuttahage for good," Iron Dog went on. "Leaving him and his pale squaw with their hearts in pieces. Is that not worse than killing them? And what a surprise, *neh*? Not to strike as they expect, instead make off with their *cian*."

"*Nyoh, nyoh*, very good. Kidnap it, run off to Massowaganine, to Night Song."

"Disappear forever." Iron Dog warmed inside. He delighted in feeding his friend ideas and seeing his reaction. Blue Creek was, as receptive as a child—and as manipulable.

"Night Song will see me walk in, the past will come rushing back, she will run to my arms. And run off with me and the *cian*."

"Where?"

"To—to the Senecas. Oh *nyoh*, Night Song will explode with happiness at the sight of me. I am the only man for her, how many times has she told me?"

"She will not believe her eyes to see you come back from the Village of the Dead."

"Nyoh, nyoh!"

Just like a child, wholly predictable, Iron Dog reflected happily. The more Blue Creek thought about it, the more appealing the idea became. Graywind's death, Night Song's departure, had filled him with pain and fired the furnace of his bitterness. This plan eased both almost instantaneously and guaranteed revenge on his two enemies.

Best of all, Night Song would be Blue Creek's at last, or so he thought. At this notion, Iron Dog resisted a sigh.

"Why wait?" Blue Creek asked. "Why not steal the *cian* right away?"

"Neh, too soon, it would die without its mother's milk. It will be months before it can digest corn and meat."

"I cannot wait so long. You say without its mother's milk it will die? Really?"

"It could."

"Wait, wait, what are we thinking? Night Song can feed it!"

"I do not think so. I think a woman can only suckle after she gives birth."

"Who says? I know, we can feed it *aque* milk."

"It is not a fawn. I do not know—"

"Milk is milk. What difference where it comes from?"

"I do not know."

"Stop saying that!" Complications cropping up were

rapidly stoking Blue Creek's temper. Iron Dog took a step backward. His friend was wild before; now he appeared uncontrollable.

"Find out," Blue Creek growled. "Ask an old squaw, they all know such things. Only be careful with your questions—no one must suspect what we are up to!"

"Please. Being clever is as natural as breathing for me!"

"Deer milk will be good for my son, make him as strong as a buck. Moose milk even better."

"Let us not rush into the *cian*. Remember, the longer you delay kidnapping him and leaving, the more Two Eagles and his squaw will suffer waiting for you to try and kill them."

"I will kill them *and* steal the *cian*."

"The *cian* is enough."

"Not enough. Kill them both!"

"*Neh*, better they suffer. Let them live to grieve their loss. Is that not more painful than death?"

Blue Creek shrugged. He suddenly seemed to resent his friend's suggestions. Out of envy of his superior intelligence? Iron Dog thought so. From under his eyelids he studied Blue Creek: his pink pate, scored flesh, the ugly stumps that once held his fingernails. And yet he did not seem self-conscious about his appearance. Was he consciously blocking out the unpleasant reality? Would sight of him repel Night Song, as it did every other woman? It would!

"Night Song will leave her husband for me," said Blue Creek confidently. "Me, her first man, her only man."

Iron Dog took another step backward. "I wonder. She has been gone a long time from here. What if by now she has a child of her own?"

"I will let her bring it along when we leave, if it is a boy. And I will have two sons!"

"And if her husband refuses to give her up?"

"If it comes to surrendering her or choking to death on your own blood, which would *you* choose?"

"What if his knife is quicker than yours?"

"No knife is quicker than mine!"

Sympathy warmed Iron Dog. He would not dream of hinting that Night Song might take one look at her one-time hero and run off screaming. Or that her husband might turn out to be as big and powerful as Two Eagles, capable of cutting out the intruder's heart and feeding it to the dogs.

"Let us go check on the other two traps," said Blue Creek. Iron Dog slung the rabbit over his shoulder and started off. Blue Creek caught his arm. "Think further about this plan of mine. I will, too. It appears excellent, but before we execute it it must be perfect."

"Nyoh."

10

Spring brought sunshine and warmth to the castle of the Oneidas, reviving long dormant activity indoors and out. But it also brought mud to the longhouse. Keeping the passageways and chambers clean was a never-ending job.

With a galaxy of flowers in readiness, summer waited patiently to replace the spring blossoms in woodland and meadow. The red-shouldered hawk grabbed his hoped-for mate's talons in midair; the woodcock spiraled upward in flight and dove to attract a partner, warbling spiritedly. A thousand creatures cavorted and courted and joined to perpetuate their species.

Benjamin grew. The black hair the breeze playfully mussed, his long limbs, broad shoulders and arresting good looks were the gifts of his father. His only resemblance to his mother was his bright blue eyes. Two Eagles reveled in fatherhood but found it hard to conceal a tinge of jealousy. It showed in his face when he watched Margaret cuddle and talk to Benjamin. Margaret noticed.

"I am not jealous of my own son," he snapped, responding to her accusation. They sat in their chamber listening to the wind howling above the creaking of the naked trees. "That is stupid!"

Margaret grinned knowingly. "It is. See here, don't be embarrassed. It's perfectly natural and it'll pass."

His cheeks colored. "I am not!"

"It's partially my fault. I give him so much attention. When before he came you had it all."

"Do not make fun of me!"

"Lower your voice. Who's making fun? I'm just explaining why you feel as you do."

"How do *you* know how I feel?"

"By the way you're behaving, of course. Oh, you don't say anything, but your face gives you away." His hand went to his face. "Doesn't it always? I'm surprised you don't know how fathers and siblings resent the new baby. Fathers, and sons in particular. It's common as clams, so don't worry."

"You resent as well."

"Benjamin? Fiddlesticks and rot." She strove to conceal a snicker.

"Resent *me*."

"That's utterly preposterous. I know we haven't slept together since he was born. But that's only because of this sadness, one that many women have after childbirth, and the fact that I'm not completely healed. I'm—sore. Don't look so, it's true. I'm not punishing you. I'm surprised you think so."

"It is your thought, not mine." He picked up the cradle-board. "Dress him. I want to take him out."

"It's clouding over, getting cool."

"He can stand rain and cool. He is Oneida."

"He's barely two weeks old; he shouldn't have to."

"Dress him!"

"*Neh!* Sit, relax and take that dumb look off your face. I can't stand that look."

"Maybe it is my face you cannot stand."

"It's that look. Every time you're crossed, you don't get your way, you pout like a child. Oh, Two Eagles, what is the matter with us, why are we squabbling?"

"It is all we seem to do since—" He jerked his chin up in Benjamin's direction.

"So he's to blame? That's convenient. It wouldn't be your envy, your impatience with me?"

"Your memory."

She stared.

"How easily you forget that you are a wife as well as a mother."

She sighed. "Look, his arrival has put a strain on us. We've had to make adjustments. Who doesn't with their firstborn? I'm tired, depressed as the devil, we're both on edge. Blue Creek's hovering about like an avenging Fury is no help."

"It is time I took care of Blue Creek."

"Stay away from him!" she ordered, her voice rising.

"Be a coward in front of my friends?"

"There's nothing cowardly in avoiding a fight. It shows intelligence."

"So now I am stupid."

"I didn't say that. It's just that it's not you and him, it's us, the three of us. You get your throat cut, and where does that leave me and Benjamin?"

He considered this and nodded. Impulsively, he hugged her; the change it wrought in their mood, the suddenness of it, surprised her. He tightened his hug. She liked it. The circle of his arm brought protection, shelter, the impression that nothing, no one, could reach or harm her. Safe she was, as safe as if she were surrounded by impregnable, unscalable walls.

A hug, merely a hug, temporary glorious captivity. No warmth of touching cheeks, no nuzzling, no murmur, no kiss, not even a peck, only his arm: devotion's compass.

She could feel his heart beat, the clock of his life; she could feel his warm breath descending and see his smile, the sweetness, his fondness pour forth.

"I love you," she whispered.

"*I* love you." He released her slowly. "Now dress him, Margaret, please? So we can go out."

She hesitated, prepared to again object, but surrendered. Let Two Eagles take him out. The unseasonable coolness wouldn't harm the baby. Two Eagles wanted to refute her accusation of jealousy, wanted to be alone with his son. Maybe it would help. She began dressing Benjamin. His father fastened him to his cradleboard.

"Not too tight," she cautioned.

He grunted. When they had gone out she went down the passageway to Eight Minks' chamber. The wind flung smoke back down through the roof holes, setting her eyes stinging. She felt miserable, abandoned by the world. Eight Minks smiled greeting out of her round pan face.

"Is he asleep?"

"He's out with his father."

"In this cold?"

"Eight Minks, I need your help. I need something to take away the soreness in my *onera*."

" 'Soreness'?"

"It feels like an infection. *Aro-go-wa*."

"It sounds like you need bearberry. An evergreen, with little white flowers smudged with red, and red berries in winter. We use the leaves."

Eight Minks selected a covered basket from an overhead shelf and crushed smooth, leathery, spatulate-shaped leaves in a bowl of boiling water, steeping the concoction for about thirty minutes. Then she cooled and strained it, telling Margaret to use it warm as a douche.

"Three times a day," said Eight Minks. "Until the soreness goes away. Take this pot, keep it covered, stir it before you set it on the fire." She angled her head and stared. "What is the matter, Margaret? Why so sad? Is it him?"

Margaret lay on Eight Minks' bed. "It's both of us."

Eight Minks smiled. "You mean it is Benjamin. Is Two Eagles jealous of his son?"

"That's part of it. It's a lot of little things: my condition, my being so down, unable to pull myself up, the attention I give Benjamin—"

"You sound like Kragequa."

"Two Eagles' mother, Swan?"

"She said the same words about his father when Two Eagles' oldest brother, Stone Knife, was born." Her forehead crinkled. "But of course it is harder for you."

"Because I'm an outsider."

"You *are* Oneida," Eight Minks protested.

"Not really. One must be accepted, like Bone. I'm not."

"I accept you. Two Eagles, his friends, Swift Doe—"

"The tribe refuses to. No surprise that. To be accepted would have been the surprise. But—"

"Knowing that does not make it easier, *neh*? I am not talking about that, but about Two Eagles. He loves you very much, very strongly. I know because I know how he felt about Graywind."

"Please."

"Let me finish. He did not know what love was before you. It was a feeling beyond the reach of his heart. He respected Graywind but had no love for her. Now he has so much it spills out of his heart, and it is all for you." She patted Margaret's forearm. "Cheer up. Like *tegenhonid*, the season of the mud, and your soreness, this will pass."

"I'll make it pass."

"You both will."

Margaret got up, wincing slightly. How she loved this old woman, her warmth and generosity. What would she do without her when the wilderness closed in and this rugged existence, this constant battle to endure, got to be too much for her? Like now? "I'm going back and take a nap. Thank you, Eight Minks, I'm sure this will help."

"It will. Take the pot."

* * *

Two Eagles came back with Benjamin to find Margaret
asleep. He ventured down the passageway to Eight Minks.
Benjamin whimpered and squirmed.

"He is wet," proclaimed Two Eagles.

"So take care of him," she retorted.

"That is woman's work."

"That is parents' work." She undressed Benjamin, dried
his privates, returning his cooing with baby talk, got down
a piece of deerskin, warmed it over the fire and put it on
him. "Very difficult, *nyoh*? Complicated, like breathing.
Did you see your friend outside?"

"He is not my 'friend.' Do not talk to me about him. He
is a dead man."

She sniffed. "One of you will be if you do not stop this
foolishness. Where are you going? Sit, we must talk." He
sat as far from her as he could, assuming an expression
that said he expected criticism if not a full-scale berating.
"I know these are not happy days for you and Margaret,"
she went on, "when you expected they would be. Just remember, it is harder for her than for you."

"You seem very sure of that."

"I am. At least you are among your own people; her
people are on the other side of the O-jík-ha-dä-gé-ga and
might as well be on the moon."

"Her people are here: her husband, her son, her friends."

"Be quiet and listen. You like to think it is like that. So
would she. But it is not. Except for a handful of us she is
treated with indifference or like an intruder. Some are sus-
picious of her; some even hate her. Put yourself in her
moccasins. In her country, among her kind. You would
feel as out of place as she does here. As all *honio?'o*[n] who
try to live among the tribes, even your war friend red Duncan, the Onondaga adoptee. Living among the Oneida does
not necessarily make one an Oneida. A fox among wolves
does not become a wolf. There is too much that is different and hard for her to understand and accept. Some things
she has given up trying. And she *has* tried, Two Eagles."

"That is not why she is unhappy," he grumbled.

"I know. She wears the tight ring of sadness around her heart that happens to a woman after she gives birth. Because she does, the feeling of being an outsider that she carries and suppresses begins to surface. Dark thoughts breed even darker thoughts. She realizes what she is up against here when before she turned a blind eye, preferring to lose herself in her happiness with you. Back when the sweet was sweeter and the bitter not so bitter.

"It is very hard for her here. It always will be. Make allowances."

"I *do*," Two Eagles protested.

"Make more, bigger. You can begin mending things between you by helping her. When Benjamin spits up, wipe his mouth. When he is wet or stinks, change him."

"Warriors do not change their children."

"That is so stupid," Eight Minks replied angrily. "Even for you, who says some of the stupidest things that have ever wormed into my ears."

"Thank you," he rasped.

"There is no chore a woman does a man cannot do, and none a man does that a woman cannot."

"A woman cannot pee pictures in the snow."

"It is not funny!"

She explained in vivid detail about Margaret's infection, how it precluded sexual intercourse. His face said that he did not want to hear, but he raised no objection.

"Your son is asleep," she said handing him the cradleboard. "Take him back. And mind what I said. Help her, she will help you. That is what marriage is about."

He left. When the flap came down behind him, she released a broad smile. Amazing how easy it was to handle one so big, so proud, so intimidating to others. In Two Eagles, the little boy she so loved was still alive and healthy.

11

The tremulous wail of the loon came floating across Lake Oneida, its haunting sound reminding Margaret of the loneliness of the wilderness. She had just returned from a walk to the lake, and with Benjamin looked in on Swift Doe. Her chamber and Bone's, separated from those of her sons by storage shelves, was scrupulously neat and mud-free. Margaret began nursing Benjamin. Eight Minks had predicted rightly: the boiled and steeped bearberry leaves had worked their magic and Margaret had emerged from her depression. So, like a bird returning from the south in spring, happiness flew back into Margaret's marriage.

Swift Doe sat applying powder made of the red dry-rot of the heart of pinewood to her skin. Iroquois women, especially the younger ones, considered reddish skin a mark of beauty. Now Margaret felt Swift Doe's eyes and looked up questioningly.

Swift Doe smiled. "What a different person you are from last week. Out of your shell and alive. So, what do you think will happen with Two Eagles and the ugly one?"

Margaret frowned. "How he looks is not his fault. We should pity him. But tell me, what was he really like before he was captured?"

"A grouch."

"But how did he look?"

Swift Doe half laughed. "Better than now. He was good-looking and would have been popular if not for his disposition. He was Graywind's puppy."

"She ran him?"

"She was more his mother than his sister. He worshiped her. He wanted to keep her all to himself." She lowered her voice. "People think there was something going on between them, that they did not act like brother and sister."

This Margaret dismissed with a shake of her head. "Did Graywind feel as attached to him?" she asked.

"In a different way. She did not idolize him. Not like he did her. She could tell him to stand on his head in a fire; he would do it and not ask why."

"Did you know their parents?"

"Only their father. Their mother died when Blue Creek was born."

"That explains Graywind's treating him like a mother," Margaret said. "What sort of man was the father?"

"Not a father like Bone or Two Eagles."

"Did he abuse them?"

"Ignored them. Walk past them without even looking at either. Fathers ignore daughters but never sons. He lived by himself in the deep woods. In a cave, some say. He was strange, and even harder to get along with than Blue Creek."

Margaret shook her head sadly.

The door flap lifted, revealing Bone, who greeted them effusively and complimented Swift Doe on her makeup. Then his hand went to his scalp lock, his expression asking her to attend to it.

Like Bone, Two Eagles had worn his hair in a scalp lock up until the time he married. Some months after, Margaret prevailed on him to let his hair grow out. His friends followed his example, except for Bone. Bone's scalp lock was *the* badge of the warrior among the Mohicans who, it was widely believed, originated the style. So he retained it even when he was adopted.

After they had found Margaret half-dead sitting in a hollow tree—the sole survivor of the Mohawk massacre of her escort—Thrown Bear, Two Eagles' now-deceased best friend, had told her Bone's story. He had come to the castle one day and explained to the chiefs that his family had been massacred by roving *coureurs de bois* and that he could no longer stand living by himself. At that time he called himself Black Wolf, but many of his bones were broken and had healed roughly, leaving him with a bumpy, knobby appearance, so his new family renamed him "Bone." Adopted into the turtle clan, he became close to Two Eagles and his friends. En route to the castle with Margaret, they discovered that Two Eagles' brother Long Feather had been murdered by a renegade Mohawk, making a widow of Swift Doe. After suitable waiting period she married Bone; he became stepfather to her three sons.

Now he produced a comb carved of bark and nodded toward the fire just outside the chamber flap. "I put stones on. They should be red by now."

"Sit until I finish," said Swift Doe, applying the red powder down her arm to the back of her hand and rubbing it in to render the color uniform.

Margaret, finished nursing Benjamin, stood. "I'll get the stones."

Using a large spoon, she placed three smooth round stones one by one on the ground beside Swift Doe. By now she had bound up Bone's scalp lock so that it stood safely clear of the surrounding hair, which had sprouted to more than an inch long. Wrapping a piece of old deerskin around her right hand and using the comb to raise the unwanted hair, Swift Doe began singeing it down as close to the skin as she could.

Bone winced. "Eeeee!"

The procedure was as tedious as it was uncomfortable. Bone babbled continuously to keep his mind off the pain.

"Two Eagles should have kept his scalp lock," he said to Margaret. "Splitting Moon and the others would have kept theirs, too. Warriors *should* wear their hair in a scalp lock. It is a badge of honor."

"In wartime, perhaps," said Margaret, "but it's going on three years since the Oneidas last fought."

"A warrior does not stop being a warrior between wars," Bone insisted vigorously.

"How would you know?" Swift Does asked. "You have never fought."

"I am always ready."

"Don't misunderstand," said Margaret, "but when yours is the only scalp lock around, it's just a fad gone out of vogue. I singed Two Eagles just the one time, I told him never again. I couldn't keep my hand still. He ended up looking mottled. Why not just shave around it with your knife?"

Bone sniffed. "Because that is not the Mohican way, not the Iroquois way."

"What difference how you remove it? It's only hair."

"Shaving is for Huron snakes and pulling out by the roots for Ottawa dogshit eaters. Ow!" He shrilled and sought a new topic. "Did you hear what happened out by the gate? Two Eagles was going out, the scalped one was coming in. They had words."

"Oh my God," sighed Margaret.

"Oh, nothing happened. But it will. Again."

"What did they say?" Swift Doe asked. "Hold still!"

"They yapped like two dogs. Fire flared up between their eyes. That is all. He hates Two Eagles. I do not think Two Eagles hates him, not as much; of course, he cannot back down from him."

"It's sheer idiocy," rasped Margaret. "They'll end up killing each other. For what?"

"Two Eagles cannot back down," Bone repeated.

"Please," snapped Margaret, "let's just drop it."

"*Nyoh,*" said Swift Doe, "*ogechta.*"

"What did I say?"

"Where is Two Eagles now?" Margaret asked.

"Gone fishing. I will be joining them when I am done here. Is there a message you want me to give him?"

"Yes. No. Never mind, I'll tell him myself when he gets back. It's so infuriating and so unnecessary!"

Swift Doe was done. She rubbed Bone's fire-red scalp liberally with bear oil and carefully treated two slight burns with additional oil. When she was done she untied his lock, leaving only the knot used to bind it in place. He eyed his reflection in a kettle of water, grunted approvingly and went out.

"Men," Swift Doe murmured, dipping her fingers into the red powder. "All are as vain as the *choonoksa*."

"The ring-tailed pheasant has a right to his vanity," said Margaret.

Swift Doe nodded. "He has more to display than scars and a silly-looking topknot."

Two Eagles drew within sight of Lake Oneida accompanied by his friends, Splitting Moon, Anger Maker, O-kwen-cha (Red Paint) and (Sku-nak-su) Fox. These were four of the six warriors who had escorted Margaret to her ill-fated reunion with Captain Lacroix in distant Quebec, in the heart of New France.

Red Paint's face, shoulders and chest were liberally streaked with war paint symbolizing his heroic exploits. It was said of him that he would rather fight than lie with a woman. He was also the most skillful scout in the group, born with the ability to read the woodlands and, according to Fox, not merely find but identify tracks even on solid stone.

Fox and Red Paint were inseparable. Neither made the simplest decision without first consulting the other. Fox, too, had fought against the French and their Indian allies. He wore a silver crucifix taken from a black robe who, trying too hard to convert Fox, had compelled the Oneida to cut his throat to stop his words. Fox also wore a French major's scalp suspended from his belt. He was greatly admired for his ingenuity in the art of torture, skills he'd used upon scores of captive French moccasins in the war. Less admired was his fondness for bedding women old enough to be his grandmother.

Two Eagles led the single file. Anger Maker walked behind Splitting Moon, whose mood of the day, as usual, was as bleak as a winter sky. Anger Maker touched the coil of fishing line draped over Splitting Moon's shoulder.

"It is as dry as shed snakeskin. It will snap at the first tug."

"It will not." Splitting Moon turned, walking backward to show Anger Maker his scowl. "It is strong enough to hang around your fat neck."

"Listen to him—I give him the benefit of my superior wisdom on fishing lines and he insults my neck. Look at his line, O-kwen-cha, what do you think?"

"Leave me out of it," growled Red Paint.

Fox laughed. On they trudged in silence. Overhead a golden eagle, the great raptor of the northern skies and Tékni-ska-je-nah's óyaron, blotted out the sun with its seven-foot wing span. Fox drew Two Eagles' attention to it. All of them watched it turn and head toward the Tree-eater Mountains until it reduced to a speck.

"Sa-ga-na-qua-de is right, Tyagohuens," said Fox, walking ahead of Splitting Moon. "Your line is badly dried out."

"Feel it," snapped Splitting Moon. "Tell me if it is!"

Fox obliged him. "Not bad. Not fresh."

"What do you know? You cannot feel any better than you can see. You know nothing about fishing with a hook. All you do is spear."

"I have fished with a line. What do *you* know about spearing?"

"Oh? I was spearing grass pickerel as big as your leg before you could ride your cradleboard without pissing yourself."

The others laughed.

"So you are old," sneered Fox, "is that something to brag about?"

"Who are you calling old, grandmother fucker!"

"Enough!" burst Two Eagles. "Can we walk without talk?"

A faint smile crossed Anger Maker's face. He had started yet another fire, stepping out of it before it burned him. Reaching the lake, they uncovered two canoes hidden in the reeds and paddled out through the sunlight painting the water. Splitting Moon had stopped about a hundred yards from shore when Anger Maker hooked a walleye as big around as his forearm. Fox deftly speared a grass pickerel; Red Paint caught a speckled trout. Two Eagles hooked another large walleye, lifted it into the canoe and watched it exhaust itself flopping on the bottom of the canoe before he brained it with Splitting Moon's tomahawk.

"What will you do about Blue Creek?" Splitting Moon asked.

"I think end up giving him the red bib he seems to want so much. In self-defense." He sighed. Leave it to Splitting Moon to shadow the day with talk of Blue Creek.

"I do not think he wants to kill you."

"Think further."

"If I were you, my friend, I would not worry about myself or Mar-gar-et. Worry about your *cian*."

Two Eagles scoffed. "He would not harm Benjamin."

"He might kidnap him."

"That is foolish talk. What would he do with a *cian*?"

"Not so much what he would do with him, more what taking him would do to you two. Break your Englishwoman's heart and your spirit. Take him and flee. Vanish. Think about it—what has he to keep him here? No woman, no friends other than Iron Dog, and him he can live without."

"He would not dare. Besides he would not want to burden himself on the trail with a *cian*."

"He could find a woman to nurse Little Otter and care for him," said Splitting Moon.

"What woman? Who would lie with that body, that face? She would have to be blind as a mole, or as ugly as he is."

"All I say is there are ways he can hurt you worse than by killing you. And Mar-gar-et. For one, just by taking Little Otter."

"Benjamin," Two Eagles corrected his friend.

"I have heard that he tells people Benjamin is rightfully Graywind's *cian*, that Mar-gar-et is an intruder who stole

Graywind's child and hid him in her belly until he was born."

"You *heard*. And trees fly and sticks turn into snakes by the light of the spring moon. Why do you foul the channels of my ears with such *oeuda*?"

"Taking Benjamin, he will believe he is taking his own nephew."

"*Oeuda!* Shit!"

"Maybe, but guard your son well, or wake up one morning and find him gone. It could happen."

Bone appeared in the distance, loping along easily, waving. They waved back and cheered him on. He himself disliked fishing but enjoyed keeping his friends company. Now he drove in and swam out to Red Paint and Fox's canoe, climbing in. And immediately noticed Two Eagles' scowl.

"What bug is under his hide?" he called over, asking Splitting Moon. "Ossivendi Oÿoghi?"

"Why ask him?" growled Two Eagles. "Ask me. This one, who sees black in every rainbow, claims Blue Creek is planning to kidnap Benjamin."

"I did not say that," Splitting Moon protested. "I said it is possible."

Bone made a face as he turned it over in his mind and shook his head. "He might as well offer his belly to sheathe your knife as to do such a stupid thing."

"Tell him." Two Eagles frowned at Splitting Moon.

"So I could be wrong," said Splitting Moon.

"*Nyoh.*"

"Or I could be right."

Was he? Had he blundered onto something? Something else for him and Margaret to worry about. Should he mention it to her?

"*Neh.*"

The others looked his way. He pretended he didn't see.

12

In August, having gotten his fill of summer in London, Seth Wilson was anxious to pile aboard the coach at Waterloo Station, heading down to Clapham Junction and out the Kingston Road toward Southampton. Altogether, inside and on the topside baggage rack, sixteen passengers bunched as snugly as herring in a tin, grousing, sweating, reading, eating, snoring. Seth sat with his back to the driver, facing a happy-looking man wearing thick spectacles, a soiled collar and cravat and an ill-fitting suit. With Clapham Junction only minutes behind their dust, this final leg of the journey was already more uncomfortable than the run down from Bedworth nearly three months earlier. To add to his misery, the man facing him, their knees almost touching, turned out to be a tireless conversationalist.

"Always been a commercial traveler," he began. "Sold everything under the sun. You name it, I've sold it. Fascinating line of work, selling."

Seth sought refuge in his thoughts. What sort of woman would Margaret Addison turn out to be? Would she listen to reason? Probably not. Definitely not. He'd have to do his monumental best to talk her into returning with him. He disliked the thought of pulling her heartstrings. It seemed so shamefully devious. Could she be deranged? Made so by all she'd been through? Her father hadn't mentioned that possibility, but whatever else possessed her to take up with a savage in the wilderness instead of coming straight home from Quebec? Her red Indian must be a man indeed. And did his tribe accept her? Blonde, fair-skinned, now knowing their language, their ways? And to top it off she'd actually married this ... what was his name? He got out the copy of the letter her father had given him.

The commercial traveler chattered on relentlessly. "Always preferred men's clothing to anything else. Except, perhaps, farm implements. Taught me everything there is to know about farming. Know what a box drain is? Made of stones arranged in the bottom of a trench to form a hollow channel about six inches square. Fascinating, eh?"

Impervious to his listener's lack of interest, the salesman continued. The passengers sitting on either side of him drooped their heads in sleep, but Seth read to himself:

Dearest Daddy and Mother,
I've no way of knowing if this will ever reach you; I can only hope and pray it will. You'll think that I've lost all reason, became completely insane, but it's not so. There's nothing wrong with my brain, I'm in the best of health. The fact is I've found a life and love here in the wilderness, as outrageous as that may strike you. I'll explain how it came about. Our ship ran aground partway up the Hudson River, and we were attacked by Mohawks. I fled for my life and, as it turned out, was the sole survivor.

I was found by Oneida hunters, a tribe related to the Mohawks who attacked us. I shan't bore you with what followed, but through everything, good and bad, I remained determined to get an escort to take me up to Quebec, to Pierre. Eventually I did, and we were reunited. But then everything went awry. We discovered we'd made a chaotic mistake. (I know I did.) Pierre turned out not to be the man for me, nor was I the woman for him. So I left Quebec with my Oneida escort and returned with them to their castle (village). I asked to be adopted into the tribe and my rescuer, Two Eagles, and I were married. In a formal ceremony, Mother.

Did all I'd been through affect my brain? Did I

lose my sanity? No, all I did was fall in love. Since you will never meet him, let me describe him. He is very tall, very handsome, uncommonly stubborn and single-minded. He can be petulant, he has no sense of humor, and he's excruciatingly literal, as are all Indians. He's a know-all, he can be quarrelsome, sour-tempered, overbearing and as sullen as a six-year-old denied his favorite toy. I adore him, and he adores me with equal fervor. We're happy. Life here is harsh, dirty, difficult, often dangerous, but all in all beautiful and marvelous in many ways. Because we are together.

I realize all this must come as a frightful shock, one I've no right to inflict. I love you both and would never want to hurt you, but I have to go with my heart. So I beg you to try and see what I've done through my eyes, if you can.

"All drains use flat stones on the bottom, of course. Walter Blith recommended digging stone drains three to four feet deep, in which the lower layer of faggots is covered by turf, then fifteen inches of stone. Fascinating, eh?"

Two Eagles would look preposterous in a gentleman's jacket and trousers, in button shoes, a brim hat and cravat. At the dinner table he'd use his fingers. He doesn't believe in God, none of them do. In church he'd be unable to carry a tune. Sitting still for five minutes he'd fidget like a small boy. He'd sleep, he'd snore, he'd embarrass you to tears. I could never make him over into a proper gentleman. I'd never try; I'd never tamper with perfection.

I wanted happiness with Pierre, I yearned for love, faithfulness, a tender and sensitive husband who would think of me first, as I would of him. A man whom I could trust, one who cares and is not afraid to show affection.

The man I wanted wasn't Pierre, it is Two Eagles.

This was no snap decision and definitely not an easy one. I believe it was fated to turn out so from the first. I've been here many months and not once have I felt the slightest twinge of regret. Nor do I think I acted precipitously, that having "lost" Pierre I jumped into another relationship to relieve the pain, to clear my head and my heart. Two Eagles and I were in love before we got to Quebec, and looking back on it there was no way I could have seen him off and remained with Pierre.

"Stones comprising a stone drain are ideally less than two-and-a-half inches in diameter. Know how they measure them? I'll tell you—the stone breaker passes each one through a ring of that diameter. Fascinating, eh?"

I love you both and always will. I miss you, home, the family, my friends, Bedworth and expect to till the end of my days. But I made a decision, a good one. In my heart, as I write this, I know it was right. I beg you both, please don't send someone to track me down. He'll only return to you without me. I'm happy beyond all expectation. I'm so deeply in love sometimes it dizzies me. Please, please, try and understand and accept it.
   Love, love, love,
   M.

"I beg your pardon, are you listening?" the commercial traveler asked.

"To every word. Drains, drains, as you were saying—"

II

THE BLACK CLOAK

13

The leaf of the white oak had grown to the size of the red squirrel's foot; the Oneidas' fields were ready for planting. The soil was raised into hills three feet apart and imbedded with *signoc* shells. Three or four kernels of corn were planted in each hill, as well as seeds for pumpkins, squash, beans and tobacco.

Benjamin grew, too. His mother delighted in him. His father hunted, fished and played with him by the hour. And wondered about Blue Creek. Did he still consider Benjamin Graywind's *cian*? If so, Two Eagles reflected, Blue Creek's mind had to be as battered as his body.

Far from Onneyuttahage, across the Atlantic in Southampton, Seth Wilson's coach arrived in all its dusty majesty from London, reaching its final stop barely a day before the *Deliverance* was scheduled to embark. Seth took a room at the Admiral Pew Hotel and, after a brief nap to refresh himself, got up and prepared to inspect the city, in particular the West Bay docks where the *Deliverance* would be dropping anchor.

After locking his door he descended to the lobby and approached the desk. The lounge was crowded, its patrons surrounding tiny tables. The crowd filled the room with smoke, discussion, argument and laughter. Conversation ceased abruptly as Seth entered. He set his hands on the desk, and the clerk fashioned a smile around prominent incisors.

"My ship docks tomorrow," said Seth. "I don't know the exact time. Do you by chance have a schedule of arrivals and departures?"

"Oh yes, sir."

From under the desk the clerk produced a massive, dog-eared notebook.

"The *Deliverance*," said Seth. "Out of Boston. Due in tomorrow. Morning, I hope."

The clerk's jaw dropped slowly. "Oh dear, I'm afraid the *Deliverance* won't be arriving morning or afternoon."

"What?"

"She sank. Just the other day. About four hundred miles west of Land's End. Lock, stock and barrel at the bottom of the ocean. Only two hands saved."

Shock settled in Seth's heart. "Oh my god." He indicated the book. "May I look?"

"Oh, she's listed all right, departure and arrival and *was* due in tomorrow." The clerk showed him. Seth groaned aloud. "Now don't upset yourself, sir. See that gentleman with the pegleg over in the corner? That's Joshua Conklin, first mate aboard the *Sea Robin*. He knows the whole story firsthand. It was the *Sea Robin* rescued the survivors."

Joshua Conklin did not bother to remove his wooden leg from the little table, hemmed in as it was by assorted mugs, tankards and glasses. Nearly a dozen men crowded around him, and Seth had a hard time pushing up close. Conklin smiled toothlessly, grasping the outstretched hand, closing his own completely over it. He smelled strongly of tobacco and slightly of fish.

"Sit, lad." One of his visitors obligingly rose to leave. Seth took his stool. As he spoke Conklin got out a battered briar pipe, filled it, tamped it with his thumb and lit it with the table candle. He cleared his throat. Everyone leaned forward.

"We was 'hind her by a full day but the seas was still choppy by the time we got to where the blow struck, and we made our way through. We came upon the first bits of wreckage about six bells of the afternoon and within the hour picked up the only two hands what didn't drown or get their heads bashed in. They had some story to tell." He shuddered.

"You're sure it was the *Deliverance*?" Seth asked, crossing his fingers.

"Oh yes, we knowed she were ahead of us even before we spotted the two in the drink."

"I was told she'd be virtually the last ship to return to Boston, it's so late in the summer."

" 'Tis for a round-trip. But I know for a fact at least one more ship'll be putting out."

"Are you sure?"

"The *Deliverance* was the Cooksey-Draper Company's like my ship, the *Sea Robin*. Just this morning I heard that Captain Evan Box will be taking the *Dauntless* over with the passengers that would have taken the *Deliverance*. A bit dry in the keel, the *Dauntless*, been out of service for some time, but she's seaworthy and they's no better or more experienced captain than Evan Box." He leaned forward, bringing his listeners in closer. "I understand the managing partners offered him a pretty penny to come out of retirement and get back to sea."

"I absolutely must be on her!" exclaimed Seth.

"If you was booked on the *Deliverance* I'm sure you're guaranteed passage on the *Dauntless*. Cooksey and Draper's port office is just up the way. I'll walk you up, introduce you to George Latchford, the manager. George and I go way back. You'll get to America, lad." He laughed. "If you're sure that's what you want."

The others laughed.

14

A cockroach scurried across the bare floor as Seth turned to the full-length mirror hanging beside a cheap chest of drawers. He watched the creature scuttle to a hole in the floor down which it vanished, and compared his approaching voyage to the insect's travels. From Boston he would venture westward and, like the cockroach down the hole, vanish into the wilderness.

He put on a black cloth suit and green woolen stockings, fastening the latter to his breeches with points of black galloon. His wide-brimmed hat was black felt circled with a narrow band of ribbon and a shiny silver buckle. He put on a mandilion lined with fustian, then started to sweat. Hat, mandilion and jacket he removed and placed in his portmanteau.

He surveyed himself in the glass. He looked fun-loving, carefree, as if in him there was laughter that wanted to get out. Passersby, after a quick glance, might take him for a man of business, a politician, a solicitor; only his attire confirmed him as a man of God.

Out of his valise he got his letter of introduction to the Colonial Missionary Society. He read it for the sixth time, restored it to its envelope, wrapped his nonclerical clothing in heavy paper, secured the bundle with cord, and closed the portmanteau and valise. At the door, giving the room one last look around, he also glanced toward the hole the cockroach had taken.

"Farewell, my friend. Wish me good journey."

Downstairs, he gestured to the desk clerk, who was engrossed in a newspaper. He came up smiling, then mild surprise crossed his face at sight of Seth's clothing.

"Did you enjoy your stay, Mr.—Reverend Wilson?"

"Immensely." He set a parcel on the counter. "I'll need a boy to take this to the nearest mail carrier for me."

Dipping a quill in the inkpot he scribbled Benjamin Addison's name and address on the parcel, then Seth put down money for his lodgings. The clerk woke a boy sitting in a cubbyhole office behind him who came out yawning and fisting his eyes.

"What's your name?" Seth asked.

"Christopher Augustus Middleborough, sir, at your service."

"Well, Christopher Augustus Middleborough, if you can carry all those letters you can carry this." He tapped the parcel. "To the mail carrier. Fast as you can leg it. The postage will be paid at the other end." Seth produced a shiny shilling. "For you, Christopher Augustus."

"Yes sir, right away, sir!"

"Mind you, get a receipt and bring it to me at the West docks straightaway. I'll be by the *Dauntless*. We sail in one hour, so shake a leg."

"Yes sir, yes sir."

Off he ran.

"Tell me something," said Seth to the clerk, "have you ever crossed the ocean?"

"No sir, never had the pleasure."

"Me, either; I wonder, will it be a pleasure?"

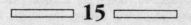

15

West Bay docks offered the stench of rotten fish, bird and horse droppings, fetid bilge water, dead rats and other vermin, cooking cabbage, rotten refuse, sour rum and countless other odors combining in one vast overwhelming assault on nostrils and eyes.

Horns, whistles, whipping canvas, men shouting, birds shrilling, cattle lowing, sheep baaing, dogs barking, fishmongers screaming, horses clopping, the wind, the washing waves assailed the ear. A colorful panorama of goods—bales and barrels, wagons and carts and crates, signs, flags, acres of sail, a forest of masts, an agitation of humanity buying, selling, working, idling, leaving, arriving—attacked the eye.

The stinking, eye-dazzling, ear-dinning activity impressed Seth Wilson, who had never even seen a port, much less crossed an ocean. Less impressive was the *Dauntless*, snugly hawsered, the gaskets loosed, ready to be hauled up. A three-masted, square-rigger wearing leagues of rope, she looked ancient to Seth. He envisioned the dark, limitless depths and wondered would this groaning, barnacle-studded derelict ever reach Boston, would it ever get as far as Land's End?

Passengers were already boarding. He watched a middle-aged man and wife ascend the narrow gangplank, followed by a pretty, buxom girl chattering animatedly. The man laughed at something she said. Reaching the deck quite out of breath he was greeted by the captain, then helped his wife and daughter aboard.

Others started up the gangplank.

"Sir, sir . . . !" Christopher Augustus came running, waving a yellow slip of paper.

"Good boy." Seth rewarded him with a second shilling.

"Good voyage, sir, don't get seasick." He waved and vanished into the crowd. Filling his lungs, fear slightly hastening his heartbeat and weakening his legs, Seth started up the gangplank thinking, would he ever come down it? He envisioned the *Deliverance* at the bottom of the sea.

Bloodshot eyes, bulbous nose, mottled skin and foul breath testified that Captain Evan Box drank. He carried his vast overweight low and entirely in front. Consumed with doubts, Seth nonetheless took the hand Box offered.

"Welcome aboard, sir. Captain Evan Box at your service."

"Delighted, Captain. Reverend Seth Wilson."

The captain turned his attention to the two passengers behind Seth, who gestured to a sailor with tattooed forearms and a hook for his left hand.

"Excuse me, how does one get down into the hold?"

"Down the companion ladder, sir." He indicated it with his hook.

Seth started down it into Stygian darkness. His feet found the floor and he looked about, slowly accustoming his eyes to the absence of light, save for the little coming down through the open hatch. There was no ventilation, so close was the air it pressed. The cargo, unloaded hours earlier—mainly hides and furs—left behind a rank odor that mingled with the fetid smell of bilge water.

Now he could dimly see about. The upper hold—for there was a second hold under the floor—looked discouragingly small, cramped, with a ceiling so low anyone over six foot could barely stand upright. Bunks lined the walls. The area was cluttered with boxes filled with bundles of clothing, cooking utensils, baggage, guns, tools and food for the voyage. These, he assumed, would be consigned to the hold below to make living room for the emigrants. The ship's pinnace had been dismantled and the boards would be used for dining tables. Piled to the low ceiling in one corner, occupying nearly a quarter of the space, were barrels of hardtack and oatmeal. There was barely, wheat, peas and other vegetables for planting in the New World. There were boxes stenciled tinned biscuit, salted meat, dried fish, cheese and dried vegetables. And beer with which to wash it all down. Where, he wondered, did they keep the fresh water? And how long would it stay fresh under such conditions?

So this dark, dank, miasmic wooden pit was to be home for the next two months. Sighing, he selected a bunk and shoved his portmanteau and valise under it, first removing the letter of introduction from the valise and slipping it into his inside jacket pocket. Then he ascended the ladder to the deck, breathed deeply and spied the sailor with the hook for a hand. He was grinning.

"You'll get used to the stinks, the dark and the roll of the sea."

"Have I a choice?"

The sky was pale blue with not a single cloud. With all eighty-two passengers safely aboard, the *Dauntless* prepared to depart. The lines were loosed and hauled in, the blocks rattled and the sheaves creaked as the boom swung lazily across the deck. Up went the foremast sail, flapping and filling as the breeze picked up. Up went the main- and mizzen-mast sails. Away slipped the *Dauntless*, the crowd cheering, horns and whistles sounding.

Seth stood aft watching the dock retreat. Down the Southampton water they glided, creaking and groaning in every seam, down the Salent past the Isle of Wight and out into the channel, where the wind blowing from the east-northeast found their canvas. Tacking, they headed west-southwest.

Some hours later, they passed the Manacles, turning a few points onto a northwesterly heading, and began to pitch in the long, rolling swell of the Atlantic. Before they slipped by the Scilly Isles, the last land of England, most of the passengers were suffering from seasickness.

Among them, Seth Wilson.

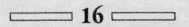 16

Summer had moved almost halfway through the lazy days of August; nature fell prey to a lethargy that would prevail until the chill nights of late September. The

katydids, grown fat from seasonal gorging, chirped list-
lessly in the long twilight, goldenrod flourished in the
fields, and the wild bergamot flaunted its purple loveli-
ness. In the woodland, tall, hay-scented ferns stood garbed
in the pale green of the wood duck's crest.

Margaret, out with Benjamin to pick blueberries, found
a number of bushes heavy with fat ripe fruit at the foot of
a weed-infested outcropping. Locating a thick stick, she
thrust it deep into a fissure in the rocks and hung Benjamin's cradleboard on the projecting end. The breeze began
rocking him to sleep. From the woods behind her came the
low hooting of a spruce grouse and the drumming of
wings. Overhead, a robin serenaded her: *cheer-up, cheerily
cheer-up, cheerily.*

Margaret's elm-bark bucket filled rapidly. Suddenly, she
heard dry grass being crushed underfoot. She was standing
at a right angle to the outcropping, but the sound turned
her slowly, warily to her left. The spruce grouse was silent, the robin had flown off. She gasped and dropped her
bucket.

Then she stiffened and swallowed. Blue Creek stood
staring icily. Margaret's throat constricted so she could not
utter a sound. His eyes rounded hugely, his hand shot to
his knife. Up it came, the blade catching sunlight. Straight
at her face it flew.

17

She felt the blade slice her cheek, she was sure. But
there was no blood. He wasn't aiming at her.

At Benjamin! She screamed and spun around. The knife
had struck, piercing the upraised head of a rattlesnake. It
was stretched down the ledge and starting out along the

stick supporting the cradleboard. The creature dropped, the knife dislodging, falling harmlessly to one side. The snake twitched and died.

"Dear God, dear God . . ." she murmured.

"Dear God," he said sneeringly. "Carry your *cian* on your back where he belongs and no snake can get close to it."

He spoke in Oneida. She began gushing gratitude, all but falling to her knees to kiss the hem of his breechclout. He did not even look at her. Retrieving his knife, he walked off. Margaret did not see where he headed, having turned full attention to Benjamin, holding him hard against her breasts.

He awoke crying out irritably.

— III —
THE CRUEL SEA

18

The corn in the fields of the Iroquois was approaching full ripeness as, nearly three thousand miles away, the *Dauntless* moved steadily north-westward under full sail and a blistering sun. The sky showed no sign of impending change in the beautiful weather. But as Captain Box pointed out to Abner Keaton, his wife Leonora, daughter Hannah and Seth Wilson, bad weather would "show its ugly face beyond the halfway point as sure as the Devil makes rocks and shoals." As Box spoke, he kept an eye on the sky to the north.

Seth was getting his sea legs and could now walk the deck in the gentle roll of the vessel as surefooted as any crewman. The threat of rough seas did not worry him nearly as much as that of prolonged confinement below. The rats were not many but active, and every day a few were dispatched, but birth kept their numbers from diminishing. The crush of passengers added their body odors, vomit, excrement and urine to existing stenches. Buckets provided the only sanitary facilities, and privacy was nonexistent. One slept with one's eyes watering beneath closed lids.

Some unfortunate passengers took sick even before they sighted the Manacles and were to remain that way through seven more weeks of suffering. In the persisting heat, the water supply was rapidly turning foul. Fever and dysentery threatened. To remain out on deck as much as possible be-

came everyone's most sought-after goal. Many exercised;
others played games to pass the time; a few tried to muster
competition in ninepins, in defiance of the rolling deck.

Passengers cooked on deck when seas were calm, in
small braziers set in boxes of sand to catch the sparks. The
crew worked tirelessly caulking leaky seams, readjusting
rigging, pumping out the bilge and at other chores. The
deck was holystoned daily.

The route the *Dauntless* followed was that which fisher-
men had taken to the Grand Banks for the past two hundred years, according to the captain. The ship headed north
toward Greenland to avoid the opposing flow of the Gulf
Stream. Once beyond its influence, Box planned to head
west, tacking into the wind, and move with the Arctic current toward Newfoundland before steering south to the
New England coast.

Seth was spending much of his time in the Keatons'
company. Abner Keaton was a bookseller and was bringing four large crates of volumes, planning to open a shop
in the center of Boston. The property had already been
purchased through an agent and Abner was eager to get
there and establish his business.

"Third largest port in the world, after London and Bristol,"
he said proudly. "Population of seven thousand souls."

"Will you be staying in Boston, Mr. Wilson?" Hannah
asked, eyeing him warmly and turning on her magnificent
smile. Sight of it inspired weakness across Seth's chest, a
constriction of his throat and wobbliness in his knees.

Her smile tempted him to throw his arms around her.
She was the most desirable female he had met in ages. But
he warned himself not to harbor thoughts so inappropriate
for a man of the cloth.

He liked all three Keatons. Abner had graduated from
Oxford and had considered teaching before settling into
selling books in Knightsbridge in London. He jokingly
called himself a bibliomaniac, so fond was he of his chosen vocation. Influenced by both her parents, Hannah was

an avid reader, her tastes eclectic. When settled in the New World, she planned to teach.

"What are your plans when you disembark, Mr. Wilson?" she asked as the four of them stood watching Captain Box lecture a young crewman for carelessly tossing a bucket of slops overboard into the wind.

"He drinks, that one, he smells like old cask kindling," Leonora muttered.

"Will you be staying in Boston?" Hannah went on.

"Not for long," replied Seth. "Once I'm cleared for assignment I'll be heading into the interior."

"To convert the savages?" cried Hannah. "How exciting!"

"How marvelous," said Leonora.

"How dangerous," added Abner. "Mind you keep your hat on, lad. I've always thought bald chaps would make the best missionaries to the Indians. Temptation removed, so to speak."

"Which Indians?" Hannah asked.

Seth was reluctant to specify. Where he was heading—and why—was no one's business, not even friends'.

Abner saved him from replying. "Stay clear of the Iroquois," he cautioned. "I understand they're the fiercest of the fierce."

Hannah sounded intensely curious. "How long do you go out for? Six months? A year? And must you convert a certain set number?"

"We do what we can in the time allotted us. Or we request. Some missionaries stay in the field ten years, even longer."

Hannah grinned. "Not you," she said confidently.

Seth feigned surprise. "Why not?"

"I don't know. You don't seem the St. Augustine sort."

"You mean on fire with zealotry? What makes you say that?"

"Are you?"

"Mustn't pry, my dear." Abner affectionately admonished her, taking Leonora's arm. "Let's go for a stroll, Lee."

"Sorry," murmured Hannah sheepishly when her parents were out of earshot. "I didn't mean to be so personal."

"You weren't." He looked after the Keatons. "Your mother and father are jewels."

"And your parents? Where are they?"

"My mother's dead. My father's in Edinburgh, in building construction, last I knew. We haven't seen each other in years."

"Pity. Do you stay in touch?"

"No."

"So—you're alone in the world." Hannah studied him. "Forgive my nosiness, but how was it you became a clergyman? Was there a—divine call?"

She *was* getting personal. And if he let her go on she'd be getting him into lying. Her doubt as to the strength of his commitment disturbed him. She was the first person he'd gotten to know well since putting on his black cloak in the hotel room in Southampton. He smiled uncomfortably.

"I'm sorry, there I go again, nosy Hogan," Hannah said cheerfully.

When she suggested they walk around the deck, Seth offered her his arm. He continued disturbed by her seeming skepticism; clothes, evidently, did not make the missionary. He must be more careful in talking about religion. Maybe he should never let her see him without his Bible? No, he'd feel uncomfortable, even hypocritical, suddenly carrying it about.

It occurred to him that since he'd bought it in London upward of two weeks ago he had yet to open it.

19

Seth soon changed his mind. He began reading his Bible publicly in the hope that Hannah would notice and elevate her opinion of his commitment.

He was smitten with her. She had much more than beauty. She offered intelligent conversation and companionship, she took his mind off the rigors and apprehension of the voyage, and her mere presence seemed to ease the strain of the hours in the hold. Many of their fellow passengers, unwilling or unable to cope, resorted to continuous complaining.

"I don't understand them," Hannah remarked as they stood at the starboard railing watching the churning sea. "That Mr. Dustin and his wife never open their mouths but to whine. We're all saddled with the same inconveniences and discomforts."

Seth had anticipated this as a subject for conversation. " 'How long will ye vex my soul, and break me in pieces with words?' " he asked.

"That's from the Bible."

"Job, chapter nineteen, verse two."

"Job had good reason to complain. Jeremiah, too, except when he bewailed getting old. I think he got a bit whiny over that, don't you?" Hannah asked.

"I—ah!—"

"That verse that begins, 'My flesh and my skin hath he made old.' Everybody's flesh and skin get old, it just happens; you can't do anything about it. What else did Jeremiah complain about? You must know."

"Everything, everything, worse than Job," he said hastily. "Breathe this sea air. It's ambrosia! Would they could pipe it down into the hold at night. Your father tells me your mother is a bit under the weather."

"It's the food. She has a very sensitive tummy. Eats like a bird always and not much of anything these days. You've seen. She'll likely starve herself when we hit bad weather. Has the captain mentioned when that will be? The sky was red last night. Does that mean anything?"

Seth looked north in emulation of the captain. The sky was clear all the way to the horizon. "I think fair weather," he predicted.

"I hope. For her sake. For us all. I have visions of the sea convulsing furiously, tossing us about in the hold like peas in a sieve. I'll tie me to a mast before I go through that, bother the wind and the sea."

"Perhaps it won't be that bad. 'The Lord *hath* his way in the whirlwind and the storm.' "

"Are you trying to impress me with your knowledge of the Bible?"

"Not at all, I just have a habit of falling back on it, there are so many pearls."

He could feel color rising in his cheeks.

"Let's walk."

Passengers were washing their clothes on deck, using buckets of seawater and homemade soap. Small children toddled about on leashes, the free ends tied securely around their mothers' wrists. They spied Abner and Leonora. Mrs. Keaton did not look well to Seth. She was paler than usual, dark circles under her eyes, her lips ivory, her walk unsteady. Hannah ran to help Abner support her. Her mother shook them both off.

"I can walk, my dears, thank you all the same." As if to prove it, she stepped ahead of them, then suddenly grabbed the railing for support. As Hannah joined her, Abner told Seth, "There'll be bean soup for supper. One of our neighbors is making up a batch and invited us to share it. Lee's problem is she can't seem to get food down down below, what with the glorious stench."

* * *

That night after a dinner of salt meat, hardtack and some of the soup, Seth lay abed listening to the creaking of the ship and the snoring all around him when suddenly a strange odor made its way through the customary stenches.

Smoke.

Fire crackled in an empty bunk directly opposite him, the only light in the entire hold. People came awake and began shouting. The tumult grew louder as people scrambled up the ladder. The fire appeared to be contained in the bunk and one man had the presence of mind to beat at it with a blanket but was unable to extinguish it. As Seth threaded his way toward the flames, another man joined the first one, thrashing the flames with a fine piece of canvas. Seth pulled a blanket off a bunk and joined the effort. A woman fell screaming from the ladder. Those beneath her caught her and pushed her to one side while they clamored up as she shouted angrily.

Seth and the others got the fire out. By now the hold was filled with smoke, everyone choking, coughing, complaining bitterly. The hatch cover had been shoved aside, letting in moonlight. Seth looked about vainly for the Keatons, then assumed they were already up on deck. Before long the hold was completely empty, the passengers assembling on deck, many still coughing and choking but no one seriously hurt in the stampede topside.

But there would be no returning to the hold this night; the hatch cover was left off to let out the smoke.

At noon the next day the smell of smoke was still strong, discouraging most of the company from venturing back down the ladder. Seth, Abner and a number of other men discussed the incident with Captain Box as he came down the ladder to his cabin.

He was in a foul mood. "I warned every man jack of you before we passed the Isle of Wight that smoking belowdecks was strictly forbidden. We came within a whisker of complete and total immolation. Had it not been for your presence of mind, Mr. Wilson, and that of the other two gentlemen who extinguished the blaze, we'd all

be sleeping in Davy Jones' locker. When the underwriters
get wind of this back in Southampton, and somebody's
sure to blab, there'll be the devil to pay. I want to know
who's the culprit."

"Hard to say, Captain," said Abner. "Mr. Mannix, who
occupies that bunk, was on deck at the time. Members of
your crew saw him."

Box scowled. "Then it was one of his neighbors set the
fire."

"They deny it," said Seth. "It would have been anyone.
It's so dark. Anyway, I'm sure it was an accident."

"Carelessness is no accident," the captain rasped. "Whoever he is he should be made to pay in hard coin. You find
him, I'll see he pays. I'll put him in irons! That's all I have
to say on the matter." He glanced aloft, shading his eyes
with his gnarled hand. "The wind is backing onto the beam.
It'll blow tonight; the seas'll be restless. And inside of two
days the glass'll drop like a shot, mark my words."

20

In the cornfields the stalks gained the height of a man;
in the green husk the corn fattened. The field cricket
sang and in the clover the bees droned endlessly. Fledg-
lings were out of the nest.

Margaret and Two Eagles sat by a stream on a grassy
knoll, their privacy ensured on three sides by tall rushes.
They had bathed; he had washed her hair. She pulled her
comb through it and watched as, like a golden sword from
heaven, sunlight plunged through the early morning mist
warming to life hordes of butterflies. Slowly the mist dissolved, and the butterflies glowed, trembling and rising in
shimmering black and orange, their flight like pattering

rain. Upward they floated languidly and curled downward, sweeping away, descending to the meadow, settling like vividly colored autumn leaves to drink the dew.

With the heels of his hands Two Eagles wiped dry her shoulders and back and hips. She turned to face him. He stroked her limbs, her body, down to her toes. She moved closer and smiled lovingly. He bent to kiss her, his moist tongue finding hers. As he drew her close the hunger of her mouth set him glowing. Easing her down on her back, he kissed her forehead, her face, her eyelids. Motes of sunlight swam in the blue depths of her eyes. Her breath came huskily. Her skin gleamed in the now full sunlight. She held him. He slipped his hand between her thighs, his finger stole inside her place. She yielded her moistness and in him desire flamed. A sweet fragrance found his nostrils, sweeter than the flowers or her hair, a musky scent that seeped into his brain and made him wild with want of her.

The black and orange meadow stretched to the dark mountains to southeast, the Ganawagehas, Catskills. The sun rose higher, gilding the morning, bathing them with warmth. His tongue dueled hers, he could feel her rising passion. He nuzzled her hair. Lowering his chest to her heaving breasts, gently crushing them, his heart touched hers and the beatings blended.

And they made love.

They lay naked staring at the sky, her thoughts unaccountably returning to earlier years. She saw herself in the orchard throwing cider pippins, gleefully watching them smash against the tree trunks.

"Margaret!"

Up the walkway shaded by bowers of motley honeysuckle she ran. Through the flower gardens: laburnum, everlasting love-in-a-mist, hosts of perennials and annuals planted in neat rectangles and enclosed by box and lavender hedges.

"Margaret!"

"Coming!"

All the relatives would be at her birthday party, everyone arriving at once carrying parcels and boxes. The
dining-room table was set, the servants bustling about arranging the centerpiece of pink and white roses, straightening the chairs, the place settings. Soon they'd be
bringing in heaping platters of her favorite dishes: steaming roast beef, tiny potatoes still in their skins, fresh beans
and parsnip, and for dessert custards and ices and cookies
and fruit and the most splendid birthday cake ever baked.
She'd peeked into the kitchen and seen it: six layers tall,
armored in thick, delicious chocolate frosting. Nine can-
dles. Make a wish!

In poured her cousins and aunts and uncles, her grandparents. "Happy birthday! Happy birthday!"

Daydreams of home came infrequently. It was nearly a
year since the last one. She wished they wouldn't come at
all but she had to expect one once in a while. Did her conscience demand it? What if she had gone back, what
would life be today? Would she have eventually met
someone? Probably. Fallen in love, married, settled in or
near Bedworth. Children and church, teas, parties, fairs,
shopping. And sending her husband off to the office every
day, welcoming him home with sherry and dinner. She
glanced at Two Eagles. His eyes were closed; he was almost asleep. She could search from the Orkneys to
Penzance, she'd never find a man to equal him. There was
none. Bother England, this was home.

Iron Dog found Blue Creek dozing under his favorite tree
and woke him. He was in a foul mood.

"I have decided," Blue Creek growled. Iron Dog eyed
him, puzzled. "Do not be stupid, you know. I have to get
my nephew away from them before she kills him. Already
I have wasted too much time. Come."

"Where?"

"Back to the castle. And on the way, plan. Tonight I
will take him from their chamber while they sleep."

"How will you care for him all the way to Masso-waganine? I asked you that already, remember? How will you feed him? Where will you get milk?"

"I will—bring a woman with me."

"What woman? Think, my friend: these are the same old questions we have not found the answers to. And you are running off on six trails at once. Be patient, wait—"

"For what? For him to grow to manhood? I am leaving, taking him! What?"

A sly look had crept into Iron Dog's eyes. "Maybe there is a way after all to care for him all the way to Masso-waganine—"

"To Night Song waiting for me."

"*Nyoh.* Let us go, I will explain."

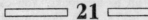

21

Iron Dog's scheme for abducting Benjamin was simple, with but one drawback that Blue Creek could see.

"Steal him in daylight?" he asked.

They sat in Iron Dog's chamber discussing the plan while the others in the longhouse slept. It was nearing the end of summer. The oaks would soon be dropping their acorns, the field crickets would move into the longhouses, the swallows would be the first birds to head south over the Ganawagehas Mountains to where Gâ'-oh never ventured.

Before any of this took place, Blue Creek would be long gone. His mind was made up.

"Daylight." Iron Dog nodded emphatically.

Blue Creek grunted. "You have said all along that when the time came one of us could sneak into their longhouse in the quiet heart of the night and while the two of them slept—"

"Not as good a scheme. Two Eagles' chamber is near the middle of their longhouse. Going in and coming out with the *cian* you would have to pass others' chambers. Who knows of Swift Doe's boys' sleeping habits? Eight Minks never sleeps. By day is best and least expected by either of them, *neh*? We must make surprise and quickness work for us.

"As I say, I have been watching the whiteskin squaw mother. Every day when the weather is fair she goes to the lake to swim, sometimes with Swift Doe. But we must act when the whiteskin one is by herself. Always, she takes the *cian* with her."

"What does she do with my nephew when she swims?"

"There are rocks where she leaves her clothes. She leans his cradleboard against the one nearest the water so she can see him. It will be easy to sneak around the rocks and, when she dives, to steal him. The maple trees are good cover right up to the rocks. You can grab your nephew, dive back behind them, flee through the trees. If you can get far enough away before she notices and pursues, there will be no swishing of branches to tell her which direction you take."

"She will not know where to begin to look," said Blue Creek. "That part I like."

"It will be all over then and there. You hide with him in a prearranged spot until after dark. I will bring Moon Dancer with milk for him."

"Do-wa-sku-ta's widow?"

"Thrown Bear, *nyoh*."

"She can give my nephew milk?"

"I did not say she will *give* it, I said she will have it. She can get it for us; she has promised."

Blue Creek looked skeptical. "Moon Dancer and I hardly know each other. Why should she do me a favor?"

"You do not remember, but Moon Dancer is my aunt. Besides, this will be a favor for my uncle, Thrown Bear. She hates Two Eagles for what he did to him."

"What?"

"Has no one told you what happened?" Iron Dog looked astonished. "He killed Thrown Bear on the Kanawage."

Blue Creek scoffed. "I do not believe that. Everyone knows they were best friends."

"They were. He killed him."

"How?"

"It is a long story. One you might better hear from Moon Dancer. Yes, she would like nothing better than to see the tall one with dirt in his mouth." He leered. "But she is willing to settle for kidnapping his *cian*."

"Graywind's *cian*," snarled Blue Creek. "*My* nephew." He was eyeing the little man with undisguised admiration. "You have planned this well, Iron Dog, very shrewdly. How am I to repay you?"

"My reward is your friendship."

Blue Creek snickered. "That and the opportunity this gives you to work evil. That is always your sweetest reward, *neh*?"

Iron Dog looked offended. "You are my friend. Do not friends do friends favors? A good turn that comes out of one's heart?"

Blue Creek grunted.

"You will make for the white caves," Iron Dog went on. "And the trail north to Massowaganine and Night Song."

"Night Song." Blue Creek's eyes sparkled. "Perfect. Except for one small detail: it is you who will steal my nephew."

"But—"

"And bring him to me at the prearranged spot behind the maple trees that shadow the cove. Moon Dancer can come by herself. Tell her. Once I have my nephew and the milk I will be on my own. Only you will kidnap him."

"If you rather."

"It will be the last favor I will ever ask of you and you will be well rewarded."

Iron Dog brightened. "How?"

"You will see. Just be careful the whiteskin squaw does not see you sneaking up. She will tear the air with her

screams. And make sure no one else is around watching
her swim. We do not want some accidental interruption
wrecking everything."

"I will be very careful."

"One other thing—do you think anyone suspects that I
will be heading for Onondaga Territory to join Night
Song?" He stiffened. "You did not tell Moon Dancer—"

"*Neh*," Iron Dog studied his friend in the dimming light:
his shinning pate, his scarred skin, his stumpy fingers. "Do
not worry. No one would dream you would go after Night
Song."

22

The *Dauntless* was nearing completion of its third week at
sea, approaching the midpoint of the voyage. The
weather continued pleasant, enough wind to belly the sails
without buffeting the little vessel about. So bright was the
sun it seemed to grow in circumference and spread over the
heavens. The sea heaved and rolled gently, the *Dauntless*
gliding through it without so much as upsetting a cup in its
saucer. The passengers crossed their fingers and prayed.
Captain Box studied the northwest horizon continually.

Seth was not normally pessimistic but he was unable to
dismiss a troubling impression, one peculiar to all ocean
voyagers: the *Dauntless* was a chip afloat in an ocean so
vast that his mind could not encompass its limits, an ocean
deep, unpredictable, powerful when aroused, extraordinarily cruel. Six inches of oak separated captain, crew and
eighty-two souls from the bottom, as he overheard one
passenger put it, and the longer the storms stayed away the
rougher they would be when they finally struck, for they
used the delay to increase their potency.

Bother such morbid thoughts, he chided himself. His mood should be ebullient. It was the sixth of September, his twenty-ninth birthday. Only it didn't seem like a birthday: no one to celebrate with, no congratulations, not a single gift. When they disembarked in Boston—assuming the ship made it—he must buy himself a gift, just so year number twenty-nine wouldn't slip into obscurity without something to recall it.

He stood at the bow with two couples, watching the vessel cleave the sea like a knife through a melon, the stem bar kicking up spume on both sides. Silently he urged the ship to greater speed. Was it conceivable they might cross without encountering a single storm? Highly unlikely, according to the first mate. Impossible, in Box's view.

Seth's thoughts went to Hannah, his mental oasis in these threatening surroundings, recalling a conversation they'd had several days earlier.

"You actually play the contrabass?"

"Why shouldn't I?"

"But you're . . . a woman."

"Ah, you noticed. I'll have you know I've played since I was five, when I had to stand on a chair."

Her favorite musical instrument: the great, fat, absurdly shaped, lank-necked, curving-headed contrabass! And Abner later claimed she was quite accomplished at it.

"I hated leaving it behind. I had to, it would have taken up so much room in the hold."

"You should have taken up the piccolo. Tell me more about Hannah Keaton."

"There's nothing very interesting. I do like to sing. Do you?"

"Who doesn't? I'm just not particularly talented. At anything."

"I love children, dancing, cooking."

"In that order? Lucky you, you're one of those who's gifted at everything he tries."

"Not really. I tried painting and failed dismally. Tried to

master German and decided to stick to French, which I'm not very good at. I've a poor ear, which makes for a poor accent. But I try."

She seemed incapable of getting down; her disposition was as bright as her smile and lifted him when they were together. Yet at the same time she had a slightly disturbing effect on him. He found he could not rein his feelings. He wasn't falling in love—he was plunging. She had to be aware of the effect she was having on him. Did she think him an utter ass?

Now he felt a tap on his shoulder and turned. Her smile ignited his own. Yes, he was plunging! She was wearing the same navy cotton jacket and skirt she'd worn when he first saw her ascending the gangplank. She also wore a short cloak, the hood down, her hair bound up in back and falling in curls on either side of her face.

She seemed to grow more beautiful every day; he could not see enough of her. In her presence his heart quickened and butterflies fluttered in his stomach. From the waist up he glowed, then stammered and blushed. "Happy birthday." She kissed his cheek. He gawked absurdly, his hand flying to his face.

"How did you—"

"Daddy told me. You two got into discussing birthdays the other day, remember? September sixth, and you're twenty-nine. Congratulations, Seth, many happy returns." She produced a small envelope. "I've absolutely no talent for such a thing, I'm afraid. It's as close as I could get."

Seth withdrew a silhouette of himself. "It's me, it's perfect! I had no idea you were so gifted!"

"Nonsense, I just drew your profile when you were standing at the rail one day, looking like Drake. Then I cut it out."

He stared at the image. "When we get to Boston I shall have it framed. I'll treasure it always. Only something's missing. You. Can you, would you make one of yourself? I'll have them framed facing—"

"If you like."

"Please do. And thank you, thank you,"

She frowned. "Can't you do better than that? Hold still."

She kissed him on the lips and walked away as the two couples at the bow watched in amusement.

That night about an hour before dawn the wind came up, blowing furiously for a time, setting the *Dauntless* rolling, spilling sleepers out of their bunks and objects off the makeshift tables. When the sun came up, it seemed to have a calming effect, for within minutes the wind lost its bluster, the sea settled within itself and the ship sped on as smoothly as before. As usual, Seth ate breakfast with the Keatons. No one mentioned the rough seas but all eyes held an anxious look.

The sea stayed reasonably calm for the next new days. When Hannah gave Seth the silhouette of herself, he placed both in the envelope containing the letter of introduction to the missionary society.

Early one afternoon the hogpen on the afterdeck was opened to remove a dead animal. The passengers watched as two muscular sailors hoisted the creature up to the railing and overboard. A man standing behind Seth remarked that an animal dying en route was bad luck.

"Aboard the *Columbine* on a voyage to the West Indies a horse died. They hit a storm off Bermuda and three hands were washed overboard. Mind what I say: when a creature dies a man will too, as sure as the Devil has hooves."

An hour later, in a spot on deck affording him reasonable privacy Seth sat with his back to the fo'c'sle, composing a poem. The crumpled sheets surrounding his feet testified to the difficulty. He crumpled yet another attempt, threw it down angrily and failed to see it bounce around the corner.

Hannah was walking on deck with her mother as the crumpled paper rolled to her feet. She picked it up.

"What is it?" Lenora asked.

Both had stopped. Hannah read: "To Hannah." Her mother grinned wickedly and moved to look around the corner of the fo'c'sle. Hannah caught her in time. They backed away. "Listen," said Hannah, " 'Since the first day when I saw your smile, my heart took wing—' "

"Go on."

"That's all there is."

Another tightly balled sheet came rolling into view. Hannah turned her back on it. "Let's go back around the other way, Mother. And don't say one word about this to Daddy."

"Perish forbid!" Leonora exclaimed.

"Please, Seth is never to find out. Promise."

"I promise."

Back around the corner of the fo'c'sle out of their sight, Seth cleared his throat and read: " 'Since the very first time I saw your smile, My heart has been singing all the while.' Dreadful. Pitiful! What the devil rhymes with smile? Tile? Pile? Rile? File? Spile? What the devil is a spile?"

It wasn't working, it never would. His words of adulation were in his heart in all their poetic beauty; he simply couldn't get them out and onto paper. Still, maybe that was good. What if he handed her the completed poem, she read two lines and burst out laughing?

She couldn't be that insensitive, though he couldn't blame her for thinking he was ridiculous. He'd been at it for more than an hour and couldn't get through the second line.

"Pathetic, old chap."

At least now he knew he was no competition for John Dryden; not even for the nameless doggerel scribblers who left their inspirations on walls and fences.

He gave up, collected his discarded efforts, got to his feet and, leaving quill and inkpot for the moment, threw his papers overboard, making sure the wind was at his back. Turning from the railing, he noticed one crumpled paper where the fo'c'sle met the deck. He disposed of it and picked up his writing utensils.

"Relax, old chap. At least this way she'll never know what a rotten poet you are."

23

Blue Creek waited restlessly at the rendezvous. Sundown was still hours away, and Moon Dancer would not be bringing the milk until after dark. She would carry it in a clay jug, which had been buried to keep the contents cool.

But long before she showed up he would hold his nephew in his arms. He had found the perfect hiding place. While he paced his heart eagerly drummed. By day after tomorrow he would be in Massowaganine, safe from pursuit.

The prospect of vengeance thrilled him. The sun would be coming up for the first time in the long darkness that had been his life since his capture.

He was so happy, so exhilarated, he began singing. Through the leaves overhead he could see the sun on its downward path. Iron Dog would be coming with his nephew any time now.

Blue Creek corrected himself. *"Not nephew! My son, mine and Night Song's!"*

Meanwhile, Iron Dog crouched behind the rocks, having taken the precaution of removing his headband with the two hawk feathers. Carefully he inched upward so he could see Margaret sitting naked in shallow water, head down, shampooing her hair. She sat facing the shore squarely. Why must she take so long and not turn, not once? Maybe he should have come earlier, when she was out swimming. Still, she'd probably go back out for one last swim to rinse out the mixture of powdered soapwort and camomile.

That would be his chance. From where he squatted he could not see the cradleboard leaning against the rocks. But it was there; she talked to her son as she washed. An indigo bunting landed on the rock . . . and lifted its voice in song.

He looked past the bird to Margaret as she made quarter turn to her left. She was rinsing her hair. She sat about ten feet from shore, the water rising to just under her breasts. Impulse seized Iron Dog: *Now!*

He crept around the rocks, keeping as low as possible, his headband in his left hand. He could not see the cradleboard without revealing himself. He would have to stretch prone and make a grab for the baby.

He threw himself forward. Margaret screamed. Pulling the cradleboard to him by the two rawhide strings, he jumped to his feet and ran for the maples. Into the trees he ran, clutching the infant, Margaret's screams ringing in his ears. He turned to see how closely she pursued him, but saw nothing and heard only her voice. He turned his eyes forward. Too late—into a tree he slammed. Still clinging to Benjamin, he fell to his knees muttering, tested his shoulder, decided nothing was broken and got up.

In his path stood Red Paint and Fox. Anger Maker came up pushing between them. They stared at him, puzzled. Dropping Benjamin, he threw himself to one side, sprinting through the trees, stumbling, falling, regaining his feet, pausing to orient himself and turning sharply left.

Red Paint retrieved Benjamin just as Margaret came running up, the sight of her baby safe stopping her screaming. Oblivious of her nakedness she snatched him from Red Paint, holding Benjamin so tightly he cried out.

24

At the crashing sound of Iron Dog's approach, Blue Creek shot to his feet.

"Ahhhhhh!" he exclaimed in anticipation.

Iron Dog came up, out of breath. "Get out of here quick. They're coming!"

"Who? What are you talking about? Where is he?"

"I will tell you, come, hurry—"

Blue Creek stood his ground, now holding Iron Dog's arm so tightly the other man winced. "Where!"

Iron Dog tried vainly to shake loose, then hurriedly explained. Blue Creek's eyes rounded as he listened; all his joy, his glow of triumph, fled him. Iron Dog's words were like hammer blows to his heart. He could not speak or move, only stand gaping in shock. Iron Dog babbled on, squirming, struggling to free himself, shrinking from Blue Creek's deepening scowl.

Now Blue Creek growled, bellowed frustration and let go of Iron Dog. But only briefly. Whipping out his knife, he slit Iron Dog's throat. Gushing blood draped him, his eyes bulged, he struggled to emit a grotesque gurgling sound. More blood spilled down his chest.

Watching him fall, Blue Creek lifted his eyes and saw Margaret and the others coming through the trees. Off he ran, leaving his friend lying on his side kicking, clutching his throat, his hands crimson, his eyes glazing in death.

Blue Creek ran, his mind whirling, recalling the failure of the scheme. Still, even had Iron Dog succeeded, his reward would have been a knife. He knew too much to be permitted to live. To leave and not silence him would have been stupid—and cruel. Two Eagles would torture him, force him to tell all. Cowardly Iron Dog screamed when stung by a hornet. How would he stand fire at his feet, or his nails pulled out one by one? Weakling that he was, he would not have survived a week in Huron captivity.

Running full speed, Blue Creek came to the white caves and the trail north. No one was behind him. He had regained his health, and was in superb condition. He would eventually outrun Fox and Red Paint. Anger Maker would not keep up with him, and Two Eagles' squaw, content to have her *cian* back, would not even pursue.

The *cian* that was not hers. Not even Graywind's.

His!

"My son, mine!"

This failure did not end it. He would try again for his son. And again until he succeeded!

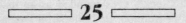

25

The days dragged by. Monotony reigned, boredom prevailed. One night a ring appeared around the moon, and a school of dolphins scurried through the gently heaving ocean. Just before dawn the waves gave way to a heaving swell.

A group of emigrants climbed up on deck to find Captain Box in discussion with his three mates, two of whom were pilots. Overnight black clouds had formed to the northwest, lumbering across the sky toward the *Dauntless*. The air grew heavy; lightning flashed in the distance. By four bells, approaching midmorning, drizzle turned into a chill rain that sent the passengers back down into the foul hold.

Captain Box descended the ladder and called for attention. "As some of you have seen topside, bad weather is coming." He drew their attention to the swell and warned that the strong winds would produce breakers huge and threatening. "You must tie everything down down here. As I speak, men are aloft furling the topsails."

"Why not keep all the sails up and run through the storm?" a man asked.

"The waves that are coming would make it impossible," replied Box. "And the winds will be fierce; they'd tear the sails to tatters."

"Can't we turn around and go back to where the weather's clear?" asked a woman. "And let the storm pass in front of us?"

"No, madam. Because it won't be *a* storm, it will be many, all rolled together and all around us. Oh, there'll be lulls, the wind will let up to a degree, but the waves won't shrink any."

"How bad can it get?" asked Abner Keaton.

"There's no predicting that," replied Box. "Or how long it'll last. Perhaps a week. I'm going to have to ask you to stay down here in the hold until the all clear." Up went a chorus of groans. 'I know, it's hard, but I can't permit anyone up on deck. My men'll be working around the clock, and we can't let you endanger your own lives and possibly theirs. So please, stay put. One other thing: if the rain gets heavy, and it likely will, I'm afraid I'll have to order the hatch covered."

Another, louder groan.

"With no air we'll suffocate!" protested a man.

Box shook his head, "I promise that won't happen. You're my responsibility. I'll take care of you as best I can. All I ask in return is that you obey orders."

"You've been through bad storms before?" asked Seth.

"Many."

"How bad it get? Truthfully?"

"Truthfully, sir, you can't imagine. But you're safe down here. The *Dauntless* may be a long time out of the blocks but she's seaworthy as they come. I wouldn't be here if she weren't. Any other questions?"

None came.

"Very well, for the time being the hatch'll stay open. But don't, I repeat, don't come up on deck for any reason. If there's an emergency, call, and somebody will come down."

"What if we take on water and start sinking?" asked a man.

"We won't," Box replied, trying to sound confident. He touched his cap in salute and started up the ladder. The Reverend McCoy, a Baptist minister with a heron's eyes and physique, lifted his shrill voice.

"May God have mercy on our souls. Let us pray."

Captain and crew worked feverishly. Early in the evening galeforce winds struck, the sea rose and the *Dauntless* found herself in the midst of a series of fierce storms. The hatch was closed. Below, the air grew more and more fetid and contaminated. Passengers fell ill, most of them with dysentery. Some well-intentioned individual took it upon himself to relieve the stench and drive out the stale air by opening the scuttles. In rushed seawater, soaking bedding, clothing and passengers. Seasickness broke out again, and in the dank, nauseating stench, conditions became all but intolerable.

Leanora Keaton fell violently ill and could not even keep tea down. Nor, by three bells, could half of her fellow passengers.

Working conditions on deck became more and more hazardous. The hogpen aft broke loose and before the men could catch it, smashed against a bulwark stanchion and shattered, freeing all eleven pigs. They ran about the deck squealing, slipping and sliding, making it impossible for the men to work. In desperation, Box ordered the creatures thrown overboard.

Then a deckhand, one Amos Wheelwright, only sixteen, whom Seth had spoken with on occasion, was manning the whipstaff controlling the rudder with another man when a wave swept over the deck. Amos's companion, bigger and stronger than he, hung on. Amos was pitched overboard. As he hit the water his hand was whipped by the topsail halliards which streamed overboard, stretching across the water. Feeling the halliards strike, he grabbed hold. The ropes were thin, he was carried under as the one he managed to cling to ran out. But he held fast. His companion at the whipstaff shouted, "Man overboard!" Four men rushed for the inboard stretch of the halliard. They caught it before it ran out and hauled Amos to the surface. He was pulled close alongside with a boathook. The roll of the sea brought him within reach, he was grabbed by the hair and belt and pulled to safety.

Down in the hold the emigrants were becoming desperate; tempers grew short, patience thin, the situation was rapidly deteriorating to a stage where it threatened to be every man for himself. Barely able to breathe, soaked with seawater, chilled to the bone, thrown about so roughly and for so long they no longer had the strength to brace themselves against each roll of the ship, half-starved, many ill, all miserable, men, women and children were prepared to give up the ghost.

Despite everything Box and his men could do, the *Dauntless* was being driven further and further to the north, pitching and rolling in mountainous waves, the wind shrieking through the rigging, spray flying across the deck whipping up spume that seeped below to add to the passengers' wretchedness.

The captain battled to maintain control, but in the wildly tossing seas he was compelled to take in every inch of canvas, leaving the vessel to drift helplessly, hammered by giant waves, bowled over time and again to the gunwales, thrown skyward, pitched forward in a steep drive. The strain of the wind on the top-hamper began splitting seams below. The ship began to leak and the steaming dampness in the hold worsened.

26

The attempted abduction of Benjamin and the murder of Iron Dog were the talk of the castle. Serious crimes were rare among the Iroquois. Even the elders could not recall the last time a child or woman was kidnapped. Tribal law authorized the death penalty for murder, but it was an act open to condonation. Still, if the family was not compensated for its loss, the accused was given up to their private vengeance. Moon Dancer was Iron Dog's only family, but since his murderer had fled, for all practical purposes the situation was closed and the crime would go unpunished.

Two Eagles disagreed. He vowed that one day he would find Blue Creek, "face him down and leave his corpse draped across Iron Dog's grave." Margaret could not even think about vengeance; Benjamin was safe, Blue Creek was gone, the nightmare was over.

But her embarrassment lingered. "I was so frantic I forgot I was naked; in front of all those men!"

She walked with Eight Minks and Swift Doe in the amber twilight. At home, it appeared she would never put Benjamin down—until she had to change him.

"You were lucky Anger Maker and the others happened by," Swift Doe said, bouncing the cooing baby.

"It wasn't luck, dear," said Margaret. "It was a miracle."

"I am surprised Red Paint and Fox gave up chasing him," said Eight Minks. "Of course, he was running for his life."

"Even if they caught him they would know better than to kill him," said Swift Doe. "Two Eagles would have broken both their heads."

"He would not kill them either," Eight Minks insisted. "Why risk being banished?"

"Blue Creek has banished himself," murmured Margaret. "Will he ever come back, I wonder?"

The older woman shook her head emphatically. "The three of you are rid of him for good. He was so stupid, so like a man. How did he expect to feed a *cian* on the trail? Change him when he got wet and soiled himself? See to his needs? What man can do that? He did not think beforehand. His hunger for vengeance clouded his mind."

Margaret paused, picked a purple-fringed orchid, and inhaled the fragrance. "I wonder where he'll go."

"Out of Iroquois Territory," said Swift Doe.

"Poor man," murmured Margaret, "poor desperate creature."

Both looked at her archly.

"How can you say that after what he did?" Swift Doe asked, sitting on a deadfall. "Not just to you and Two Eagles, but he murdered his only friend. What kind of man is that? His brain is as twisted and tangled as an old vine."

"She is right," said Eight Minks, sitting beside her. We are lucky we have seen the last of him."

Margaret thought about Blue Creek. The other woman had overlooked one aspect of his behavior. His failure to abduct Benjamin or even Iron Dog's murder on his head might not discourage him. He might try again, and again, until he succeeded.

In the open inside the castle entrance, four old squaws finished washing Iron Dog's body. His aunt Moon Dancer dressed him in his best breechclout, jacket and moccasins. Red Paint and Fox then placed a fresh moose skin around him and carried him to his grave.

Together they set him in the open grave, covering his face with his hands.

"Draw his knees up," said Fox.

Food and weapons were placed in the grave to accompany him on the journey to the Village of the Dead.

"Who will fill him in?" Fox asked, surveying the circle of onlookers. No one volunteered.

"I will," said Margaret.

"Me, too," said Swift Doe, coming forward. "You two get the pickets and put them up. After we will paint them."

27

The battered *Dauntless* lay hove-to, wallowing help-lessly in the trough of the waves. Water seeped in everywhere. The crew worked to exhaustion, tamping wadding and oakum into seams and eventually managing to stem most of the leakage.

Then disaster struck. In the middle of the night, while the emigrants slept fitfully if at all, an ominous cracking sound ran through the bowels of the ship. Within seconds Captain Box came down the ladder carrying a lantern.

When he found what he was looking for, he inspected it under the light. As one, the emigrants gasped. One of the main beams holding the hull in position had cracked.

Box got to his feet and held up the lantern. "I'm afraid it was inevitable under all this strain, this pressure from the wind and waves. It could break in two."

"Will it?" burst the Reverend McCoy. "The truth, Captain!"

"I'm afraid it will in time. When it does, the ship will begin to break up. All of you, pray that it holds. In the meantime I'll continue to hold her as steady as I can."

"Not very steady," snapped one man.

"Aren't the wind and the current running easterly, Captain?" an elderly man asked. "Why not try to return to England rather than risk holding our present position until the weather clears?" He gestured at the split beam. "In calmer waters that might hold."

"Frankly, I don't dare raise sail to attempt to turn back," said Box. "The ship's carpenter is on his way here," he added.

The emigrants looked on in apprehensive silence as a doughty-looking little man came slowly down the ladder, carrying a toolbox and humming to himself. He ran a crooked finger down the widening split.

"If we could strap her with some kind of collar to keep the split from spreading . . ." he mused.

"Have you anything suitable?" Box demanded.

"Nothing big enough for this. That beam's a foot square if she's an inch."

"Blast!"

"We could splint her easy with a post, only how do we fasten 'em together? This ain't the sorta thing a body prepares for to happen when you stock up replacement parts for a voyage."

A tall, raw-boned young man in a beaverhat stepped forward and cleared his throat politely.

"My name is Enoch Taylor, Captain. I think I can solve the problem."

The captain eyed him skeptically. "You've a metal collar big enough?"

"I've a coil of iron wire thicker than your thumb."

Off he went, reappearing seconds later carrying it.

The carpenter whistled. "That's thick enough for cable," he said. "Must weigh a hundred fifty pounds."

"What are you doing packing such a thing?" Box asked.

"It seemed a waste to leave it behind. I thought it might come in handy when I get settled."

"God bless you, my son," sang Reverend McCoy. "We're saved, we're saved!"

The emigrants cheered. Two crew members were ordered below and the carpenter superintended as they placed a stout post firmly against the cracked beam and fixed it securely, winding the wire around both to support the beam against further strain.

The leaks plugged, and the weather cooperative, sail was hoisted and the ship's bow brought around to the west and headed for Boston. The weather held for nearly ten hours before the wind revived and resumed punishing the sea. Once more the sails came down, the ship resumed pitching and rolling in mountainous waves and the emigrants were again terrified.

But by dawn the skies had cleared and the wind died, although colossal waves continued to pummel the *Dauntless*. Desperate for air, the emigrants streamed up the ladder.

Seth and Hannah stayed topside, positioning themselves out of the wind between the fo'c'sle door and the ladder to the poop deck, prepared to grab the ladder railing in case a wave struck. Neither saw Abner bring Leonora up for air.

"Look!" Seth burst, pointing forward.

Abner and Leonora moved slowly up the deck hand-over-hand along the railing, Leonora gulping air, ignoring the spray and the terrifying threat of gigantic waves assaulting the ship on all sides.

"My God!" burst Hannah. "What are they doing?"

In that instant a wave lifted halfway up the mainmast, curling, falling, sweeping over the older couple.

"Motherrrr! Daddy!"

They vanished. When again they could be seen they had separated: Leonora had been pushed clear up to the bow. On her knees, soaked to the skin, she clung to the capstan crying out feebly.

"Abner . . . Abner . . ."

Seth and Hannah rushed up the deck. Seth took hold of the dazed and drenched Abner. Up near the bow, Hannah clutched her mother. Seth started up the deck with Abner but a second wave struck, inundating both, knocking them sprawling.

On hands and knees Seth groped about, searching for

the older man. He located him muttering irritably, breathed a sigh of relief and helped him to his feet.

Up at the bow Leonora was waving futilely, screaming. Seth started. Where was Hannah? Up the deck he ran, Abner following. They reached Leonora just in time to catch sight of Hannah's arm thrust upward out of the water, her fingers flexing, clutching the air. Up came her face, her eyes staring terror-stricken. Slowly she sank from sight as Leonora screamed and screamed and Abner stood ashen-faced.

 **28**

Captain Evan Box's cabin was a dingy little chamber that smelled strongly of tobacco and rum. Leonora lay on a Chesterfield, a blanket drawn up to her chin, a damp cloth across her forehead. A seaman who doubled as the ship's doctor had given her a quantity of chloral hydrate. She slept badly, twitching, occasionally writhing under the blanket, her face contorted in agony. Abner refused any medication. He sat beside her, restoring the cloth to her forehead each time she jerked her head and it slipped off. The seaman had returned to his duties, leaving the patient, Abner, Seth, and the captain.

The tempest had moved away; the sun was out gloriously. The emigrants crowded the deck murmuring prayers of thanks for their deliverance. Back on course was the *Dauntless*, gliding westward under full canvas.

Seth stood gazing down at Leonora. Soon she would awaken to confront the reality of Hannah's horrible death, just as Abner was confronting it now. Or had it overcome him? He sat staring into space mumbling, now and then shaking his head seemingly helpless to fend off the monsters. He looked like a prisoner who had just been removed from the rack: tortured, anguished, utterly destroyed. Seth pressed the man's shoulder comfortingly, reflecting how it had taken courage for Abner to remove himself and his loved ones to America to start fresh and how Leonora and Hannah had bolstered his courage with their own. Now the poor man needed even more courage to get the two of them through the empty, painful days ahead. They had suffered a loss from which they would never recover. Hannah, sweet, beautiful Hannah, so alive, so delightful, blessing all around her with her presence.

His love.

He felt hollow, drained of all inside save his painfully thudding heart.

"Your wife is welcome to stay here as long as she pleases," Box broke in. "You too, Mr. Keaton, if you don't mind sleeping on the floor. There are more blankets."

Abner did not seem to hear.

"That's very kind of you, Captain," said Seth.

"I wish none of you had to go back down that ladder. I don't know how you've stood it this long," said Box.

"If the weather continues fair, can't some of us sleep on deck, if we choose?"

"After what you've been through I wouldn't have the heart to forbid it." Box smiled grimly. "I might find myself facing a full-scale mutiny. The good news is the glass has risen beautifully. Fair weather ahead, possibly all the way to port."

"A little late," murmured Abner.

29

The *Dauntless* continued heading westward, tacking into the wind, moving with the Arctic current toward Newfoundland before altering course to steer south to the New England coast. Leonora remained sedated most of every day for nearly a week, until one morning when she declared to Abner she didn't need the medication. He too had bounced back—physically. Mentally, would either of them ever recover? Seth was not optimistic. Hannah was their universe.

Abner did his best to console his wife but his words sounded hollow and useless. Seth held his peace, feeling he had no right to discuss the tragedy with them or even offer condolences, for fear of appearing presumptuous. It was Leonora who took the initiative.

The two of them stood at the stern, watching the white wake of the ship, listening to the never-ending creaking of hull below and masts above, feeling the sun on their faces. Every passenger had fled the hold.

"You loved her," said Leonora bluntly.

Mention of Hannah caught him off balance. "I—"

"Blind Homer could see you two moving closer and closer. And she loved you; she told me."

"Really?"

"Come now, you know she did, even if she was coy about it. We'd never known her to spark to any man as she did to you. Abner and I couldn't have been more pleased. Goodness gracious, you are a blusher."

"I—"

She laughed for the first time since the tragedy. It warmed him, a good sign.

"I loved her so," he murmured, avoiding Leonora's eyes. "If I tell you something, will you promise you won't laugh in my face?"

"Never."

"And please don't tell Abner. I tried to write a love poem to her."

"How sweet."

"Oh, it was a complete fiasco. I discovered I'm one of those poor unfortunates who knows what he wants to say but can't get it out and onto paper. I wanted to propose, too, but it was too soon, we were still getting to know each other. I thought a little poem would open the door."

"You didn't need poetry. You reach a point where your heart tells you it's time to propose. You open your mouth and out it pours."

"I just couldn't get up the gumption. I'd never been in love, it was all so new: complicated, confusing—"

"Yes, it can be complicated. When it dawned on Abner and me how we felt about each other, that it was the real thing, I must say he didn't hesitate. I didn't want him to. He blurted out his proposal. And forgot to kneel, so he knelt and repeated it."

"Abner's pluckier than I am."

"You're no shrinking violet. You'd have popped the question before Boston."

"I would have."

"Captain Box would have performed the ceremony."

"Yes." He looked off toward the wake of the ship, imagining them back to where the tragedy occurred.

"Would have, could have," murmured Leonora. She managed a wan smile and kissed his cheek. When she drew back he could see tears glistening. "You're a fine man, Seth Wilson, as good as Abner. You would have made a good husband." She fumbled for a hanky and daubed her eyes.

Abner came up. "What are you two talking about?"

"The weather, dear," said Leonora.

He looked from one to the other and knew. "The weather, yes." With this he shaded is eyes and looked out over the gently heaving sea to the west. Seth did the same. Leonora, her spirits restored, took both their hands and started up the deck.

30

Summer was nearing its end. The days became lazy; the chirp of the field cricket filled the afternoons. Smaller than its field cousin, the green tree cricket heralded summer's end by lowering the pitch of its continuous trill.

Eight Minks went out walking with, of all people, Fox, who was notorious for bedding women old enough to be his grandmother.

Two Eagles disapproved of his choice of companions. When Two Eagles' mother committed suicide after his father had been murdered by Huron hunters, Eight Minks had taken over the family and raised the three boys. Now Two Eagles, the only surviving brother, considered her his mother. What business, he asked himself, did Fox have courting Two Eagles' mother?

When he asked the same question of Margaret as they strolled outside the longhouse while Swift Doe watched Benjamin, Margaret laughed.

"You're a prude," she replied. *"Ca-hootä-wä."*

He bristled. *"Neh."*

"Be smart, my sweet, bridle your ire. Fox has more sense than to take advantage of her. Let us hope she has more sense than to do the same with him."

"Let us *hope*?"

"She's getting old and I don't think she's ever slept with a man."

"Never," Two Eagles said.

"Oh? She told you?"

"I know," he insisted.

"I doubt she has any designs on Fox; a man and woman can have a friendship without sex."

"Not Sku-nak-su."

"He wouldn't dare; he knows you'd be down on him like a hawk on a hare."

"When his spear gets hard," Two Eagles said, scowling, "he does not know anything, does not think. Except to stick it in the nearest place."

"Forget about it. Besides, whatever they do is no business of yours."

"She is my *distan*."

"Your 'mother' is entitled to do whatever she pleases with whomever, without your opinion or interference."

"I will talk to him."

"Warn him, you mean. Don't. If she hears, you'll wish you'd kept out of it."

"I do not like it. I hate it." He paused and brightened. "I know, I will take to O-kwen-cha. Get him to warn Sku-nak-su."

"*Neh.* Red Paint and Fox are close as skin. A friend doesn't tell a friend what to do, not something that personal."

"I know. You talk to Eight Minks," he urged.

"I will not."

"Then I will!"

"Go ahead. I can't wait to see what she says. Don't be surprised if she rips you up and down."

He stared at Margaret as she continued: "Not with a knife, with her tongue. Lay you out in lavender. Bawl you out roundly. *Ko-ma-sega-ah-ne.*"

"She would not."

"Try it and see."

His expression said he wasn't eager to. He leaned against a longhouse, his arms folded, chin bunched, chewing the knuckle of his forefinger, plunged into thought. She watched him and waited, fighting back a smile.

"Well?"

"I have thought about it. I think we should stay out of it. You and I."

"Coward."

"Eh?"

"Nothing."

IV

BOSTON

31

Under a dull white sun, with the shriekings of gulls ripping the air, the *Dauntless* nosed into the morning mist blanketing Boston Harbor. Griffin's Wharf teemed with activity despite the earliness of the hour.

Boston, where the Puritans decreed that husbands and wives who kissed in public were subject to a fine. Where no one in authority took the least notice of the rampant smuggling—unless they themselves were involved in it. Boston, where God was zealously worshipped on the Sabbath and mammon with equal fervor on the other six days. Boston, where human behavior was strictly monitored by biblical injunction, where the laws of England were flouted and ignored in the face of the successful individual's law unto himself.

Seth Wilson stood near the taffrail watching the gangplank placed and his fellow emigrants start down it carrying their every possession, their hopes, their fears. Locals from baseborn to gentry: villains, blackguards and wastrels crowded the foot of the gangplank impatient to get at the newcomers to dupe, defraud, and swindle them. By nightfall pockets and purses would be lighter and misgivings heavy. Seth caught himself. He had such a jaundiced view of his fellow man. Particularly for a clergyman, which to the world was what he was; hadn't he passed the test en

route? Abner and Leonora called to him and came down
the deck.

"What are you waiting for, Seth?" Leonora asked.

"Just for the crowd to thin. I'm in no rush. The Missionary Society office is open until five this afternoon and
they're arranging a hotel room for me."

"When do you leave for the interior?" asked Abner.

"Shortly, I'm sure."

"Remember what I said about the Iroquois."

Leonora brought a folded piece of paper out of her ret-
icule. "This is the address of our shop. I wouldn't know
what directions to give you, but if you don't mind asking
in the street we'd love you to stop by for tea before you
leave town. Perhaps tomorrow? Four o'clock? We should
be halfway settled by then."

"I'll be there with bells on."

She kissed his cheek. Abner shook his head, touched his
hat brim and off they went.

They were almost to the foot of the gangplank when
Seth reached in his jacket pocket and brought out the two
silhouettes.

He studied Hannah's. His thoughts flew ahead to the
day when he would take it out and look at it and it would
be so worn it would fall to pieces. Moving closer to the
rail he dropped both silhouettes. The breeze caught them,
setting them dancing briefly. Then they spun downward,
settling on the black water, floating, sinking, vanishing.

Captain Box cleared his throat behnd him. Seth turned
and clasped his outstretched hand.

"Best of good fortune to you, Reverend."

"Thank you, Captain, the same to you. Will you be returning to England soon?"

"Not until she goes in for repairs. That keelson has to
be replaced and she'll kneed scraping and caulking fore
and aft before she puts to sea again. And the mizzenmast
is in sorry shape; we've loose hanging knees and lodge
knees. But you don't want to hear a list of her infirmities.
You're rid of her forever. Suffice to say it was the most

brutal weather I've ever encountered, man and boy." Box waved and walked off.

By now most of the emigrants had disembarked. Seth picked up his portmanteau and valise, took one last look about and started up the deck.

The Colonial Missionary Society office was on the corner of Marlborough and Sumner Streets, a block from the Common. The streets were quagmires crowded with drays, wains, wagons, carts, wheelbarrows, horses, mules and pedestrians crawling along in noisy confusion. The houses with their clapboard and shingle fronts and overhanging second stories with small, many-paned windows gradually gave way to larger three-story houses, with big chimneys at each end, wider, higher windows and fanlights over the doorways. Some were built of brick that had come from England as ballast or was fired in local kilns.

Each shop had its own heavy wooden sign hanging out front describing the product for sale. Halfway up Sumner Street, his head ringing from the din, he slipped into Hoadley's Apothecary Shop. The doorbell jangling too close to his ear as he entered made him wince but the door shut out the clamor. The shelves behind the counter were lined with jars filled with the healers, soothers and restorers of humanity. Vomits and purges, salves and ointments, spices and soaps and sweets all mingling in an overpowering scent that challenged description. "Blood stones," "teeth drawers," "anodyne necklaces" to ease the birth of babies, and all sorts of medical devises and instruments were also on display.

A girl with smudged cheeks, no older than ten, evidently filled in for the clerk. She sold him two headache powders and gave him a glass of tepid water. He paid and left still in pain. It wasn't until he came within sight of the northwest corner of Sumner and Marlborough Streets that the throbbing began to ease. Up Water Street, which continued Sumner to the Common, rose Beacon Hill, crowning it the tall, gibbet-shaped beacon by which ships' masters guided their vessels through the darkness to port. Nearby Copp's Hill supported a windmill, its cumbersome sails flapping loudly in the breeze from the sea and audible above the traffic's din clear across the Common.

Behind him out in the bay the mist had fled, revealing boys in skiffs hauling cattle from one island grazing ground to the next, the beasts swimming with a line looped around the leader's horns and prodded by poles. Barges heaped with firewood, sea-coal, oats and hay moved about. Lobstermen pulled up their pots, eel pots were hauled and emptied and the Charlestown ferry bell clanged melodiously through the chill morning.

A wooden sign in the shape of a Bible with the inscription COLONIAL MISSIONARY SOCIETY swung lightly in the breeze above the entrance to a two-story brick building that looked no more than fifteen feet in width. Up the stairs trudged Seth to the second floor. At the rear of the office were two doors side by side, one of them ajar. He paused on the sill, setting his bags down. Two men in missionary black were talking, seated on either side of a pier table. One was at least seventy, completely hairless, as wizened as a dried prune, pale, with an unnatural flush to his cheeks. He was perspiring and his hands trembled slightly. His companion looked remarkably robust, at least thirty years younger, with a powerful chest supporting a thick neck. Both rose as Seth introduced himself, presenting his letter of introduction.

"Timothy Allbright," said the older man, offering a frail, veined hand. "And this is my associate, Dr. Ernest Frame. Welcome, welcome, welcome."

"How was your journey?" Frame asked as Seth sat.

He told them, without dramatizing the dangers. Allbright squinted determinedly and read the letter to himself, grunting repeatedly, which Seth took to mean he was impressed.

"He positively raves about you. And one couldn't ask for a worthier recommendation than Reverend Ephraim Colton." Shakily, he handed the letter to Frame. "If you don't mind, I've one question I ask all our successors of the Apostle Paul: Precisely what, Mr. Wilson, inspired you to become a missionary?"

"At the risk of sounding self-important, sir, I felt called."

"Excellent. You are aware that this will be an extraordinarily difficult undertaking.

"Arduous, dangerous," added Frame, "demanding in dedication beyond the call."

"Are you prepared in mind, body and spirit to assume it?" the older man asked.

"I am."

"Excellent. Let me say if success shines on your efforts your reward will be personal satisfaction in abundance. The job well done. Souls introduced to and embracing the one, the true, religion."

"Heathens converted and finding Almight God," added Frame.

"I hear the Iroquois are a particularly fierce lot," said Seth.

"No denying that," said Allbright. "We'd be less than honest if we were to lead you to think you'll be without hazards to life and limb. And the job itself won't be easy. They're as independent as Zulus and broken up into five different tribes, with each tribe further divided into clans. This is important to know because you mustn't assume that if you succeed in converting one or two the others will fall like dominoes."

Frame nodded. "Unlike some tribes, the Iroquis' conversion will be like pulling teeth: one at a time and painful."

"At least difficult," corrected Allbright. "But it has to be done." He spoke deliberately. "The French in New France have converted virtually all their tribes to Catholicism; we must match their efforts among our savages. It is our heaven-sent opportunity and obligation. Men with your uncommon zeal, your dedication, are the hope of the Protestant world."

"How many will be in our party?"

"Four," said Frame, "all about your age. You'll meet them tomorrow. A fine group; you'll get along famously. You'll be leaving day after tomorrow."

"That soon?"

"The sooner the better," said Allbright. "Your supplies and equipment are ready and waiting. Your itinerary, too."

"How long will we be out?"

They exchanged glances, and Allbright cleared his throat.

"That'll be up to you, my boy. You four will be the judges of how well it's going and whether it's worthwhile to continue. If all goes well, as I expect it will, you could be out for as long as two years. Many stay out even longer."

"Reverend Obadiah Hedgepath has lived among the Senecas for nearly three years," said Frame. "By himself, mind you. And last we heard he has converted more than a dozen chiefs and fifty warriors and squaws. Not counting children, you understand. Once their parents are converted the little ones are taken for granted. The sheep, then the lambs."

He moved to a cabinet and got out a pamphlet, handing it to Seth.

"Peruse that at your leisure. You'll note Reverend Hedgepath is the author. He's set down a number of do's and don'ts."

"You'll find them the most superstitious people on God's green earth," said Allbright. "And the most fool-hardy thing you can do is to attempt to win them over by critizing their beliefs, their spirits, the importance to them of their dreams, etcetera."

Frame nodded. "They have a very confused notion of Creation and no end of fantastic and ridiculous explanations of the beginning of life and the formation of the world. They don't believe in an omnipotent God. They answer to spirits. Good and evil as they bring good luck or bad, health and plenty, or disease, famine, death. Interestingly, according to Obadiah Hedgepath, they do believe in the existence of the soul as a spiritual entity."

"But they can't define its nature," said Allbright. "They don't understand that the soul is purely spiritual. They think it's a shadow of one's self. They do believe it's immortal and after the body dies it travels to their so-called Village of the Dead, their eternal home."

Though neither had ever set foot across the Hudson, the ministers took turns droning lectures for more than two hours, and Seth was beginning to get sleepy when Allbright got to his feet, signaling an end to the meeting.

Seth was given directions to an address on Short Street down near the waterfront.

"It's run by a Mrs. Tweed. It's not a very big room and the washstand's outside in the hall," said Allbright. "But it'll do you nicely for the two nights. Can you come by at eight in the morning? Your companions will be here. Two are from London. The other, Dwight Hopkins, is from Virginia."

"I look forward to meeting them."

He stood outside under the sign, taking the sun on his face. It had gotten chillier. Eight tomorrow morning. He hoped he'd be able to get away by midafternoon and make his tea date with the Keatons.

He reflected on his experiences of the past two months. He'd survived the voyage; snow, cold and inhospitable savages couldn't possibly be as bad. The millinery shop next door to the Colonial Missionary Society bulding displayed a sign showing the silhouette of a young girl, a muslin cap tied under her chin.

He shook his head, picked up his bags and headed down Marlborough Street.

32

Seth surveyed his companions: Dwight Hopkins was built like a barrel; he barely came up to Seth's shoulder but was all muscle, bursting with vigor. He contrasted sharply with Jonathan Wilby, who was as skinny as a pole. His face was painfully narrow; was that a fanatical gleam in his red-rimmed eyes? Wilby also had a disconcerting breathless manner of speaking; his absurdly high-pitched voice rose even higher when he got excited.

"Souls, souls, souls, to think there are hundreds, thousands out there just waiting to be taken!"

"Taken?" Up went Fisk Drummond's eyebrow. "You make it sound like we're a press gang for Her Majesty's navy."

"A press gang for God," retorted Wilby.

Immediately after introductions, Fisk Drummond, a rich man's son, had attempted to impress his companions with the sacrifice he was making propagating the faith. After all, he said, he could have stayed home in Manchester managing his father's cotton mill, "the largest in central England."

Despite this, Seth sparked to him almost the moment they shook hands. His boastfulness aside, his winning personality shone through.

"I wonder how long we'll be out," asked Wilby.

"Bring a bag, Jonathan," said Hopkins, "and when it's full to bursting with souls, sling it over your shoulder, turn around and come back."

Dwight Hopkins' sense of humor was nine parts homespun wit, well suited to his rough edges. He didn't impress Seth as missionary material; Hopkins didn't have the com-

mand, the aura of authority calculated to inspire the unen-
lightened. And he looked out of place in his missionary
black; in Seth's opinion, the man was better suited to
buckskins and coonpelt hat.

In contrast, Wilby was a caricature of a missionary
straight out of a cartoon in the *Weekly News*. Shamelessly
holier-than-everyone-else, intensely religious, he was intol-
erant of rival faiths, determined to change the thinking of
every nonbeliever and wrong-believer. Had he not appeared so ridiculous, his zeal would have been frightening.

Listening to the men sharing anecdotes about their pas-
sages, Seth wondered what drew them to Boston and this
calling. Clearly, Wilby was intended for nothing else. But
not Drummond or Hopkins. Drummond would have been
far better suited to business. Garrulous, engaging, warm
and likeable, he invested his listeners with a fondness for
him and was no doubt a charmer among the ladies. What
he was not was typical of the soul gatherers preparing to
labor in the wilds of the New World.

Guiltily, Seth knew he shouldn't have been there in the
first place. Long before boarding the *Dauntless* he'd decided that this role was only a job that paid handsomely;
the money was the only consideration.

"I very nearly got into a violent fight with one of the
deckhands on our ship," announced Wilby. "He was scrub-
bing the deck with a brush worn down to the wood. Not
a bristle I could see. I asked him what possible good it
could do with no bristles. He told me to mind my own
business. Not those exact words, but profanity meaning the
same thing. One word led to another and we nearly came
to blows. And would have had I not turned the other
cheek. Ah, me, a 'fool's mouth is his destruction.' Prov-
erbs eighteen, seven."

"It can be for sure," said Drummond tightly, "if he
doesn't know when to shut it."

" 'But a soft word turneth away wrath.' "

Drummond groaned; Seth and Hopkins laughed. Wilby
looked confused.

"Does anyone know what we'll be taking with us?" Seth asked.

"I hear half a ton of dry rations," murmured Drummond. "Which I plan to jettison my share of in the first ditch outside town. I've little appetite for sawdust in any form."

"You'll starve," burst Wilby. "You will!"

"Not I. I intend to live off the land. I'm bringing a Morton all-metal spring rabbit trap, the latest of its type manufactured in Birmingham. It's impossible to starve out there. To begin with we'll find positive acres of fruit trees."

"It's getting a bit late in the year for fruit," said Seth.

"Oh, but the tribes store it. Apples, plums, cherries, berries, nuts, everything. There'll be fish, too, and meat: venison, quail, squab. And don't forget, leaving here we'll have our Indian guides. You can bet your buttons they won't be carrying great packs of food. They know how to live off the land."

"What do they have for us for weapons?" Hopkins asked Drummond.

"Knives, I'm sure. I imagine one or two flintlocks, powder and ball. For hunting, of course. And we'll be skinning what we catch. I've read up on hunting and fishing in the wilds. Dr. Skinner has written a fascinating manual. It's easy—a child can hunt and fish. The Indian tykes are taught to almost as soon as they can walk."

They talked through lunch; most of the conversation, when they discussed the days and weeks ahead, pure conjecture, bold assumption. Clearly none of them had any idea of what actually awaited them. Seth wondered what would happen if one of them took ill or broke a leg or worse. How would they care for him out in the wilds? When the snows came how would they find their way? And what if hostile savages attacked without warning?

Unfortunately, what it came down to was that the four of them, acting as God's agents, were untested innocents,

guileless good Samaritans marching into the wilderness.
Would they one day march out?

Allbright and Frame could have done more to reduce
the difficulties. For one thing, an experienced man ought
to have been assigned to the project, someone who'd
worked with the Iroquois and knew about them firsthand,
not from Obadiah Hedgepath's pamphlet, which both
Allbright and Frame touted as the Bible of the wilderness.

He wondered about their guides. What tribe were they?
Not Iroquois, not around Boston; but the Iroquois had
made enemies of all the neighboring tribes. What were the
chances the ones assigned them might be from a tribe they
had conquered at one time or another? Defeated warriors
who hated and feared them? Still, if that were the case,
why would the guides take the job?

What troubled him more than anything else was the
feeling that preparations were all fairly haphazard. Dwight
Hopkins had been all over the southern colonies and as far
west as the Appalachians and knew how to read any map.
But he didn't think much of the maps provided them. Of
course, the guides would know the route. Yet all things
considered, it was more than a little scary.

Even now, so early on? Pleasant thought. What am I
doing here? he asked himself.

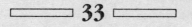

33

The four missionaries were still talking when Seth asked
to be excused. He hurried to the Keatons' address on
Cornhill Street, easily locating it in a retail district at the
center of town. The Keatons' shop sign was not yet hung
and through the dusty front window he could see the un-
packed crates of books brought from England. To the left

stretched a counter, a curtain at the rear evidently concealed living quarters. The shelves and the window display space were bare. Litter had been swept into a neat pile in the middle of the floor.

Abner and Leonora came through the curtain, and Abner ran out and ushered Seth through the shop into a small, sparsely furnished sitting room. There were, he explained, four rooms in all, with only one of the two bedrooms furnished and presentable. The four crates of books had taken up more than the space allotted them in the hold, so they'd brought only one other item from England, apart from clothing and furniture; a lovely silver tea set. Leonora produced a tin of bohea tea.

She smiled. "Did you know they've been selling tea here for nine years? Boston has two licensed dealers, one just around the corner, so we shan't have to stint."

She made him feel welcome, but something about her had changed since they last spoke aboard ship. Her eyes had difficulty focusing on him; her smile looked painted on. As well, Abner seemed uncharacteristically fidgety and could not seem to muster a smile.

Seth glanced about the room. An oval rag rug centered the puncheon oak floor. There was little furniture, only a fourth chair and small table. Not even a clock, though the bare walls and molding had been painted.

He sensed that it was being left to him to get the conversation going.

"When will you be opening for business?" he asked.

"We hope to open the day after tomorrow," said Abner.

"Will you be specializing in any particular types of books?"

"Not right away. We do plan to import, of course. England's the only source. Eventually we'll get into publishing: books, pamphlets. There's money to be made in printing, too: blank forms for bonds, certificates, documents and the like."

"Abner wants to get a government contract to print official documents, don't you, dear?"

"I'm afraid that's a vain hope, but we might get business printing public news sheets."

Leonora poured the tea. Seth took cream. It was getting stuffy, and the conversation was now lagging, although the three of them had never had trouble finding things to talk about aboard ship. From Abner's expression, Seth began to get the impression that he wasn't wanted here. Suddenly Abner clapped his hands on his knees. "So—when do you leave?"

Seth told them about the meeting he'd just left, not mentioning his reservations about the project.

Suddenly Leonora excused herself to go into the bedroom. "I've something for you, Seth. A going-away gift."

"She was up half the night knitting them," said Abner. "Seth." He lowered his voice to a whisper. "She's had a setback. I'm worried sick. The doctor says—"

He stopped as she came back in with a pair of mittens.

"I guessed at your size. I said to Abner after we got off the ship—we were checking to make sure the crates had been unloaded and the rest of our baggage—I said he'll be going off into the woods in the dead of winter, he'll need warm clothing."

"They're splendid, Leonora."

"But do they fit? I guessed at your size."

He tried one on. "Splendidly."

"I thought navy would be nice. Did you know it's Hannah's favorite color?"

Listening to her, and watching Abner, he saw him raise his eyes, shake his head almost indiscernibly and clear his throat. Seth finished his tea.

"I should be going."

"No, no, no, not so soon," she protested. "Just a little longer. Have another cup." Before he could stop her she was pouring. "Hannah'll be here soon now."

"Leonora—" began Abner.

"She'll want to see you, to give you a proper good-bye. Not secondhand through us. Do you know how long you'll be away? She'll be waiting on tenterhooks. Watching the two of you on board, as the days passed, was charming. And Abner and I couldn't be happier for you. Delighted! Isn't that so, Abner?"

"Yes."

She laughed lightly. "Listen to Mr. Enthusiasm. But I'm embarrassing you, Seth."

"Not a bit."

"I promised Hannah long before we landed I'd keep it Abner's and my little secret. But now I've blurted it out. She'll be furious with me. I did warn her she could wait for you as long as two or three years. You know what she said? She said, 'I don't care if it's ten, I'll wait for him.' And she will, she's as tenacious as they come when she makes up her mind. Oh dear, now I really am embarrassing you." She mimed locking her lips and tossing away the key. "But did they tell you how long you'll be?"

"It's impossible to say; it appears to depend on how successful we are."

"I wonder what's keeping that girl. I told her you'd be here at four o'clock."

"My dear," said Abner, "I think we're keeping him."

"We are, aren't we? Leaving the way you are so soon, with so much to do to prepare, you must be up to your ears." She stood up. "We won't detain you a moment longer. I'll explain to Hannah; she'll understand. Seth?"

"Yes?"

"If you don't think it too forward of me, may I—kiss you good-bye for her?"

"Of course."

She kissed his cheek and moved to squeeze his hand affectionately but he was still holding his cup. He set it down.

"Delicious tea, that's only one thing I'll miss out there. And thank you again for the mittens, Leonora. I'll think of you both every time I put them on."

"You'll think of all three of us," she corrected him.

"Yes, of course. Oh, I'm forgetting—" He drew a

sealed, somewhat bulky envelope from his pocket. "Hold on to this for me, would you, Abner?"

"Certainly."

"I'll pick it up when I get back, whenever that may be. Just please put it in a safe place."

"I shall."

"Thank you. Good-bye, Leonora; good-bye, Abner. And thank you for coming into my life." He started for the door.

"Aren't you forgetting someone?" Leonora asked.

He glanced at Abner, abject and helpless as he studied the floor. Leonora cocked her head admonishingly. "You must say a good-bye I can pass on to her for you."

"Of course, sorry. Good-bye, Hannah."

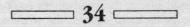

34

"Nip-muc? Do they eat mud?" whispered Hopkins to Seth. The four missonaries, packed and ready to leave, stood with the Reverend Allbright outside the office watching the Reverend Frame coming up the street with two Indians dressed in filthy buckskin vests and white men's trousers, their faces painted, their heads shaved up to scalp locks decorated with frazzled feathers. Carrying backpacks they seemed to be doing their utmost to look fierce but failed to draw even a passing glance from pedestrians. One Indian looked like a boy on the threshold of puberty; the other, only half a head taller, looked tipsy. They grunted and nodded to Frame as they approached.

"The town's infested with Nipmucs, Wampanoags and Narragansetts," said Allbright. "Their fathers fought in King Philip's war twenty-five years ago; there was a good deal of bitterness for a long time but there's been no trou-

ble with any of the tribes the past few years. Nothing or-
ganized." Seth stared gauging their ferocity and wondered.

"Are they Christians?" asked Wilby.

"Nominal Christians. They'll tell you they are if they
think it'll get them something, but few attend services regularly. Our work goes on and never gets any easier. Here
we are." His voice dropped as Frame came to stand before
him.

"Gentlemen," announced Frame, "permit me to introduce Sko-sko-wro-wa-neh, Great Branch, and De-hat-ka-
dons, He-looks-both-ways."

Great Branch, the shorter and younger of the two, did
not look "great" in any respect. His companion extended
his hand and all four shook it in turn. Although Seth had
seen many Indians wandering about town, it was his first
close contact with any of them. These reeked of body odor
and He Looks smelled as if he'd been swimming in liquor.
They impressed him as being about as competent as two
stray dogs to guide them through the wilderness.

He Looks spoke proudly. "Welcome to America, Reverends. We will guide you good to where you are going,
have no fear. We know the woods and the tribes. Great
Branch speaks Maquen."

"Maquen?" asked Drummond.

"The Iroquois word for Mohawk," explained Frame.

"Mohawk," repeated He Looks. With this he reached
under his vest to his armpit and brought out an insect of
some kind, grinned, popped it into his mouth, swallowed
it. Wilby gaped, Hopkins chuckled, Seth snickered to himself. It promised an interesting association.

"One last thing before we wish you godspeed," said
Allbright. "Obadiah Hedgepath has apprised us by messenger that Ska-na-wa-di and Dē-yoh-ron-yon-kah, principal chiefs of the Senecas, have sent word to the chiefs of
the various castles to expect you and to treat you with
courtesy and kindliness. A most unusual gesture. A first.
One might take it as a milestone in our progress. And you
four are to be the beneficiaries. Congratulations."

"Could you write down those names, sir?" Drummond asked.

"Already have." He handed him a slip of paper. "Pronounce them just as they sound."

"Castles?" asked Wilby. "They live in castles? Is that a joke, sir?"

"Not at all," said Allbright, defining a castle for him. "When our people first visited their lands, that was the term they brought back. The Iroquois have evidently used it since Europeans first arrived in this part of North America."

"Where did they come from?" Seth asked.

"No one really knows," said Drummond. "Possibly down from Canada."

"The Congregational church has set its sights on the Iroquois," said Frame. "Obadiah Hedgepath has opened the door. It's up to you gentlemen to build on what he's begun. The Jesuits have tried for a hundred years to convert the five tribes and have made little progress, other than with the Mohawks who migrated north to the St. Lawrence. Not the Mohawks you'll be visiting, nor the other tribes."

"The soil's virgin, the plow's in your hands," Allbright told them, beaming with enthusiasm. Bowing his head, he continued. "Gentlemen, let us pray. Almighty God, bless this mission and its purpose, help these your servants to bring thy Divine light to the savages and their immortal souls to thee, amen."

"Amen."

After a pause, He Looks belatedly said, "A-men," and nudged his friend with his elbow.

"A-men," Great Branch agreed hurriedly.

"Godspeed," said Allbright.

With which the four missionaries shouldered their equipment and supplies and trudged off after their two guides.

35

Two Eagles woke up one morning, sniffed the air and smelled deer; the hunting season had arrived.

Hatho, the frost spirit, had visited during the night, leaving skin ice on pots and kettles of water. Two Eagles and his friends assembled, disrobed and took turns in the sweat lodge. They heated stones red hot and plunged them into water to create steam to draw the impurities from their bodies.

Splitting Moon came out of the lodge gleaming with sweat, his face as red as a grosbeak's breast.

"You look cooked," said Two Eagles. The others laughed.

"See how you look," Splitting Moon snarled. "How long you can take crouching inside a fire?"

Inside the lodge, sweat poured from Two Eagles as he pushed a cheek against a sliver opening in the bark siding for a breath of air. Emerging, gasping, he was given an emetic made of the bulbs and leaves of adder's tongue, then a purgative made of the bark and leaves of the ash tree, both prepared by Eight Minks. Lastly he bathed in clear water in which sweet fern had been mixed. Their bodies made clean and all human odor removed, the sweet fern gave them a woodsy perfume calculated to deceive their quarry.

Heading into the woods, Anger Maker—puffing his ashwood pipe crammed with a foul-smelling combination of tobacco, dried sumac leaves and red willow bark— walked at the rear of the line. Now he called a halt alongside a hickory sapling. The winter before he had selected a branch, split it and set in it a sharpened stone tomahawk head. As the tree grew and the wood healed around the stone, it became locked tightly in place. In a little more than a year from now he would cut off the branch and have a fine handle for his tomahawk.

The trail widened as they resumed walking. Two Eagles walked with Fox on one side, Anger Maker—done smoking—on the other.

When Two Eagles glanced at Fox, Anger Maker noticed. "You look at Sku-nak-su like he is *oeuda*," he said.

Two Eagles bristled. "I do not!"

"You do," said Fox. "Shit."

"Because you spend so much time with his mother," Anger Maker told Fox, pointing accusingly.

"With, with!" burst Two Eagles, stopping short. "What does that mean?"

Anger Maker winked. "What do you think?"

"Ogechta!"

"Shut up, yourself."

"He is not saying anything everybody in the castle does not know," observed Splitting Moon behind them.

Two Eagles whirled on him. "Who asked you? What have we here, *two* old squaw gossips? You think Sa-ga-na-qua-de is not up to the job? He needs your mouth?"

Red Paint spoke. "Quiet down, all of you. You will scare the *aque*."

"He resents my spending time with Tékliq?-eyo," growled Fox resentfully.

"With your *mother*," said Anger Maker to Two Eagles, leering.

"As much a mother to me as yours was to you!" rasped Two Eagles.

"And a fine woman. Sku-nak-su knows. Tell him, Sku-nak-su," Anger Maker taunted.

"She is marvelous," sighed Fox.

Two Eagles flared. "What do you mean by that?"

Anger Maker laughed.

"What are you laughing at?" Two Eagles demanded.

"What is all this?" Bone asked wearily. "Did we come out to argue or to hunt?"

"You disapprove of my keeping company with her," said Fox. "Too bad. Only that is our choice. What you think matters about as much as bird *oueda*."

Two Eagles riveted him with a scowl. "You think? I warn you, grandmother fucker, you touch her and I will cut your heart out and feed it to the dogs!"

"And if you do, maybe she will cut yours out and do the same," said Anger Maker.

Fox laughed. Two Eagles started for him, but the others caught and held him. He shook them off.

Fox sighed and studied him. "We are friends, you and I, almost since the cradleboard, *neh*? If my seeing her upsets you, if you would prefer I stop seeing her——"

"I did not say you *had* to," Two Eagles retorted.

"Look at me, Sku-nak-su," said Anger Maker. "If you break off your friendship she will know why, and who caused you to." He shuddered. "You want that, Tékni-ska-je-a-nah? Her fire in the channels of your ears?" The others laughed.

Two Eagles stared at Anger Maker, then at Fox, and looked sheepish. "She is my mother in the moccasins of my womb mother. I—feel protective of her. Because it is you——" He frowned at Fox. "What you do to old squaws!"

Fox smirked. "Ah, what do they do to me?"

"He is right, my friend," said Red Paint. "It takes two to make a fuck."

Two Eagles winced. "Enough! I do not like this talk."

"I will tell her as soon as we get back that you disapprove of us," said Fox.

"*Neh, neh,* do not say anything."

"But if it displeases you——"

"Just drop it."

"You!" Fox snapped, his voice suddenly hard. Two Eagles looked down at his friend's finger waggling under his nose. "Do not threaten me like that ever again. We are friends. Friends trust each other. If you mistrust me——"

"I did not say that."

"*Her,* then——"

"I did not say that either! You are putting words in my mouth. Just drop it!" Brush swished loudly to their left. A fine buck showed its imposing rack for a brief instant. Splitting Moon was the first to react, nocking an arrow, letting fly. But despite the sweet fern, the buck had caught the strong scent of humans and bounded away.

They went on deeper into the woods and paired off to hunt. Two Eagles and Bone moved crouching six paces apart through the underbrush, arrows at ready. Neither uttered a sound. They moved into the breeze, and Bone signaled a halt; Two Eagles froze and watched him kneel and examine the ground. When he got up he mouthed the word *oeuda.* Whitetail droppings, black and pointed at one end, were easily differentiated from those of rabbits and hares.

They continued on, Two Eagles narrowing the space between them. They found tracks, the distinctive pear-shaped imprint of a whitetail hoof. The creature fed most heavily before sunrise and after the sun went down. At midday it bedded down; now, approaching midmorning, it was most active. Its home range was small; bucks generally wandered within a range of only half a league. The indentation of these hoofprints suggested weight, a fully grown animal.

It had warmed up as the morning progressed, and the sky was cloudless: conditions that tempted the whitetail to move about. Bone paused to look over the terrain. The breeze had shifted so that they now approached it at an angle. Other than the occasional cawing of a crow somewhere overhead, they could hear no sound.

Two Eagles sighted a rack, a fine buck ahead and slightly to his right, possibly the same deer Splitting Moon had shot at and missed. Bone too saw it and started to circle, as Two Eagles circled on the other side. Moving stealthily they approached to within fifteen paces before the creature moved, starting, crashing through the underbrush directly in front of Bone. Its white tail flashed. He let two arrows fly in quick succession. One struck a tree at a bad angle and fell harmlessly. The other found its mark. They rushed forward. The arrow had driven through the animal's neck up to within a span of the fletching. The deer lay dead, its huge eye staring. Its coat was already beginning to turn from the reddish brown of summer to a grayish brown, its underside remaining as white as its tail year round.

It was a superb rack, the separation between antlers as long as a man's forearm. Bone set about removing the head, lessening the weight to carry back. Two Eagles bled the animal. Excited by their good luck, he now lapsed into a serious mood.

"I had a feeling last night deep down in my gut," he murmured. "So strong I consulted my óyaron."

"Are we back onto Sku-nak-su and your 'distan'?" Bone laughed.

"*Neh,* I am talking about Ossivendi Oÿoghi, Karístatsi Sateeni's murderer."

"What about him?"

"I know where he has gone. My óyaron agreed. To Massowaganine."

"Why would he go there?"

"Before the red days started, back when he looked like a man, he was very close to a woman: Ganõda, Night Song. When she learned of his death she went into mourning. Later she met an Onondaga warrior, Quane Gachga, Tall Crow. A big man, taller than I am, wider than Tyagohuens. They were married and live at Massowaganine."

"You think Blue Creek went to see this woman?"

Two Eagles touched his gut with one bloodied hand. "This tells me he did. He is there. Or he stopped there. I am going after him."

"But he must be long gone from there."

"She or her husband must know where. His trail should not be hard to pick up."

Bone made a disapproving face and shook his head.

"What?" Two Eagles asked.

"You cannot go after Blue Creek. Margaret would not permit it."

"I do not need her permission!"

"What you do not need is her anger. She will burn your ears black with words. Let me do it. I will go to Massowaganine for you."

"*Neh.* Swift Doe would not like that."

"She does not have to know my reason. I can tell her the chiefs have asked me to take a message to the chiefs of the Onondaga. I will find out for you where Blue Creek has gone. Then you do what you like about it."

Two Eagles mulled this over. "You would go there for me?"

"Why not? Would you not do it for me?"

"*Nyoh,* of course."

"That settles it, I do not like deceiving Swift Doe—I have never lied to her—but this is important to you. Even if she learned the truth she would understand. How far to Massowaganine?"

"Four sleeps there and back. It is up near Lake Ne-ah-gä-te-car-ne-o-di."

"The lake the lace-cuffs call Ontario," Bone murmured.

"You pick up the trail north near the white caves. Follow it to there." Two Eagles lay his bloodied hands on Bone's shoulders. "You do not have to go."

"Someone has to or you will chew on it until your teeth break." He laughed. "And all of us will have to listen. Besides, I have another reason. I want you in my debt."

Both laughed. Two Eagles wiped his hands on leaves and shouldered the decapitated buck. Bone picked up the head, and they started back to the trail. Thoughts of Blue Creek tumbled through Two Eagles' mind: he saw him fleeing, running ahead of the pursuing Red Paint and Fox, arriving at Massowaganine. He thought back to the peace conference two years before, how he and Splitting Moon had gone there to consult with He-big-kettle, how they had arrived and were watching a spirited baggataway match when Governor-General Frontenac and his contingent came marching in.

From the beginning the peace negotiations had not gone well. And two days after they began, someone—it was never determined whether it was an Onondagan or a Frenchman—set fire to the Council House. The whole castle went up in flames and was eventually rebuilt north of the old site. He-big-kettle was among the victims of the fire and the two sides were still haggling over terms, with peace as elusive as ever.

"When you get there," said Two Eagles, "ask for a close friend of mine from the war. Gordon Duncan. He is an adoptee like you. His tribal name is Gä-de-a-yo."

Bone snickered. "Lobster?"

"Because he is red: his skin, his hair like a torch. He is a good man, Bone, you will like him. He will help you. I am certain in my gut that Blue Creek told Night Song where he is heading when he leaves there. He will leave a trail."

"You think she might desert her husband to go with him?"

"Never. But he sees himself as what he looked like before, not the turtle skin he is now. His bitterness has turned his brain upside down in his head."

"He may walk into a knife. We may be talking about a dead man."

"Ask for Gordon," said Two Eagles.

They rejoined the others. The hunt had been successful: three fully grown bucks. The days would grow colder and provide more bounty for the winter.

Two Eagles felt his chest warm with satisfaction. No more wondering where Blue Creek had gotten to. Bone would find out what had happened to him, where he was heading.

And when Bone returned he would go after Turtle Skin. No matter how much she carried on, how vigorously she protested, Margaret would have to allow him. She would, she would understand.

He hoped.

36

Bone lost no time leaving for Massowaganine, departing within the hour after returning from the hunt; first taking pains to make certain Swift Doe was looking on when he spoke to Chief Ho-non-ses. He explained that he would be doing Two Eagles a favor and His Longhouse agreed, if reluctantly, to help in deceiving Swift Doe, although he preferred that Two Eagles let the thing rest. Since this appeared not possible, he agreed to cooperate with the two warriors' plan.

He would tell Swift Doe that Bone was taking a message to To-do-da-ho, He-great-wizard, and Ta-ha-nah-gai-eh-ne, Two-horns-lying-down, principal chiefs of the Onondagas.

Bone told Swift Doe that he would return in four sleeps at most. All Two Eagles had to do while waiting was control his impatience and avoid raising Margaret's suspicions before he disclosed his intentions. But his patience was unexpectedly assaulted from another quarter. And it was Margaret who triggered the attack. He was carrying Benjamin, sleeping over his shoulder, as husband and wife walked by the stream. Margaret carried a half-filled jug of blueberries, the last of the summer crop.

"I've something to tell you," she said gently. "Promise you won't get upset."

"What? What?"

"Calm down, let me at least start. Just hear me out before you explode."

"Is it Eight Minks?"

"She is baking marriage bread."

He exploded, shouting, setting a flock of starlings beating away out of danger. She snatched Benjamin from him.

"She cannot marry Sku-nak-su, I forbid it! It is . . . it is . . ."

"Ridiculous? Unseemly? Unbelievable? What? It's what they want. Obviously what they need. What they don't need is you sticking your oar in!"

He was unfamiliar with the term. She started to explain; he interrupted.

"I will talk to her," he muttered, clenching and unclenching his fists.

"I'm sure she wants to talk to you. In fact she said she did."

"She has no shame."

"Because she's twice his age?"

"More. The day his mother dropped him squalling in the woods, Eight Minks was already nearly forty summers old."

"So what? Listen to me and try to understand. They like each other. For all I know they share a passionate love. You know what passionate love is." She laughed and poked him good-naturedly. "It's what we used to have. Back when we got married."

"Everything is funny to you. This is not funny, it tears my heart."

"Fiddlesticks and rot. Stop being so melodramatic. Talk to her. Not him. Not till you talk to her. Listen to what she says, tell her what you think. She'll be receptive; after all, you are her nephew."

"Her *son*," Two Eagles corrected.

"Her son. Let's go back and get it over with."

Two Eagles had split the skull of the buck Bone had shot. Eight Minks had removed its contents, dissolving them in warm water. Now she was crushing the mass with her fingers, making it into a fluid paste, as she sat cross-legged on the floor of her chamber.

Two Eagles entered. He immediately saw that she appeared uncharacteristically nervous.

"Sit," she said patting the ground beside her.

"I will stand."

"Sit!" she commanded. He sat. The decapitated deer lay nearby. She pulled Two Eagles' knife from its sheath and handed it to him, and wordlessly he began skinning the animal.

Eight Minks spoke calmly. "Sku-nak-su has asked me to be his wife. Even though I am old enough to be his grandmother."

Two Eagles sniffed.

"Shh, just listen. I know what you think, what everybody thinks." She leaned closer. "I do not care. My life is lonely. When I am with him he chases the loneliness like summer rain chases heat. He makes me feel wanted for the first time in my life."

"My brothers and I did not make you feel so?" Two Eagles asked sourly.

"That was different; you were little boys."

"He is a *rocksongwa*."

"He is as much a man as you are! Maybe more. We are not stupid—I know I am too old for a first *cian*. We are not marrying for a family; we are marrying to have each other. To bundle close on cold winter nights. To walk together in the woods in the spring. To eat and laugh and just be together. I am weary of living with my shadow for companionship."

"You are not alone."

"I know, I have you and Margaret. You are wrong. She has you, you have her. The two of you have Benjamin. All I have is my shadow. I am like an old owl watching two wolves on the ground below enjoying each other.

"The wolf mates for life, *neh*?" she went on.

He grunted. He continued skinning the buck, and she went on squeezing the brain paste.

"Like wolves he and I will be together for what is left of my life. As for you and me, our relationship will not change. Why should it? You would not know, but loneliness is like a wound, like pain that stays with you, never goes away. To have to live with it all the days of your life is unhealthy, as bad as a fever or headache. It hurts, Tékni-ska-je-a-nah. To be not wanted, not needed."

"We need you."

"He does not? Is he not alone, too?" Eight Minks countered.

"Him alone? He and O-kwen-cha are like two halves of the same nut. Will O-kwen-cha move in with you? He will expect to."

"You talk stupidly. O-kwen-cha will be no problem for us. Do not make him one for yourself."

"Sku-nak-su's reputation does not bother you?"

"It is *gó-dio-diá-se.*"

"*Neh*, not a 'lying tale.' He sleeps with every old woman he can find," Two Eagles snapped.

"Before, when he was young and foolish and wanted to prove his manhood," she said. "Those days are long under the dust. He will be as faithful to me in marriage as I to him." She shook her head, eyeing him questioningly. "Anything else you do not like about this marriage? Speak up, it's getting late." Her look changed to a puzzled expression. "Why do you disapprove? The real reason. Because of what others may think of us? Does that embarrass you?"

"Does it not *embarrass* you?"

"I do not care. Nor does he. People with nothing better to do can always find something to pick on in others. With you it was Margaret. With us, for the difference in our ages. If not that, the gossips would find something else. Look at me. Do not hang your head like a guilty boy caught stealing honey. I want your approval. It is important to me. So tell me, tell your mother that you accept him, you approve."

"I will have to think about it," he muttered, unable to meet her eyes.

"Your brain is exhausted from thinking about it. Say it!"

"All right, all right."

"Say the words and mean them. Welcome him into our longhouse as I welcomed Margaret."

The flap lifted. It was Fox. Seeing Two Eagles, he turned to leave them in privacy.

"*Neh, neh,*" said Eight Minks, her eyes sparkling at sight of him. "Come in, come in." She gave Two Eagles a prompting nod.

He cleared his throat. "Sku-nak-su, my mother has told me of your intentions. I approve. I welcome you, my friend, brother, into our longhouse."

"Father—" Fox added, grinning.

Two Eagles frowned, then his features softened slightly, recognizing the attempt at a joke. "My friend, my brother."

37

Shortly before midday on the missionaries' third day on the trail, it began to rain. Carrying more than fifty pounds in supplies and equipment had already taken its toll on Seth Wilson. Every bone in his body felt shifted out of position. His feet felt broken and so swollen he could barely get his shoes on each morning. The rain persisted up the Taconic mountains and down the other side, which to everyone's surprise and disappointment was far harder on the legs than ascending the eastern slope. They made their way through Mohican Territory without incident, arriving at the edge of the Hudson Valley. Dwight Hopkins appeared to be enduring the rigors of the journey better than the others and did his best to keep their spirits up. However, his efforts were wasted on Jonathan Wilby.

But by the time they reached the Hudson River all four were much improved, in condition to cope with the long distances ahead. That night on the riverbank they lit a campfire with some difficulty, for it had resumed raining, and ate sparingly of tinned beans and biscuits.

"Are the mountains in Virginia as high as the Taconics?" Drummond asked Hopkins, who sat enjoying his pipe, holding his hand over the bowl to keep his tobacco dry.

"Higher," he said. "Both the Blue Ridge mountains and the Appalachians. I climbed them in midsummer. It's pleasantly cool up top, not freezing cold like the Taconics."

"We should have started out a month ago," said Wilby.

"We didn't," said Seth, "and we all know it. There's no point in beating that drum." His impatience surprised even him.

Wilby stirred the fire with a stick. The wind made the rain feel like sleet. The cold crept through Seth's mandilion, sneaking into his bones. He Looks and Great Branch sat apart from them, talking in their own tongue in hushed tones. Drummond looked their way.

"Not very friendly, are they?" said Seth.

"All Indians are aloof."

"I don't trust them," whispered Wilby.

"Shhhhhh." Hopkins set a finger to his lips. An owl hooted plaintively close by. "In case you haven't noticed, we're stuck with them. Let's keep peace in the family. They've gotten us this far—I'd say they're doing nobly."

"I wouldn't worry about them, Jonathan," said Drummond to Wilby. "I'm sure the society engages only the ones who come recommended."

"Who by?" asked Seth. "And I wonder what they think of missionaries. Not much admiration there. I'm sure they think we're as much interlopers as colonists."

Hopkins yawned. "Who cares what they think of us? We don't need their recommendation to the Iroquois."

Wilby looked about them and shivered. " 'This is the land of darkness and the shadow of death.' Job ten—"

"Oh shut up," said Drummond.

Hopkins got up and summoned He Looks and Great Branch.

"How far to the nearest Mohawk castle?" he asked them. Great Branch held up two fingers. "Two days? Ahhhhh."

"Good, excellent," said Drummond.

"More immediately," said Seth, "how do we get across the river? It must be at least a hundred yards wide."

He Looks told them that all the supplies and equipment would be tied to two deadfalls lashed side by side and that he and Great Branch would guide them to the other side.

"And I suppose we swim for it," said Seth.

"Yes, swim. You can swim?" asked He looks.

"Not terribly well," said Wilby.

"I'll help you," said Drummond. "Just take it easy. Don't panic if you swallow a little water, and we'll be across before you know it. Not much of a current here. Nothing dangerous in these waters."

"You'll make it," said Seth to Wilby, clapping him encouragingly on the back.

"Tonight we take turns staying awake," said Great Branch, indicating He looks and himself.

"Why?" asked Wilby. "Is it dangerous?"

Wolves began baying in chorus upriver. Drummond grunted, impressed.

"How did you know?" he asked the guides.

Great Branch grinned toothlessly and pointed at his nose.

"I can't smell a blessed thing," said Wilby worriedly.

"Your nose no good."

"I'll sleep with one of the flintlocks," said Drummond, "if nobody minds."

"I'll sleep with the other," said Hopkins. "We'll bed down outside of you two." He snickered. "Keep you from walking in your sleep."

"Good, good," said He Looks. "All of you stay together."

They retired early, all four falling asleep within minutes of each other. Seth dreamt of Hannah. He saw her
running up the heaving deck of the *Dauntless* toward
Leonora, the wave washing her overboard, his heart
wrenching at the sight, her arm thrusting out of the water
like Excalibur. He awoke feeling miserable. It had
stopped raining but a dampness hung over the woodlands.

He stayed awake for a time, listening for the wolves,
but heard nothing save the wind. He thought about
Leonora; Hannah's death had unhinged her. Was it permanent? Abner hadn't said. He glanced over at the two
guides. He Looks was lying on his belly snoring; Great
Branch sat with his knees drawn up, staring at the ground.
Seth went back to sleep.

All four were awakened by the shrill cawing of crows
overhead. The river eased quietly by, mist rising from it.

Seth rubbed his eyes, looked about and gasped. Their
guides were gone!

"They've taken everything!" Drummond burst out.

Everything necessary and important, it appeared after a
quick survey. The weapons, both axes, knives—excepting
Drummond's and Seth's, who happened to be wearing
them. They left most of the food only because they apparently didn't eat black cloaks' food. Wilby took one look
around and lost control.

"Deserted! Abandoned! Left like lambs in a lion's den!"

"Oh shut up," snapped Drummond. "Hysterics won't
help. Let's calm down, discuss it, decide what to do."

"I'd like to chase after those two miserable wretches,"
said Hopkins. "They can't have gotten far."

"Thieves travel fast," said Drummond.

"He's right, Dwight," said Seth. "And who knows
which direction they took. They could even have crossed
the river."

"I doubt that," said Drummond. "My guess is they
planned this from the first and never had any intention of

crossing. They're probably deathly afraid of the Mohawks. Accursed heathens! May they rot in hell!"

Wilby looked predictably shocked. Hopkins grinned.

"Let's forget about them," said Seth. "Spilt milk. So, what's it to be? What do we do?"

"We go back, of course," said Wilby.

"Of course?"

Drummond had gotten to his feet and was peering through the mist toward the opposite bank. "Great Branch said two days to the first Mohawk castle."

"He was lying!" Wilby shouted.

"Why would he lie?" Seth asked. "Fisk, are you suggesting we continue on our own?"

"I don't know. I do dread climbing back over those accursed mountains, dragging all the way back to Boston, having to start all over again at some future date."

"But," said Wilby, "it's the only sensible course."

Hopkins rubbed his chin thoughtfully between puffs on his pipe. "Do you think we might get a couple of guides from the Mohawks? I mean, after we've converted a few and gained their confidence?"

Drummond nodded. "You're reading my mind. Two days can't be far. Down to the corner for a loaf of bread. Dwight, let's have a look at the maps."

He traced the main trail on a map. "Here. This X. O-ne-ka—"

"Honck-a," Hopkins finished. "Castle number one. There'll be three before we get to the line separating Mohawk from Oneida territories. We must be about here." He indicated. "We cross, move north along the bank and here's the main trail. I say we go on."

"I say we take a vote," said Drummond.

The others were all for it, but Wilby was dead against continuing on. He grudgingly ended up deferring to the majority, although not until he'd limned some of the more fanciful dangers he expected ahead. "I knew they'd desert us," he added. " 'Father, forgive them for they know not what they do.' Luke twen—"

"They knew," interrupted Drummond. "Forgive them if you like; I'd like to wring their grimy necks."

"Amen," said Seth.

38

It's freezing!" Wilby withdrew his rapidly reddening hand from the water.

"And the river's starting to get turbulent from all that rain," said Drummond.

Hopkins nodded. "It had to have rained even harder up above. The current's running faster."

"We mustn't dare cross until it's back to normal," said Wilby. He scanned the sky; it promised a beautiful fall day. "It's not going to rain again. Yes, by all means let's wait."

Hopkins shook his head. "We could dawdle here for a week. I say we get across as fast as we can. In an hour it'll really be swollen."

Seth agreed. "Let's find some deadfalls."

They quickly found three fallen trees all about the same dimensions. Long dead, their limbs broke off easily.

"We can tie them together with our mandilions," suggested Drummond.

"Too bulky," said Hopkins. "They'd be impossible to tie tightly."

"What do you suppose our friends the Nipmucs intended to use?" Seth asked.

"Probably their breechclouts. They're long enough and would tie a good tight knot. Let's use our trousers."

"They'll get absolutely soaked," protested Wilby.

"I don't see as we have much choice, Jonathan. We can't risk these logs breaking apart in midstream. We'd lose everything. We can build a fire on the other side and dry our clothes. Let's get to work."

By the time they stripped down to their underclothing and packed the raft, the river threatened to become impossible for even the strongest swimmer. The sun was well above the horizon but seemed no warmer.

"It's freezing, all right," muttered Hopkins, stepping into the water. He crossed his arms and shivered. "The only thing I can't abide is cold."

"Jonathan," said Drummond to Wilby, "just try and relax. You won't drown. I'll be holding you across the chest all the way."

"Will we make it?" he asked.

"If you two run into any trouble, I'll help," promised Seth.

"Don't count on me," said Hopkins. "If one of us doesn't hang onto this contraption all the way across, it'll be swept downstream in a trice. Here we go!"

A hundred yards, perhaps more. Seth set forth, picking his way gingerly across the descending bottom, mud oozing between his toes. He paused when the water reached his hips. He was shivering, his teeth chattering wildly. Hopkins plunged ahead, diving in. He surfaced, groaning loudly, and came back for the raft.

"Pray the bloody thing floats, Seth."

Together they pulled the raft into the water. Each held a protruding end under one arm, Hopkins at the front guiding the raft. To their right upriver about fifteen yards Wilby and Drummond had already set out. No sooner was Wilby completely immersed than he discovered he was over his head. He began thrashing wildly.

"Stop it!" boomed Drummond. "Just relax. Kick your feet, don't move your arms. They'll just get in my way. I said *kick*! Help me."

Wilby blurted something, choked violently and resumed thrashing in near panic. Then he got hold of himself, kicking and swimming with his right arm only, matching Drummond's left arm. Meanwhile, Hopkins guided the raft toward the far bank, kicking hard against the current to keep the front end heading straight for a bare patch between two large stones. Seth pushed at the other end.

Drummond and Wilby were well ahead of the raft and closing in on the opposite bank when Drummond suddenly shouted in pain.

"My leg!"

"What is it?" called Hopkins.

"A cramp, vicious! Dear God, I can't move my leg. It's all knotted up. Excruciating!"

Panicking, Wilby began splashing violently, churning the water and screaming. Drummond let go of him. Horrified, Seth and Hopkins watched Drummond as he screamed in agony and his head sank below the surface. Up he bobbed, choking, sputtering.

"Help—me!"

Down he went. Barely three yards from him, Wilby screamed and splashed and kicked furiously. Touching bottom he surged forward, throwing himself down on the bank.

"There!" called Seth to Hopkins, pointing to where Drummond had gone down.

"He'll come up!" shouted Hopkins.

Drummond's broad back and shoulders showed briefly; his head remained submerged. As the two of them looked on, he was swept helplessly away around a bend and out of sight. Seth started for him.

"No!" shouted Hopkins. "He's drowned, he's dead!"

They finally got the raft to the opposite side, staggering up the bank, dragging it partway out of the water. A few yards away Wilby lay on his back, staring upward, the color drained from his cheeks. For a moment Seth imagined his heart had given out. Then Wilby sat up.

"Give us a hand here," barked Seth.

Wilby looked about anxiously. "Where's Fisk?"

"Swept away," said Hopkins. "Didn't you see?"

"Dear God, dear God, dear God!"

"Shut up!"

"I heard him shouting about a cramp. He let go of me."

He gawked at one then the other. "You didn't expect me to help him? I can't swim."

Seth grunted. "Never mind. Nobody's blaming you. You fellows unpack," he added. "Make a fire, dry out our things." He untied his trousers used to fasten the logs together at the center. He retrieved his shoes and mandilion. "I'm going downriver to look for his body. It may have snagged on something."

"Maybe he didn't drown," shrilled Wilby. "He survived, caught onto a branch, pulled himself out!" Seth and Hopkins exchanged glances.

"The least we can do is give him a Christian burial," said Seth.

"I'll come help you," said Hopkins.

"No!" cried Wilby. "Don't leave me alone!"

"I can do it," said Seth. "I'll get him to shore and we'll bury him there." He buckled his shoes and closed his mandilion around him.

"Be careful," cautioned Wilby. "These woods are crawling with all sorts of deadly creatures. . . ."

Seth ignored him and headed downriver. Drummond was dead. Seth and Hopkins had seen his body vanish around the bend. Was it an omen, a warning to turn back here and now? He couldn't; he'd made a pact, he must see it through to completion.

They had to go on.

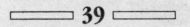

39

Eight Minks had convinced herself that Red Paint would not pose a problem in her marriage to Fox. She made it clear to her husband-to-be that his friend would not be allowed to hang around the house like dried apples from the rafters. Fox must have so informed Red Paint, for he abruptly shed his disinterest in the marriage and took to openly complaining about it. It was obvious to Margaret that his feelings were deeply hurt. He felt that his friend was abandoning him.

Marriage proposed and accepted, Eight Minks presented her husband-to-be with the traditional unleavened corn bread; in return he gave her fresh venison. In everyone's eyes they were now man and wife. They were that easily joined because neither had a mother to arrange a more complex ceremony.

There was no wedding feast, no guests, no one else even present when the gifts were exchanged. Margaret and Two Eagles' marriage ceremony was only slightly more involved. When Eight Minks as Two Eagles' mother, had produced a piece of rawhide as long as Two Eagles was tall, Margaret and he sat cross-legged facing each other surrounded by women. Each woman tied a knot in the rawhide; lastly, Eight Minks joined the two ends and draped the loop in a figure eight over bride and groom.

Margaret understood why Eight Minks and Fox were married privately; they preferred not to draw undue attention to the unconventional union.

Two Eagles had no desire to discuss the marriage with Red Paint, but the latter brought it up. As Two Eagles sat on the ground with Benjamin in his lap, watching the entrance gate for Bone, Red Paint's shadow fell across him. Two Eagles looked up to see his friend, bright with fresh paint, fists on hips, staring down gloomily.

"Do you believe it?"

"Believe what?"

"I sent word inside asking him to go *ochquari* hunting with me; he refused. I spotted a fine full-grown bear in the stream!"

Two Eagles suppressed a smile. "Perhaps he has better things to do?"

"Are you saying he and his *odasqueta* cannot be out of each other's sight for half a day?"

Two Eagles bristled. "My mother is not an old woman!"

"She is *exhecta*, a young girl?"

"She is my mother. Careful what you say. They were married yesterday. For a while they want only each other's company. That is natural."

"He has not shown his head out the door."

"Leave him alone. Be patient. He will go *ochquari* hunting with you when he gets around to it."

"By then our bear will have found itself a cave to hide from us. Get up, go inside, and tell him I am waiting."

"*Neh.*"

"You refuse?"

"*Nyoh.* And you do not go inside either." Two Eagles got wearily to his feet. "If you insist, I will go hunting with you."

"I want *him*."

"He is busy."

"How much fucking can they do?"

"Let me give Benjamin to his mother and get my bow. Where exactly did you see this bear?"

Red Paint looked sheepish. "I do not remember. Get Sku-nak-su for me and we will go and look."

"My company is not good enough for you? Give it up, my friend. I am not going inside after him. He will come out only if the longhouse burns down."

Five days passed and no sign of Bone. The snake of worry glided faster through Two Eagles' mind. Six days, seven.

Finally Swift Doe came to him, with Moon Dancer. She was widow to Thrown Bear, Do-wa-sku-ta, Two Eagles' best friend, who had accompanied him, Splitting Moon and the others when they escorted Margaret to Quebec.

Moon Dancer looked not at all like a dancer. She was dumpy, flirting with obesity, with a face as round as a melon and beady eyes surrounded by puffs of flesh.

"Moon Dancer has something to say to you," said Swift Doe.

Two Eagles avoided the older woman's eyes. They had not liked each other even before he had shot and killed her husband to put him out of his agony. Every time Two Eagles saw her, that chilling episode came back: Thrown Bear perched on a rock, hands and feet cut off by the Ottawas, suffering horribly, beyond endurance even for an Iroquois, begging his friend to kill him.

"You remember when I predicted Do-wa-sku-ta's death," she said, "that if he went with you up to the Kanawage he would be killed by you?"

"Do you ever let anyone forget it?" Two Eagles snapped.

The prediction had established Moon Dancer's reputation to virtually everyone except Two Eagles and Margaret. Two Eagles simply refused to comment on her prescience, and Margaret considered the prediction coincidence.

Moon Dancer waddled closer, Swift Doe anxious at her side. The sun was bright, the air unseasonably warm; the lands of the Iroquois thirsted for rain. Children played with a puppy at the spot where Iron Dog's body had been prepared for burial by the squaws.

"My husband is not coming back," lamented Swift Doe, flashing a sidelong glance at the older woman.

"He is," said Two Eagles.

"Is he?" Moon Dancer smirked. "*Neh.* He cannot. He is dead." She raised one fat finger for emphasis. Swift Doe looked devastated, and began trembling.

"He is alive and will be here before the lake swallows the sun," said Two Eagles.

"Dead," repeated Moon Dancer. "Murdered. Once more Swift Doe is a widow. This time because of you." She leveled the finger accusingly. "He went to Massowaganine not for the chiefs but for you."

"He went after Iron Dog's murderer," added Swift Doe.

Margaret, who had come out of the longhouse, overheard this. She came running up. Two Eagles resisted an urge to throw up his hands in disgust and walk off, as Moon Dancer tapped his chest brazenly.

"When Blue Creek left here that is where he went: Massowaganine."

"Did he?"

"Everybody knows that."

"Let's talk in private," murmured Margaret to her husband.

"Leave me along, all of you. I did not *send* Bone anywhere," he said to Swift Doe. "He—offered to go."

"And you let him," said Margaret, "because I wouldn't let you do your own dirty work."

Chief His Longhouse came shuffling up. "Your husband must be delayed in returning from his mission for us," he said to Swift Doe.

"Do not bother to lie, Sho-non-ses," sneered Moon Dancer. "We all know the real reason why he went there. Tékni-ska-je-a-nah just admitted it."

His Longhouse's jaw sagged. He fixed Two Eagles with a betrayed look.

"This is *oueda*," snapped Two Eagles. "I have things to do!"

"Inside," commanded Margaret. She took him by the arm, leaving the others staring at them.

Two Eagles sighed to himself, recalling the day he and the others had brought him word that his brother Long Feather, Swift Doe's first husband, the father of her sons, had been murdered by a renegade Mohawk. How stoically she had reacted: holding back her tears, her hands on her stomach round with her unborn third child. She had mourned and picked up the traces of her life. Months after the baby's birth, she accepted Bone's proposal of marriage.

Now this. And the women were right: he was to blame. Had Moon Dancer guessed right? Had Blue Creek sighted, ambushed, and killed Bone?

Margaret sat on the bunk. If she was still angry she hid it well. When she spoke, her voice had lost its edge.

"Tell me what this is all about."

"First you must understand. I—have to finish what Turtle Skin started. He cannot get away with murdering Iron Dog. He must pay."

"Stop it! You don't care two pins about Iron Dog. Be honest. You have to have your precious vengeance!"

"That is the way of our people."

"The way of all people, all *men*," she sneered. "That doesn't make it right or necessary. It's stupid as a goat. You are! Pray Bone gets back here unharmed, because if he doesn't—"

"I am to blame, I know!"

"Don't shout!"

"I will give him until sundown tomorrow. Eight sleeps for a four-sleep journey. If he does not show up, I will go looking for him."

"How convenient."

"What do you mean?"

"You can look for Bone and Blue Creek at the same time. Or find Bone, let everyone back here think you're still looking for him and the two of you keep on after his nibs."

"If Bone is not dead he may be badly hurt. I must go out."

She stared at him. "Mmmmm, I'd say you've little choice. Only don't even think about going alone."

"I will ask Splitting Moon. We will leave right away."

40

Moving at a steady lope, Two Eagles and Splitting Moon passed the white caves on the northernmost path to Lake Oneida and turned north for Onondaga Territory. Their journey to Massowaganine two years before replayed itself to both warriors.

"Remember back when you killed Cahonsye-rú-kew for murdering your brother? And got in that bad trouble with the chiefs and elders?"

"He deserved my knife!"

"You stirred up a hornet's nest. That was the last time we took this path. To go up and talk to Kah-nah-chi-wah-ne, He-big-kettle, at the peace conference, remember?"

"How can I forget if you keep reminding me?"

"And to ask him, too, what should be done with Margaret."

Two Eagles' grunt and frown ended the conversation. The two arrived late in the afternoon of their second day on the trail. Almost the moment they entered the Onondaga castle, Splitting Moon caught sight of Gordon Duncan, Gä-de-a-yo, Lobster. He was hard to miss: he stood six foot five, with shoulders wider than Splitting Moon's, a mass of fiery red hair and full beard, with mischievous eyes as blue as the sky.

"Duncan!" Two Eagles called warmly.

Sergeant Gordon Duncan, formerly of the 2nd Scottish Highlanders, came pounding toward them, shaking the ground, seizing Two Eagles, then Splitting Moon in his powerful arms.

"Lord love a duck, if you twa are nae a sight for sore eyes!"

Two Eagles had never completely understood Gordon's English, but the Oneida could not help but like him more than any other English—which Duncan bridled at, explaining that he had "nae a drop of Ainglish blood in any vein."

Into nostalgia they plunged: the attack on Fort Vercheres, the Battle of Schenectady, the defense of Toniota, the many raids on the St. Lawrence—then their rescue of Margaret and her Oneida escort from *coureurs de bois* and Ottawa poachers in the woods just south of Fort Frontenac, discovery of Thrown Bear on the river- bank. Splitting Moon, seeing Two Eagle's face fall, changed the subject.

"We are looking for Bone, the Mohican," he said to Duncan. "You met him when you rescued us from the Ottawa dogshit eaters. Tall, broken cheekbones, he still wears a scalp lock."

"I remember him. What about him?"

"Have you seen him?" Two Eagles asked.

"Nae."

"But he came here." He held up one hand splaying his fingers. "Five, six sleeps ago. I told him to ask for you."

"I dinna see him. What was he after?"

They told him about Blue Creek, about Night Song and their relationship, the attempted kidnapping, Iron Dog's murder.

"We think Blue Creek was coming here to see her," said Splitting Moon.

"Night Song I ken. She is morried to Tall Crow."

"Take us to them," said Two Eagles. "Something is very wrong here. Maybe they can help."

As Duncan led the way between longhouses, Splitting Moon described Blue Creek in detail. Recognition lit up the giant's face.

"Aye, he came a few days bock. Looking like he'd run a gauntlet all the way from Onneyuttahage. I dinna speak to him, but Night Song and Tall Crow moost have."

He led them to their chamber. Tall Crow was alone lying down. Two Eagles and Splitting Moon barely knew him, having seen him only once and that three years ago when he came to Onneyuttahage to ask Night Song to marry him. Years before he had proposed, but Night Song turned him down, telling him that she planned to marry Blue Creek.

Duncan introduced the two visitors, asking Tall Crow about Blue Creek. He nodded slowly and was about to speak when Night Song came in. She was as pretty as Two Eagles remembered her; she resembled Swift Doe, the same dark, beautiful eyes, perfect skin and sensuous mouth. She carried a baby older than Benjamin. Tall Crow motioned for the child and spoke to her.

She went out. Tall Crow did not even look down at the squirming baby. Night Song returned carrying a heavy kettle of what smelled like *o-gon'sä'-ganon'-dä*, green corn scraped from the cob and thrown into a pot of half-cooked beans, simmered together with salt and bear grease.

"Ahhh," said Duncan licking his lips. "Sooccotosh, my favorite."

They ate. Between mouthfuls Tall Crow filled them in

on the fugitive's visit. Night Song listened, silent and apprehensive.

"He wanted Ganõda to go with him," laughed Tall Crow. "At first I thought he was joking. But he really did, he wanted her. His brain was upside down in his head." He set his fingers against Splitting Moon's throat. "I lifted him up, set him down, swung my hand around the back of his neck like so and walked him to the gate. Outside he turned to say something; he was very *aquinachoo*."

"Angry," murmured Duncan, translating the Onondaga word. "On fire."

"So he left then," said Two Eagles.

"*Neh*. He hung around, although I myself did not see him again."

"I did," said Night Song.

Her husband frowned her into silence. "Others say they saw him, too. Hanging about outside watching the castle. Then he must have given up and left."

"Where did he plan to go?" Two Eagles asked Night Song.

Tall Crow shook his head. "He did not speak to her after he asked her to leave with him." He leered. "How could he speak with my hand at his throat?"

"He did not even hint where he might be heading?" Splitting Moon asked Night Song. After a timorous look at her husband, she shook her head.

Sensing that the subject had exhausted itself, Duncan stood up. "We will go," he said to Tall Crow. "And thank you and Night Song for your *o-gon'-sä'-ganon'-dä*. It warms our stomachs and gives us strength."

Splitting Moon started to protest, but Two Eagles silenced him with a frown. Outside Duncan set his massive hands behind his neck and stretched his arms.

"I am sorry, Twa Eagles. I could ask around if anybody happened to see which direction the bostard took when he left, but I doobt anyone noticed. Being a fugitive, he'd be careful not to let anyone see."

Troubled, Splitting Moon. looked from one man to the other. "What now?" he asked.

Two Eagles did not answer. He looked off in the direction of distant Lake Oneida and rubbed his chin thoughtfully.

"Bone never got here," he said quietly. "Blue Creek killed him before he could."

"Hoo ken ye that?" Duncan asked.

"Think like Blue Creek. He knew he was being followed; what he did not know was that Fox and Red Paint gave up. He kept an eye back down the trail. He either spotted Bone and killed him before he got here and went through that business with Tall Crow and Night Song or spotted and killed him after leaving. One way or the other, Bone is dead."

Splitting Moon held his breath, his face grim.

"Was Bone married?" Duncan asked.

Two Eagles explained. Duncan shook his massive head. "Widowed a second time, no less. Dreadful. And you have to be the one to go back and tell the poor lass."

Two Eagles grunted. "*Nyoh*. But first we must find Bone's body."

— V —
WILL

41

Seth made a cross with two sticks at the grave, a monument to Fisk Drummond, heir to an industrial fortune, missionary to the Iroquois, abruptly no longer either, drowned at twenty-three.

"Rest in peace," murmured Wilby. He looked down a moment longer, shuddered and restored his hat. "What now?"

Hopkins got out the maps, studied them briefly and pointed north upriver. "I make it roughly five leagues, at which point the Mohawk River flowing from the west joins the Hudson. When we come within the sound of the Mohawk we should turn sharply left. With luck we'll find a path that'll lead us to the main trail. We follow it from then on. We should be able to see all three Mohawk castles and the one Oneida beyond from the main trail to the north of it."

When they were ready to move out, Hopkins looked about and back to the rude cross. "Sleep well, Fisk, you're a martyr to the cause."

Wilby sighed. "Will he turn out to be the lucky one?"

Despite his promise to himself to overlook Wilby's whining and inanities, Seth flared. "If you don't want to go on, Jonathan, don't! Swim back across and hike back to Boston."

"I'd have to go all by myself," Wilby protested. "I couldn't."

"Then stop being so bloody negative!"

As they set out, the air felt like early winter. The red squirrels they saw showed coats paler than normal. They passed snakes twined together in the feeble sun on a rocky hill. They saw deer and vermin, and once Wilby insisted he glimpsed a bear through the underbrush to the west.

They stopped to rest midafternoon. Hopkins smoked, Wilby read his Bible, Seth removed his shoes and dipped his feet in a nearby pond. Then they resumed hiking.

When the coppery sun had lowered to nudge the horizon, the party heard the churning sound of the swollen Mohawk directly ahead. Once more Hopkins consulted the maps, then directed them toward the west. They found paths all leading in the same direction. Puzzled, they looked around the woods, then between matching immense oaks.

"The main trail!" Hopkins pointed.

According to their maps, it had to be. It was wide enough to march ten men abreast. Gradually the woodlands retreated on both sides, leaving dun-colored grasses, fading green weeds and occasional patches of rampant wild pinks, shaggy fireweed, straggling beggarweed.

They had traveled about fifty yards up the trail, straight into the dying sun, when Indians suddenly appeared at the edge of the woods to the right. Seth counted nine, evidently a hunting party, all armed but carrying no game. They looked to be Mohawks. The missionaries held their breath as the Indians drew closer.

Their upper bodies were garishly painted and tattooed with geometric designs, a double-curve motif and clan crests on chests, shoulders and faces. All wore bracelets and armbands and were naked to the waist despite the chill air. Their buckskin leggins came up above their knees and they wore twined corn-husk moccasins.

As they assembled in the middle of the trail, facing them, Wilby gasped. "What do we do?" he muttered.

"What we don't do is panic," cautioned Seth.

The Indians stared curiously, pointing, jabbering to each other.

"They must be from Onekahoncka, the nearest Mohawk castle," Hopkins speculated.

"They look like they'd slit their mothers' throats," said Seth. At which Wilby's hand found his own throat. "Stop that," Seth chided angrily. "And when we get up to them, try not to show fear."

Five paces from the hunters, the missionaries stopped.

Hopkins held his palm outward. "We come in peace. We are missionaries of the Congregational church. Your chiefs have been told to expect us by the Seneca chiefs—ah . . ." He turned to Seth. "Where's that paper with the two names Ernest Frame gave to Fisk?"

"In his pocket, I'm afraid."

"We are at your mercy, oh great warriors!" burst Wilby. "We are harmless men of God, his emissaries come to bring you His light in the one true faith—"

Seth whirled on him. "Shut up!"

The eldest of the hunters had stepped forward. His eyes were spellbinding. His long hair was pure white, his features sharply cut; he was good-looking but his face was riddled with pockmarks.

"Shut up," he repeated, grinning broadly.

No surprise to Seth; they had been told that virtually all Iroquois warriors spoke English. The white-haired hunter addressed a ruggedly built younger man in Mohawk. Off he ran.

"I am Joshú-we-agoochsa," said the older man. "Hole Face. These are our hunting grounds. Why are you here?"

"We are on our way to Onekahoncka to speak with your chiefs," said Hopkins.

Hole Face ran a hand down the front of the missionary's mandilion and felt the material. He spoke to the others, who all laughed. One said something that elicited a smirk from Hole Face. Seth was beginning to feel uneasy.

Clearly all of them were warriors and must have fought with the English.

"We will take you to our castle," said Hole Face. Hopkins' and Seth's eyes met. "It is all right, no harm will come to you." A man behind Hole Face spoke; the others tittered. *"Ogechta!"* snapped Hole Face, and the speaker's smirked fled. "You look tired, hungry. Come."

The party turned and started up the trail. Seth and Hopkins hesitated, then fell into step, Seth deciding they had no alternative. Wilby stood rooted, then caught up with them at Seth's murmured urging. They went on in silence, Hole Face in the lead. Seth tried to subdue his fears. If the three of them could get to the Mohawk chiefs and explain their mission, mentioning Obadiah Hedgepath's name, it was possible they'd be safe. After all, they posed no threat. That should be obvious.

No, he tried to reassure himself, it would turn out fine.

42

The gray rectangular castle of Onekahoncka stood slightly elevated in the center of a clearing. As one approached it, the end of a large field was visible, its cornstalks stripped. The last of the squash and pumpkin still awaited harvesting. From the river behind the castle on the near side, two women carried a deer on a pole. It was still alive, twisting futilely in its bonds. As the missionaries drew closer to the open gate their escort slipped back, hemming them in. Seth noticed, his heart quickening. Hole Face grinned and nodded.

Inside the entrance, a gauntlet waited, men, women and children standing in two lines holding clubs, sticks, birch rods, rawhide whips. Hopkins groaned. "The filthy beggars!"

Wilby cried out; the hunters hemmed them in, brandishing their knives.

"Take off your clothes," growled one and, seized the side of Wilby's mandilion, ripped it off. Instantly the missionaries' clothes were pulled off, leaving them naked, shivering in their shoes.

"How fast can you run?" bawled Hole Face. A current of excitement shot through the crowd. Up came clubs and whips. The leader pushed Seth forward, toppling him, and suddenly the Mohawks fell on him, beating him mercilessly. Pain struck from every side. Struggling to fend off blows, he staggered to his feet and ran. Clubs pummeled him, sticks struck smartly, whips stung, leaving bloodied cuts, rods sliced deep. He had covered no more than ten yards before he began to stagger and felt himself pushed upright from both sides. On he ran, bleeding all over, head ringing with pain, ugly welts rising on his shoulders, chest and back. The torture went on until it felt as if his wounds had become so many they lost distinction, merging into a single all-encompassing pain.

To his blurred sight, the gauntlet appeared to have no end. Around the corner of a longhouse the double line headed back, and those who had already beaten him ran around to the end of the line for a second chance.

A gray pall descended over his throbbing, whirling head, and through it each separate blow burst red. On he staggered until he could no longer thrust one leg ahead of the other, and down he fell into the blackness.

43

Certain as to what they would find, Two Eagles had no heart to search for Bone. Saying good-bye to Gordon Duncan, leaving Massowaganine, he thought of Swift Doe's boys, at the loss of their natural father; in time they had come to idolize Bone. Now he was taken from them.

They started for the trail leading back to the white caves near Lake Oneida. Splitting Moon tried to console his friend.

"You did not force him to go. It was his idea."

"Does that change anything?" Two Eagles fisted his heart. "Not in here. I only know I have sent a friend to the Village of the Dead before his time."

"What about Turtle Skin?" Splitting Moon asked.

Two Eagles stopped short. "What about him?" he rasped. "We find Bone, you take him back to Swift Doe, I will go on."

"Where?"

"I will pick up Blue Creek's trail."

"You think he will leave one for you? He knows you are coming after him." He knotted his homely face in a frown. "Where do you think he went from here? South to the Susquehannocks? North to the Kanuwage? Not up past the big lake—Ne-ah´-gä-te-car-ne-o-di. Not back to the Huron snakes."

"Not south. We have fought the Susquehannocks too many times. They hate all Iroquois; they would feed him their knives before he could get a word out."

"How would they know he is Iroquois? He is scalped, he has no tattoos, no paint."

"I think he has headed north."

"Into Gâ'-oh's teeth, with *augustuske* coming? Maybe he doubled back toward the Shaw-na-taw-ty. The Mohawks would welcome him."

"One thing at a time. First we must find Bone. Pick up your moccasins."

Still within sight of Massowaganine they began searching both sides of the trail, venturing deep into the woods, returning to the trail to compare notes. There was no sign that Bone had passed through the area. When darkness wrapped the woodlands, Splitting Moon made a fire with smoldering punk—grass and fungus wound in a tight cylinder inside a hollowed-out corn cob. As they satisfied their hunger with a handful of cornmeal, Splitting Moon got onto the subject of the recent nuptials.

"Why did your mother not make the usual *gon-ni-ta-o-a-kwa*? The two balls with the neck connecting them, wrapped in a corn husk and tied in the middle? That is traditional."

"Wedding bread is wedding bread. Baked for the man to eat. What difference what shape it is?"

"Tradition. And she should have baked twenty-four loaves, not just one."

"You think Sku-nak-su cares? You think he married her for her bread?"

"*Neh,*" Splitting Moon said uncertainly.

"So if it does not bother him, why should it you?"

"I have to *oeuda*."

"Downwind," Two Eagles snorted. "We have to sleep here."

Splitting Moon walked off into the darkness, and Two Eagles stirred the fire. They had to find Bone's body if it meant searching all day tomorrow and the next day. Blue Creek, he speculated, had arrived at Massowaganine, tried and failed to get Night Song to leave with him, had hung around outside the castle for some time. Probably then he had caught sight of Bone approaching—near the castle, not this far away. Should they go back in the morning and start covering the same ground a second time?

He started. Splitting Moon was calling loudly up the trail and off to the left. He ran toward him. Splitting Moon came running up all excited.

"Come!"

Two Eagles' heart jolted. Bone was tied to a tree, his feet inches from the ground. An arrow protruded from his chest, a second from his forehead. His eyes stared so, Two Eagles was constrained to look away. Two feathers were stuck in Bone's mouth. Two Eagles removed them. They were white at the base of the quill, black at the tip.

"These are the feathers of a young golden eagle," he murmured.

"Placed there for you to find," added Splitting Moon unnecessarily. Reaching up he closed the dead man's eyes.

"Do you think you can carry him back by yourself?" Two Eagles asked.

Splitting Moon frowned. "*Neh*, he is too heavy. You must come with me. You must tell Swift Doe. I cannot speak for you."

He was right. Responsibility for Bone's death was Two Eagles'. Only after he explained could he set out after Blue Creek. He twirled a feather in each hand. Find him, return him his feathers. A fair exchange for his black heart.

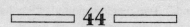

44

Consciousness threaded its way to Seth and he hesitantly opened his eyes. Faint light made him wince. He groaned. Looking down, he found himself lying in his own blood on the dirt floor of a longhouse chamber. The odor of putrid meat struck his nostrils, nauseating him momentarily. He saw a star, visible through a slit between the bark panels just below the roof, and the glow of the passageway fire beneath the deerskin flap at the entrance.

He lay in agony, his body a mass of slowly burning pulp. He felt every bone was broken; even to draw a shallow breath sent pain radiating through his torso to his aching privates. The portions of his body that he could see were crisscrossed with lacerations, riddled with bruises. He concluded that only his eyes and teeth had escaped injury. Ears, nose and lips were shredded and bleeding; his head was crammed with pain.

As his sight cleared, he sensed that Hopkins and Wilby were nearby, but he had neither the will nor the energy to look about him.

He tried to swallow, but pain struck his throat like a knife, and when he cried out his lacerated ears rang at the sound.

He heard a noise.

"Seth?" It was Wilby.

"How are you making it, Jonathan?"

"Is Dwight dead?"

"Very nearly," murmured a feeble voice from a corner.

"Don't talk," murmured Seth. "Save your strength. Make them think they did a thorough job. Maybe they'll leave us alone for a while."

The effort of so many words took its toll. Seth closed his eyes, and immediately the pain intensified.

Enveloped in agony, he wondered: How had they survived? Was it intentional? It must be. What next? Fisk Drummond, with his fascination for Indian lore, had told them of reading where the Iroquois kept prisoners barely alive for as long as a week. Was that the plan?

And why? They were no threat; they were utterly harmless. But did the Iroquois, particularly the Mohawks, need a reason to torture prisoners other than for the pleasure of it? Hopkins read his mind.

"The Powhatans, the Chickahominies and the other tribes in Virginia don't torture," he said. "They kill prisoners, but swiftly. None of this."

"Do you remember what Fisk said about the Iroquois?" Wilby asked. "How they drag out their torturing? I won't be able to stand it, I know I won't. I don't want to die—"

"Shhhhh," said Hopkins. "Do you think we're looking forward to it?"

"We've got to get out of here," said Seth.

"Don't talk nonsense," scoffed Hopkins. "Shhh, somebody's coming."

In strode three warriors wearing pieces of the missionaries' clothing, looking both ridiculous and menacing. All carried bark buckets. Without a word each man tossed the contents of his bucket over one of them. Wilby screamed. Seth sniffed and made a face.

"Smells like walnuts."

"It does," said Hopkins. "It doesn't burn or sting; actually it feels rather good. Do you suppose it's to help us heal?"

Seth grunted. "Assuming they do want to keep us alive."

Ignoring their nakedness, an old squaw came shuffling in carrying buckskins, setting her burden down in the middle of the floor and going out.

"Maybe it's over," said Wilby. "They want us to get dressed so we can leave."

"Don't hold your breath, Jonathan." Seth groaned. "God, but it hurts."

"Anything broken?" Hopkins asked.

"I don't dare move to find out."

A second woman came in with a large wooden bowl. She set it down near the clothing and exited. Wincing and groaning, Seth dragged himself to the bowl.

"Smells like corn and beans." He sniffed and poked at it. "And there's meat of some kind."

"Don't eat the meat," cautioned Hopkins. "Savages don't know good from putrid."

Nevertheless, famished as they were, they ate, tentatively at first, then wolfing it down.

"It's good," said Seth. He glanced at the pile of clothing. "Do they really expect us to put on those rags?"

Hopkins picked up a worn breechclout. "Rotten. And crawling with lice. Is either of you getting the feeling we're not exactly welcome here?"

"We're dead," said Wilby. "We should make our peace with God and prepare for the worst."

"Jonathan," said Seth quietly. "We know what we've gotten into here. Please, if you can't say anything hopeful or positive, hold your peace."

"I can't stand pain even the slightest. Owwwww—"

"Try, there's a good fellow." Seth paused in his eating and dragged himself to the entrance, peering up and down the passageway. "No guards, Dwight."

Hopkins scoffed. "We wouldn't make it to the outside door."

"Is there a rear entrance to this place, do you think?"

Hopkins shrugged. "Could be."

"Then why did those two women carrying the deer come all the way to the front?" Wilby asked.

"Good point," said Hopkins. "Seth, let's put escape to one side for now; it just strikes me as impossible. I think we should try and get to the chiefs. Tell them why we've come, make them understand we're no threat."

Seth shook his head. "The hunters could see that."

"Just the same, their chiefs must know the Seneca chiefs; don't you think they'd respect their wishes? Let me try. It's best if one of us speaks for all, don't you think?"

"Go ahead. Just don't get your hopes up."

Two warriors came in. The missionaries recognized Hole Face. He ordered them to put on the clothing. When the lice and the body odor made Wilby throw up, the Mohawks laughed.

Hole Face gestured. "Come with us."

"Where?" asked Hopkins.

Hole Face ignored him. They were escorted up the passageway and outside. The grounds were deserted, but torches burned overhead on the palisade platforms.

They were pushed inside a longhouse at the rear of the castle. Seth caught sight of a rear entrance. They were marched down the passageway to a double chamber at the end and ordered to sit. Two men came in; from their attire—more ornate than that of Hole Face and the others—and their ages, they appeared to be chiefs. They took their places opposite the three missionaries and sat staring. Then the older one raised his wrinkled hand and the escort withdrew, leaving only Hole Face standing behind the three prisoners. Light came from torches on either side of the chiefs. Their skins looked deeply bronzed and their eyes were angry.

"English whiteskins," said the younger chief, about Hole Face's age, "why do you come to our place?"

Hopkins explained. "We humbly ask your permission to stay here among your people. We have crossed the ocean on a mission. Our mission is to bring the Mohawks to Christ."

"You are black robes?"

"We are missionaries of the Congregational church, honored to bring to you and your people the priesthood of all believers."

His listener grunted and turned to his companion, who shrugged. Hopkins went on. Seth realized the Virginian's strategy: Petition them for the chance to convert the people. How much better than to attempt escape against almost certain failure.

"All we ask is your permission to speak to your people," added Seth. "We Congregationalists are a people brought together not by nationality or station in life but by the commoner lifestyle."

The older chief held up his hand and spoke to his companion, who spoke in turn to Hole Face. Then the older chief pointed to Hopkins. Seth held his breath. Slowly the chief's finger moved to him. And finally settled on Wilby.

"Ke-da-toh."

Hole Face called up the passageway and two warriors came running in.

"Táktahte?," rasped the chief, his finger still leveled at Wilby, who had begun shaking, his eyes rounding with fear. He was seized and dragged out. His screams echoed up the passageway.

"I warn you, don't hurt him," said Hopkins, gesturing to the old chief. "He is God's agent, protected by Him from all harm. To hurt him is forbidden."

"For—" The chief frowned at Hole Face.

"Ne-gash-á."

The chief's frown deepened to a scowl. He beckoned to Hopkins. As Dwight stood his ground, Hole Face pushed him up to within six inches of the chief, who rose unsteadily, pulled out his knife and held it straight up less than an inch from Hopkins' face. Seth swallowed. The chief slowly lowered the knife and spat at Hopkins full in the face.

"Táktahte?!"

They were taken outside, to the other longhouse. In front of the three longhouses standing opposite the main entrance a platform had been erected. Torches burned at the four corners. In the center stood a six-foot pole. Tied to it by the neck, wrists, waist and ankles was the hapless Wilby.

"They're going to torture me—I can't stand it!"

Seth and Hopkins had stopped. Hole Face pushed them forward.

"You can't do this!" Hopkins cried.

Hole Face grunted, leered and pushed them on.

45

You're not going after him. Not now, not ever!"

"Do not shout and do not tell me what to do."

Husband and wife had been arguing since Two Eagles had returned. He rose wearily to his feet.

"Where are you going?" Margaret asked.

"To tell Swift Doe. She was not in her chamber when I came down the passageway."

"I'll go with you."

"*Neh*, this has nothing to do with you."

"Listen to me." Margaret set a hand on his shoulder then brushed his hair back from his eyes. "I know how you must feel, but you're not to blame for what happened."

"He went to Massowaganine for me, a favor for a friend. Blue Creek hardly knew him. He would not have harmed him if there was not this thing between us. He killed Bone to spite me. He wants me to pursue him. He will leave a clear trail so I can follow him easily."

"That in itself should be enough to discourage you. You'd be playing right into his hands."

"I do not care. I only know what I have to do. Trying to kidnap Benjamin was bad enough; killing Bone—"

"Go! Go!"

He went up the passageway to the chamber of Swift Doe, who had returned with Hare. When his father, Long Feather, was killed—Hare had been ten at the time—he could not wait to step into his father's moccasins to dominate and discipline his two younger brothers. When his mother eventually married Bone, Hare willingly accepted his stepfather, to everyone's surprise. In time the boy came to idolize Bone, for he could see and appreciate how the Mohican restored Swift Doe's lost happiness.

Now twelve, Hare was tall for his age, a man struggling to get out of a boy's body. He was strong, a superb athlete in every sport and game except those that required speed of foot, for he suffered from a congenital condition of the right hip. His infirmity seemed the bane of his existence.

Swift Doe searched Two Eagles' face, her own filling with fear.

"So Moon Dancer was right," she murmured. "My husband is dead."

Hare started, his eyes rounding. *"Neh!"*

"Leave me with your mother, Tantanege," Two Eagles ordered.

"He can stay," said Swift Doe. "Once more he is the man of the family."

Two Eagles related what had happened. "Splitting Moon is outside with his body—"

"You killed him!" burst Hare and attacked him. Two Eagles did not move even when Hare struck him in the face with his fists, though Swift Doe quickly pulled him off. Hare finally backed into a corner, sinking his face into his hands. Then he glared at Two Eagles and ran out.

"Hare! Hare!" his mother shouted. But he was gone.

Two Eagles' mind flew back to the day he and the others returned with word of Long Feather's murder. He had found Swift Doe out berrying with Hare and Dawn Maker, his youngest brother. She was pregnant. Then, too, she had told Two Eagles of her husband's death before he told her.

"Tantanege is right," Two Eagles murmured. "*I* killed his father. He died because of me, it is the same thing." He drew his knife and pricked his palm, closed his hand and opened it. "I will avenge his death; by my blood I swear it." He flattened his hand against his heart. "In this hand I will bring you Ossivendi Oÿoghi's black heart."

"And what should I do with it?"

"Keep it as proof that I kept my word."

"Is that as important to me as it seems to be to you? Will either of us sleep better knowing he is dead? Did I sleep better when you avenged Long Feather's murder by killing Burnt Eye's cousin? Did that bring Long Feather back to life? Will killing Blue Creek bring back Bone?"

"I cannot rest in my heart until Turtle Skin sleeps with dirt in his mouth."

"Then go and kill him. Only you will do it for you, not me. Not my sons. What does Margaret say?"

"Nothing."

"She says the same as I. Admit it! Let it go, Tékni-ska-je-a-nah. Bury it with Bone. You could spend half the moons of what is left of your life searching for Blue Creek. Depriving Margaret of a husband with your absence, depriving Benjamin of his father, depriving you of both. Some rivers are not worth the time and effort to cross. The deer are no fatter on the other side."

"I am sorry, Swift Doe." He glanced at his palm. The wound had clotted. "I would willingly give all my blood that this did not happen."

"Just as foolish. You should die so Bone can live?"

"I will go take care of his body."

"I will."

"Then I will go and talk to Tantanege."

"Not yet. Let his fire die down." She touched his cheek. "He gave you a bad bruise. He is very strong when angry. He goes wild. I will talk to him first, then you."

She went out, leaving him staring at his bloodied palm, his knife still in his hand.

He felt foolish.

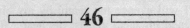

46

Swift Doe's tears fell inside her skin, down the cliffs of her cheeks. Bone's remains were prepared for burial. With a solemnity belying his years, Hare dug the grave; later he would erect the low palisades around it and paint them red. All the Oneidas attended Bone's burial. Two Eagles stood with Margaret, Splitting Moon and others of their friends. Hare found a place between his mother and Splitting Moon.

Bone's body was wrapped in a moose hide, lowered into the grave in a sitting position and food and weapons were placed around him. Fox and Red Paint filled in his grave and the crowd was dispersing when Splitting Moon spoke. He had taken Bone's murder as hard as had Two Eagles.

"We will go back out and find Turtle Skin," he muttered.

"*Oeuda,*" snarled Hare beside Splitting Moon. "Your moccasins are too slow to catch a slug, mush belly."

The insult was overheard by all. Splitting Moon's stomach could not tolerate meat or fish. He had subsisted from childhood on corn in its various forms. He hated being teased about it, and his scowl burned into Hare. He reached to grab him, but Two Eagles stepped between them, pushing Splitting Moon back.

"Go back inside," said Swift Doe to Hare. "Wait for me in my chamber."

"Mother—"

"Go, we will talk."

As Hare walked off, his mother said, "I am sorry, Tyagohuens. I will see that he comes to you in your chambers and apologizes."

Splitting Moon grunted.

Margaret walked back with Swift Doe and Eight Minks. Two Eagles assembled Splitting Moon, Anger Maker, Fox and Red Paint and waited until they were alone. "Listen to me," he said, "we are going after him."

Anger Maker chuckled. "Will Mar-gar-et let you?" Two Eagles glowered at him. "Don't look so, I was just poking your ribs."

He was. He was also drawing attention to Two Eagles' problem. Two Eagles had two choices: sneak off, or confront Margaret and tell her straight out that he was leaving and had no idea when he'd be back. He glanced aloft as an eagle passed high overhead, bringing back to mind the two golden eagle feathers placed in Bone's mouth—a scornful message to Two Eagles.

He must catch up with Blue Creek; never had he wanted an enemy on his knife as badly as this, not even Long

Feather's killer. If he had to bind and gag Margaret so he
could get away after him, he would do it!

As if he could . . .

A young golden eagle sat on a branch about fifteen feet
from the ground, staring down at him. He stared back. It
turned and flew off, but before its talons released the
branch he noticed that two of its tailfeathers were missing.
Still is soared high, then began circling. Slower and
slower. Then it took off to the north, straight up the trail
to Massowaganine.

If flew low in plain sight; even had the day been
overcast—and it was golden bright—he would have been
able to see it clearly. It seemed to be making sure he
could. It flew sweeping slowly from side to side. Then
lowered and landed on a branch directly ahead, turning to
eye him, letting him catch up.

He was almost up to it, he could see it clearly: its
golden lanceolate hackles, dark eyes, yellow cere, gray
beak. And supporting its feathered legs, large yellow feet
and powerful talons. He could almost reach up and touch
it and was about to try when it took off again, flapping
close over his head, circling wide and resuming its northward flight.

His imagination rested. He lay abed. It was not yet dark out
but he was very tired. Would this struggling with his conscience ever end? He had not discussed his leaving with
Margaret since Bone's burial; not yet. She sat changing Benjamin, talking in low tones to him. Two Eagles turned on his
side to watch them. He would be leaving with no idea when
he'd return. Swift Doe was right. He'd be depriving both
wife and son. And himself. His son could be walking and
twice as tall by the time he returned home.

Blue Creek. How could one man wreak so much havoc
in their lives? Now the flap lifted, revealing Eight Minks
and Swift Doe. Both looked worried. Two Eagles sat up.

"Something wrong?" Margaret asked.

Eight Minks nodded. "Hare . . ."

"I lectured him for insulting Splitting Moon," said Swift Doe. "I ordered him to go to his longhouse and apologize. I saw Splitting Moon a while ago. Hare did apologize, only he never came back. I have not seen him since. It has been half the day—"

"Is he still as upset as yesterday?" Two Eagles asked.

"Worse. He has gone after Blue Creek, I know it."

Margaret gasped. "How can you be sure?"

"His pack and weapons are gone from under his bunk."

"We will go catch up with him," said Two Eagles. "Bring him back. If we have to we'll carry him on a pole like a deer, but we will not harm him. Only his pride."

"He has been gone a long time," said Eight Minks. "Who knows in which direction?"

"By now he is on the trail north to Massowaganine," said Two Eagles. "If we hurry we can catch up with him before he gets halfway there."

"See that you bring him back," said Margaret. "Don't simply send him back and go on yourself."

This was precisely what was running through Two Eagles' mind. "Someone will bring him back," he murmured.

She frowned. "I'm warning you!"

"Do not start fighting now!" Swift Doe exclaimed. "Go, Two Eagles, please. Find my son, bring him home safely."

"Nyoh."

Onekahoncka was bright with torches. The hapless Jonathan Wilby had been tied to a stake on the platform for four days and nights. His rags had been torn off, leaving him with only an ill-fitting breechclout to hide his na-

kedness. Though he had been fed bread and water, he
looked wretched, and half dead to Seth and Hopkins, who
were forced by their captors to stand all day, every day, in
full view of the victim. Wilby called repeatedly to them
until Hole Face lost patience and ordered him gagged.

Now the entire castle turned out to watch. To the right of
the platform four men sat thumping tom-toms. Children
were pushed to the front of the semicircle so that they could
see better. The very young perched on their fathers' shoulders. His eyes imploring, trembling with terror, Wilby mumbled behind his gag, pleading with Seth and Hopkins to
intervene. Hopkins, no longer able to stand it, whirled toward the two chiefs seated on the ground to his right.

"This is barbaric! You can't permit it! In God's
name . . ."

The chiefs' eyes met, but neither understood him. Hole
Face translated. The chief who had earlier spit in Hopkins'
face got to his feet and stood facing him. For a moment
Seth imagined he would spit in his face again; instead, he
poked his chest.

"You watch. You next."

"Animal!"

"For heaven's sakes, Dwight, what good will that do?"
Seth asked.

The gate behind the platform opened and in came a warrior carrying two spears, holding them upright. On the point
of each was a dead porcupine. As the women and children
ran to him, he lowered his spears, dropping the two animals;
the crowd fell upon them, pulling out their quills. As the naked carcasses were kicked to one side, the women and children formed a line at the foot of the platform steps. Seth
watch in horror as one after another they ascended the steps
and plunged their quills into Wilby's exposed flesh. He
screamed behind his gag. The vein in his forehead protruded
so it threatened to rip through the skin. Sweat poured off
him. The quills were pushed in as deeply as possible. He
bled profusely. Within minutes, his body—with the excep-
tion of his skins but including his feet—was a human pin-

cushion. Hole Face removed his gag. He screamed horribly, the drummers beat harder, the crowd yelled in delight.

When Wilby passed out, the two warriors ran up the steps with buckets of what Seth assumed to be the walnut liquid the missionaries had been splashed with earlier. As Wilby came to, moaning pitifully, Hopkins shook his head and muttered, "He won't make it through the night."

The warriors who had revived him now took out their knives and each went to work on a hand, cutting away the flesh anchoring his fingernails, and extracting them with mussel shells. One after another they were held up for the crowd to see while the shouting drowned out his screams.

Seth couldn't believe his eyes. Was there no limit to their viciousness? As he watched, the warriors drew out Wilby's toenails. He stood with bleeding stumps, covered with quills, blood seeping from hundreds of punctures. His nails were collected in one of the empty buckets. A bowl of what appeared to be corn mush was handed up to one warrior. Seth watched as he dropped the toe- and fingernails into the mush, stirring it with a spoon. The other warrior then pried Wilby's mouth open and the concoction was forced down his throat to the raucous cheering of the onlookers.

"We come to bring these brutes to the Lord's table," murmured Hopkins. "Saving is the last thing they need. They should be exterminated like plague rats."

Hole Face leered and addressed the two chiefs, and Hopkins' tormentor looked his way and shook his head.

"To the devil with you!" burst Hopkins.

At which Hole Face stepped forward and gagged him, at the same time looking Seth's way as if asking if he too wanted a gag. Seth lowered his eyes. The warrior feeding Wilby had forced the last of the mush down his throat. Seth eyed the captive's stomach, touched his own, sighed and shook his head.

So much for long, drawn-out torture.

48

Seth and Hopkins were returned to their longhouse, and Wilby was brought in and laid on the ground, quills and all. He was still alive but suffering hideously. Even when Seth took off his gag, Wilby could only mumble. He seemed out of his head. They set to work extracting the quills as gently as possible. When all of them were removed he was rolled over on his back and they covered him with some of the ragged buckskins. Hopkins bent close to his ear.

"Try and sleep, Jonathan, the worst is over. You'll make it. You will!"

Seth stared at Hopkins with a sour look and when the Virginian rejoined him in the corner opposite Wilby he lit into him.

"What are you saying? Can't you see he's a dead man?"

"Is there any harm in making him think he'll survive? At this point, it's all he has left. He doesn't know he's dying."

"Of course he knows it. Look at his eyes." Seth imagined the nails churning in his own stomach, bleeding in a dozen places. He lowered his voice. "He won't last till sunup, poor soul. And one of us is next. And soon. They enjoy the spectacle too much to delay. We must at least *try* to get away."

"It'll be light in a couple hours," said Hopkins. "We won't stand a chance in daylight."

Seth nodded. "True."

"They'll start work on me first thing."

"On second thought, maybe not. They put poor Jonathan off until now. It's got to be well past midnight.

Maybe they'll wait until dark before they resume; it does add a mysterious effect."

"Look." Seth followed Hopkins' nod toward Wilby in the corner. They went to him. Hopkins examined his eyes and flattened his ear against his heart.

"He's dead."

"May God have mercy on your soul, Jonathan, poor, poor chap."

"Shhhh!"

Two warriors came in, and the two missionaries scuttled back to the other side of the chamber. The Mohawks ignored them, crossing to where Wilby lay and kneeling to examine him. Hopkins pointed at one's knife hanging from his belt, then at himself. Seth nodded.

Could he do it? Kill a human being? Seth answered by snatching out his guard's knife, slitting his throat cleanly. Hopkins was having trouble with his man; the warrior had turned just as he landed on his back, throwing Hopkins to one side. Clutching his knife, Seth lunged at the Mohawk, stabbing him between the ribs, pushing all the way up to the haft, pulling the knife out dripping.

"Thank you kindly," murmured Hopkins, righting himself. "Let's put on what we can of the rest of those buckskins; it's bitter cold out. God help us, it could begin snowing anytime."

They dressed and started for the rear entrance to the longhouse, sneaking past snoring occupants. At the door Seth held Hopkins back and peered out.

"All clear. Let's try for the rear gate; less traffic."

"Go."

They crept out, passing down the side of the longhouse behind theirs, pausing at the end to wait for a squaw to go back inside. At the end of the fourth and last longhouse in the line they paused again. About forty feet of open ground stretched between them and the gate.

"What do you think?" Seth asked.

"Go!"

They ran, Seth dropping a moccasin halfway to the gate,

retrieving it, hopping on the other foot as he restored it, catching up with Hopkins at the gate. They stood leaning against it catching their breaths, and suddenly felt the gate pushing. They leaped to one side, knives up and ready. In plodded two old squaws—who took one look, screamed and dropped their bundles. Seth and Hopkins dashed past them and out, slamming the gate behind, muffling the continued screaming.

They ran.

 **49**

Night. Hare's hip hurt; since sundown he had been fighting off the pain. Just before it struck he had found and turned onto the north trail. He had planned on traveling all night, which should bring him to Massowaganine early next day, and there he hoped to question everyone. Someone must have seen Blue Creek leave there and could tell him in which direction.

But now his hip pleaded for rest. What if it stiffened up overnight and the pain came back even worse in the morning?

Still, nothing must delay him from finding the *seronquatse* who had ambushed and killed his father. Tears streamed down his cheeks as he saw Bone's smile in the darkness, felt his arm around his shoulder. He swiped his eyes clear and stopped, sitting down hard, out of breath. He sat panting, then lay down, rolling over onto his good hip.

Seronquatse. Evil man, evil as a snake. *Oeuda.* The shit who had crushed his mother's heart and his own. Blue Creek would not recognize him right off. That would give

Hare a precious edge, a moment to run his knife into his gut before it dawned on him who he was.

Kill him, scalp him. Ideas came in droves. Cut out his heart. Wrap it in the old piece of buckskin he'd stuffed into his belt just before leaving, bring it home to his mother as a trophy of the chase. His first test of manhood: find and kill his father's murderer. Two Eagles had scalped the first Huron snake he came upon, avenging *his* father's death. Hare could do better; he'd find the actual culprit. Blue Creek's heart would be his mother's, his scalp his.

He sat up, kneading his hip with his fist. Then he scanned the star-strewn sky; how many hours till dawn? A gibbous moon sailed swiftly through white-rimmed black cloud shreds. They were not fat, no threat of rain for the time being. His stomach spoke and he remembered that he hadn't eaten since yesterday; he'd left in such a rush he had completely forgotten about packing food. In the morning he'd find apples, perhaps grouse eggs.

He got to his feet, setting his afflicted leg down tentatively before putting his full weight on it. It hurt, but not nearly as badly as running on it would. Could he walk? He sucked in a deep breath and tried; the pain came swiftly back. He got off the trail, pulled up handfuls of dried grass, added leaves and made a bed under an old white ash. The breeze rested. He pulled his cover over him and lay down.

Lying back, he closed his eyes. Had he kept them open a split second after his shoulders touched down, looking straight upward he would have seen the limb directly overhead and noticed the dark shape sprawled along its length, its head tilted down.

The lynx had climbed to its night perch only minutes before Hare arrived. Normally, like all cats in the wild, it did not attack humans, contenting itself with birds and small animals, taking an occasional deer. But now it was angry, for it had earlier been chased by wolves from the rabbit it had caught for supper, and it was ravenously hungry.

Tufted ears erected, it lowered its broad, short head, resting its beard on one outstretched leg. Its tongue lolled out. Slowly its claws slid from their sheaths, and even more slowly, balancing precariously, it rose on the limb.

A soft, low rumble issued from its throat as it brought its head up. Its fangs gleamed in the moonlight. It stared down, slavered, tensed, sprang.

Miscalculating slightly; landing on Hare's legs, its momentum sent it sprawling to one side. Hare's eyes snapped wide glimpsing the tawny coat, the head twisting; the creature's vicious snarl ripped the silence. Hare's hand flew to his knife. The lynx wrenched about, tensed, sprang. Up came Hare's knife catching it full in the throat. It twisted to free itself and fell full weight on him.

Dead.

He pushed it off and rolled over. Not until then was he aware that the cat had clawed him above his left knee, through his legging, piercing flesh and bone.

Belatedly pain struck like a driven arrow; he screamed. Whipping off his headband he tied it around the wound, hoping to close it so the blood would clot. But the binding wasn't tight enough. Fighting off his mounting agony he retied it tighter and passed out.

 **50**

The shredded black clouds had vanished with the moon; dawn was tinting the sky in the east when Two Eagles and the others came upon the unconscious Hare and the dead lynx lying beside him. Anger Maker examined him and pronounced the boy near death from loss of blood. As Hare came to, Splitting Moon was standing over him.

"Do you not look around you for animals before you lie down to sleep? They look around for you, you should have as much sense."

The others laughed. Two Eagles grunted. "He killed himself a good-sized *adiron*."

"You came a long way, boy," said Anger Maker. "It's just as long back." He undid Hare's headband and threw it aside. Blood still seeped through the boy's legging.

"How bad?" Two Eagles asked Anger Maker in a whisper.

Anger Maker did not answer him immediately. He carefully cut away Hare's legging. Blood gouted, and the boy stared at it ashen-cheeked.

"Somebody find me some couch grass," said Anger Maker. He folded the piece of legging into a pad and held it against the wound. Hare winced but made no sound, even as blood appeared at the sides of the pad.

The couch grass Anger Maker applied to the wound, inducing clotting, and he helped fashion a litter. While Anger Maker, Fox and Red Paint gently lifted Hare onto it, Two Eagles and Splitting Moon spoke together some distance away.

"Fox and Red Paint can take him back," said Splitting Moon. "We three will go on."

"*Neh*," muttered Two Eagles.

"You are going back?"

"I must. His running off happened so fast. I did not have a chance to talk with Margaret."

Splitting Moon's expression was critical. "Who wears the knife in your family?"

"It is not that. I am his uncle, stepping into his father's moccasins, in a way. Besides, I cannot sneak off behind her back like a thief."

Splitting Moon smiled grimly. "She expects you to. Why disappoint her?"

"I know her, she does not expect. She trusts me, I am going back. I have to do what is right."

"Catching up with Blue Creek is right. And she knows it. So go back with Red Paint, the rest of us will go on."

"*Neh*, you cannot. That is what Bone did. This would be the same kind of favor and the same thing could happen to you."

Splitting Moon scoffed. "You think I fear Turtle Skin? Besides, there will be three of us. He will be the one to worry." He stared stonily. "Bone was as much our friend as yours; we have as much right to his murderer as you. This is our *ola•na•*, our soup; we will eat it. It is not for you to deny our stomachs."

He was right. It occurred to Two Eagles that like hooking a giant fish and ceding control, he had lost it over this situation. Now Blue Creek was the one in charge, manipulating all of them.

"We will go on to Massowaganine," Splitting Moon went on. "Talk to everyone, even the children. Find out which direction he took."

Hare was conscious; hearing this, he began to smile.

"We will bring him back to you alive," said Red Paint as he came up.

"Maybe," said Splitting Moon, running his thumb over the tooth in the ball of his tomahawk.

It was decided. Splitting Moon, Anger Maker and Red Paint would go on. Two Eagles and Fox would carry the wounded Hare back to Onneyuttahage to Eight Minks.

Two Eagles went over to where Anger Maker was skinning the lynx. Anger Maker held up its bloodied pelt. "Take this back with you for him."

"What do you think, can his leg be saved?"

Anger Maker glanced over at Hare and lowered his voice. "His wound is deep, very bad." He shrugged.

Two Eagles looked over to see Hare's face contorted with pain.

More heartache for his mother, more worry, more suffering. All thanks to the fugitive. So many debts to settle.

51

Eight Minks took one look at Hare's wound and sighed discouragedly. To her chamber, Hare had been brought sweating from the pain. Most of the way home he had been unconscious, as he was now.

"Very bad," murmured Eight Minks.

"We know, we know!" snapped Two Eagles.

"Can you heal him?" Swift Doe asked.

Eight Minks knelt to examine the wound more closely. "The couch grass stopped the bleeding but will not help to heal it. That scab should come off. The wound should be kept open."

Swift Doe laid a damp piece of deerskin across Hare's forehead. "Do what you have to do," she said worriedly.

"You may not want to watch."

Margaret came in with Benjamin.

"It is getting too crowded in here," Eight Minks snapped. "You two, Fox, *ísene,* out. Swift Doe, you stay."

The three obeyed. Swift Doe heated Hare's knife over the passageway fire. When his brothers came running in from playing, Swift Doe shooed them out. Eight Minks carefully removed the scab. Hare sighed in his sleep as blood oozed.

"This will hurt even more," she said. "I must try to see inside."

As gently as she could she pulled back the edges of the wound. The boy was drenched with sweat, and Eight Minks frowned in concern. "Perhaps we should be in no hurry to let it heal. The muscle is badly mangled, a tendon torn. Better to keep it open to make sure the flesh knits properly. It is very bad, like a knife stuck in and swung around."

"Will he lose his leg?"

"It is too early to tell." Eight Minks shook her head.

"What?"

"This is beyond my skills, Swift Doe. A fever, a cough, sick stomach anyone can cure. But this is something for the False Faces."

Swift Doe scoffed. "They cure only toothache, nose-bleed and the like."

"I have seen them heal a spear wound to the stomach that spilled enough blood to fill a stew pot. And the man lived. Hadondá he•hä′, Shoulders-a-log, a close friend of your father's before you were born. The spear drove so deep it almost reached his spine. He could not eat, sleep; he was so weak he could barely breathe. And the pain was intolerable. No one could help him."

"Not even Ronyadashayouh?"

"The medicine man? That one could not even cure his own earache. His death saved more lives than he ever did. Hadondá he•hä′ took his wound to the False Face Society and went through the ceremony. Within a month he was walking about as healthy as ever, showing everyone his scar."

"He became a False Face?"

"All who are cured by the False Faces join the society."

"Even a boy?" Swift Doe asked.

"Hare is the man of the family now. He certainly tried to prove he is." Eight Minks nodded with finality.

"Can you arrange for the ceremony?"

"*Nyoh*, of course. In the meantime he must sleep as much as he can. And he looks starved. When he awakens see if you can get some *ohnekákehi* down him. Let him sleep so he can dream. He needs *orenda*, the essence of life, to give him strength, power to help the False Faces heal him."

"Can they?"

"If he believes in their power they can. Do you?"

"*Nyoh, nyoh*, anything," blurted Swift Doe.

"That is not believing, that is hope." Again Eight Minks examined his wound. "*Nyoh*, we will keep it open. And perhaps I can straighten the muscle and the ripped tendon so that they heal properly. Not like poor Bone's bones. It will hurt. It will be like no other pain he has ever felt."

"He can stand it. Moon Dancer is the *go-ga-so-ho-nun-na-tase-ta,* the Keeper of the False Faces," murmured Swift Doe.

"*Nyoh.*" Eight Minks nodded.

"The other day I could sense that she does not like our family."

"She hates Two Eagles, but that may be pretense; deep down she understands that he did what he had to do. I will speak with her."

"When?"

"Patience. We must work in stages. First I will try to repair inside the wound. I will make a drain so that it remains open."

A stick was found and placed between Hare's teeth, so he could bite it. He woke, his eyes widening.

"Listen closely, Tantanege," said Eight Minks. "What I am about to do will hurt very much." He nodded. His mother rearranged the cloth on his forehead. "But it has to be done. Hold very still. If you move I may damage it more in there, do you understand? Now take a deep breath and hold it."

Two Eagles and Margaret with the baby in their chamber stiffened and started at the heartrending scream that came ringing down the passageway.

"Poor Hare," murmured Margaret. "Can she save his leg, do you think?"

He grunted.

She eyed him. "You came back."

"Splitting Moon and the others went on."

She set an arm around him. He stiffened as if mildly resenting the gesture.

"What is it? Are you angry with yourself for not going on? Angry with me?"

"With everything. This will not end until he is dead!"

"*Neh,* it's ended, they'll never find him. He's dropped out of our lives, isn't that enough? Aren't you satisfied? I am."

Eight Minks and Swift Doe came in. Both looked gray with worry.

"How is he?" asked Two Eagles.

Eight Minks shrugged.

"Not good," murmured Swift Doe. "He is asleep."

"Will he lose his leg?" he asked Eight Minks.

"Who knows?" snapped Eight Minks. "I know I have done all I can."

"The False Faces will heal him," Swift Doe assured the older woman.

Margaret threw up her hands. "Those wild men jumping around screaming, shaking their silly rattles?"

"We believe in their powers to heal and cure," said Two Eagles.

"*You* don't!" Margaret rasped.

"*I* do," said Swift Doe softly, "and he is my son."

"I'm sorry," said Margaret. "I shouldn't run them down, but they really are absolute charlatans. In England we'd call them quacks." The three of them stared at her, not understanding either word. "I don't know the word in Oneida. *Seronquatses?*"

"Evil people?" Eight Minks asked. "You think the False Face Society is evil?"

Margaret lowered her eyes. She was treading on sacred ground, like deriding another's religion. "It just seems to me that flinging ashes at him is not going to heal anything."

"What do you suggest we do?" Two Eagles asked.

"I—don't know."

She should be quiet. They knew how she felt about many of their beliefs. Why remind them? She looked down at Benjamin. What if he were to become seriously wounded or ill, with no doctor for leagues in any direction? What would she do, stare helplessly down at him hour after hour, watching as his life drained away?

Or call in the False Face Society?

VI

WHITE HELL

52

Seth had never known such paralyzing cold. It had struck them within minutes after fleeing Onekahoncka and had stayed with them since, penetrating their ragged clothing, invading their very marrow. His heart felt like a chunk of ice, and burying his fists in his armpits failed to ease the tingling frigidity.

On they plodded, following the Mohawk River west, already too tired to talk. Hopkins in the lead stumbled repeatedly. He fell. Seth came up to him. Hopkins lay panting, sending up great clouds of breath. Seth turned him over. In his companion's frost-lidded eyes Seth could see capitulation; he was already giving up less than two days on the trail.

As Seth helped him up, Hopkins groaned. "We'll never make it. We don't even know where we're going, that's the worst of it, don't you think? No destination, no place to shoot for."

"But we do. The Oneida village—"

"They're Iroquois, too. Even if we get there they'll only finish what the Mohawks started. It's hopeless. I can't go on, there's no point."

"You must."

"I've never been so cold."

Seth managed a weak smile. "Not like Virginia, eh?"

"I'm slowly freezing to death. If I move I'll shatter."

"Nonsense. Dig in your heels, I'll help you up." Seth got him to his feet. Hopkins stood teetering. Seth caught him. "Deep breath."

"I can't, it'll burn up my lungs."

"Breathe!"

"We need food in us. We'll die of starvation before the cold gets us."

"Chew on this." Seth handed him a piece of deerskin. Hopkins shook his head. "Do it. You'll at least get taste out of it. And it'll give you something to occupy you."

Hopkins sighed and began chewing. "God in heaven, what I wouldn't give for a slab of hot roast beef!"

"Let's not think foolish thoughts. Let's just go on."

"They're probably right behind us, you know. The joke's on us. They'll catch up and find us frozen stiff."

"Keep going, Dwight, and stop that talk. You surprise me. I figured you for the optimist of the group."

"Only an imbecile could find optimism in this."

53

Swift Doe sat cross-legged bedside Hare's bunk as he watched her make twine. Over the past few days his pain had eased, the sharpness supplanted by a dull aching. But if he moved even slightly, as he sometimes did in his sleep, back it came like a hot knife stabbing.

Swift Doe fashioned her twine of basswood fiber. Mainly she wove it into rope and harnesses designed to carry heavy burdens. She had stripped the bark the previous spring when the sap was running, peeling the bast from it in narrow strips six to eight feet long. Then she bound it, tied it in skeins and left it to dry out.

Eight Minks came in. "They are making the rounds of

the castle," she said. She crossed to Hare and felt his forehead for fever. "We can expect them anytime now. Lucky for you, Hare, you had the dream."

As required, Hare had dreamed of a False Face. Eight Minks had so informed Moon Dancer, and he was accepted by the Society. Joining was payment for the society's cure, whether it worked of not. Eyeing him, thinking about it, his mother could only hope as she wove the fishing net for him out of twine.

"I just want this over with," murmured Hare.

A hand drew aside the door flap, and Moon Dancer waddled in looking as self-important as always, assuming immediate command of the situation. Swift Doe's heart lifted.

"*Ísene,*" Moon Dancer snapped to the two women.

"Let his mother stay," pleaded Eight Minks.

"You, *ísene.*"

As Eight Minks departed, Swift Doe took her work to a corner. In filed the False Face Society members, garbed in tattered blankets and carrying mud-turtle shell rattles, their faces hidden behind grotesquely carved masks. Swift Doe recognized one she had painted, the rough face His Longhouse had carved out of basswood, and wondered who was behind it. The masks were painted red, black or both, decorated with strands of hair, scowling eyes, crooked mouths—some grinning bizarrely, others purse-lipped. One displayed a hideously protruding tongue. Eight members came in, transferring Hare to the floor and forming a circle around him. Moon Dancer spoke: "*Odé ka'.*"

A False Face carried a bark tray outside and brought in a portion of the passageway fire, setting it in the center of the floor. As wood was added, smoke rose, setting all eyes stinging. Moon Dancer gestured. One of the False Faces knelt beside Hare and moved to stroke his wound. He sucked a breath in sharply. The man hesitated.

"Do it!" she snapped.

The False Face rubbed his hand lightly over the afflicted area while another man blew ashes in Hare's face. He sneezed as more ashes were blown at this face, then all over him, even in his open wound. One man stood guard at the entrance; any interruption at this stage could disturb, perhaps even nullify, the healing process. The False Faces sang incantations, shouted and shook their rattles to drive the evil spirit out of the wound. Hare kept his eyelids tightly sealed as more and more ashes were flung at him.

The shaking rattles and incantations stopped abruptly. The ceremony was over. The patient lay covered with ashes. Eight Minks, waiting outside, came in with a tray of tobacco and a bowl of *gago^n' să odijis'kwa*, False Face pudding: boiled parched cornmeal mixed with maple sugar. It was considered a powerful influence for pleasing the masks.

She and Swift Doe looked on in silence as Moon Dancer gorged herself along with her companions. While the others gathered up their rattles and removed the fire to the passageway hearth, Moon Dancer had a final word for Hare.

"Remember, boy, that you are now a False Face yourself. When your wound is healed and you can get about, you will be expected to carve a face for yourself and paint it. If you carve it in the morning, it must be painted red; if in the afternoon, black. If when the sun is overhead, red and black. You will be expected to take part in the ceremony."

Hare's expression showed no enthusiasm.

"He will, he will do everything properly," said Eight Minks. "You will, Tantanege. And thank you, Go-ga-so-ho-nun-na-tase-ta, thank you all. We are grateful. He will heal now. He will walk again, he will run."

Moon Dancer fixed her beady eyes upon Hare. "If he believes he will, he will. Only if he has told the truth about his dream and truly believes."

Now Hare was restored to his bunk, and Moon Dancer left with the others. When their steps had faded up the passageway, Swift Doe spoke for the first time.

"What now?"

Eight Minks shrugged. "We wait."

"How long?"

"You should have asked Moon Dancer." Eight Minks started for the door, motioning Swift Doe to follow. Outside they lowered their voices.

"They got ashes in his wound," said Swift Doe worriedly.

"Leave them there. How are they to work if they do not touch it?" Eight Minks filled her lungs and beamed. "I have a good feeling about this, Swift Doe. He will recover completely, watch."

"Mmmmm," she said noncommittally, wondering, *When? How long?*

54

Margaret sat by the frigid stream, which was already partially skinned with ice. A small fire warmed water to rinse her hair. *Augustuske* had one foot onto the lands of the Iroquois. The squirrels' drays were crammed with acorns and their tails had become bushier, rabbits had grown thick fur around their feet and the screech owl's plaintive hooting took on a sorrowful tone that resembled a woman's weeping.

She had finished rinsing her hair and was drying it when Swift Doe approached. Though she was still in mourning, now her expression showed another emotion: worry bordering on despair.

"Come see. The white flesh around the edge of Tantanege's wound is turning gray."

Margaret gasped. "It's mortifying, I knew it. It's those filthy ashes! They should have been washed off the instant Moon Dancer went out."

"Eight Minks forbade me to clean them. Otherwise, the ashes' power would not work."

"Fiddlesticks and rot! Let's go back. We'll clean it thoroughly, every last smudge!"

"Eight Minks—"

"Bother her! If we don't get busy, by this time tomorrow his leg will be so bad it'll probably have to be amputated."

"*Neh—neh—*" Swift Doe moaned.

"Either we take over or we don't, it's up to you!"

"*Nyoh.*"

"Good, come along. We should have done this days ago. Pray it's not too late."

Hare was awake, his face twisted in pain. Margaret took one look at his wound, clucked loudly and moved Swift Doe out of his hearing.

"It's a holy mess. Get water and clean cloths. What do you use against mortification? *Kha-enga-da?*"

"Snake lily. It is blue, it blooms in May." She described the blossom.

"It sounds like iris."

"Eight Minks uses the root and the fat part—"

"Rhizome," said Margaret.

"She crushes them into a powder and mixes it with water to make a medicine."

"Tincture. It's also mixed with boiling water to soak a poultice. Back home we use it too," said Margaret. "Eight Minks must have it. You know what it looks like, get it."

"*Neh.* She will want to know what it is for. I will have to tell her."

"Never mind. I'll go. You boil the water."

Down the passageway slipped Margaret to Eight Minks and Fox's chamber, girding herself for a rousing argument. But when she lifted the flap no one was in. She got down both medicine baskets from the overhead storage shelf and, poking through them, found a single dried blue flag attached to its root-studded rhizome. Restoring both baskets she went out hurrying to the entrance of the long-house. Eight Minks and Fox were nowhere to be seen.

How much time would she and Swift Doe have? When Eight Minks walked in, the first thing she'd do would be to look in on Hare. She could easily catch the women treating him. She'd be furious with Margaret for poking into her baskets.

Margaret knew little about the progress of infection in such a wound but assumed that it had to be rapid. She and Swift Doe bent over the kettle, hurrying the water to boiling. When it did Swift Doe added the crushed rhizome and root to the boiling kettle. Hare drank a full cup, gritting his teeth as his mother moistened a cloth with the mixture and cleansed his wound. He sweat furiously but made no sound. She soaked a second clean cloth, folded it and held it in place with two rawhide cords.

"He looks disgusting," said Margaret. "We must sponge him clean from head to foot."

"*Neh*, Eight Minks would see. The *che-gasa* on his wound we can cover with his bear robe."

"I suppose. And hide that kettle." Margaret sniffed. "There's a faint odor of iris."

Swift Doe crushed a handful of mint leaves to mask the odor.

"The robe is hot," protested Hare.

"You'll have to put up with it for now," said Margaret.

"Somebody is coming," Swift Doe whispered.

Margaret pulled the robe higher on his chest. "Pretend you are asleep."

She and Swift Doe started for the flap. In sailed Eight Minks; Fox waved and continued down the passageway to their chamber.

"How is he?" Eight Minks walked between them up to Hare.

"He just fell asleep," said Margaret.

"Let me see his wound."

"*Neh*," said Swift Doe, "you will wake him. He did not sleep last night, he is exhausted."

Eight Minks set a hand to his forehead. "He looks pale. Has he been eating?"

"Yes, yes," said Margaret.

Eight Minks looked from one to the other; Margaret thought she recognized suspicion on the older woman's round face.

"Eating very well," said Swift Doe. "He just needs sleep."

"Mmmmmm."

Swift Doe cleared her throat. "I—was thinking of washing the ashes off the upper part of him."

"*Neh! Neh, neh, neh,* leave them just as they are. All over him. Even the soles of his feet. The more ashes that stick, the stronger the power of the False Faces." Margaret rolled her eyes. Eight Minks saw. "I know, you think it is foolish and the whole ceremony nonsense."

"I haven't said one word."

"You had better not. Because you do not understand our ways does not give you the right to throw dirt on them." She paused and sniffed. "What is that smell?"

"Mint," said Swift Doe.

"Why? What for?"

"It stunk in here."

"Mmmmm." Eight Minks stared at Margaret, who avoided her eyes. Swift Doe held her breath. Hare feigned sleep. Eight Minks went out. All three sighed.

55

The season's first snow fell in great quantity on the lands of the Oneida. Gâ'-oh filled his lungs and blew his icy breath down from the north with intimidating ferocity, turning white the breaths of men and dogs and keeping the hickory wood fires burning continuously in the longhouses.

Snugly warm, Margaret and Two Eagles played with Benjamin in their chamber, tickling him, eliciting happy gurgling, tickling and pinching one another.

Now Two Eagles positioned himself behind her on the bear robe, his legs outstretched on either side of her. He walked his fingers up into her hair, into the tumbling golden mass, digging higher, higher, describing tiny circles, stimulating the flesh. Upward and back down until he reached the base of her neck. There he applied a small quantity of cream made from the root, green bark, berries and white flowers of the elderberry, stroking her neck with the flats of his fingers and proceeding outward toward her shoulders.

She could feel a warm tingling radiating, loosening the tension, enlivening her flesh. As he moved outward, her neck and shoulders seemed to melt beneath his touch. Now he returned to her nape, applying the cream in light, rapid circular strokes, infusing her with a delicious warmth. A third time he moved outward toward her shoulders, clenching the cords, releasing and massaging them, causing her to fleetingly wish he might stroke every inch of her in such fashion. So gentle yet pervasive was his touch, it brought a drowsiness that heavied her upper lids. A languid feeling possessed her; she sighed. He paused.

"Are you all right?"

"Don't stop, don't stop . . ."

The flap lifted. In stormed Eight Minks, her outstretched finger stabbing at Margaret's face.

"You! I have seen what you did to his wound. You stole medicine from my baskets. That *che-gasa* you put on his wound smells of snake lily. You washed off the ashes, destroyed their power!"

"His leg was mortifying," snapped Margaret. "He could lose it, thanks to your precious ashes!"

"*Ogechta!* You deliberately destroyed their power. Now

he is doomed. He will never walk again! You should be
whipped raw for this. You and his mother!"

"She did nothing. I was responsible."

"She has told me everything. I made her."

"Quiet down!" said Two Eagles. "You are loosening the
rafters. What did you do to him, Margaret?"

He looked at her ominously, and she told him. Eight
Minks stood clutching her elbows, rocking on her heels,
scowling.

"You should not have interfered," said Two Eagles.

"His wound was mortifying! Can't either of you get that
through your heads? He could lose his leg in two days, he
could die, and those filthy ashes would be to blame. You
really think I'd stand idly by—"

"*Nyoh!*" burst Eight Minks. She shook a finger under
Margaret's nose. "*Now* he will never walk again. Your
fault, not the ashes. Why is it you cannot keep out of what
is none of your business? You join our people, we welcome you and what do you do? Make your own rules, re-
ject ours, refuse to obey them."

"That's not so!"

"It is. You select what you will go along with, ignore all
else. You think us stupid, superstitious. Ridicule us behind
our backs." She pushed her face closer, her eyes burning.
"Why do you stay here where you do not belong? Do not
fit? Do not want to? Where no one wants you?"

"Enough!" Swift Doe had slipped in unseen by the others. "Leave her alone. She was trying to help; his leg is
very bad. The snake lily powder could save it, the ashes
were killing it. I am going back now and wash him clean
of every speck!"

"*Neh!*" screeched Eight Minks. Benjamin screamed.
"Leave him alone. You do not believe any more than she
does. You are not fit to look after him. You cannot be
trusted. Keep away from him. I will care for him."

"You stay away from him." Swift Doe glowered. "I take
care of my own, you stay out of his chamber!"

"Please," said Two Eagles, "all this shouting is giving

me and Benjamin heads like drums. *She* is his mother," he said to Eight Minks. "Do as she says, leave him alone."

"You dare tell me?"

"*I* dare!" snapped Swift Doe.

Eight Minks threw up her hands and stomped out.

"It's all my fault," said Margaret.

"*Our* fault," said Swift Doe. "Only there is no fault, no blame. Thanks to you his wound will heal. They were bad ashes, they had evil power."

Two Eagles scoffed.

Swift Doe glared. "You have part in this. Are you forgetting what Moon Dancer thinks of you?"

"You think she cursed the ashes deliberately?" he asked. "That is too stupid."

"You could see them eating into the raw flesh and inside the wound."

"I have never seen Eight Minks so upset," he said. He turned to Margaret. "You should not have—"

"I asked her to," hissed Swift Doe. "Drop this. Eight Minks will get over her anger and when Hare is fit again and can walk, what will she say then?"

He shrugged. Margaret shook her head and looked away. By her actions, despite her convictions, she had repudiated the powers of the False Face Society and embarrassed Eight Minks. Her reluctance to accept many of the tribe's ways had been a sore point between them since she first arrived. Eight Minks saw Margaret's refusal as arrogance. To her, Margaret should either accept the Oneida's ways or not; not set up her own standards and pick and choose.

Would Eight Minks tell Moon Dancer? Would the whole tribe know about it before noon tomorrow? Too many already refused to accept her. This could only reaffirm their disapproval and bring others into their ranks.

Worst of all, it destroyed the close friendship she shared with Eight Minks. It alienated Swift Doe from the older woman, as well, for which Eight Minks would blame Margaret. And it brought Margaret's biggest problem into sharp focus. Since joining the tribe, not once had she ever felt as if she truly belonged.

And what about poor Hare? What if the snake-lily cure had come too late, and his leg had to be amputated anyway? Eight Minks would hold Margaret responsible and punish her. It all traced back to Blue Creek. Didn't all their troubles these days?

By now Benjamin had quieted down, and Margaret held him. Swift Doe withdrew. Two Eagles looked at his wife grimly. Resignedly? Accusingly? Or pityingly? Still, he managed a smile.

"Do not look so, it will be all right."

She kissed him. In every problem, in the final analysis he invariably came down on her side, the two of them against the world. It helped so very much. He returned to massaging her.

56

Margaret remained deeply troubled over her falling-out with Eight Minks. Meanwhile, Hare's wound healed, his fever and pain left him. His mother's relief seemed to alleviate her depression over the loss of Bone. She continued to mourn him, but not as intensely as earlier.

When friends visited Hare, he boasted about the lynx and proudly displayed its pelt. Swift Doe came to Margaret for advice almost daily. She praised her to others, insisting she had saved Hare's life, not realizing that she was only adding fuel to the fire.

Two Eagles brooded over his problem, more than ever convinced that he should have been the one to go after Blue Creek. Even now Splitting Moon and the others had not returned.

Before he and Fox had started for home with the wounded Hare, he had asked Splitting Moon as a favor to limit the search to determining Blue Creek's destination, in the belief that he would remain there. When the searchers returned, Two Eagles and Fox planned to join them and all five would go after the renegade.

As he leaned against the longhouse while Benjamin crawled in the snow, Two Eagles recalled that none of the three had actually promised to return after pinpointing Blue Creek's whereabouts. Anger Maker's final words on the subject were a cryptic "We shall see."

Now Margaret came out of the longhouse, snatching up Benjamin, and brushing him off. "What are you doing, letting him crawl about in this dirty snow?"

"He likes snow."

"Filthy." She scowled, studying him. "What's eating you? Still brooding about their not coming back?"

"Neh."

"Face it, they're your friends, not hirelings. They don't live and die by your command." She cuddled Benjamin. "I'm worried about Eight Minks. She isn't in her chamber. Fox doesn't know where she is, only that she slept poorly again last night."

"The last I saw of her was when it thundered just after the sun rose. She was on her way out the gate. She may have gone to her place near the white caves to consult with Ah-ke-so-tah."

Ah-ke-so-tah was the thunder, Eight Minks' paternal grandfather and in her estimation the source of all wisdom, in whose counsel she put great value. Lightning held no significance for the Oneida, but thunder, when it rumbled across the heavens, was the voice of Ah-ke-so-tah, a god and her father's father. Margaret assumed Eight Minks had gone to ask him what she should do about the situation with the interloper, Margaret.

"She and I have to talk," said Margaret. "We can't go on like this."

"*Neh,* it is too soon. Let her anger weaken and die before you approach her."

"It's too infuriating! How can she be so small-minded? It's unlike her."

"She feels foolish."

"You mean *I* made a fool of her?" Margaret snapped.

"Can you blame her for feeling so? It does not help that Hare's wound is getting better. I do not criticize you, Margaret. You were right in what you did for him, but sometimes to be right is wrong."

"Wrong to save his leg?" She threw up her hands. "You people!"

He jerked his head, his eyes narrowed. "Us savages?"

"I'm sorry, there I go again. It's just that I get so frustrated." She handed Benjamin to him. "Get his cradleboard, would you? Hang him wherever you please. Just don't let him get down in this filthy snow."

She left, visibly disturbed, as upset with herself as with the situation. She really had a knack for letting her tongue run away with her thoughts, thrusting the needle in without considering the irritation it inflicted and how it made her look in others' eyes. Was it thoughtlessness or deliberate? Could it be that deep down she felt holier-than-they, so puffed up over her "standing in civilization" she felt obliged to flaunt it, while at the same time belittling these people's primitiveness? Did she consider herself the white voice in their wilderness, missionary to their minds, invading them to correct their mistakes, clear their thinking, abolish their superstitions?

She wearied of thinking about it. Going on, she passed the white caves, the forked path, the left way leading to the lake, the right turning sharply north toward Massowaganine. Clouds the color of mussel shells sailed overhead. Gâ'-oh had struck furiously during the night; the almost full moon resembled a ball of ice. The trees moaned in an unending chorus, in a dirge that had sent a shiver up her spine as she lay awake silently arguing with Eight Minks.

Augustuske had already brought snow, remarkably early; she would welcome a blizzard. If enough fell, Two Eagles would be forced to postpone his pursuit of Blue Creek, even if his friends did return with his whereabouts.

So many clouds in her sky—but this quarrel with Eight Minks was the blackest. She couldn't go on this way. They must have it out.

The harsh winds of the previous night had flushed out the last of the legions of insect eaters. Red polls, finches and red crossbills trafficked the barren woodlands. She spied a black-beaked woodpecker and heard the deep booming *whoo*s of a great gray owl, repeating ten times in a gradually descending scale.

Finally Margaret came upon Eight Minks sitting on a rock, her back to her, her head raised slightly, eyes closed, staring sightlessly at the feeble sun. She appeared in a trance. Margaret stood watching her, hesitant to speak for fear of startling her. Finally Eight Minks lowered her head and turned around.

"I—want to talk," said Margaret.

No warmth found its way into the older woman's expression, no sign of forgiveness or relenting.

"Tantanege is better," she murmured in Oneida.

"Nyoh."

Eight Minks went on in Oneida. "So it seems your meddling turned out good; you saved him from Moon Dancer and the False Face Society. I know. The flesh around his wound was turning gray. And you think if you did not act he would lose his leg, maybe his life."

"I did," Margaret admitted in Oneida.

"Still, now no one will ever know."

"Isn't it a relief to know he's getting better?"

"That is an unfair question, and beneath you. You still do not understand. Our people have had many medicine men down through the years back to long before the whiteskin showed his face and his guns here. Some were successful healers; some, like Ronyadashayouh, frauds."

"*Is-ga-há*, that's the word I was looking for: charlatans."

"Is not that what you called the False Faces? But we do not think of them as such. We hold them in the highest regard. The dancing does not always succeed. In treating some illnesses they fail, but that does not affect our respect for them or for the ceremony on the ashes. Long before my grandfather's grandfather opened his eyes for the first time, the False Faces were entrusted with the healing of the sick and wounded. And so will they be forever, despite what you may think of them."

"I understand, I do!" Margaret insisted.

"But you still do not respect them."

"May I ask a question? If I had not intervened, and if his wound worsened and his leg had to be amputated to save his life, would that have been the right thing? For me to stand by and do nothing?"

"*Nyoh.*"

Margaret started. "I don't believe you!"

Eight Minks shrugged. "I have tried to explain that the Society is bigger than any one patient's ills. If our spirits of life and death decide that Tantanege should not recover, that has to be the way of it. The ceremony works or it does not, but either way we believe in it, rely on it. Just as you rely on your god. Tell me, do you pick the situations where you ask your god for help? Or do you give over your life completely to his protection?"

"I—completely—" Margaret stammered.

"In a sense the False Faces are our god of healing. They have our trust and faith. We believe, Margaret. Swift Doe did, until you turned her brain in her head."

"I see your point. But I, too, have a point. I looked at his wound, the festering. Maybe he wouldn't have died, but he would have lost his leg."

"You seem very sure."

"His hip is already deformed. He's twelve years old. Would you rather he be carried about on a litter by his

friends the rest of his life, simply to preserve the people's
respect for the False Faces?"

"*Nyoh.*"

Margaret threw up her hands. "We'll never get together.
Let's just accept that and put it behind us. Can we? Or do
you plan to hold it against me the rest of my days?"

"It *has* raised a wall between us."

"Is it impregnable? Insurmountable? Let's not lose sight
of one thing here. I love you, Eight Minks. You love me.
Without you my life here would have been far more difficult. We're friends. I can't lose you. I won't—not over a
difference of opinion. Moon Dancer is no loss to me, she
never was my friend. Others turned their backs on me
early, and I can't do a blessed thing about that."

Eight Minks stared long and hard at her. In her eyes
Margaret could see misting. She would not cry; the Oneidas almost never surrendered to such obvious displays of
their feelings.

"I love you, Margaret, and I do want to be your friend
again."

Margaret embraced her, but Eight Minks held her at
arm's length. "Still, you must never again interfere. All it
does is reinforce the bad opinion some of the people have
toward you. And even now, after more than two years, you
are still trying too hard to fit in. So hard it shows."

"I know."

"Do you? Then get control of it. Do not be so overly
friendly with women who are cold toward you. And do
not talk to men like you are their sister. Their women do
not like that. You should know by now that among us, except for husbands and wives, men and women keep separate.

"Let Benjamin play with other babies. He is old enough
and they will not contaminate him. If he plays with another baby you will get to talking to its mother about your
children and perhaps make a new friend. Smoothly, effortlessly, without trying. Two Eagles does not talk about
these things, not because he does not care but because he

is blind to their importance. I tell you because I see and we are friends."

Margaret kissed her and took her hand, then abruptly released it. "I interrupted you. Are you done here?"

"*Nyoh.* Do you know why I came? Of course, Two Eagles told you. You might be interested in what Ah-ke-so-tah said about you. He said you are *de-a-go-ah-nah-se.* Do you know what that is?"

"A moose in a longhouse." Margaret laughed. "In England they say a bull in a china shop. Blundering about, breaking everything."

"You are still fitting in and will be for some time. Always keep that in mind."

"*Nyoh.*"

"Be more careful, that is all. It is curious. Unlike Two Eagles you usually *are* more careful, you do not jump into things. Tantanege you jumped into. I know, because you thought time was his enemy. Maybe not. It could have been at a stage that the ashes would have cured. And the healing would have begun shortly after you interfered. Is that not so?"

This Margaret didn't believe by any stretch of the imagination. But she nodded. *"Nyoh."*

Approaching the open gate, Margaret and Eight Minks saw a crowd gathered inside, dogs yapping around the perimeter, excitement charging the air. Margaret was delighted to see Anger Maker; all three searchers were dirty, disheveled and yawning with exhaustion. Two Eagles was firing questions, and Splitting Moon struggled to keep up with him.

"An old squaw at Massowaganine claimed to have seen him heading north. She was returning home from digging roots and he passed her. She described him perfectly. We followed him, found a dead cookfire."

"And after that he got off the trail," said Red Paint. "We followed his tracks west all the way to Lake Ne-ah'-gä-te-car-ne-o-di. Right up to the water's edge. He stole a canoe and set forth and left no tracks, no cookfire ashes on the water."

"Did he head north?" Two Eagles asked.

They shrugged. "He could have gone anywhere except toward the sunrise, *neh*?" Anger Maker pointed east, then west. "In the opposite direction to the lands of the Neutrals, north to the Montagnais seal fuckers, up the Kanuwage to Sokoki Territory."

"Not to the Hurons!" exclaimed Two Eagles.

"Maybe south to the Wenros or the Susquehannocks."

"Neither. Nor the Munsees, either," said Two Eagles. "All are our enemies."

The crowd around them listened in silence. Margaret was tempted to advise Two Eagles that it was possible Blue Creek hadn't gone to any particular tribe, but instead to a place where he knew he could live in solitude. It was even possible he'd returned to the Hurons. True, he'd been their prisoner and they'd tortured him, but he'd been with them two years and eventually they'd given him his freedom. It was possible he'd made friends among them. Prisoners often ended up adopted by their captors. But she would not interrupt.

Two Eagles' disappointment took the form of sarcasm toward his friends. "You should have stayed alert and stolen a canoe of your own so you could look for him on the lake."

At this Splitting Moon scoffed. "He was half a moon ahead of us. It would have been like looking for a fishhook at the bottom of the lake."

Two Eagles absently bit the knuckle of one finger, thinking hard. "He is heading north. Definitely."

"Oh?" said Splitting Moon. "When did you dream that?"

"Think about it. He would not take to water if he was heading south. And forget west. He has fled up to Fort Frontenac, past it up the Kanuwage. Maybe all the way up to Quebec."

"*Neh*, not into the arms of the lace-cuffs."

To Margaret, Two Eagles seemed no more satisfied now than before the party returned.

When the discussion broke up and the crowd dispersed, he handed Benjamin in his cradleboard to Margaret.

"Satisfied?" she asked.

"Do I look satisfied?" he retorted.

"Once and for all, darling, forget about him. Wipe him out of your mind, out of our lives. Please."

He grunted.

"And what does *that* mean?" Eight Minks challenged him.

"It means *nyoh*. What she says makes sense."

Margaret brightened. "Do you mean it?"

He grunted again. Then Benjamin grunted. Everyone laughed. Even Two Eagles.

 57

Gazing straight upward into the descending snow it looked to Seth as if the sky were filled with feathers. Then the wind flung the snow furiously in all directions.

Now the missionaries could not see ten feet ahead and repeatedly they ran into low branches, misstepped against rocks or slipped into holes. To Seth, the snowfall brought a curious tingling warmth, seeming to heat his perspiration. But Hopkins was not warmed. His arms tightly wrapped around him, he stumbled forward, shivering with the cold, gasping for breath. They ran until they fell. Seth lay flat on his back. His companion knelt panting like a bellows, unable to speak. Then he found his voice.

"Will they come after us?"

"We left two of them dead, Dwight."

"But would they follow us in this?"

"Who knows?"

Hopkins shook his head resignedly and resumed shivering. "Sorry to be such an old woman. It's nerves. I'm all knots and tangles. Shouldn't we go on?"

"In a minute."

Hopkins sighed. "Freezing to death has always been my worst fear. I don't fear dying, just freezing to death. Starting with my toes and fingers, fighting for breath, my lungs burning. And when it gets to my heart it turns it to ice."

"All right, all right." Seth got to his feet and, pulling a deerskin from around his midsection, ripped it in half and tied the pieces around his moccasins. Hopkins did the same.

"Ever since childhood I've had the same dream," he went on. "I could burn at the stake, fall off a cliff, be shot or stabbed, none of them is half so harrowing as freezing to death."

"Dwight . . ."

"I'm sorry."

With a crack like musket shot, freezing sap split a nearby tree, startling them both.

"Let's go on," said Seth. "Maybe we can find a cave where we can hole up, get out of this bloody wind. It's the wind that's the problem, not the snow."

"Not a cave, that'd be the first place they'd look . . ."

"Look at you, you're rattling cold and we've hours till dawn," said Seth. "What choice have we? Keep your eyes peeled; I'll keep an eye on you. Just keep moving. Don't stop till we find something."

"Yes, yes, you're a decent sort, Seth. I feel heaps better that you're here."

Seth managed a dry laugh. "I don't."

They had brought along every stitch of the buckskin from the pile, wrapping pieces about them head to toe until both looked like medieval beggars. They had even tied pieces of the foul-smelling leather over their faces up to their eyes.

The snow's depth of six inches made headway difficult, and the wind was becoming a gale. Neither had eaten since the stew brought into the chamber. Both were exhausted, stumbling more frequently now, grabbing for branches to keep from falling. The blizzard gave no sign of letting up. They followed the path paralleling the Mohawk River, wandering off it repeatedly. They could neither see nor—when the wind rested and the trees ceased their creaking—hear any pursuers. Which, as Seth pointed out, was no reason to get careless.

They saw no caves, no possible shelter of any sort. Drifts, which had to be skirted, frequently slowed their advance. Seth lowered his head as the wind attacked. Cold needled his throat through his improvised muffler. His calves and thigh muscles were tightening. He had never known such crushing weariness. It was like a huge vise slowly closing, pressing, and it was all he could do to keep his eyes open. Hopkins closed his, stumbling, falling, lying looking dead asleep. Seth roused him.

"Up, keep going!"

"I'm so tired—" the other moaned.

The wind caught Seth's muffler, ripping it off, sending it flying out over the river. His face exposed, the wind set fire to his cheeks, chasing up his nostrils, stabbing like needles. Lowering his head, he bulled forward, pushing Hopkins on. Then suddenly stopped.

"Dwight, look!"

A large spruce had fallen, coming to rest at an angle against a towering maple. The heavily needled boughs of the deadfalls spread in all directions, affording shelter, albeit meager. They staggered to it, testing it to make certain it could fall no farther, then scuttled under, sweeping away snow. Using his knife, Seth hacked away at branches until there was ample room underneath for both. The lopped-off branches he then placed on top. It wasn't much protection, open as it was on three sides, but the snow failed to penetrate it, even though the wind did easily.

"It's coming from across the river," said Seth, "from the

north. Let's cut off more branches and hang them there, make a wall of sorts."

"Yes, yes—" Hopkins gasped.

When they cut additional branches and hung them on the angled trunk, they huddled inside.

"I wouldn't fall asleep if I were you," cautioned Seth.

"I've never been so tired," Dwight mumbled.

"Only a couple hours till daylight. Hang on."

"I don't know if I can."

Seth pointed south. "Tomorrow we'll head in that direction. Find the main trail."

"Then what?"

"Return to our original plan. Follow it west."

"Oh no—we'll be set upon and captured again, tortured. Besides, it's wide open. We'd freeze to death in ten minutes."

There was no disputing that. Seth pondered the situation. The snowfall showed signs of letting up. They could now see the trees around them and out across the river. Even before deciding which direction to take and whether to risk the main trail, they first had to find food. All the game in the area had likely gone to ground. Any fruit trees would be bare, as would berry bushes. He had seen a gray fungus hanging from trees back along the path. Was it edible? And what about bark? Which bark was poisonous and which edible? How did the Indians survive on the trail in such conditions? Of course, they knew better than to set out without so much as a crust of bread for provisions.

"What are you thinking about?" Hopkins asked.

"We've got to find food."

"I'm starving."

"Come daylight, it'll be the first order of business."

"We used to trap rabbits in the woods in Virginia. They're delicious slow roasted over an open fire and seasoned with herbs."

"Please. Under the circumstances I think hunting is out of the question."

"Trap them. We have our knives. It's easy to make a spring snare. You fashion a noose."

"Out of what?"

"A slender length of this skin."

"It's rotten," said Seth. "The slightest pressure and it'll snap."

"Then we use a twig, use anything. Cut a pole, fasten the snare at the end and set it under the end of a second pole." He explained in detail.

"It sounds a bit complicated."

"It's not, I've made dozens. The question is, what do we use for bait?"

"Let's put it aside for now." Seth leaned out from under the cover and studied the snow. "It's letting up. When it stops, won't the animals come back out of their lairs?"

"Yes, yes. I've another idea. We'll cut poles and sharpen them for spears."

"Have you ever thrown a spear?"

"It can't be difficult, the most primitive tribes use them. With a little practice—"

The ideas tumbling one upon another raised both their hopes. They sat gazing out at the storm. Seth glanced overhead. "It's building a layer; it should make it warmer in here." He flexed his hands in their wrappings. "Do you know that I had a perfectly marvelous pair of mittens when we left Boston? The gift of a friends."

"I had an engraved *Rhemes and Douay* Bible, a treasure. It was my grandmother's. Now look at us, the two beggars of Baghdad."

Seth managed a grin through his weariness. "I think I'll doze off. Maybe dream of a steaming hot steak-and-kidney pie, a tankard of good stout."

"Not me. I'll take pheasant simmering in its own juices, skin so crisp it shatters, succulent as ambrosia. And wine, a fine claret."

"Mmmmm."

Seth lay back and fell asleep immediately, and dreamed not of steak-and-kidney pie but of Hannah. She was giving

him a silhouette of himself then the one of her to match it.
He saw the boiling sea and her arm upraised, slowly sinking, then the pieces of both silhouettes fluttering down into
the dirty water. And a grinding sadness overcame him, until she reappeared on deck. Only the deck was the aisle of
a church and she was in a bridal gown, holding a bouquet,
sparkling with happiness, gliding toward him in all her
beauty.

The shrieking wind woke him; he looked over at the
snoring Hopkins. What would become of them? Would
they find something to eat, perhaps trap a rabbit, as
Hopkins suggested? What about fish? Could they break
through the ice of the river and spear a fish? Roast it? That
would be capital! Skin and roast two or three, bring them
along. Get on the main trail and fast as they could get to
the border separating the Mohawk and the Oneida territories. There was only one Oneida castle.

There she'd be.

The wind howled, pushing their makeshift cover but not
dislodging it. It had almost stopped snowing entirely. It
was growing colder, bitter. He leaned over Hopkins and
rearranged his rags to better cover his chest and shoulders.
On he snored.

 **58**

Margaret, Two Eagles and Eight Minks were visiting
the much improved Hare when a warrior of the wolf
clan, Sho-deg-wa´•shon', came into the chamber. Margaret
knew him only by sight. He pointed to her.

"Come with me."

"What for?"

"O-dat-she-dah wants you. Come."

"I will come with you," said Two Eagles.

"Neh," said the messenger, "just her."

Margaret bundled up and followed him out, trailing him through the snow to the wolf clan chief's longhouse. Inside she was confronted by His Longhouse, He Swallows and Carries-a-quiver sitting in a row. Behind them sat the fourteen tribal elders. In front of the chiefs Swift Doe was already seated. She looked anxiously at Margaret but said nothing.

"What do you want with me?" Margaret asked.

The chief of the bear clan, her own and Two Eagles', smiled affably. His Longhouse, twenty years younger than the other two chiefs, was a notorious lecher whose wife had long ago left his bed to a succession of younger women.

"You will see," he said.

"Do not speak," said Carries-a-quiver, who was partially blind and suffered from chronic headaches. He Swallows stared without speaking, as did the elders.

Margaret glanced at Swift Doe, beside her, who looked extremely agitated.

"Carries-a-quiver will explain," said His Longhouse.

The chief cleared his throat. Like His Longhouse and He Swallows, he spoke only in Oneida, for the older men of the tribe, not having fought in the recent war, knew little English.

"The *go-ga-so-ho-nun-na-tase-ta* of the False Faces has lodged a complaint against you. She claims that you deliberately removed the sacred ashes from the body of one of the Society's patients, destroying their power, exposing the boy Tantanege to grave illness and possible death. Did you remove the ashes?"

"Nyoh."

His Longhouse looked downcast, as if expecting denial; Margaret assumed that he would prove understanding and sympathetic when she explained. Providing they let her explain.

Carries-a-quiver went on. "You admit it?"

"Nyoh."

The elders reacted in mild shock and began whispering. Carries-a-quiver held up his hand, quieting them.

"Why?" he asked.

Margaret's explanation appeared to have no effect on either chief nor on His Longhouse. What she did was monstrous, a crime and intentional, for which she must be punished.

"May I speak?" asked Swift Doe.

"You are the boy's mother," said Carries-a-quiver. "Did you know about this?"

"I—asked her to help."

As one man the elders sucked in their breaths sharply, rolling their eyes.

"I do not understand," said Carries-a-quiver.

"His flesh was rotting away; the rotting was getting into the wound. The ashes were bad ashes, evil."

"Are you a medicine woman?"

"Neh."

"Are you?" Carries-a-quiver asked Margaret.

"Neh. It did not take a medicine woman's skills to see that the flesh was rotting. I had to do something. If that makes me guilty of a crime, so be it. The *crime* would have been not to lift a finger."

"What you did was unforgivable. Both of you must be punished."

"Carries-a-quiver," said His Longhouse, "this one is a recent widow, still in mourning. The loss of her husband compounded by the wounding of her son has been hard on her. She was confused."

"I was not," said Swift Doe. "I was desperate. The ashes were useless, I tell you, evil. His wound was festering, he was in agony. Now, thanks to Margaret, he is almost completely healed and feels no pain."

Carries-a-quiver stared at her in silence. "Your confusion is understandable, but inviting her to interfere is not. You must be punished. Moon Dancer has asked our permission to remove your son to her longhouse, to her care until he is healed and can walk again."

"Neh!" burst Swift Doe. "I have lost my husband. You will not take my son!"

"The *go-ga-so-ho-nun-na-tase-ta* has spoken and he is her patient." He eyed Margaret. "Not yours, you had no business interfering. As for your punishment, you will be banished until the ground softens and the trees bud."

"Neh!" Unseen by either Margaret or Swift Doe, Two Eagles had pushed aside the messenger and come in. "Moon Dancer will not take Tantanege," he snarled. "And my wife stays."

"Tékni-ska-je-a-nah," responded Carries-a-quiver, "you have no business here. Leave us."

"Neh." Two Eagles drew his knife. "If you force my woman to take one step out the gate, blood will spill. I swear it. She saved the boy's life. She should be rewarded not punished. You do not know what you are doing, you have only the fat one's word for it. You have not seen Tantanege's leg. These two saved his life! Margaret, Swift Doe, get up."

"Tékni-ska-je-a-nah—" growled Carries-a-quiver.

"Both of you, go, I will handle this."

They left. Anger narrowed every eye focused on Two Eagles, save those of His Longhouse.

"You want to deal out punishment? Punish me!" Two Eagles snarled. "Not two helpless women who only did what was right." He extended his hand, pointing to each chief in turn and moving down the line of elders. "We have a law you all know of. A law that says that any time, in any case, anyone may step forward and assume the punishment for another. Is that not so?"

"It is," said His Longhouse.

"Then here I am. Punish me in place of them. Now, today. Do it. Put an end to this nonsense."

"We do not consider it nonsense," said He Swallows, speaking for the first time and eyeing Two Eagles savagely.

"As you wish," said Carries-a-quiver. "We will let Moon Dancer decide the punishment, as the widow of the man whose heart your arrow found."

It was stifling hot; he was suffocating. He woke up drenched with sweat, a piece of deerskin covering his nose and mouth, making it all but impossible to get a breath. He was shivering uncontrollably. It was so cold in the lean-to, he felt encased in ice. Snow had fallen all night long.

"Dwight?"

No response. Raising himself on one elbow he looked over. Hopkins was gone. Seth rose to a sitting position, bumping his head on the bough ceiling; snow sifted down. Checking his buckskins to make sure no part of him was exposed, he crawled outside and got unsteadily to his feet. Dizziness struck and he stood with his head whirling and the emptiness all but echoing in his stomach. The snow drifted about him, in some places to a height of six feet and more. No wind, not a whisper, and the enfeebled sun seemed barely able to shaft light through the dense woodlands. Then abruptly it broke through, smashing against his eyes; he winced, blinking rapidly. About twenty yards to his right a rabbit stuck its head up, assessed him, ducked and bounded out of sight.

Never in memory had he encountered such crushing cold. He resumed shivering; one cheek where the cover had fallen away felt puffy. He covered it quickly. Such extreme cold could be fatal.

Where had Hopkins gotten to? He took a step forward, sinking to just under his knee. Shading his eyes from the glare, he peered a slow circle about him. No sign of him. Then he noticed footprints heading outward, turning, circling around behind the maple against which the deadfall rested. He followed the tracks, his heart coming to life, thumping loudly.

Against the tree sat Hopkins staring straight ahead. Seth knelt and gripped his shoulders. "Dwight—Dwight!" Hopkins fell, lying on his side, eyes gaping, his face a sickly blue. "Oh, my God!"

Seth got up, staring at him.

"Poor fellow."

And now there was one.

60

Neither Margaret nor Swift Doe was permitted to accompany Two Eagles to Moon Dancer's chamber to hear his punishment. Only His Longhouse and Carries-a-quiver entered with Two Eagles. The chamber smelled of fern. False faces hung from one wall, and the center of the dirt floor was worn from her dancing. When the three men entered she did not look up as she continued breaking buff-olive ring-necked pheasant eggs into what looked to be wood ashes in a bowl. The three stood watching her. Two Eagles' patience failed him.

"Moon Dancer?" he snapped.

Not until she stirred in the last egg and set the bowl to one side did she acknowledge her visitors' entrance.

"Your punishment, *nyoh*," she said to Two Eagles, narrowing her beady eyes and leering. In her tone was triumph. "I have given it much thought." Her glance strayed to the two chiefs, then she turned her back on all three. "I think often and sadly of my poor nephew, my long-dead sister's only son, Karístatsi Sateeni. And his murderer. The day Ossivendi Oÿoghi fled he took with him any hope I had of avenging Karístatsi Sateeni." She faced Two Eagles. "Now that hope is revived, *neh*? And the punishment I require is actually no punishment, only a task. You will go and search for my nephew's friend and murderer. Find him, bring his head back to prove it is Blue Creek, and I will set it at the foot of Iron Dog's grave and all will be right again."

Two Eagles' heart beat faster. This was no punishment, it was reward! And Margaret couldn't object, nor Swift Doe. *Nyoh,* go and track north, find Benjamin's would-be kidnapper, bring back his head. He resisted the urge to seize Moon Dancer's hands and squeeze them gratefully. He would leave at once, taking Splitting Moon and Anger Maker.

Moon Dancer went on. "You will go on this quest alone. You will leave when the first ice leaves Lake Oneida and return with his head before next winter's ice closes the lake. I hope you succeed. If you fail, do not bother to return. Ever."

His Longhouse sucked in a breath. "That is harsh punishment, too harsh for the offense."

Anger filled her eyes. "Was it given to me by you two and He Swallows to decide? This is my decision. I do not need your opinion, His Longhouse. I need no one's." She shifted her attention back to Two Eagles. "Do you understand it?"

"*Nyoh.*"

"And you will do it?"

"*Nyoh.* Only I see no reason to wait until the spring thaw to leave."

"I do. You will not leave until the ice has left."

He glanced at His Longhouse, then at the bowl on the ground. "*Nyoh.*"

"One thing," said Carries-a-quiver. "If he fails to find the murderer in the allotted time but continues to search and eventually does find him, should he bring his head back then?"

"*Neh.*"

"But you will still get the head you want so badly," protested His Longhouse.

"*Neh!* You have until next winter's freeze. Not a day longer. I will go with Eight Minks and others to the lake each morning and determine when the last ice has gone, and when the next ice is in place. That is all, *isene.*"

Margaret and Swift Doe were waiting with expressions that feared the worst as they stood at the entrance to the longhouse, their breaths whitening the air. Apprehensively they followed Two Eagles and His Longhouse down the passageway to Margaret's chamber. There Eight Minks held Benjamin as she waited with Fox.

"What's your punishment?" Margaret asked.

"It is not so bad," he replied, pausing before entering their chamber to place two logs on the fire.

"I'll bet. She despises you!"

"She wants me to find Blue Creek and bring back his head."

"Oh dear God!" Margaret rolled her eyes, threw up her hands.

"Within a time limit," said His Longhouse, eliciting a glare from Two Eagles.

"Time limit?" Swift Doe asked.

His Longhouse explained.

Margaret stared wide-eyed at Two Eagles. "Is it true? If you don't find him before next year's freeze you're to be banished forever? You agreed to that!"

"Not banished—"

"I'd like to know what you call it!"

"She is right," said His Longhouse. "You would be risking banishment."

"I will find Turtle Skin long before next winter."

"You don't even know where to start!" burst Margaret. "He easily lost Splitting Moon and the others. Now his trail is cold as ice. He might as well have walked off the earth. Of all the devious—"

Swift Doe nodded. "This punishment is too severe for saving Hare's life. Unfair."

"I could strangle her!"

"I said it was too severe," said His Longhouse. He glanced at Two Eagles and back at Margaret. "I had better go. When you decide, Tékni-ska-je-a-nah, come to my longhouse and we will talk."

"It is decided," snapped Two Eagles. "Were you not listening?" He paused, pondered and brightened. "I can leave right away."

"Neh." His Longhouse shook his head. "You heard her."

Two Eagles' eyes narrowed slightly. "Not to look for Blue Creek, only for his trail, where he left Lake Ne-ah'-gä-te-car-ne-o-di. He went up the Kanuwage, I am sure, but how far? He must be living with some tribe, but which? I will consult my óyaron."

His Longhouse had paused at the entrance, lifting the flap.

"Neh. Do not deceive yourself. Looking for his trail would be looking for him before the time she gave you to start. She will not permit that. Do exactly as she instructed, that is the only way."

He left. Two Eagles glowered after him, muttering.

61

It was early morning of the fourth day since the death of Dwight Hopkins. In the clear, bright, bone-shrinking cold, Seth had been unable to bring himself to remove any of the buckskins from Hopkins' corpse. Additional clothing he had no need for; what he needed was food. He had taken Hopkins' knife and dragged his corpse into the lean-to. Closing his eyes, he had murmured a brief prayer for the salvation of his friend's soul and resumed walking. He found the going increasingly difficult, trudging through snows that came well above his knees; he rested more often than had he and Hopkins during the blizzard.

Displacing the cold and the difficult going was the threat of starvation; his head rang, his energy level dropped precipitously, his gnawing hunger was beginning to affect his eyesight. The path blurred, double images hovered and swam before him. Lifting his legs was lifting stone. He thought about retracing his steps to where they'd seen the fungus hanging from low branches in their path. Some fungus was edible, others were poisonous. Could he test some without killing himself? It was also risky heading back toward Onekahoncka; what if the Mohawks were out scouring the woods for them? Clearly his only hope of survival was to get over the border into Oneida Territory.

Over the past two days he had tried eating various types of bark; all were hard chewing and he found that elm bark was the only kind he could get down. But when he'd consumed a quantity his stomach rebelled, and he projectile vomited.

The path gradually rose. Directly ahead a tall tree stood perilously close to the edge of the bank, which dropped straight down to the frozen river. He was within five strides of the tree when dizziness seized him. He stumbled and fell hard, rolling off the path, dropping a good six feet. He landed on his face in the snow; it revived him at once and he rolled over on his side. His sight swam so he could not see two feet in front of him and he found himself desperately weak.

Suddenly he gasped. At the base of the tree was a gaping hollow that exposed the roots. He pulled himself inside and could see that it was opened to a depth of about five feet. The walls around him served to support the weight of the tree.

He found charred firewood, two halves of a broken arrow and a second shaft missing its flint head. There was also a log with one end badly scarred and split it two places, suggesting it had been used as a club. He found that he could sit erect without bowing his head. He looked out on the snow-manteled river, realizing this was better cover than the lean-to, despite the fact that it faced the wind. The sky was free of threatening clouds.

Hefting the club he ventured forth unsteadily. Clearing away a path of snow about a meter in diameter, he struck the ice with all his might. The club bounced harmlessly, but he kept at it, and just as he felt his strength giving out he managed to break through. The hole was jagged and only about a foot across, but it would be all he'd need.

Getting out his knife he cut a branch, carving a sharp point. He then ripped off a small piece of buckskin and began chewing it. It tasted foul, but his saliva quickly rendered it pliable. He tore a strip from a skin wrapped around his leg, tied the chewed rawhide to the spear about eight inches up from the point, and let the bait drop into the water.

He hadn't the least idea what kind of fish swam the river, but they had to be more edible than elm bark. As he fished sitting in front of his shelter praying for luck, he salivated uncontrollably. His heart quickened in anticipation. He'd start a fire and roast his catch. Clean it, eat every morsel. Only slowly; wolfing it down as he had the bark would only risk upsetting his stomach again.

Periodically he would check his bait. Almost at once a fish took it. Down came the spear—he pulled it out. Wriggling on the point was a fat speckled trout. He shouted gleefully, smashing it on the ice alongside the hole, nearly losing it in the water, snatching it up.

He laid it aside and gathered leaves and sticks in a small heap. Finding a stone, he rubbed it briskly against the blade of his knife but no sparks showed. He tried rubbing blade against stone with the same result. He rubbed both knives together. He tried and tried.

It was useless. Picking up the fish, he examined it. It was covered with slime as protection against cold. Carefully, he scraped away the slime, cut off the head, bled the fish as thoroughly as possible, then set about removing the skin. Again his grinding hunger distorted his vision; for a time he could barely make out the fish in his grasp. Then his eyes cleared and he finished skinning it.

He cut out a cube of flesh, holding it before him on the knife blade. He took it in his mouth. Very slowly, he began chewing it. It tasted a trifle rubbery but clean, fresh. He stiffened and let it slip down his throat, holding his breath, waiting. To his relief it did not make him ill. He downed a second and third piece. Then he waited, mindful that he mustn't gorge.

He resumed eating; the sun was high overhead when he was done, leaving a neat rack of bones. He felt no nausea. He got up and climbed to the path, trudging a few steps, marveling at how well he felt, how his energy seemed to be returning.

Before leaving, he caught two more fish, using a portion of the first trout's head for bait. When he'd cleaned and bled them, he stuffed them under the buckskin tied around his chest, then resumed his journey.

Two days more he trudged westward; for fear of roving Mohawks, he didn't dare to turn south to seek the main trail. He had no map, only the memory of the ones that designated the border between territories with a scraggly line running north to south, and an "X" marking the site of the Oneida castle just over the border.

Shortly before twilight of the second day it resumed snowing; enormous flakes floated lazily earthward to dust the crust of the previous blizzard. Was it another blizzard?

"Dear Lord . . ."

Seth bowed his head and trudged on. Luck was his. It stopped snowing before dark and the cloud that dispensed it floated on ahead toward the horizon, leaving in its wake an ultramarine sky. He stopped to eat, taking out his one remaining fish. It smelled as if it were beginning to rot. He threw it away.

He looked about for shelter for the night. The wind was up, sweeping up the snow dust and flinging it about. The only shelter he could find was behind a rock out of the wind. He dug down to bare ground, heaping the snow around him in a half circle, curled into the fetal position, and went to sleep. It was not nearly as cold as the previous night and those before that. Ice clinging to branches had begun melting before the snow came and the temperature dropped. But when it stopped snowing the temperature rose once more, and he felt he was growing used to the cold.

The sun was well above the horizon when his grumbling stomach wakened him. Something to quiet it would be the first task of the day. Before him stood a large double tree; it looked much like a linden, bearing a dense crown of many small, drooping branches. Its two trunks were identical in size, and the smooth, dark gray bark was burrowed into scaly ridges.

On impulse, he cut some bark and chewed it. It was tough and fibrous but it had a clean taste. He satisfied his hunger and cut a supply for emergency rations, placing it in a piece of buckskin at the small of his back, avoiding the place in front where he'd kept the fish.

He was preparing to leave when he heard screaming from the other side of a ridge ahead and to his left. He made his way to the ridge, throwing himself flat, peering warily over the top. In a large clearing he saw savages in teams of six men each heading toward the river, hauling roughly hewn sleds piled with game.

From three sides they were being attacked. Screaming at the tops of their lungs, Mohawks came trudging through the deep snow wielding tomahawks. They attacked furiously; in seconds the snow was drenched with blood. The poachers, though armed with iron axes, were taken by surprise and found themselves badly outnumbered.

Seth looked on in horror as the carnage continued. Not content to dispatch the hunters, the Mohawks seemed bent on chopping them to bits. A warrior stood astride his dead victim, decapitating him, severing his limbs, cutting up his trunk, reducing him to gore.

Seth's stomach churned in revulsion. Only three men managed to escape, fleeing across the river, one missing his arm, blood spurting from his shoulder. Another took an arrow full in the spine and fell. The one-armed man and the third one scrambled up the opposite bank into the trees.

The attackers now set about scalping the dead and dying, laughing, joking, working methodically with the sure-handedness of accomplished surgeons. One not fifteen feet from Seth made a neat circular incision around the pate of his victim and pulled the scalp away from the fleshy layer of the skull. Another Mohawk knelt on a fallen poacher's back and while the man screamed, alternately pulled and peeled the scalp from his head before dispatching him.

Then the Mohawks looted the dead before dividing into groups and hauling away the sleds. They set off toward the southwest; the site, littered with body parts, red on white bathed in sunlight, the scent of death rising like mist from a meadow, stood silent.

When he was certain none of the attackers would return, Seth climbed over the ridge. Searching the dead, he found hard, dry cornbread, some studded with cranberries, others with beans. He found salted venison, as well as mintlike leaves pressed into a block. He found a short, hollowed-out stick crammed with a smoldering mixture of grasses, useful for lighting fires. He took an iron-bladed ax, apparently the only one overlooked by the Mohawks.

Lastly, he stripped off his rags, washed his shivering body in clean snow and put on blood-stained fur trousers, fur jacket, a bearskin robe and a ragged pair of boots. They were heavier and higher than those of the Mohawks.

He also took a pair of hickory-deerhide snowshoes. Quickly he discovered how to slide across the snow in them. He speedily got the hang of it.

Gagging now and again, he made his way through the scattered corpses and reached the woods, finding the path that followed the river. As he slid speedily along, he sampled some of the cranberry bread. He found it delicious, once it softened and became chewable.

He remembered that after Onekahoncka there was supposedly two more Mohawk castles, the third and last close to the border of Oneida Territory. Had the attackers come from the middle castle or the last one? Since there was no way of determining, he chose to continue along by the river. Its course had scarcely deviated since he and Hopkins came to it after fleeing their captors earlier. On their maps, it had appeared to head eastward, to join the Hudson.

Before long he came to the river's turning. It headed north-northwestward around a deserted camp: he could see tumbledown shacks, lean-tos and racks for drying pelts, but it looked as though it had been deserted for years.

The two poachers who'd escaped the Mohawks had headed north, so their home must lie in that direction. None of the poachers had worn buckskins, all were garbed in furs. About thirty of them had fallen to the Mohawks; not a single Mohawk had been killed, although a few had incurred wounds. He got out the iron-bladed ax and examined it, running his thumb along the edge. It was razor sharp. Did they make them themselves or trade for them with the French?

It was late afternoon when he decided to turn south and seek out the main trail. It should be windswept by now, making travel easy; perhaps he would not even need the snowshoes. When Hopkins and Wilby and he had come onto the trail near the Hudson, they'd found it unexpectedly wide, with the woodlands set well back on both sides. That meant he'd be able to see any attackers approaching from ahead or behind, giving him time to run for cover.

He now had two knives and the iron ax; all three he'd trade for a decent musket or brace of pistols, but better Indian weapons than none at all. Darkness was descending

in the lowering sky by the time he came within sight of
the main trail. It stretched westward, as straight as the horizon, into a gray mist. How far to the Oneida castle?

The sky was clouding over rapidly. More snow? He
shivered at the thought. Still, his situation had improved
dramatically; he had ample food, excellent clothing and he
was near the Oneida border. Only who was to say the
Oneidas were any less savage than the Mohawks?

One worry crept to mind: Fisk Drummond had mentioned that the Iroquois had conquered most of their neighboring tribes. Any Iroquois hunters seeing him in furs
would assume he was an enemy.

And shoot him dead from thirty yards away!

62

It had been snowing heavily since shortly after nightfall.
High drifts buttressed the palisade inside and out. The
sullen sky appeared to lower. The snowfall snuffed out
torches and chased the hardiest dogs inside. The Oneida
bundled into their robes and moved closer to their fires.

On one family the weather had no effect; husband and
wife were too engrossed in arguing. They were in Swift
Doe's chamber, where Margaret had come to discuss the
situation with her friend and was followed by an irate Two
Eagles. Their shouting could be heard all the way up the
passageway to Eight Minks' chamber.

"For the last time," Margaret shrilled, "I—am—going—
to—her! We'll have it out."

"There is nothing to have out, I tell you. It is all settled."

"It is not! It's supposed to be my punishment and Swift
Doe's. You had no business horning in. Oh, but you love

the idea. She's put the official stamp of approval on your wild-goose chase!"

"I do not understand what you mean."

"You understand. And it won't work. Swift Doe, are you coming with me?"

"Coming, coming."

"Do not do this, Margaret," said Two Eagles. "Do not embarrass me in Moon Dancer's eyes."

"If anybody's going to be embarrassed it'll be her, I promise you."

Bundling her robe about her, she stormed out, Swift Doe padding after her, pretending fear and grinning for his benefit. As they exited the longhouse, they drew their robes over their heads. Margaret fell, got up seething, went on. Moon Dancer's longhouse was the second one behind theirs. The passageway fire outside her chamber crackled merrily. She was asleep. Margaret shook her; her eyelids parted, a scowl darkened her face.

"Get up. We have to talk."

"How dare you? I was in the middle of an important dream."

"Up!"

By the time Moon Dancer's pudgy feet found the ground she was furious.

"I'll make this short," hissed Margaret. "Two Eagles is not going anywhere. If you simply have to have your pound of flesh you'll get it out of me, not him."

"You are too late. It is all decided."

"I'm the guilty one. I'm the one who'll be punished. That's my decision."

"Too late, I tell you."

Margaret glowered at her. "You bloody witch!"

"You loudmouth! And stupid! This was Two Eagles' idea and Carries-a-quiver agreed. Why put it on my head?"

"Why don't you be honest? You're still bitter over what happened up on the Kanuwage. Admit it."

"He murdered my husband!"

"It wasn't murder! I know. I was there. If their positions were reversed, Thrown Bear would have done the same. He begged Two Eagles to put him out of his misery."

"That has nothing to do with this. Blue Creek murdered my nephew, my only living blood. Am I not entitled to revenge? Two Eagles has offered to get it for me, for which I am most grateful."

"I'll bet!" Margaret sneered.

"Why are you so upset? It is not as if I was sending him to his death. It is not even punishment. He looks forward to it with great eagerness. He has as good a reason to execute Blue Creek, as I do. I could have asked that he be beaten at the post, buried up to his chin and smeared with honey for the red ants. He—"

She paused and glanced at Swift Doe. "Have you nothing to say? Or are you just here to listen? Blue Creek murdered your husband, too. Do you not want to see him punished? Will you not be delighted to hold his head and spit in his face?"

"I would like nothing better in my life than to see Blue Creek punished, but not if it means putting Two Eagles' life at risk. What is this foolishness about banishment if he does not return on time? Tell me that isn't *your* revenge against him for Thrown Bear.

"None of us deserves any of this. If there is to be punishment, you should be the one to receive it. You and your evil ashes nearly killed my son. Now, thanks to *her*, his wound is almost healed. She saved his life. If she did not act when she did, I would not be showing up here now with mild words in my mouth. I would show you a knife and leave here with it sticking in your heart."

Moon Dancer sniffed and turned away.

"All we ask," said Margaret, "is give me back the punishment."

"And me," said Swift Doe.

Moon Dancer looked from one to the other. "Tell me, English, have you discussed this with Two Eagles?"

"That doesn't concern you. All that matters is that we

are the transgressors here, the ones who should be punished."

"Oh?" She glanced at Swift Doe. "You just finished saying that *I* should be.

"Will you listen?" demanded Margaret.

"*You* deserve the punishment, I agree. But now Two Eagles stands in your moccasins. He wants to go, he will. Now, if you do not mind, *I* would like to go back to sleep."

"Moon Dancer—" began Swift Doe.

"That is all. *Ísene.*"

They left. Outside the snow was still coming down heavily. Margaret shook her head. "He can't go. If he does I'll never see him again. I know, I feel it!"

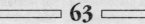

63

Two Eagles was not superstitious. In that respect he was a rarity among his people. To the "fear spirit," he made only one concession. He consulted his óyaron regularly. Even that he would not acknowledge as superstition. Instead, he considered it his counsel and guide, and he dared undertake no important mission, nor reach any important decision, without its advice.

He started out from the longhouse early the next morning, taking pains to avoid waking his wife and son as he dressed. It had stopped snowing but the sun rose into bitter cold.

It was not necessary for him to venture far into the woods. Behind him he could still see the gray, gloomy, abandoned-looking castle against the sky. Reaching an open space he took off his robe and knelt on it. He removed his feather, the tailfeather of *ska-je-a-nah*, the great golden eagle. Holding it horizontally at eye level he began chanting. The frolicking wind tossed snow powder at him, covering the robe, except where he knelt. The watching trees groaned protest at his intrusion among them. The cold bit his exposed flesh.

He set the feather down and out of his belt brought a pouch of tobacco, laying it before him: a gift for his guiding spirit. Once more he lifted the feather, chanting loudly, invoking his óyaron. The ceremony lasted only a few minutes; then he got up, restored his feather and put his robe back on, leaving the tobacco pouch on the packed-down snow.

He started back. There as no point in continuing to argue with Margaret. He would not be leaving until spring; were they to be at each other's noses all winter? He smiled to himself. Her concern over him was one of the things that nurtured his affection for her. If she had her way she would keep him as close as she kept Benjamin. In that respect she was like Eight Minks had been when he was younger. In his troubled young life he had treasured her fondness for him and his brothers. Just as he now treasured Margaret's affection.

It was strange. If they never argued, if the two of them agreed on everything, they probably wouldn't have been nearly as close. It was the differences, the concessions each extended the other and the efforts to solve their problems that tightened the bond of their relationship. They would eventually solve this problem, like all the others. And there was time.

Within sight of the castle entrance he spied Eight Minks and Fox coming toward him, taking the early morning air as had become their custom. Both wore snowshoes. Fox slid ahead effortlessly, while Eight Minks pushed forward in mincing, unsteady steps, fearful of falling. Fox was well ahead of her when she called to him to slow his pace and waved to Two Eagles.

As he came up to them, she asked, "You have consulted your óyaron?" He grunted. "And?"

"Nothing. I did not learn anything I do not know already. He has gone north into Gâ'-oh's teeth. I must dream."

"I will make you some water pepper tea. It will fill your head with dreams."

Two Eagles smiled appreciatively.

Until Eight Minks added, "It is all wrong, but I do not have to tell you that. You have no business taking their punishments on your back."

"I should turn my back and let my woman be banished?"

"You will be the one to be banished."

"*Neh*, I will find him."

Fox shrugged. "It will not be easy."

"You will be venturing into the lands of your enemies," said Eight Minks. "By yourself. A lone Iroquois among Hurons, Ottawas, Montagnais, Abnakis."

"Blue Creek did."

"He had an advantage over you. He was so long among the Hurons he learned their language. Without his scalp, scarred all over like he is, he does not even look like an Iroquois, not like any tribe. Not so with you."

Two Eagles grunted.

She mimicked him. "What does that mean? That you understand? I make sense?"

"I do not leave until the spring. Much can happen between now and then. War could break out."

"And how would even that change anything for you?" Fox asked. "You would still have to go."

"I am just saying that all of us should put it aside until the ice breaks."

Eight Minks shook her head. "Margaret is very upset with you."

"I cannot do anything about that."

"You could stay home."

"That would not solve a thing."

She sighed dramatically. "Why do I work my mouth? Why bother?" She shook her head, fixing him with her most critical gaze. "You always end up doing as you please. As you will in this. And leave your wife a widow and you son fatherless." She flung her hands in dismissal and went on past him. Fox shrugged and followed her.

64

The sun stood straight overhead. Splitting Moon and Two Eagles were standing outside Two Eagles' long-house, stamping against the cold, talking about Blue Creek, when to the surprise of both Hare appeared in the doorway. As he stood with his trophy pelt around his shoulders to ward off the cold, Two Eagles noted his scar: slightly pink, but the flesh was even, suggesting that in time the scar would disappear completely.

"What are you doing out of bed, lynx hunter?" Splitting Moon asked.

"I can walk," said Hare, his eyes shining.

"You had better not let your mother see you," said Two Eagles.

"She is with Margaret and Eight Minks. Look—" He walked inside the longhouse and came back to the entrance. "No pain, only stiffness in my good hip. From not walking in so long, *neh*?"

"You have tested it enough for one day," said Two Eagles. "Back into bed."

"Not yet. I have to talk to you. Man to man."

Splitting Moon grinned.

"Now!" said Hare, ignoring him.

"You get back to bed and I will be right in," said Two Eagles.

"Now. It is important," Hare called over his shoulder as he went inside.

"You know what he is going to ask you," said Splitting Moon.

"To go north with me." Two Eagles shook his head. "Not a chance. It is not a hunting party. It is my punishment."

"Some punishment. I envy you. Go, see how he approaches it. He is a clever one."

Two Eagles found Hare sitting on the edge of his bunk, flexing his leg gingerly. "It is stiff."

"What do you expect? To answer your question: Will I let you come with me? *Neh*."

"Listen to me," said Hare, his eyes turning wistful. He paused and looked past Two Eagles at the chamber flap, to make sure no one was eavesdropping. "By spring I will be thirteen and a man. The age you were when you killed your first Huron snake. You were accepted by all as a man, you deserved to be called a man. Just as I will be." He fisted his chest. "The man of *this* family. Do you deny that?"

"That is not the point, Tantanege."

"What is?"

"If I were allowed to take someone with me, it would be Tyagohuens or Sa-ga-na-qua-de, but you know it is forbidden. I must go alone."

"I could leave the day before and meet you where the trail turns north to Massowaganine."

Two Eagles smiled and winked. "Are you sure you want to go up that trail again?"

"I am serious!"

"So am I. The answer is *neh*. Two moccasins will pursue Turtle Skin, not four."

Hare narrowed his eyes and smiled thinly. "We shall see, Tékni-ska-je-a-nah."

"*Nyoh*. I will say this for your ears only." Two Eagles lowered his voice into a menacing tone. "If you go ahead of me, if you follow me, if I see your face between here and the Kanuwage, I will beat you so you will not be able to crawl after me, much less walk. Do you understand?"

Hare chuckled, then laughed.

Two Eagles went out. For the life of him, he could not
understand young people.

I t was late in the afternoon of Seth's third day on the
main trail when he decided instead to follow the line of
trees paralleling it to the north. He got off just in time; he
was moving along at a steady pace, swinging around a
large elm, when he caught sight of a hunting party directly
ahead. Immediately he ducked into the trees, moving
deeper and deeper. Then, stopping, he retraced his steps to
where he was hidden but could see the party passing.

He counted eight men, all carrying game, evidently on
their way home to the Mohawk castle located just before
the Oneida border. Then it occurred to him that heading
eastward, as they were, *could only mean they had already
passed the third castle*. Meaning he had already crossed
the Oneida border or would soon do so.

He held his breath as he watched the last man in the line
pass, and when the mist had swallowed them, he turned to
continue in the opposite direction. But then he heard a
thrashing of brush behind him. Panicking, he fled, crossing
the trail to the cover of the opposite side and working his
way westward until he was clear of the approaching savages' path, should they too decide to cross over.

He got behind a tree, peering back. Two Indians appeared, then a third, all heavily armed, none carrying any
game. As they turned up the trail he backed deeper into
the trees, slipping and falling loudly into bushes. The crisp
air carried the noise to their ears, and they turned and
loped straight for him.

Off he slid, not daring to look back, crashing through brush, locating a path and striding up it. They could follow his snowshoe tracks easily, he told himself—he had to stay well ahead. If they didn't catch up with him right away they might give up and go on.

The wind came up, flurrying the snow and covering his tracks. But he was slowing, his calf muscles tightening, his legs growing weaker by the stride, until it took all his strength to push one snowshoe ahead of the other. Behind him the wind continued obliterating his trail, but this was the only path in sight; once they found it they'd know he'd taken it.

Ahead, the mouth of a cave yawned darkly. Ducking, he scrambled inside, breaking a lace in the rush to hide. Inside smelled so foul it was all he could do to keep from throwing up. He glanced back at the opening. Did this make sense? Wouldn't it be obvious to them, when they saw no sign of him, that he'd ducked inside? His heart sank. It would take precious seconds to get back out; by then they'd be within sight of the entrance.

He would stay. Turning, he slid slowly forward, lost a snowshoe and fell over something solid. In the pitch darkness he could see nothing; on his knees, he thrust out a hand to feel—fur.

He gasped and swallowed. A hibernating bear. It lay perfectly still, not a sound coming from it, not even breathing. He could hear voices outside. Would his pursuers come in? Only the first few feet of the floor of the cave were visible in the daylight. And his snowshoes didn't show tracks in the leaf mold and other debris covering the floor. Yet by the time they got that far they wouldn't need a trail to follow. He was trapped.

He was dead.

Taking a deep breath, he snuggled up against the creature on the side furthest from the entrance, at the same time slipping off his other snowshoe and throwing both aside. Now he could hear his pursuers just outside. A torch flared suddenly, filling the cave with orange light, defining its dimensions: about seven feet high and at least five times that much deep, hollowed out straight back.

The torch was removed. He crouched lower, waiting. One of them shouted: *"Ochquari!"*

An arrow whirred, thumping into the sleeping bear. A second. Seth backed away on hands and knees retrieving his snowshoes, backing, backing until his feet struck the rear wall. He estimated he'd moved ten or twelve feet from the bear. Assuming the fetal position against the wall, he waited, holding his breath.

The hunters had come in leaving their torch sticking in the snow just outside. Congratulating themselves loudly, they began dragging out the carcass. Only then it occurred to Seth that, crouching as he was in his bearskin robe, his faced concealed, *he must look like a bear.*

The dead bear's mate!

If they brought the torch inside, they'd see him in an instant.

Did bears hibernate with their mates? He was as ignorant of the woodlands and its creatures, nature's tricks and traps, as poor Wilby had been. Would he live long enough to learn anything? Would he survive the next six seconds?

They had gotten the carcass outside. Now, no doubt, they would skin it, cut it up, shoulder the pieces and be on their way. Hopefully!

He waited, afraid to raise his head to see what was going on. Cramps seized him. Still he didn't dare budge. It was growing dark outside. They finally finished skinning the bear and carving it up, dividing the pieces, shouldering them and leaving.

Still he waited, so cramped every muscle below the waist felt twisted. Slowly he ventured back to the cave mouth, where he could hear nothing save wind and trees. He crawled outside, gulping fresh air, struggling to rid his nostrils of the vile stench. He tried to stand but could not, so knotted was he with cramps. Lying on his side, he stretched one leg then the other and, with great effort and much discomfort, flexed them, got the circulation started and pulled himself upright.

It was as dark as the cave outside. No moon, no stars. Sleet began falling straight down, pricking his cheeks painfully.

Bracing himself for the stench, he crawled back inside the cave.

66

The sleet storm was uncommonly severe for early winter. It was still sleeting on the morning of the third day when Splitting Moon lifted the flap of Two Eagles and Margaret's chamber and woke them.

"Come and see—a *coureur de bois* just came wandering in. Come watch me cut his stinking throat!"

Both pulled on their clothes as Splitting Moon waited in the passageway. By the time the three of them got to the longhouse door, other early risers had gathered to gawk at the visitor. By now the sleet had stopped, and the sun had broken through, lending a dazzling brilliance to the crystal-clad woodlands.

To Margaret the man teetering just inside the gate looked carved of ice, as if a single blow of a tomahawk would shatter him. Splitting Moon pushed through the gathering, Two Eagles and Margaret behind him. Unsheathing his knife, he knelt to slit the man's throat as he fell.

"*Coureur de bois.* Thieving French *oueda!*"

Margaret had seen *coureurs de bois* in their encampment at the Carrying Place inside the northward turning of the Mohawk River. They brazenly robbed the Iroquois' traps, stealing their beaver to sell to their countrymen traders in Quebec and Montreal. This one looked like a *coureur de bois* and wore a beard like theirs, but there was something about him that distinguished him from the French trappers.

"Wait," she burst, gripping Splitting Moon's arm, "he's trying to say something."

"I give—you—my—word, Hannah, my—solemn word—I—will—return."

"He's not French! He's English. Pick him up, get him inside! He's freezing to death."

Grumbling, the warriors nonetheless complied and put the stranger to bed in an unused chamber of the longhouse. His icing had begun to melt, and within minutes his bunk was soaking. Margaret and Swift Doe mopped it dry, and Margaret removed his robe, moccasins and trousers and covered him with a dry bearskin.

"He's very flushed," she murmured. She set a hand to his forehead. "He's running a fever. Wake up Eight Minks and tell her to make him some camomile tea."

"The *Dauntless*. She looks dauntless; she looks like another ten minutes and it's straight to the bottom. I'm to trust life and limb to this hulk? Ah me, Seth, old chap, what a man doesn't do for filthy lucre."

Swift Doe had paused at the flap on the way out. She looked confused.

"Seth," mused Margaret. "So we know his name and that he's recently arrived. He's no *coureur de bois*. What in the world is he doing out here in the back of beyond? And by himself?"

Two Eagles came in with Benjamin. "We are going out to chase rabbits." He nodded toward the newcomer. "What do we do with him?"

"Do?"

"I think take him back outside when he is well and push him north. The nearest whiteskins are the lace-cuffs up at Fort Frontenac, at the headwaters of the Kanuwage."

"We do no such thing!" Margaret retorted. "Besides, he's English."

"Ahhh, even worse." With a black look toward the man, Two Eagles shifted Benjamin to his other arm.

Seth resumed babbling, profoundly delirious. Margaret could see that he was deathly ill.

Eight Minks entered with Swift Doe, who reported that the tea water was heating.

"It looks like pneumonia." Margaret shook her head resignedly.

"He is too sick. Camomile will not help him," said Eight Minks.

"Can't you do something?"

Eight Minks shrugged. "If I try, will you stop me in the middle of treating him and take over?"

"Please don't start on that. For pity's sake, *do* something for the poor soul."

"Go back to my chamber and tell Fox to give you some blood-root. Grate it fine and steep it in boiling water."

"This is good," said Two Eagles. "Get him on his feet so he can walk out of here." With one more glare at Seth, he stalked out with Benjamin.

Before giving the steeped root to the patient, Eight Minks added the resin of the plant and powdered leaves and seeds. Swift Doe held his head while Margaret fed him; in vain, he tried to fight them off.

"His throat must be on fire," said Margaret.

Eight Minks shook her head. "Very sick. Let us let him sleep."

Suddenly the flap lifted and in waddled Moon Dancer. Without a word of greeting to them, she brought her fist out from behind her back, opened it and blew wood ashes in Seth's face.

"Stop that!" burst Margaret.

Moon Dancer ignored her, bent and examined him. "They will not help him. He will sit with dirt in his mouth before the next sunrise."

She went out.

* * *

For the next two days Seth's labored breathing persisted, and his skin kept its faint bluish cast, which alarmed Margaret. When awake he coughed without sputum and in his delirium complained of chest and abdominal pain.

Early in the evening of the third day, Margaret was feeling his forehead for fever when he groaned and woke.

"How am I doing?" he asked, seemingly lucid.

"You sound coherent for the first time. That's a good sign," she said. "Up to now you've been raving." When he started up on one elbow, she eased him back down. "How do you feel?"

"On fire, from my throat down to the pit of my stomach." He coughed, grimacing with the pain.

"Easy. It looks like your color's improving. It's hard to tell, but I think your fever's starting to come down, too. Apart from your pain, are you comfortable?"

"Reasonably. Sick as six dogs, but I'll live, I hope."

"Do you feel up to talking?"

"See here, where are my manners? You saved my life, you're nursing me, waiting on me hand and foot, and I haven't even told you my name," he said.

"Seth," she said.

"Wilson," he added.

"I'm Margaret Addison, formerly of Bedworth in Warwickshire, now an Onneyuttahagen by way of Quebec."

"I'm from—Southampton."

"You don't seem sure."

"Southampton." He eyed her questioningly. "What on earth are you doing here?"

She detailed the experiences that had brought her to Onneyuttahage to stay. He listened openmouthed.

"You're married to an Oneida? You have a child?"

"Benjamin. After my father."

"And do you—fit in here? Are you happy? Content?"

"Very."

"Astonishing."

"Is it? I suppose. Tell me about yourself."

He told her his experiences since his arrival in Boston,

dismissing the crossing with a couple of sentences and skipping over the Keatons. He described the missionaries' ordeal as prisoners of the Mohawks, his and Hopkins' escape, the Virginian's death on the trail. He brought her up to his arrival.

"And who is Hannah?" she asked. He looked surprised. "You mentioned her several times in your babbling."

He told her about Hannah and her tragic death. "How terrible." Margaret shook her head. "And you're a Congregational missionary." She grinned.

"You find that amusing?"

"Incongruous. When you showed up at the gate, the way you were dressed, your beard—everybody assumed you were a *coureur de bois*. They infest these woods; they steal the tribes' furs and cheat them in trading. A wicked lot. The outside gate was very nearly as far as you got."

"I'll say it again. You saved my life."

"Not exactly."

"You're saving it now; my ministering angel. 'I was sick and ye visited me.' Matthew twenty-five."

"I'm curious. Was Onneyuttahage your original destination? Or did you just happen by, driven here by the storm?"

"It was our planned destination."

"And you've come all this way to try and convert the Oneida?"

"That was our assignment. It still is mine."

"I wish you luck. Our people are not exactly clamoring for religion."

"A skeptic," Seth smiled.

"I'm just being realistic. The Jesuits have been trying for a hundred years, with scant success. Only the Canadian Mohawks up on the St. Lawrence have become Christians, actually, the Caughnawagas. There's been a little success with the Onondagans. I don't know about the Cayugas and Senecas. I do know about us."

"Interesting."

"What?"

"You say 'our' and 'us.' You really do consider yourself an Oneida?"

"Of course."

"Of course. Why wouldn't you? It just strikes me as so—unusual. You're not a prisoner, you weren't abducted. It's your own doing, purely voluntary it was. I know there've been men who joined Indian tribes, but a woman—"

"Purely voluntary."

"Let me guess. Are you Church of England?"

"Yes. Non-practicing." She gestured toward her surroundings. "No vicars here, no hymnbooks, prayer books, Bibles."

"I know of no religion that comes from books; it's all in the heart. Which, if you think about it, means there's nothing to prevent you practicing your religion."

She got up, averting her eyes. "Am I embarrassing you?" he asked. "Sorry."

"You must understand one thing, Mr. Wilson, Reverend. I made a clean break with my family, with England, with everything in my past. I've become as Oneida as anyone born here. Oh, I don't deny God's existence. I don't worship Oneida spirits. My religion is—personal."

"Isn't everyone's? The Congregational church strongly emphasizes individuality. We have no fixed liturgy. We're disposed to emphasize the free and active movement of the Spirit in worship."

"Can we talk about something else?"

"I'm sermonizing, I'm sorry. What *shall* we talk about?"

"First, are you hungry?"

"Famished."

"Another good sign. There's a kettle of venison broth on the fire." She filled a bowl and sat and fed him. "*Aque ohnekakeri.*"

"*Aque . . .*"

"*Ohnekakeri.*"

"Are you fluent in their language?" Seth asked.

"I get by. Still learning. They have some words as long as our sentences. Keep swallowing, Seth, you've got to get down as much as you can, reduce your fever. You won't really start mending till it's normal."

He touched his neck. "My throat's viciously sore."

"Finish this and I'll get you a gargle."

"What sort of gargle?"

"It's perfectly safe. I've no intention of poisoning you," she said. "It's made of the leaves of the bur marigold. Very efficacious."

Two Eagles returned and, without looking at either of them, went to the corner and put Benjamin down.

"Two Eagles," said Seth, "I apologize for dropping in on you uninvited, burdening you like this, disrupting your lives. I must be honest. I planned to come, to preach the gospel of Jesus Christ to you and the others, to bring one and all to the Lord's table. To enlighten."

Two Eagles' grunt said he was unimpressed.

"With, to be sure, the help of your dear wife."

"Oh no!" cried Margaret. "I'm no missionary. By the way, you'll be needing the chiefs' permission to go among the people."

"Oh, I'll get it, I'll get it," Seth said.

"Just don't plan on drafting me to assist or interpret. I really can't," Margaret warned. She made to protest further, but Two Eagles, eyeing him with all too evident disapproval, interrupted.

"How did you make it this far in this weather?"

"A miracle on the par with the loaves and fishes." Seth laughed. Then he winced, his hand going to his chest. "It really was a miracle. I'd never been in any woods before, certainly not like this forest primeval. I don't know the first thing about living off the land. I found out one thing: Necessity actually is the mother of invention."

Two Eagles' face reflected his confusion.

"Babe in the woods," explained Margaret.

"Exactly. I was reduced to eating bark. Only I had no idea which trees."

"Basswood bark you can eat," said Two Eagles. "Not elm bark unless you are really starving. It is too bitter."

"As I think back on it now, I could have sampled one that was poisonous." He went on, detailing his experiences. "You remember my telling you about the bear's dean I ducked into? It was filled with all sorts of vile stenches: rotting vermin, rotting fruit, plus the bear himself. But oddly enough there were no droppings. How could that be?"

She repeated this to Two Eagles.

"Tappen."

"What did he say?" Seth asked.

Two Eagles explained in Oneida, slapping a hand against his backside.

Margaret translated. "He says that when the bear goes in to hibernate in early fall he stuffs his rear end with leaves, blocking the intestine. He doesn't eat, doesn't release droppings. The people call it *tappen*; it means obstruction."

"Fascinating."

"This is fascinating," said Two Eagles. He picked up one of Seth's winter moccasins. "Where did you find these?"

"You remember my telling you about the Mohawks' ambushing the deer poachers?" Seth asked Margaret.

"Where?" Two Eagles asked, turning the moccasin over, rubbing the fur and smelling it before casting it aside.

"I can't pinpoint the exact spot. Wait, when I went on my way afterwards it wasn't long before I came to where the river turned north-northwest."

"The Te-ugé-ga."

"The Mohawk," said Margaret.

"Yes, and on the other side I remember seeing a camp of some kind: shacks, lean-tos."

"Da-yä´-hoo-wä´-quat," said Two Eagles to Margaret.

"The Carrying Place," said Margaret to Seth. "Where the *coureurs de bois* assemble to dry their pelts before turning them over to the traders who come down from Quebec."

"The ambush you saw was in Maquen Territory," said Two Eagles.

"No, I'm sure it was Mohawk."

"Maquen *is* Mohawk," explained Margaret.

"But these winter moccasins are not Mohawk," said Two Eagles, retrieving one. "Not buckskin, not moose-hide. Sealskin."

"Seals live in the St. Lawrence," said Margaret.

"Cha-go-tenta," said Two Eagles.

Margaret picked up the other moccasin and examined it. "Which tribe up there wears this type?"

"Montagnais," Two Eagles answered. "The Iron Axes. They live on both sides of the Kanuwage in birch-bark wigwams and in the winter under the ground. They are bad people, they are our enemies."

"Why would they come all the way down here to poach?" Margaret asked.

Two Eagles shrugged. "Perhaps this winter the hunting is poor up around the river. Perhaps they just got their bellies full of seal blubber and fish."

"Only two of them got away," said Seth.

Two Eagles' face clouded. "That is bad. The Mohawks should not have let any get away to report back to their chiefs. They will come back in great numbers and avenge the massacre."

He went out. Margaret said to Seth reassuringly, "Not something you need be concerned about."

"It really is ironic how all those deaths saved my life. I'd never have made it halfway here without their furs and dry food. Do you know, I'm feeling better by the minute. How long do you think before I'll be fit enough to get up?"

"I'm no doctor, but you show all the signs of pneumonia," Margaret replied. "I know them; my mother was stricken with it four years ago. It's winter. Better to prepared to spend at least a month in bed, maybe six weeks."

He began coughing suddenly and was red-faced and glistening with sweat before he could get it under control.

"Let me get that gargle," said Margaret. She paused at the flap. "But first you must promise you won't try to convert me."

"I wouldn't dream of it. Besides, you're already a Christian."

"And don't count on me to help you."

"That, I'm sorry to say, mystifies me."

"Think about it. If you're successful here, all well and good. If you fail and in the process perhaps rub some people the wrong way and then leave, I'll be staying. I'm not too popular around here already. I'd prefer not to aggravate the situation."

"I understand."

"I'll ask Eight Minks to speak to the three chiefs for you, get their permission to go among the people. That's the best I can do."

67

Two Eagles was helping Splitting Moon stuff moss in the chinks in his chamber walls, against the winter cold. Fox, Red Paint and Anger Maker also helped, but repairs went slowly: the work was secondary to the opportunity to talk.

"I should have slit his throat when he walked in and collapsed," growled Splitting Moon. "Then when it turned out he was English and not French, I would have apologized to Mar-gar-et."

Two Eagles jeered. "That would have been almost as stupid as this, waiting until winter is half over to chink your walls."

"To let him into your longhouse was stupid," responded Splitting Moon. "Now how do you get rid of him?"

"He is sick."

"He could be sick into spring," said Anger Maker. "And pretend to be for many moons longer, maybe even until you come back with Blue Creek's head. I would not like a whiteskin stranger living in my longhouse with my whiteskin wife while I was away."

"You have no wife," said Two Eagles, "so you cannot have an opinion."

"He wants to convert our people to his Christianity," said Fox. He threw a clump of moss at Splitting Moon, who ducked. Red Paint, who was less quick, caught it in the face and threw it back.

"Under his furs he is a black robe?" Anger Maker asked.

"Neh," said Fox. "Black cloak."

Red Paint frowned. "What is that?"

"The English religion," said Two Eagles. "Margaret's."

"What do we need with their religion?" Red Paint asked and spat. "What do they think is wrong with ours?"

"When he is well again, tell him to go," said Splitting Moon.

"You. But be prepared to go through Margaret," said Two Eagles. He went on to tell them about Seth's sealhide winter moccasins.

"Those Iron Axes could come back and destroy whichever castle the Maquens came from," observed Red Paint.

"I told him that," said Two Eagles. "I doubt they were from Onekahoncka," he added, squishing a handful of moss into a slender tube and stuffing a crack. "They must have been from Schandisse or Tenotoge."

Anger Maker grunted. "If, as you said, the ambush was near Da-yä'-hoo-wä'-quat, it would be Tenotoge. They had better sharpen their knives, post guards on their high platforms and keep their eyes on Gâ'-oh's teeth."

68

While Two Eagles and the others chinked the walls of Splitting Moon's chamber Margaret hovered about her patient like an anxious mother over her ailing first-born. In the meantime, Eight Minks had taken Seth on as a personal challenge, dosing him with all kinds of medications out of her extensive collection. But recovery eluded him. His fever had come down, but not as much as Margaret would have liked. He lost the bluish tint to his skin, but healthy color did not take its place. Most worrisome of all was his seemingly incurable cough. His throat and chest were not being given a chance to heal, and she feared that his lungs would be permanently scarred.

She went down the passageway to Eight Minks seeking optimism, but Eight Minks could offer little. "It is *augustuske*'s favorite illness."

Margaret shook her head resignedly. "It's got such a hold on him, he just can't seem to throw it off. I worry so—"

"Why? I know you are both English, but you do not share his blood. You do not even know him. Besides, whether he gets better or worse is up to the spirits. I have done all I can."

"On top of everything else he's lost his three friends and everything he owns. A missionary without even a Bible." Her forehead creased.

"His religion is all in his head, like a black robe. Why are you making that face? What is it now?"

"I don't know. Something just isn't right. He *says* he's a missionary and I believe him, but he's unlike any cleric I've ever seen."

"What is wrong with him?"

"He's just not—I don't know—professionally solemn, grave enough. And he lacks fire, much less that glazed, near-fanatical look that most of them get when they're talking about God. And he's not all that holier-than-thou."

"What is that?"

"A superior attitude, as if God is speaking directly to a particular individual."

"Why would he pose as a missionary?"

"Why not? It at least gets him access to the castles."

"Could he be a *coureur de bois* after all?"

Margaret shook her head emphatically. *"Neh."*

"One thing I do not understand," said Eight Minks. "Why come straight to Onneyuttahage? Why bypass the three Mohawk castles?"

"He didn't bypass Onekahoncka. The three of them didn't get a chance to. Obviously their run-in with the Mohawks would discourage them from dealing with any." She paused. "Still, you do have a point. Seth did say Onneyuttahage was their original destination setting out from Boston. Let's go see him."

Seth was awake, not looking too well but up to managing a smile of greeting. Margaret gazed straight at him. "I'm curious," she said. "Why did you start out from Boston to come directly here?"

"This was to be our starting point. Our information was that the Oneidas were ... less hostile than the Mohawks toward strangers. Reverend Allbright and Reverend Frame felt that if we met with success here, we could work our way back toward the Hudson, go back to the first Mohawk castle over the border, perhaps bringing with us two or three converts from here to help pave the way."

"Is that still the plan?"

He hazarded a light laugh and grimaced. "I really can't think that far ahead, not yet."

Eight Minks, who had gone out, returned with two bear robes, and dropped them on the floor. She stood over the patient.

"The embers in your head are not cooling fast enough. And your cough is like a thorn branch in your throat. You should not be lying down. Better you sit up." They propped him up on the folded bear robes. "Stay in a sitting position all day, all night. No more lying down."

"You're the doctor," Seth grinned.

She looked to Margaret.

"Doctor, *Anna-ha-ta-toa*."

Eight Minks grinned and went out.

"I've been thinking about Benjamin," Seth said. "I know he's just a babe, but one is never too young to accept Christ. Infant membership in the Congregational church isn't the result of baptism. It results from the covenant relation already acquired by birth in a Christian household. That gives rightness to the sacrament. And, happily, it only takes one parent to be a believer."

"A Congregationalist you mean," Margaret said flatly.

"Any recognized church. You'll find us much more tolerant than some. You're a Christian. You'll want your son to be, I'm sure. Which leaves Two Eagles."

"I very much doubt he'll want to become a Christian."

"Has he said he doesn't?"

"I know my husband." She folded her arms across her chest.

"Well, all in God's own good time. That's one of what you might call the most convenient things about accepting Christ—there's never any rush. Tell me, do you by any chance have a Bible?"

"No, I told you I didn't. I came back here from Quebec with the clothes on my back, nothing else."

"Except your first communion ring."

"This? It's just my birthstone: beryl for October."

"A gift from your parents. Bit of England around your finger."

"Mmmm."

"I remember now you did say you had no Bible. Pity. When Benjamin gets a little older, what better, more fascinating stories to read him than Bible stories? Daniel in the lion's den, Noah and the ark, David and Goliath."

"I think I can trust my memory," she said.

"Of course." He continued. "Let's get back to Two Eagles."

"I wouldn't approach him if I were you; I'm sure you'll find others more receptive."

"You wouldn't know their names, would you?"

"No," she said, "it just stands to reason there'd be some."

He smiled. "I'm to be on my own."

She smiled. "I thought we'd already agreed on that."

69

Six weeks passed. *Augustuske*'s grip appeared to be loosening. The sunny days were unseasonably warm, the chill wind at night blew less frequently, less fiercely. Seth began improving. He followed up on his earlier request to Eight Minks: would she speak to the chiefs for him, asking permission for him to introduce the people to the gospel of Jesus Christ? She agreed but with little enthusiasm.

Two days later she came back with disappointing news. "Sho-non-ses, Chief His Longhouse does not agree, does not disagree. But sees no harm in it. Chief Hat-ya-tone-nent-ha, He-swallows-his-own-body-from-the-foot, and Chief O-dat-she-dah, Carries-a-quiver, refuse you permission."

"But why? What reason did they give you?"

Eight Minks shrugged. She had set out a pile of fungus and mushrooms on a robe and was sitting cross-legged separating them.

"I don't understand. Did you tell them that I'm English, remind them that their warriors fought on the English side, that we're longtime friends?"

"That," said Margaret, "may be your problem."

"Problem?"

"It's true the Iroquois fought alongside the English against the French, but when the war ended and it came time to formulate a peace treaty, the English deserted us."

"I never heard that."

"Listen to her," said Eight Minks.

"Just before the two sides got together at Massowaganine, Sir William Phips sent word to the sachems. The English colonies no longer could supply material support to the Five Nations to help defend their lands against French colonists and their Indian allies. Unfortunately, that support was the reason why the chiefs had originally backed the English. So suddenly the Iroquois weren't negotiating a peace but would have to sue for whatever crumbs the French would give them.

"The two sides are still wrangling. I don't know what your superiors back in Boston told you about the tribes, but they no longer have any fondness for the English, that I can guarantee."

"That's not important." Seth paused to ponder, then resumed. "It's not that I'm English or French or Scandinavian that matters. It's that first and foremost I'm a missionary of God. Nationality doesn't enter into it. Our Father in Heaven recognizes no nationalities; all men are brothers in Christ. The chiefs must be made to understand. I must speak to them directly."

Eight Minks looked up from her sorting. "They are not interested," she said.

"Ask them to let me explain. Please."

"I will ask, they will refuse. As Margaret says, you are still an English who deserted us."

"Just please ask. I appreciate it, I really do." He paused. "What is that gray fungus? I saw it on the trail; I passed it up, I was afraid to taste it."

"It is good, *ana-tag-a*; very tasty." She held some up. "Try it."

"I'll take your word for it." He shook his head. "To think I nearly starved to death because I was afraid to try it! The wilderness is no place for the fainthearted. What are those?" He indicated silk-puffball and little mushrooms with white gills and smooth, silvery stems.

"*Oně^n′ să′ wá ně′* and *oně^n′ să.*"

"Everything you see are what you might call emergency rations," explained Margaret, "useful on the trail in winter. They keep forever."

Eight Minks smiled. "Almost." Seth was staring at her.

Reluctantly, she yielded. "I will talk to the chiefs. But do not expect them to change their minds."

As she went out, Margaret lay a comforting hand on Seth's. "She'll work on His Longhouse, he'll work on the others. She'll get around him. She's very clever at getting her own way."

"I pray."

She smiled. This new friend was having a distinct effect on her. He was not just the first white man she'd seen in going on two years, but English, in tongue, in heart and mind. England, Warwickshire, Bedworth, home. Back they came. Home, the dark ancient Arden forest, the farmsteads, the cattle lowing late on a summer afternoon, the trees heavy with fruit in the orchards near the Valley of Evesham; the beautiful Avon River of Shakespeare's inspiration, splendid Warwick Castle, the ruined Kenilworth, the spires of Coventry. Home, the parties and balls, fairs, and festivals, holidays and the joy and contentment of life in the heart of the Midlands. So many golden threads of memory gathered in his fist and tugged at her heart as he reminisced about their England. Since settling here, as she expected, she had been prey to nostalgia; it came and went, she dealt with it. But now he nurtured it, and it grew daily, flooding her thoughts.

Even though she'd carefully made her decision to stay

with Two Eagles forever, with no possibility of ever returning home, regret at leaving her family lingered.

Now Seth was bringing England and home rushing back. Curiously, though, he never mentioned Warwickshire or Bedworth. He was very clever; too clever?

70

To Margaret's surprise, Seth Wilson was granted his audience with the chiefs. It confirmed Eight Minks' extraordinary powers of persuasion. Margaret suspected that Eight Minks had challenged the chiefs, telling them something to the effect that Seth's God was the English spirit: "They have but one god. Are not our spirits powerful enough to overwhelm him? Would they not welcome the chance to prove their superiority?" But now it was up to Seth to complete the job.

Margaret volunteered to interpret for him. She did not feel she'd be intruding; in fact, it was the least she could do. Her run-in with Moon Dancer was a closed issue. The chiefs, she knew, would not hold it against her. Unlike some Englishmen, Indians did not nurse grudges.

He Swallows had fought on the English side in the war and knew some English, but he could hardly be expected to use it purely for Seth's convenience. Carries-a-quiver and His Longhouse spoke next to no English. The audience was held in the same chamber in which Margaret and Swift Doe had been tried, but this time no elders were present.

Margaret explained her presence in Oneida, which, she could immediately see, pleased them. Seth opened with his request and his reasons supporting it.

* * *

Margaret had coached him. He knew from the Reverend Allgood and Reverend Frame that the Iroquois had no form of divine worship or prayers of any kind. They had no knowledge of God. Their religion was based exclusively on myths. To them, the spirits who influenced human destiny were birds, beasts and reptiles. Spirits dwelt in waterfalls, lakes and rivers, which gave ear to man's pleas and influenced his life for good or evil. A mysterious and inexplicable power rested in inanimate things, which also listened to man's appeals. Through all of Nature's works and those of man, nothing existed, however seemingly trivial, that might not be endowed with power for good or evil.

Carries-a-quiver opened the questioning. "Who are your gods?"

"We have but one God: the Father, Creator and Sustainer of the universe, infinite in wisdom, goodness and love. And we believe that in Christ He reconciles the world to Himself."

He Swallows grunted, understanding Seth's English before it was translated. "Only one god? We have many. We have Areskoue, god of the sun, who becomes Ondouetaete, god of war, when we need his power. A-ke-so-tah is our god of thunder; Tarenyowaga, the god who speaks to men in their dreams. Many, many gods, not just one."

"And spirits," added Carries-a-quiver. "Like the spirits of the Quarters of the four winds. Gâ'-oh is the north wind, the Wind Giant; at the entrance to his longhouse are a bear, a panther, a moose and a fawn. When the north wind blows strong, the Bear is prowling the sky; if the west wind tears the sky, the Panther is whining. When the east wind blows chill with rain, the Moose is spreading his breath and when the south winds wafts warm breezes, the Fawn is returning to its Doe."

Out of the corner of her eye, Margaret studied Seth for his reaction. He looked properly impressed. A good start. She had heard that many missionaries made the mistake of disparaging the people's myths, even to condemning them as sinful.

"Have you giants and monsters in your religion?" He Swallows asked.

"No."

All three chiefs reacted almost pityingly. His Longhouse shook his head.

"We have many," said Carries-a-quiver. "We have dwarfs, too."

"Our God stands alone, he needs no assistance. By himself he embraces all human dreams and desires, meets all needs. He is a god of all mercy, all goodness. And a just god in this world and the next."

His Longhouse punctuated Margaret's translation with a grunt. "Our gods do not dispense justice in this world or the next. Our spirits control justice. Good spirits give good luck; bad spirits give illness, wickedness, misfortune, everything bad."

"What else do you believe?" Carries-a-quiver asked Seth.

"We believe in the immortality of the soul."

Carries-a-quiver nodded. "We believe in the soul. We were the first to."

"When you die," He Swallows asked, "is your soul removed to the Village of the Dead, to be rewarded or punished as it deserves?"

"We call the places of the afterlife heaven and hell. But they are not places of bliss or torment. We believe that physical death is not the end of life, that God's justice cannot be escaped, and that it will be heaven to be with God and hell to be without Him."

"They have no concept of heaven or hell," whispered Margaret to Seth.

"All spirits in the Village of the Dead sit in the posture of the sick," said His Longhouse. He demonstrated, crouching. "All day. And when night comes they hunt the shades of animals with the shades of blows and arrows among the shades of trees and rocks."

"These are just some of our beliefs," added Carries-a-quiver. "We have many, many. They are like the stars. What else does he who lives in the sky tell you to believe?"

"To define our faith in Him. Also, we believe in sin and salvation."

"What is sin?"

"Opposition or indifference to the will of God. God, however, as Jesus revealed Him, is willing to forgive. When a person repents in faith, God accepts him—and when God has accepted a person, he need have no fear of his future in this world or the next. We say that he is saved."

Their faces said that they didn't altogether understand this and Margaret could see that Seth wasn't eager to go into detailed explanations. What they didn't understand tended to impress them. They asked him many questions; he was quick with every response and brimmed with self-confidence. He knew his subject well; there was no hesitancy, no uncertainty. They could not help but be impressed.

"If you speak to our people of your god," said Carries-a-quiver, "you will make them forget their own gods and spirits."

"Not so," Seth protested. "All I would ask is that they consider the one, true—ahem, consider *our* god, what He offers, how He nurtures and protects. I would never ask any man to abandon his beliefs. I tell him about God, I answer his questions, that is all I do. People *come* to the Lord's table, they are not pushed to it."

He Swallows shook his head, pushed down the corners of his mouth and furrowed his brow. "There is a great difference between you and us. You whiteskins have a different look and ways and customs. Everything about us is different, because our worlds are different, with the Wide Water between us. Is this not true?"

"It is," said Seth.

"Since the difference between us is so great in so many

things and ways, is it not sensible to believe that we should have a different religion in accordance with our understanding?"

"It is true that our differences are many. But what of our similarities? We both have heads with brains, legs, arms, feet, hands. Like you, we experience joy and sorrow, pain and illness; the same illnesses the world over. Like you, we argue with our neighbor and make war and make peace. We both use the things around us. Nature gives us the water, the wind, the sun, the trees and their wood, the rocks and their strength, the fish from the waters, the sun and rain for our crops. The things that are the same on both sides of the Wide Water are too numerous to count. Is this not true?

"Why would Nature give us so much that is the same if she didn't see us as the same, as brothers? And don't brothers have the same father? Our father is father to all nations, to all men, wherever they live, whatever their color.

"Our God is a god who asks only that men believe in Him and in His only begotten son, Jesus Christ. And how can any man not believe in a god whose hand has made and framed the whole fabric of heaven and earth? He has hung out the globe of this world, resting it on nothing. He has drawn over the canopy of heaven. He has created that fountain and center of light, heat and influence in this lower world, the indefatigable sun. The stars, the moon, the seas and vast mountains are His work, all wrought by Him."

Margaret translated, worried lest Seth's words sound effusive and self-serving. Surprisingly, they had the reverse effect. Whether it was his sincerity or the suddenness of his declamation, after speaking so softly for so long, he impressed his listeners deeply. Their expressions clearly showed it.

They talked briefly among themselves; Margaret and Seth were dismissed.

* * *

His Longhouse came to the head of the passageway. "Wait for me. I will come back shortly and tell you our decision."

Just inside the longhouse entrance, out of the wind, Margaret and Seth stood waiting. His Longhouse came shuffling back, nodding and smiling at Seth.

"You can talk to anyone who is willing to listen. But only those willing to, no one else. And you will have a time limit."

"How long?" Margaret asked.

"He will know that when he is told to stop."

Off he padded. Seth raised a fist in triumph. "Hallelujah!"

Seth's performance had surprised her: he'd proved shrewd, tactful, resourceful, skillfully deflecting their arguments, piquing their curiosity, responding with explanations that went down easily, gradually eroding their fears of invasion by his "foreign" god.

She put to rest any feelings that he was not what he claimed to be. Now she believed him, accepted him. He was a missionary exemplar, God's agent equipped both intellectually and spiritually for the task. He might just end up converting the whole tribe.

They started back to the longhouse. Dripping icicles and melting snow crust testified to the balminess of the day, which brought thoughts of the ice breaking in Lake Oneida and the consequences for Two Eagles. There would be no stopping him, Margaret concluded. At stake was his honor.

They were preparing to enter the longhouse when Seth was seized by a wracking cough. By the time she got him into his bunk his face was crimson, and, to her dismay, for the first time since he arrived at Onneyuttahage, he spat up blood.

VII

NIGHT OF THE IRON AXES

71

The physical effort required for Seth to persuade the chiefs had clearly been too much for him. Not until four days later did his bleeding stop, and six days after that he was able to get out of bed to stay. Eight Minks was pleased, Margaret overjoyed. More critically, Two Eagles took the recovery as a sign for Seth not to begin proselytizing but to leave.

Husband and wife discussed it in bed late one night.

"Let him at least try," she said. "After all he's been through, he's at least entitled to that."

"A waste of time. No one is interested in hearing about *Gai' wiios'-tŭk*," Two Eagles grumbled.

"The Christian religion is my religion, too. Don't demean it."

"*Augustuske* is over. Your Seth will not have to fight storms to get back, like he did coming. Tell him to start out right away."

"I will not! What he does is none of my business," she protested.

"You have made him your business, caring for him, interpreting for him, befriending him. I want him to go."

She propped on one elbow, smoothed back his hair and waggled a reproving finger. "You're jealous."

"I am *not!*"

"You are. What's more, you're afraid."

"Of him? That is stupid!"

"Of me. You'll be leaving soon. You're worried, afraid of what might happen while you're away."

"What would?"

"You're disgusting!"

"Me?" he burst.

"You know what I'm saying. You don't trust me. Something very nice for a wife to find out about her husband. Congratulations!"

"I trust you," Two Eagles said.

"Not with him around, you don't. It's really ridiculous. Ludicrous. With Seth and me it's not like that."

"Like what?"

"We've become friends, that's all. Isn't it perfectly natural we should? He's English. We talk and talk. How can we avoid becoming friendly? And what on earth is wrong with it?"

"He does not belong here."

"I do?" Her stare in the dim light challenged Two Eagles.

"*Nyoh.* You are my wife, and Oneida. He is a nosy black cloak blundering in where he is not wanted, to turn people's brains in their skulls. I do not understand the chiefs, to give their permission. Old age must be shrinking their brains." He eyed her suspiciously. "What did you say to make them change their minds?"

"Nothing. When we sat down he did all the talking. This is insane, what are we squabbling about?"

"Him."

"There's no reason—" Margaret insisted.

Two Eagles frowned. "He must leave. I went fishing this morning when you were with him, as you are all the time. The ice is beginning to soften. Far out there is a hole starting. The sun will make it grow. In half a moon the water will swallow the ice and I will be leaving."

"I know—" She nuzzled him playfully, pulled his head down and kissed him. "Go, my darling, find him, come back. Quick, quick, quick."

"Quick, quick, I will do my best."

"I could strangle Moon Dancer!"

He grinned. "Do not do that. The elders will order my throat cut."

He seemed to have momentarily forgotten about Seth and his unwanted presence. Two Eagles sent his hand down her back and began gently stroking her buttocks; she could feel her place beginning to tingle and, seizing his mouth with hers, she probed for his tongue. His body came alive in response; they locked together, entwining their legs, rolling slowly about under the bearskin. He kicked it off. She felt his member hard against the plane of her stomach and willed it downward to slip between her thighs, touch her place, ignite it and slowly enter her.

And it was clear to her that he, only he, was why she was here, why she would stay forever. To be with the only man alive for her.

Silence held the night. Their heavy breathing invaded it as passion took possession.

A thud. They glanced upward; another. An arrow dislodged a piece of bark siding. A fire arrow flew through the opening at an angle, crossing the bed, shuddering to rest within a foot of the sleeping Benjamin.

Two Eagles jumped up: *"Oetseira!"*

72

The surprise attack came from all sides. Fire arrows rained down, hideous screaming rent the air. Her heart thundering, Margaret threw on clothes with trembling hands, grabbed Benjamin and followed Two Eagles up to the entrance. On the observation platforms at the two front corners of the castle both guards had been killed, one taking an arrow in the throat, and falling to the ground, the other sprawled on his platform with two arrows in his chest. Fire arrows continued whirring in over all four walls. Flames leaped at the top of the entrance gate. Already, roofs had caught fire, Two Eagles and Margaret's longhouse among them. She gawked in horror as the flames spread quickly. Swift Doe emerged sleepy-eyed and yawning with her boys; Fox hurried Eight Minks up the passageway to join them.

"Out," bawled Two Eagles above the din. "Now!"

"How?" yelled Fox. "There is fire all around us. Who is it, who would attack us?"

"Huron snakes, who else?"

Two Eagles threw a glance toward the rear entrance. Fire had already partially consumed the gate. Now the palisade on all sides was sending up tongues of flame. A ring of black smoke encircled the castle, rising, blotting out the stars. The screams of the dying were all around them. The corner where the slain guard lay on his platform was burning furiously; they watched as it collapsed, bringing down platform and corpse. Margaret pointed across the way. Fire was eating a hole in the timber uprights, flames licking upward to create an opening.

"Run!" snapped Two Eagles.

Margaret clutched Benjamin close as they sprinted across the open ground, throwing themselves through the hole, stiffening, expecting a fusilade of arrows. But only a few came whirring at them from both sides, and the billowing smoke afforded the Oneidas cover. Then Eight Minks, whom Fox was dragging along by one arm, was struck in the breast. She froze, her face exploded in terror. Gurgling escaped her throat as her hand started for the arrow—she dropped and fell dead.

"Run!" yelled Two Eagles to the others who had stopped, staring.

Fox was screaming; he snatched up Eight Minks, staggering under her weight, struggling forward to catch up. Two Eagles fell back and took Eight Minks' body from him. Fox looked deranged, eyes bulging from their sockets, mouth gaping, shaking all over, and wielding his tomahawk at invisible foes on all sides as he stumbled forward.

Into the woods they fled. In time the din behind them grew fainter. Looking back they could see only occasional flames licking high up and the smoke obscuring the sky completely. Margaret sat down comforting the crying Benjamin.

"Eight Minks . . ." gasped Swift Doe, dropping down beside Margaret in a daze, holding her younger sons, one in each arm. "Eight Minks!" Fear rounded the boys' eyes. One whimpered.

Two Eagles arrived, setting down Eight Minks' body. Margaret groaned. Releasing her sons, kneeling beside Eight Minks, Swift Doe began swaying and keening.

"Where's Seth?" burst Margaret, looking about frantically.

The others looked dumbly at one another; in the confusion he had been forgotten.

"He must have got away," said Two Eagles.

"He would have had to come out the same hole we did," rasped Margaret. "Didn't anybody see him?"

Before anyone could speak he came crashing through the underbrush. Hare, who had led the flight to safety, turned toward him, smiling—then out of the darkness an arrow flew, catching Hare full in the chest. Swift Doe screamed, shooting to her feet, lunging for him. A second arrow flew. Seth threw himself against her, catching it in the shoulder. A warrior came running up screaming, swinging his ax. Two Eagles' knife flew across the open space, finding the attacker's stomach. He doubled over and died babbling, crimsoning the snow at his feet. Two Eagles wrenched his ax from him.

"Iron. He is an Iron Ax." He jammed the ax in his belt and looked about. "We are not safe yet, we must move on. Toward the stream. Can you walk?" he asked Seth.

His expression said he was willing to try. Fox had recovered and pulled the arrow from Seth's shoulder. Pain twisted his handsome face. Margaret tore a piece from her skirt, folding it into a pad. Fox applied it to the wound, and Seth held it tightly under his shirt, grimacing. Fox returned to mourning his loss. Down on his knees, he held his head between his hands, shaking it slowly, staring down at his dead wife. Swift Doe was kneeling, holding the dead Hare in her arms, rocking, sobbing. Margaret went to her. Two Eagles picked up Hare's body, Fox picked up Eight Minks'. They started out.

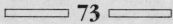

73

Considering the suddenness and ferocity of the attack, the Oneidas' casualties turned out relatively few. The great clouds of smoke that gathered around Onneyuttahage helped greatly to cover the people's escape. But the destruction was complete: every timber in the palisade, every longhouse. Black rubble blanketed the site when Two Eagles, Margaret and the others wandered back long after the attackers had withdrawn.

Twenty-one bodies were found, eleven of them children. Two Eagles' ax and bare hands dug graves for Eight Minks and Hare. Their unwrapped bodies were buried. Swift Doe now had three loved ones in the burial ground. Her mourning period for Bone had ended; now Hare would command her grief. His Longhouse had quick-wittedly climbed into a food storage hole in the floor of an adjacent chamber, covered himself with a wet mooseskin and waited until the attackers withdrew and the last fire died. He Swallows and Carries-a-quiver had fled into the woods with most of the others.

Two Eagles was examining the iron ax he had taken

from Hare's killer when Splitting Moon and Anger Maker came up to him.

"The Iron Axes did this," announced Splitting Moon, ever the oracle of the obvious. Two Eagles accorded him a pitying look and grunted. "Why?" Splitting Moon went on, "Why should the seal fuckers attack our castle?"

"I think they made a mistake," said Two Eagles. "I think these were from the same tribe of Iron Axes that the Maquen ambushed near Tenotoge. They came seeking vengeance thinking Onneyuttahage was Tenotoge."

"How could they make such a stupid mistake?" said Splitting Moon. "Onneyuttahage is not even close to Tenotoge."

Two Eagles shrugged. "Who knows how?"

"We can ask them when we catch up with them," said Anger Maker. "We must avenge this, go after them while their tracks are still fresh in the snow. Their winter village should not be hard to find. It has to be up by the Kanuwage."

"How do you expect to find men you do not know?" Splitting Moon asked.

"I will know them when I see them," said Anger Maker. "Some of their faces are stamped on my brain. There is one with one eye halfway down his cheek; I have never seen such a face. Another with his whole head painted red and the tip of his nose cut off."

"What difference which tribe we track down?" said Splitting Moon, thumbing the tooth of his tooth-ball tomahawk. "Right tribe or wrong, they are all Iron Axes."

Two Eagles was chewing on the knuckle of his index finger plunged into thought, staring at the bloodied snow between two charred timbers. "You two want to go running off after them and leave our families with this?" he murmured. "Everything destroyed, not so much as a kettle holder still standing? *Neh*, I say let the Iron Axes wait. We must first rebuild."

"You rebuild," said Splitting Moon. "I am going after the murdering seal fuckers."

"My friend," said Two Eagles, "you talk like a small *rocksongwa* with his first bow. Shooting before you aim. We will go after them. It does not have to be right away. First the walls, then the Iron Axes."

The chiefs assembled the warriors and asked for volunteers for a raiding party. Two Eagles counted 102 able-bodied veterans of the seven-year war against the French and proposed a plan whereby two thirds of the warriors would remain to protect the people and help rebuild Onneyuttahage at a site yet to be selected. The remaining thirty-four men would arm themselves and set out for Montagnais country in the north.

Two Eagles returned to the campsite the survivors had made by a stream and explained the decision to Margaret.

"Why you?" she asked.

"Splitting Moon is going," he said. "Anger Maker and Red Paint."

"What about Fox?"

"He—has already left."

"You mean you let him?"

"How could I stop him? They killed his wife."

"I ask again, why do you have to go?" Her voice rose in exasperation.

"Why not? Should I not help to avenge this slaughter and when that is done go on and find Blue Creek? I was going after him anyway, *neh*?"

"You think anybody cares about him now? After this?"

"This has nothing to do with Turtle Skin. I agreed to go, I go; it is a matter of honor."

"Well, I admit I was reconciled to your going after him. At least when—if—you find him, it'll just be the two of you. An even match, presumably. But going up against the Montagnais, and in their own backyard—"

"We will surprise them as they did us. There will not be much danger."

She shook her head. "It's all so impulsive. You're re-acting, going off half-cocked."

"I did not set the time we are to leave."

"Another thing—when you get up there you'll probably find yourselves outnumbered ten to one."

"That would be three hundred warriors; there are not that many Iron Axes in all of Canada. I must go, Margaret. I was going anyway." He stood like a small boy waiting for permission.

"When?"

"Before dawn tomorrow."

"Oh—my—God. This is insane. And wrong. I feel it. Must it be so soon?"

"The men do not want to delay; they feel we may be lucky and catch up with them before they reach their village. I do want to catch up with Fox. He is out of his mind with grief. He could get himself killed."

She held him, searching his eyes. "You must promise you'll be careful."

"Careful, *nyoh.*"

"I mean it. Don't go taking unnecessary chances. You're not alone anymore. You've a family. We want you back safe and sound."

"I will return with a present for you: Turtle Skin's head."

She made a face. "Give it to Moon Dancer."

They could hear branches moving behind her, and Seth came up. Margaret had washed out his wound and devised a sling for his arm, which had to be kept immobilized so that the flesh would knit.

"Swift Doe's sitting over there by herself," he said. "She's taking Hare's death very hard. I try to talk to her but she doesn't seem to hear."

"I'll go to her," said Margaret and left them.

Seth and Two Eagles stood awkwardly, exchanging stares. Then Seth attempted a smile.

"I came here a burden. I still am."

Two Eagles grunted.

"I know you'd like nothing better than to see me out of here. I'll eventually leave, I promise."

"Our castle is burned, we have lost everything," said Two Eagles, striving to keep the hostility from his tone. "The last thing our people need is your Christ. You are in the wrong place at the wrong time."

"I'm sorry, I don't agree. God's word is every man's most urgent need, regardless of his situation. And isn't that for the individual to decide? Moreover, in times of great stress people tend to be more receptive. Their need is greater."

"To pester them at this time would be shameful."

"I'll be trying to help them. I do have the chiefs' permission."

"How long will it take you?"

"Until His Longhouse stops me. I agreed."

"Then?"

"Then I leave."

"Good."

Seth eyed him. "You don't like me very much, do you?"

"I do not dislike you. To me you are a fly in the sweat lodge."

Seth grinned. "Don't look so downcast, look ahead. By the time you get back I will be gone."

"Good."

74

To fell trees for new palisade, faggots were heaped around the trunks and ignited so that the flames ate their way into the green wood. The Oneidas plastered rings of clay around the trunks to keep the fire from rising too high. When it burned out, the charred wood was hacked away, leaving fresh wood in a ring for a second fire.

The site for the new castle was about one hundred yards to the northwest of the old one. Everyone worked at rebuilding, with the raising of the palisade the first priority.

The raiding party did not leave before dawn of the second day as planned. Eagerness gave way to practical considerations. Time was needed to prepare weapons. Every man still had his knife and tomahawk, the latter the first thing he reached for when the attackers struck. But bows, arrows and quivers had to be made to replace those lost in the fire. Arrows had to be cut, tipped and fletched, a job even more tedious than felling trees. By the fourth day following the night of the Iron Axes, most of the men gave up making arrows in favor of sharpening sticks into spears.

"Our hunger for vengeance is our sharpest weapon," Two Eagles said to Margaret as they sat by the stream watching the winter sun, white as the snow crust, edge upward from behind the Tree-eater Mountains. Two Eagles held Benjamin on his lap. "Did I tell you I saw your friend talking to Sho-deg-wá-shon' yesterday? The man who took you to the chiefs? That black cloak is so stupid."

"I disagree. I think he's very bright. And a good man, darling. His heart is as big as your own. Lest you forget, he saved Swift Doe's life. He's also helping with the rebuilding."

"With one arm."

"I think it's cute." He looked up from sharpening the iron ax with a smooth stone. "You're still jealous," she continued. His face clouded. "There's no reason to be; I should be very upset with you, but I think it's cute. And it may surprise you, but he knows about it."

"You talked to him about me!"

"Shhhh, he talked to me about you. You're all wrong about him; he's actually quite the starry-eyed innocent. Who but an innocent walks boldly into Mohawk Territory with no more protection than a Bible and his personality?"

"He is no innocent; he is *a-ga-wa-sen-to-ro*."

"Calculating? Seth?" She laughed merrily.

"He knows what he is doing," Two Eagles went on. "He had better keep an eye on his step."

She got up. "I have to go to work."

"What are you doing?"

"Scooping out postholes for the palisade timber. We've a mattock with no handle, it got burned away. Look at my hands."

"What is he doing? Besides pestering Sho-deg-wá-shon'."

"Working with me."

He bristled. "Why him?"

"We're all digging in teams. One loosens the dirt, the other scrapes out the hole."

"Why does he not work with someone else?"

"I asked him to work with me."

His eyes widened. "You did?"

"Please, enough's enough." She sobered. "Darling, I'm worried about Swift Doe."

"About what? She is in mourning."

"I think she's thinking about suicide. *Ka-ega-da.*"

He scoffed. "*Neh.* She has lost not one but two husbands, now a son; she is toughened."

"I think she's weakened, stood all she can and can't take anymore."

"She would not kill herself and leave Little Elk and Dawn Maker."

"That may be the only thing stopping her. And who knows if it will? Losing Eight Minks didn't help any. She was so good in situations like this. She had a positive gift for reasoning out people's problems, pointing out what they can't see, helping to solve them."

"I will talk to Swift Doe."

"*I* will. You wouldn't know what to say."

"I will tell her not to commit *ka-ega-da.*"

"That's what I mean. I must go. What are you doing to-day?"

"Helping to make arrows, like yesterday. We will need all we can make; those who refuse to make them and are sharpening spears are stupid."

"Why, aren't spears effective?"

"If you are within sight of your enemy, you can shoot him with an arrow, *neh*? But with a spear you have to get close. If you get close you have your tomahawk and your knife. What do you need with a spear? Stupid, lazy."

They walked together toward the building site, Two Eagles carrying his son. "We will be leaving day after tomorrow," he said.

"It'll be postponed just like before."

"*Neh*, that is the time, it is decided. We will have enough weapons. Everyone has made snowshoes. We are packed and ready to go."

They planned to backtrack the route taken by the attackers. The many Montagnais had probably left a wide path with broken bushes on both sides leading through the foothills of the western slopes of the Adirondacks all the way up to the St. Lawrence River. The Oneidas agreed that the attackers had probably come not from Montagnais lands north of the St. Lawrence but from a clan living on the south bank. Those living north of the river had probably not crossed it to hunt, like those who had come down to be ambushed by the Mohawks. Instead, they had spread out to the northeast and southwest, perhaps venturing as far as Fort Frontenac into friendly Huron Territory.

"The Kanuwage does not freeze solid between their lands; it would have been hard crossing in the heart of winter. And they would have had to abandon their canoes. They use birch-bark canoes; they do not stand the winter as well as our elm-bark canoes. *Neh*, the ones the Maquen attacked drifted down from the south bank, found the deer plentiful and set about hunting. And these are the same."

At the building site, she took Benjamin from him. "I will see you at noon," she said; "we'll eat." Seth called and waved greeting to Two Eagles, who reacted with narrowed eyes and an annoyed expression.

"Be nice," snapped Margaret.

He grunted and walked off, swinging his iron ax. He had cut Blue Creek's name into the handle, explaining that it was appropriate: wasn't the ax intended for his neck?

Seth came up to Margaret.

"Have you seen Swift Doe?" she asked.

"Not since last night."

"Oh dear—"

"Anything wrong?"

"I don't know, I must find her. You can start. Watch Benjamin for me, I'll be back."

Margaret found Swift Doe sitting on a stump, Little Elk and Dawn Maker on the ground, knees drawn up, chins resting on them, looking anxiously up at their mother.

"Can we talk?" Margaret began.

"*Neh*, my heart is too sick, I do not want to."

"Aren't you going to help with the work?" Swift Doe shrugged. Margaret studied her. She didn't look to be in mourning, she looked angry. Then she saw that she was holding a knife.

"What's that for?"

Swift Doe threw it away.

"Listen to me," said Margaret, kneeling beside her. "Please. Granted, you've endured far more than flesh and blood should have to bear. It's just rotten, rotten luck."

"Last night I had a dream," murmured Swift Doe.

"Are you sure you want the boys to hear this?" Margaret asked urgently. Swift Doe sent them back to the worksite.

"I dreamt I saw a woman lying on the ground wrapped in a white robe, her whole body, even her head. Only her face could be seen. I moved closer to her. It was fading day, getting dark. I had to bend close to see her features. It was me. Dead. On my face was a smile; not a smile but—"

"*Or-ga-we-di-o*, contentment."

"*Nyoh, nyoh!* Beautiful contentment, like feeling sun-

shine flow from your heart all through you. I have not felt
that sunshine inside me for years. *Or-ga-we-di-o*. It is a
butterfly that I can see: beautiful, inconstant, elusive. I
chase it, reach for it, touch it, it gets away. I will never
catch it in life, never. Only in death. Is dying so bad?"

"I think it is."

"For me, do you think? How can it be worse than life?
My life is one long night: all storm clouds, constant rain,
never any sun, not since Long Feather was killed."

"Bone brought you happiness. And what about your
boys?"

She sniffed. "Bone sleeps with dirt in his mouth. And
the boys would be better off without me. They sit looking
up at me; all they see is gloominess, misery. My misery
makes me ache all over. I sob but I cannot cry, I am beyond tears."

"You feel sorry for yourself." Swift Doe looked up
sharply. "Do you ever think about what you have rather
than what you don't? Your two beautiful sons, your health,
your friends. You're blessed. Compared to Moon Dancer
you are, compared to many women. You have me, your
friends."

"Eight Minks—"

"Also your friend. Look at me, you're my best friend.
You have your talent for making masks, for painting and
sewing. You're sweet, you're kind, you're beautiful—"

"I am a *gachga*."

"A crow? Really." Margaret pulled her to her feet and
made her kneel by the stream. "Look at that face. Beautiful, extraordinary."

"It is all outside. Inside I have turned to stone. My heart
is as hollow as an old gourd. Any love that is in me was
given away long ago to Long Feather and Bone. To
Tantanege. I am empty. It is over for me, all I want now
is what I saw in the dream; *or-ga-we-di-o*."

"Fiddlesticks and rot, that's not contentment, it's surrender. I'll hear no more of this. Get up, you're coming with
me, we've work to do. I can't let you sit about moaning,

looking for gray clouds and feeling sorry for yourself. It's so unlike you. And it's indecent. Work, be with others, take your mind off your troubles and yourself. And watch, all your heartache and grief will gradually fade away."

"Not this time. I cannot live without Tantanege."

"Nonsense, come!" Swift Doe moved to retrieve the knife. "Leave it!" Margaret snatched it up and threw it as far as she could.

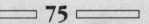

75

Margaret held Benjamin for Two Eagles to kiss good-bye. He demurred.

"Oneida warriors do not kiss their children. Kissing is for when we are fucking."

"Kiss your son good-bye," she hissed.

"Everybody is watching." He lowered his head, looking left and right.

"Kiss him."

He groaned. Again he looked both ways, then kissed Benjamin. Quickly and awkwardly. She grinned and kissed Two Eagles. "Do you have everything?"

"Nyoh."

"It's so stupid, this eye for an eye."

"We have been all through that. Are you Oneida?"

"Of course."

"This is the way of our people, of all Iroquois. We are not bugs to be stepped on."

"I packed your other knife."

"Good."

"It looks like rain, it'll probably sleet. Wouldn't it be wiser to put it off a day or so?"

"Neh, we have already delayed too long."

They stood outside the partially erected wall with the others in the raiding party and their families. It reminded Margaret of a painting she'd once seen of soldiers about to board ship for war on the continent. His Longhouse came up to them.

"Moon Dancer has asked me to remind you about Ossivendi Oÿoghi."

"I have this to remind me." He held up the iron ax with Blue Creek's name carved on the handle.

"You are getting a headstart. All the ice has not yet drowned in the lake."

Two Eagles showed him the buckskin he had folded and stuck in his belt. "This is for the Turtle Skin's head."

Margaret looked away, her expression disgusted. His Longhouse stood watching as she threw her arms around Two Eagles' neck and kissed him soulfully, hugging him so tightly he grunted. Other couples nearby stared; none of them kissed.

76

Down came the rain, thick, pelting, icy. Two Eagles glanced upward at the swollen clouds, so low the tree-tops seemed to impale them. Night sifted through the gray-ness. The Oneidas had departed without even a war dance to heat their blood with vengeance. It was not needed, they were on fire. Weapons and a daily handful of charred corn sweetened with maple sugar were all they required. They kept moving. They would go on until the darkness was firmly in possession of the woodlands. They would cover the rugged terrain stretching northward to the St. Kanawage in no more than four sleeps.

Despite his protests, Two Eagles had been chosen to lead the party, at the insistence of Splitting Moon.

The Oneidas had been backtracking the raiders' south-bound trail since leaving Onneyuttahage before sunrise, stopping for the first time when the sun stood straight overhead. At noon they had taken their one meal of the day, getting back onto the trail and tracking into weariness. On and on they went through the shadows of the great round peaks of the Tree-eater Mountains, through thick forests of snow-clad spruce, pine and broad-leaf trees. Exhaustion was creeping into Two Eagles' legs when he studied the faces of the men nearest him and called a halt.

"Why are we stopping?" asked Splitting Moon, running up. "It's too early, we can still make another full league."

"*You* make another full league yourself and wait for us. We will sleep here until the crows wake the sun tomorrow."

The others, crowding around them, nodded, and Splitting Moon snorted but said nothing further. Anger Maker and Red Paint sat with Two Eagles, the three of them huddling under the freezing rain.

"I wonder how far Fox got?" speculated Red Paint.

"He must be following this trail," said Two Eagles. "We will catch up with him."

Anger Maker looked overhead, the rain spattering his face. "It could be worse," he murmured. "It could be snow."

"It will be by morning," said Splitting Moon behind them.

Two Eagles readied the ground around him for sleep and considered their situation. Every man among them had been hurt in one way or another by the Iron Axes; all hungered for revenge. But few really had much stomach for the trek—well over fifty leagues to the St. Kanawage—particularly in winter, even though spring was only days away. For all their thirst for blood they were walking into enemy territory. The Montagnais would have hunting parties out. They could easily spot the Oneidas and ambush them as brutally and effectively as the Mohawks had ambushed their hunting party near the Te-ugé-ga.

"We should split up," said Two Eagles.

"What for?" demanded Splitting Moon.

"Remember when we were out searching for my brother Long Feather? We spread out in a line so thin each of us could barely see the man on either side. If we spread out the same way here we would be protecting ourselves. If we run into any Iron Axes spread out like that they won't be able to tell how many we are. And we can signal each other with a bird call, the *ká-ká-cow-cow* of *tite-ti*, the yellow bill."

Splitting Moon snickered. "Two Eagles become one little yellow bird."

"It makes sense."

"Which of us gets to follow the trail?" asked one man. "You?"

"None of us. They will be watching it like an *ochquoha* watches his next meal."

"I like the idea," said Anger Maker. "With more than thirty of us the line will be very wide. *Ká-ká-cow-cow. Ká-ká-cow-cow.*" Everyone laughed.

"We will talk further in the morning," said Two Eagles. He glanced skyward. "If it comes. Tonight looks like the end of the world."

The rain fell harder, colder, the Oneidas shivered, crawled deeper into their skins and slept.

Two Eagles woke suddenly, his hand flying to his knife. Slowly he released it. Soaked to the skin, he was shivering. Most of the Oneidas' clothing had burned in the fire and the warriors had not taken the time to scour the caves in the area for bears and new warm robes. Someone suggested that the first thing they would do when they finished massacring the Iron Axes would be to confiscate their clothes.

Two Eagles thought back to Seth and the furs he had been wearing when he showed up at the gate. The gate had

been burned, his clothing. All he had left unscathed was
his zeal, honed and ready for the people. What luck would
he have? No doubt discouragingly little, but he didn't
seem the sort who discouraged easily.

How could Margaret like such a man? What was the at-
traction? He who had never swung a tomahawk in his life,
never drew a bow, who took to bed when he was ill, who
ate with a spoon like a woman instead of with his fingers,
who was soft and white as a fish, and never lost his temper. *Was* he a man?

Still, he'd risked his life saving Swift Doe, whom he
hardly knew. And Eight Minks had liked him, she who
could see inside people's heads even better than could
Bone. He did hope Seth was being truthful, that he'd be
gone before they got back. He still wasn't comfortable
with the idea of leaving him with Margaret. She liked him
too much.

Splitting Moon came over to Two Eagles, stretching, sitting down beside him.

"Are you thinking about Mar-gar-et back there with the
black cloak? I would be if I were you."

"Ogechta."

"Ah, you are. I was just about to say, Mar-gar-et you
can trust. But him I do not know. He is not much of a
man, but he has a stone stick and two balls and he likes
her. What more do they need? And have you noticed the
way he looks at her?"

"She can handle him."

Splitting Moon snickered. "He can handle her, he would
like to."

Two Eagles swung at him; Splitting Moon ducked out
of the way. The disturbance woke the sleepers, and soon
the party set out in single file. They would not spread out
in a horizontal line until they drew near Iron Ax country.

The Oneidas knew little about the Montagnais, apart
from their wigwam dwellings, use of birch-bark canoes,
iron axes and their name, which their friends the French
had given them. It meant "mountaineers," although the

southern branch of the tribe did not live in mountains. From Seth's description of the ambush and the clothes he had taken, they appeared to dress much like the Iroquois: winter furs, breechclout, leggings and moccasins. No one in the party could add anything significant to these meager facts, except that the Iron Axes' reputation as fighters was purportedly the equal of the Hurons.

At this observation, Anger Maker grunted disdainfully and held his knife up for all to see. "Huron snake or Iron Ax seal fucker, neither has a knife that fights like this knife."

"Keep your knife sharp," said Two Eagles. "It may be very busy a sleep or two from now."

The castle palisade was completed, rising more than twenty feet to sharp points. The people turned their efforts to the longhouses, cutting and trimming crotched corner posts, eleven-foot- and fifteen-foot-long roof posts, crotched pieces for gable supports, short, straight poles for connecting the corner posts and roof rafters. They also cut sixty small poles to stiffen the sides of each dwelling, along with roof "stringers" to hold down the elm bark. From darkness through daylight to darkness; in clear weather and in the rain, the Oneidas labored.

It was early in the year to peel the bark sheets, four feet wide and six to eight feet long. Since the sap was not yet running in the elms, the bark was not easy to remove. But gradually the rectangular frames and rounded roofs took on covering.

With the tribe so involved in building a new castle, Seth decided to postpone his attempt to convert the Oneidas. As he worked alongside Margaret, mounting bark siding, he confided that he still thought it unwise to avenge the attack.

"I understand risking one's life for honor, but they could be slaughtered up there."

"The people wouldn't look at them with the same eyes if they didn't go. They know that."

"All the same, Margaret, aren't you worried about Two Eagles?"

"Of course. I hate it, but I'd never have been able to talk him out of going. And I'd be the only wife protesting. Not a particularly enviable distinction.

"If you think about it, from their point of view, it's necessary for more reasons than just to save face. The five nations are surrounded by enemies, all of whom they've conquered and subjugated at one time or another."

"Five? I thought the Iroquois was one nation."

"A confederacy of five separate, autonomous nations: the League of the Iroquois. The Oneidas and the Mohawks you know about, the Onondagans to the west, farther west the Cayugas and lastly the Senecas, the Keepers of the Western Door. They've been together in their confederacy for two hundred and fifty years."

"Fighting everybody else."

"Everybody within reach."

"Even before the ship docked I learned that they're considered the fiercest warriors in all of North America."

They raised a bark sheet into place, lashing it to a cross pole.

"As fierce in battle as the Spartans of old," said Margaret. "Two Eagles once told me that at the height of the war, when both English and French were pouring in troops and France's Indian allies were like leaves on the trees, the Iroquois never put more than twenty-two hundred men in the field. And yet it was they who turned the balance in favor of the British, who showed their gratitude by walking away from them at the peace table, as you know."

"It's hard to believe the Oneidas and Mohawks are

blood brothers. They're so different. The Oneidas are so—"

She smiled. "Civilized?"

"Certainly compared to the brutes we ran into. There was no limit to their savagery. I kept asking myself why; they could see we were all but unarmed, helpless civilians who meant no harm whatsoever."

"Your clothing did you in. You looked too much like Jesuits. They despise the black robes. The Onekahonckans lost nearly half of their fighting strength early in the war without a single shot being fired. Half the castle fell under the influence of the Jesuits, embraced Catholicism and left Onekahoncka, moving up to Caughnawaga on the St. Lawrence, and ended up fighting on the side of the French against their own people. The bitterness is still strong, and the Mohawks put all the blame on the Jesuits."

"But we told them explicitly we were Protestant missionaries," he protested.

"The distinction's a bit fine for them. You're both the Christian religion."

He shook his head. "The little things they didn't tell us back in Boston."

"I doubt your superiors know much about Mohawk history. If they did, they would have sent you to convert the Munsee basket weavers." She frowned. "You shouldn't be lifting with that shoulder."

"It's all right, my wound's almost healed. I can't get much done with one arm." He was staring at her. "Margaret, I've been meaning to ask. I've seen how you fit in here. You really admire these people, don't you?"

"Very much. If you only knew what they have to contend with; everything's against them: Nature, their neighbors, the whites, their own failure to improve their lot over the past five hundred years, the harshness of life, and yet they cope. And they're happy, content. They never complain, they treat their women well—better than most Europeans—they're kind and generous to their children, they're fair to each other, they're honest in their dealings.

They get along really quite splendidly, discounting the odd
bad apple, like Blue Creek.

"Life can be crashingly boring, muddy, dusty, depend-
ing on the season—noisy, smelly, with no privacy. There's
stupidity and blindness, superstition and unreasoning fear
on all sides, but all in all, I find them exceptional human
beings. And somehow I've learned to fit in."

"Thanks to him."

"Because of him, Seth."

"You love each other very much, anyone can see."

"Is it that obvious?"

"I watched you saying good-bye. It was touching, it was
beautiful. I envy you both. I sometimes feel like I've been
alone since the cradle: no siblings, no girlfriends—"

"What about Hannah?"

"She wasn't that sort of friend. We were growing closer
but then ... 'Who is the wise man who may understand
this?' Jeremiah nine. What are you smiling at?"

"Nothing."

"Something."

"I met a boy once who was forever quoting scripture. I
was quite impressed until a friend told me that he'd mem-
orized a dozen or fifteen quotes and whenever the opportunity came up in the conversation to spring one that
suited, out it came. It made him very popular with parents."

Were his cheeks coloring slightly? It was hard to tell.

"We'd better go cut more bark sheets," he murmured.

"Yes."

78

"*Ká-ká-ká-cow-cow-cow-cowlp. Cowlp.*" Two Eagles lowered his cupped hand from around his mouth and listened as the call was repeated left and right of him, as it had been for the last half league of their journey. The yellow-billed cuckoo, *tite-ti*, was an inconspicuous bird, rarely seen, only occasionally breaking into its long call; a suitable signal bird.

On Two Eagles went, the only sound the soft grating of his showshoes over the old crust. Patches of pine needles showed here and there where the snow was beginning to melt. The wind rested, the air was cold but not frigid. Milder weather was definitely on the way.

He thought about home, Margaret and Benjamin, how much he missed them already. With luck he would be back before the dogwood blossoms broke their buds. He stopped, knelt, adjusted the fastening on one snowshoe and straightened up. An arrow sang by his ear, shuddering into a tree five paces ahead. He froze and swallowed. Loud shouting broke out coming from both sides up and down the line. Not Oneida; a language he did not understand. Shouting and struggling came on both sides of him. To his right he dimly saw two figures fighting, an ax raised, descending sharply, bushes thrashing, silence. The hairs on the back of his neck raised as he became aware of someone approaching from behind. He turned.

The Iron Ax was short, stumpy, resembling Splitting Moon but not as powerful-looking, fat, the pouches of his cheeks sagging heavily. With his bow drawn, an arrow nocked, he approached.

"*Je-na-sagga-ta! Je-na-sagga-ta!*"

Two Eagles dropped his iron ax and knife in the snow. The warrior kicked them to one side and retrieved them. He was fur-clad, his high moccasins identical to those Seth had taken, and when the two halves of his robe parted there was no mistaking the ax in his belt. He shoved Two Eagles' ax in beside it.

Men were approaching from both directions in pairs: one Oneida, escorted by one captor, coming up quickly. Two Eagles sighed. The soup spilt: his plan for approaching Montagnais territory had collapsed. Evidently the Iron Axes had seen them, let them pass by and fell in behind them one on one. Eighteen Oneidas were rounded up. Where were the others?

Their leader strutted forward to confront him, jabbering in a squeaky voice. Two Eagles eyed him disdainfully, despite the knifepoint now pricking his spine. The Montagnais flew into a rage, pushing him down. Straddling him, he threatened him with his ax. An older warrior hurried up. Speaking Oneida, he ordered Two Eagles to his feet. He then addressed the leader, whose wild eyes were circled with black, as were those of most of his men. But he had taken personal adornment a step further, adding a bright red swipe trailing down from his lower lip, over his chin, down his throat to a necklace fashioned of human teeth. Two Eagles got to his feet, towering over the two of them.

Red Chin broke into a grin. *"Ká-ká-ká-cow-cow,"* he sang and burst out laughing. The interpreter explained.

"That is the call of the yellow bill. There are no yellow bills in these woods in winter. Not till the ground softens when the white oak sprouts its green tassels and its leaves are the size of a mouse's ear. Not till then does yellow bill come back." He pushed closer smirking. *"Ká-ká-ká-cow-cow-cow-cowlp!"*

The Montagnais laughed. The Oneidas stared at Two Eagles. He glanced upward at a white oak; not a single leaf had opened.

79

The Windigo towered five times the height of a man in the center of the encampment, a monster with a blood-red mouth, no lips and long jagged teeth. Its forelegs were claws, and like its mouth, its eyes and feet were painted blood red. It was an awesome sight in the glow of the many cookfires: the Montagnais' giant, stalker of the winter woods, who sought humans to devour.

Around its feet was a scattering of wigwams in various stages of completion. They were covered mostly with birch bark, with moosehide pieces filling in the gaps. Squaws sat stirring boiling kettles, children played, dogs yapped unceasingly and chased each other. A partially cut-up bull moose lay at the bloody feet of the Windigo. Women scraped hides; men tended to their weapons or stood around talking.

The noise and activity ceased abruptly as the Oneidas were led in by their captors. None was tied, a too-obvious invitation to attempt escape. The Montagnais gawked as all eighteen were shoved into a ragged line before the Windigo. It was made of wood, bark sheets and parcels of tightly bound grass; the face was a single piece of bark with the features cut out and painted. Its hair looked to be clumps of the slender long filament of the inner bark of the slippery elm, which the Oneidas used to make rope.

But it was the people's expressions, not the Windigo, that finally took Two Eagles' attention. They showed indignation, superiority—the smirk of triumph—and a few displayed an unmistakable eagerness for blood.

"O-kwen-cha," called a thin voice off to the right be-

hind a group of warriors standing talking. "O-kwen-
cha—"

At the sound of his name, Red Paint started. It was repeated a third time. The men blocking his line of sight
stepped aside, and the Oneidas saw who was calling.
Buried up to his chin, his head dusted with white powder,
was Fox. His voice was feeble. His eyes dull with fear, he
looked half dead. Red Paint started forward but was
stopped by an ax set hard across his chest.

"Sku-nak-su," he called. Struck with the flat of the ax,
he was sent reeling. Splitting Moon caught him, held him
upright.

Two Eagles' brain whirled. A desperate feeling gripped
him. His stupid attempt at cleverness—suggesting the bird-
call signal—was responsible for all this; already nearly
half their number had died, and the rest would go shortly.
Four or five would be selected, and one a day would be
tortured for the amusement of the tribe. To the left, between two completed wigwams, Two Eagles saw bodies
stacked like firewood, the remains of the sixteen Oneidas.

Their heads had been chopped off. Squatting in front of
one wigwam were a man and two women with stones,
busily knocking teeth out of heads and dropping them into
a kettle to boil away the flesh and render them clean for
piercing. Two Eagles' eyes strayed to the necklace Red
Chin was wearing.

A drum began beating. Everyone was silent. All eyes
turned to the tallest wigwam. Smoke issued from the top.
Five men came out, led by a well-built, powerful-looking
chief, missing one leg from the knee down, supporting
himself on a crotched stick. His mouth was toothless; his
upper arm was badly mangled and a diagonal scar crossed
his face from above his left eye to below his right cheek.
In his gleaming, greasy hair were red-tailed hawk feathers.
Like Red Chin, he wore a human tooth necklace, also a
porcupine-quill bib and moosehide shirt, breechclout and
leggings. His skin glistened like polished bronze. It was
smeared with seal oil against the impending arrival of

mosquitoes and black flies. The others, similarly garbed, followed him out.

Sight of the last man to emerge jolted Two Eagles' heart.

Ossivendi Oÿoghi.

Blue Creek.

80

Blue Creek appeared to be in the same buckskins he had worn the last time Two Eagles saw him. But he now wore a headband and carried a long Montagnais bone knife, with the distinctive, tightly wound rawhide grip. He approached the captives, grinning sadistically. Obviously, he had gained a position of some stature among his hosts. Like the Hurons to the west, the Montagnais were Algonquins. Since Blue Creek spoke fluent Huron, the similar Montagnais tongue would be easy for him to master. He brought other assets: he came to them fleeing from their enemies, his own hatred of the Oneidas coinciding with theirs, and he could at least pretend to know the tribe's secrets. By now, he'd proven himself a traitor, but a valuable one. He came up to within two paces of Two Eagles, triumph setting his dark eyes glowing.

"So, Tékni-ska-je-a-nah, what delayed you?" he asked.

"Turtle Skin," muttered Splitting Moon. *"Sateeni oeuda."* He spat at Blue Creek's feet.

Blue Creek turned toward him, smiling. "Tyagohuens. And Sa-ga-na-qua-de, O-kwen-cha. Everybody except the bony Mohican."

Two Eagles started forward but caught himself as Blue Creek leered. Two Eagles contained his trembling.

"Your friend Sku-nak-su has been waiting patiently,

O-kwen-cha. See him there? Now that you are here, he would like to perform for you. For all of you."

He spoke to Greasy Skin, who jabbered back, laughed; the others who had come out of the wigwam joined in. The people laughed, the dogs barked, Two Eagles' heart shrank.

Into a semicircle in front of the hapless Fox, the Oneida were herded. An order was called, three stakes were driven into the ground forming a triangle around Fox's head. A squat little squaw carrying an elm-bark bucket waddled forward, stood with her toes against his neck and carefully poured the contents over his head. He sputtered and spat at the honey slid down his face.

Two Eagles could feel Red Paint's eyes burning his cheek. He could not understand; Fox's predicament was the only situation he wasn't responsible for. Could it be Red Paint wasn't thinking of Fox but of himself? Three black bear cubs were dragged up and each one tied to a stake with a ten-foot tether.

"A torture so old it has bark on it, *neh*?" Blue Creek asked. "Old but effective. And fascinating to watch. His screaming will be heard halfway back to Onneyuttahage. Watch."

"You!" snapped Two Eagles. "Watch your treachery bring death to a proud warrior of your own tribe."

Blue Creek sniffed. "The Oneida ceased to be *my* tribe when they banished me."

"No one banished you, Turtle Skin," murmured Splitting Moon. "You fled from your crimes like a dog caught fire."

"Really, Tyagohuens, you expect me to live with the people who refused to punish my sister's murderer? And accept her as an Oneida? Your whiteskin *cannawarori*, Tékni-ska-je-a-nah."

"*Ogechta!*" snapped Anger Maker. "You are the whore, foul dog! Traitor, betrayer of your own people, snake in the skin of a turtle!"

Blue Creek broke into loud laughter. The Montagnais

stared. Two Eagles averted his eyes as the bear cubs wandered up to Fox's dripping head and began licking it. The crowd whooped approvingly. Soon every bit of honey was licked from his flesh and hair and the cubs began bumping each other for position to lick his eyes. One clawed an eye partially out of its socket, blood spitting. Another bit his cheek, tasted blood and with a single swipe tore off his nose. Blood geysered, subsiding, blackening the ground around his chin. The crowd hooted and shouted gleefully. Two Eagles' hand stole to his stomach. He shuttered his eyes.

Throughout the ordeal, Fox did not utter a sound. Then a soft, prolonged gurgling issued from his throat; he tilted his head back and died. The cubs persisted in their attack, reducing his head to a pulp.

Two warriors stepped forward and began kicking his head. It broke free and was kicked through the dust over to the pile of heads from which the teeth were being extracted.

Two Eagles threw a sidelong glance at Red Paint standing on the other side and slightly ahead of Splitting Moon.

Red Paint was distraught. He gulped shallow breaths, trembling, opening and closing his fists, his face reddening under his redder stripes. He leaned forward slightly, his body rigid as if ready to explode.

But he held himself in check, clearly disappointing Blue Creek, who had not taken his eyes off him, not even to watch the torture.

81

The prisoners were confined nine to a wigwam, left with their wrists bound behind their backs, the free end of

the cord fastened to a stick buried horizontally about eight
inches in the ground. As he was pushed inside the wigwam, Two Eagles noticed ten or more rawhide strands
coming from the ground.

There was no fire inside, although he could see the
smoke hole where the pole frame was bound together at
the top. The wigwam was mainly covered with birch bark,
with old moosehides thrown over two large holes. It was
stuffy inside, and dark, the only light the orange painted
on the bark covering by fires just outside. Two Eagles
found himself with his friends; with Red Paint, still shaken
over the execution-by-torture of his lifelong friend, muttering threats of vengeance, vowing to annihilate the entire
village.

"They will take one of us at a time," announced Splitting Moon, in a tone that suggested enlightenment of momentous importance. "Each death different."

Two Eagles grunted. "Turtle Skin arranged this, every
step, ending up with this show for his seal fucker friends."

"He was here when the survivors came home from the
ambush that the black cloak watched near the Te-ugé-ga,"
said Anger Maker.

"*Nyoh,* of course," said Two Eagles. "They wanted their
revenge. He advised Greasy Skin. They sent raiders back
down to us instead of the Mohawks at Tenotoge."

"To the right castle for his purposes," said Anger
Maker. "Knowing we would retaliate and you, Two Eagles, would be in the party. He is a crafty one."

"What *seronquatse* is not?" growled Two Eagles. "But
he has not won yet."

Splitting Moon snorted. "He is very close to winning."
He groaned. "The dirt is already in our mouths; we are
just not in our holes."

"We never will be," muttered Anger Maker. "Did you
see the others' bodies? They will not be buried. They will
be eaten." At this Splitting Moon scoffed. "It is true. Everybody knows that the seal fuckers are cannibals.
Windigo is a cannibal. When some of them get him inside

them, he possesses them and all they eat from then on are the hearts and flesh of captives." He snickered. "You, Splitting Moon, who cannot stomach meat, will end up meat for one of them who is not so finicky, *neh?*"

"Ogechta!"

"We are not finished yet," said Two Eagles. He lowered his head and his voice. "I have a knife."

"They took all our weapons," said Splitting Moon.

"An extra knife Margaret gave me. I removed it from my pack and slipped it into my right legging when we started out—a seal fucker knife I took from Hare's killer when I took the iron ax. In my legging."

"What good will it do you there?" Red Paint asked, speaking up for the first time. "Your wrists are bound behind you. There are guards outside."

"Only one guard. And if we back up to each other we can untie our wrist bindings. We must escape soon. The killing resumes tomorrow. And it will have to be every man for his own escape. Get away, head for the river."

"That is north," said Splitting Moon. "Not me!"

"Use your head," Anger Maker retorted. "They think you will head south for Oneida Territory. North makes sense. How far to the river do you think, Two Eagles? You cannot hear any water sound here."

"They fish for *ghekeront* and spear seals," he said. "It has to be nearby. With my knife in the guard outside, you can all get away. The prisoners in the other wigwam are on their own, I am afraid."

"What about you?"

"It will be trickier for me," Two Eagles admitted. "I cannot leave without Turtle Skin's head."

Splitting Moon scoffed. "Forget his head, save your arse."

"I cannot return home without his head. I gave my word to the chiefs and to Moon Dancer."

"So get away and come back later," said Anger Maker. "He will still be here. Just catch him by himself. Take his head, leave the rest of him for Windigo."

The flap was thrown wide revealing Blue Creek, who carried a torch with a sharpened end; he jammed it into the ground, knelt in their midst, looked about, leered. The torch set shadows dancing on the walls.

He shuddered, pretending fear. "I feel the air thick with plotting. Please try and get away. I bring news: one of you dies tomorrow. Can you guess which? Not you, Tékni-ska-je-a-nah—you I am saving for last. Those in the other wig-wam will have their throats cut. You, Tyagohuens, Sa-ga-na-qua-de, O-kwen-cha, will die one a night. Lastly you, Tékni-ska-je-a-nah." He laughed. *"Ká-ká-ká-cow-cow-cow-cowlp.* Some signal. Very effective—it called our warriors to you. What has happened to your brain to do such a stupid thing? And look at your hands." He peeked behind his back. "You cannot see, but they are gloved with blood: Oneida blood. And now they will get a fresh coat daily. *Ká-ká-ká-cow-cow-cow . . ."*

Two Eagles interrupted his taunting. "Tell us, what did Ganōda say when you barged in on her at Mas-sowaganine? Was she pleased to see you? Was her husband?"

The leer left Blue Creek's face; his eyes gleamed evilly. His jaw grew taut.

"What will your whiteskin *cannawarori* say when word gets back that all of you have given your teeth and your hearts to the hated Iron Axes? Maybe after all of your bodies are added to the pile outside we will return to Onneyuttahage and burn down your new castle, kill more of you. Next time, I will go. I will find your *cannawarori* and your *cian* and bring them back here."

"What do you call your chief?" Two Eagles asked. The question surprised Blue Creek. "Greasy Skin, One Leg?"

"Why do you want to know? You will not be speaking to him."

"Maybe I will. Maybe he would like to know that you sent his warriors to Onneyuttahage instead of Tenotoge. To get vengeance you were too cowardly to take yourself.

They adopted you and you used them for your own purpose."

"Shot Sky would not believe you. You think he would take the word of an Iroquois child-killer over that of a loyal adoptee?"

"He might. Men facing death are known to be truthful. He would know I have nothing to gain by lying."

"He does not want to talk to any of you; you will not get close enough to tell him anything." He leaned close to Two Eagles, his eyes glittering with hatred. "And something else: you four I have asked for, and he has given you to me to devise the manner of your executions. All he asks is your hearts and your teeth."

He roared laughter, then summoned guards. Five prisoners were removed, leaving four: Two Eagles, Splitting Moon, Anger Maker, Red Paint.

82

Spring had come early to the lands of the Iroquois. Millions of passenger pigeons roosted in the beeches. The people netted them and picked squabs out of their nests with long poles, to be fried in sunflower oil and the meat packed in elm-bark tuns.

The longhouses were completed. Margaret selected the same chamber she and Two Eagles had shared in the old house. Setting about making it livable, sadness filled her. Never again would Eight Minks' shrill laugh ring down the passageway; never again would Hare come bursting in with some momentous news that only a thirteen-year-old thought important. Fox's gruff voice was gone, Two Eagles', too. She wondered *when* they would return. She wondered *if*.

Seth selected a chamber between Swift Doe's and Margaret's, on the opposite side of the passageway. He came upon Margaret, in what should have been Eight Minks' chamber, sitting glumly on the edge of the newly constructed bunk.

"Are you worried about them?" he asked.

"Terribly. The St. Lawrence has always been bad luck for Two Eagles. Too many bloody battles up there during the war. The trip from Fort Frontenac to Quebec was frightening, dangerous. The lot of us nearly drowned half a dozen times. That river is cursed."

"And I thought you weren't superstitious." He shook his head.

"Who isn't about some things? Added to which the Montagnais hate and despise the Iroquois. They should. The Five Nations came close to exterminating the ones living on this side of the river."

"Two Eagles and the others will have surprise in their favor."

"I don't think so. The Montagnais know they'll retaliate sooner or later. They could easily walk into an ambush." Her brow creased.

"Two Eagles is far too clever to let that happen. He's an exceptionally bright man. Fine analytical mind. And he's absolutely bursting with experience."

"I know," said Margaret, "I just can't help thinking the worst. Like what you saw in your ambush: one or two of them getting away, returning home with the news. To make matters worse, he's determined not to come home without Blue Creek's head. Danger piled on danger, it's all so exasperating: starting with Graywind's death, one bad thing has led to another. Now suddenly it's all coming down on us.

"The worst of it is, he and I have never had time to be happy, to relax, do as we please, live as we like. A bone is forever showing up in the soup. I could get really superstitious and assume that Fate just doesn't want us together, doesn't approve and is doing everything in her power to discourage us."

He smiled. "You knew it wouldn't be easy."

"Maybe that's my problem: I had it too easy before. Not a care in the world, nothing my parents couldn't deal with. Now Fate's compensating." She laid her hand on his. "Forgive me, Seth, you're the last person I should complain to, after what you've been through. You never complain."

"Just not out loud."

"You're a good man, Seth Wilson, a good friend." She patted his cheek. "Now, if you'll excuse me I should go and look in on Swift Doe."

"I've noticed she hasn't seemed as down lately."

"She's still not doing too well. How much heartache can a person stand?"

She found Swift Doe sitting on the floor with a knife in her lap. Margaret snatched it up, shoved it in her belt.

"I wasn't going to kill myself," Swift Doe protested.

"Don't you dare. You're needed around here. For one thing, you can start making up medicine baskets to replace the ones we lost. We're a smaller family now, but still a family. Isn't that so?"

"I dream about him every night. I see his smile; he had a wonderful smile. I see how he was on the day he realized he had beaten his wound and would recover. He was so filled with joy he could not sit still. He wanted to run around shouting the good news to the whole castle. And even lying in his sickbed he became the man of the family. He would have been as brave a warrior as his father, as Bone. What a loss; he was the life of our people, Margaret, the next generation coming along to keep us strong."

Margaret sat beside her, her hand on her shoulder.

"Little Elk will grow straight and tall like him, like their father. And you'll be as proud of him and of Dawn Maker."

"And they will die, one then the other. All my men die, Margaret; that is my curse in life. Moon Dancer is right.

When you lose your man, do not take another, for he, too, will be lost. And do not bear sons; they are doomed.

"If you are born to live alone, do so. Do not take men inside the circle of your life to their doom."

Margaret patted her shoulder, studied her face and, for the first time, saw tears glistening in her eyes.

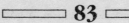 **83**

The Oneidas struggled with their bonds all night long, but none succeeded in freeing himself. At dawn they were untied and led outside to see the pile of headless corpses, now grown larger, the fourteen Oneida prisoners added to their number. The sight was like a knife finding Two Eagles' heart.

"My fault, all mine."

Blue Creek approached, commenting affably on the warmth and sunny promise of the day, and summoned two muscular warriors, who took Anger Maker away at knifepoint. The three remaining Oneidas were made to sit in a semicircle before Windigo. Presently Anger Maker was brought back naked and was forced to sit before them.

The village awakened slowly, families emerging from their wigwams and assembling to watch as Anger Maker's wrists and ankles were staked down. He looked at Two Eagles, forcing a smile, unwilling to give his captors the satisfaction of seeing him surrender to his suffering. He would die as he lived, a proud and valiant warrior. With this knowledge, Two Eagles' heart ached. His guilt was complete.

An old woman set a moose bladder filled with water on the ground. A maiden who resembled Swift Doe and was just as beautiful approached Anger Maker, knelt before him, produced a knife and proceeded to gouge his eyes out. He did not flinch or utter a sound. Two Eagles looked away, convinced that the other captives were thinking about him, although they all focused on Anger Maker as his eyeballs were forced down his throat with water pumped from the bladder.

Cheered on by the crowd, the girl deftly sliced off his genitalia. These, too, were force-fed him, after which the bleeding was stanched. Then the crowd dispersed, leaving the prisoner sitting in agony to await the next phase.

The sun stood halfway down its afternoon path and the Montagnais had returned to watch. Two men with knives approached the prisoner from the rear, kneeling and skinning inch-wide strips of flesh from his shoulders down his back. Even in such excruciating pain, Anger Maker did not tremble or make a sound. A thin smile masked his agony.

One by one the strips were peeled away and thrown to the dogs. A blanket was produced; it gleamed, suggesting it had been rubbed with some substance. The Montagnais dumped the contents of a pot on it; then they gathered the blanket up, shook it vigorously, and carefully laid it on Anger Maker's broad back.

"*Ge-na-ka-a-di-a-wa*," whispered Splitting Moon. "Caterpillar hunters."

Two Eagles sighed. A handful of caterpillar hunters could reduce a squirrel to fur and bone in two hours.

Despite Anger Maker's agony, his posture was stiff and unmoving, his lips remained clamped tightly in the suggestion of a smile, his emptied sockets stared.

He lived almost to sundown before slumping backward, falling over. As the crowd broke up, Blue Creek approached the Oneidas.

"Sa-ga-na-qua-de was as brave as Sku-nak-su." He looked at Splitting Moon, then at Red Paint. "Which of you will be next?"

"I will," growled Splitting Moon.

"I!" snapped Red Paint.

"Do not argue, let me choose. And you, Tékni-ska-je-a-nah, look tired. A bad night? Awake all night struggling to free yourself? Try again tonight. Maybe your luck will be better."

"Hope that I do not get free, Turtle Skin; if I do you will be the first one I come after!"

Blue Creek laughed and barked an order to three men standing with the chief. They brought Two Eagles, Splitting Moon and Red Paint back to the wigwam. Splitting Moon shook his head discouragedly.

"Poor Sa-ga-na-qua-de, poor Sku-nak-su—"

"*Ogechta!*" burst Two Eagles. "On top of all else must we listen to your wailing?"

"All I said—"

"We heard!" Two Eagles glanced Red Paint's way, looked away and looked back. "What are you grinning at?"

Red Paint eyed the flap, making sure it was secure. "Look what I found." He swung around, showed his bound wrists and opened one hand, revealing a mica-studded piece of sandstone in the rough shape of a tomahawk but much smaller.

"Back up to me," whispered Splitting Moon.

"Wait," cautioned Two Eagles. "Until dark. We cannot leave till then. Stay as you are."

The sun was setting, its downward journey visible through a crack at the top of the flap. Twilight settled over the village, and finally, night fell. It was time. Two Eagles watched Red Paint saw and saw at Splitting Moon's bonds until his fingers became so cramped he could no longer hold the stone. He rested, he resumed; Splitting Moon's wrists became bloodied. One thong finally parted, then another, until the sixth and last one was cut through.

"My right legging," whispered Two Eagles.

Splitting Moon got out the knife and freed both.

"I have decided," he murmured. "I am heading for the mountains in the east. They know we would not dare go south back down the trail. They will think we will try to flee north."

"Go where you please," said Two Eagles. "I must find Turtle Skin."

"I will come with you," said Red Paint.

"All right, all right," snapped Splitting Moon. "We will stick together. We will find him. But if they find us first, it is suicide!"

"Then save yourself, do not come!" snapped Two Eagles.

Splitting Moon sighed and reached for the flap. Two Eagles caught his arm.

"Outside, run for the Windigo. We will use its long shadow to cover us until we reach the trees. You two can reach safety. I will find the traitor by myself."

"Come on!" urged Red Paint.

He took hold of the flap but suddenly heard movement on the other side. Blue Creek stuck his head in. Two Eagles' knife stopped his yell midthroat. The blade in his chest, Blue Creek dropped to his knees, his eyes saucering. Two Eagles returned his stare, and in that instant the hatred that bound them seemed to dissolve. The soft rattle of death sounded in Blue Creek's throat and over he fell. Two Eagles retrieved his knife and, kneeling, prepared to sever his head. But hesitated.

"Cut it off!" insisted Red Paint.

Two Eagles got to his feet. "*Neh.* I have his life, that is enough."

"What are you saying? You cannot change the punishment. Moon Dancer demanded his head—"

"I will place *her* head on Iron Dog's grave if she does not shut her flapping mouth, end all this! Blue Creek is dead; she has her revenge and I mine: for Bone's death, Hare's wound and death, for all he has done to us.

"Thirty are dead here thanks to my stupidity. And Fox. Thirty deaths clinging to my conscience like burrs to leggins. Do either of you think I care about Moon Dancer and her demand? She is a bug under my moccasin. Take his knife and ax, come."

It was deserted outside. Torches thrust into the ground

licked the darkness around the Windigo. They circled their
wigwam and headed for the woods, the monster towering
close by and just beyond it the two grisly piles. Two Eagles threw a final look at the brave Oneidas, the veterans
of the seven-year war who had come all this way to their
deaths. Anger Maker, Fox—

Crouching, moving along without a sound, they crept
into the Windigo's shadow and were almost to the trees
when warriors rose up to block their way.

VIII

INTO THE HEART OF DARKNESS

84

In his cave the black bear stirred; to the southeast, beyond the jagged crest of the Ganawagehas, the sparrows were in flight; the velvety fiddlehead pushed through the earth and the adder's tongue opened its mottled brown and green leaves to show its yellow bell. In Lake Oneida the last of the ice dissolved, the sun grew warmer daily and in the now completed castle the people waited worriedly for word of the fate of the mission against the Iron Axes.

Margaret rose each morning and carried Benjamin up to a rear corner platform to look northward for the Oneidas' return. With each morning's disappointment, she returned to the longhouse to join Swift Doe in her chamber. Margaret was spending most of every day with Swift Doe, cheered by her steady improvement. Gone from her eyes was the wild, unpredictable look, gone the profound depression. Gradually, her inner strength and toughness prevailed.

This morning Margaret found her weaving a round washing basket of black ash strips. Finished, it would measure about eighteen by eighteen inches.

"Worrying about Two Eagles will not bring him home any faster," said Swift Doe in deference to the obvious. "They may not come back for another whole moon."

"I wouldn't be so anxious if it weren't so dangerous up

there. Not just the Montagnais, but the Hurons, the Crees, the Abnakis—"

"They fought there before, they know the area. They will be all right. You will be so proud when he brings back Blue Creek's head for Moon Dancer."

"Proud?" Margaret muttered, "More like revolted."

"How is Seth?"

"Not doing terribly well. The people listen, he's just not getting through. There's no commitment. He'd love to get one or two into arguing, get their curiosity aroused."

"Maybe he's just not very good at the converting."

She had completed the bottom of the basket in an open sievelike weave. She inspected it, straightening two plaits.

"I don't understand it," said Margaret. "He was near spellbinding when the chiefs interviewed him. He really surprised me. Still, he keeps at it, hoping lightning will strike."

"I hope not," said Swift Doe.

"It's an expression, dear, like *de-oné-a-wä-di-nah:* the slim chance. He may impress somebody enough so that they'll agree to embrace Christianity and that will be a start."

Swift Doe was building the basket up from the bottom, skillfully slipping the plaits over and under the upright warp.

"I have seen him talk to people," she murmured. "I think he does not have his heart in what he tells them. It is as if his mind is on other things." She smiled mischievously and winked.

"Nonsense!"

"The way he gazes at you you can almost hear his heart pounding in his chest. I am sure he lies awake night thinking about you: *she-ga-ka-do-e-sa-o-neh.*"

"Fantasizing? About me? Fiddlesticks and rot!"

Swift Doe peered intently at her friend. "It is true, Margaret. You have turned his brain around inside his head. He is sick like a sighing boy with love for you."

"It's just that he's lonely. I'm sort of his oasis in the

wilderness; we're both English, we talk about everything under the sun."

"Has he—?" Swift Doe looked suggestively at Margaret.

"*Neh!* He's a perfect gentleman."

"Mmmmmm." Swift Doe's nimble fingers flew, slipping the plaits tightly into position, leaving two openings for handholds on opposite sides near the top. "How do you feel about him?"

"I keep telling you. As I would toward any friend. As I feel toward you."

Swift Doe smirked.

"It's true. Only you, I love. I don't love him; we've become good friends and that's all."

"That is all. He makes you think about England. He makes you homesick."

"Not homesick, it's more ... nostalgia; I don't know our word for it. Homesickness tugs at your heart, nostalgia just nudges it."

"Two Eagles does not like Seth."

"He has no reason to dislike him. As far as that goes, what Iroquois warrior isn't bitter against the English?"

"I am not talking about the English, but about Seth. Two Eagles is jealous."

"He is," said Margaret. "I can't do anything about that. I've given up trying. The way things are going, Seth probably won't convert anybody; in time he'll give it up and leave. I mean, His Longhouse won't let him go on forever."

Seth burst in red-faced with excitement. "Margaret! Margaret! Success!"

"Calm down," she said. "Sit. Tell us."

"It's Chief His Longhouse!"

Swift Doe's jaw sagged in surprise. "Sho-non-ses has agreed to become a Christian?"

"He's very interested. Extremely. I don't know why I didn't approach him right off. He asks all sorts of questions; he's really interested. You may not believe it, Margaret, but I had a feeling about him when I sat before the chiefs. I sensed he was on my side, and when I answered their questions, explained things, I could see he looked interested. Don't you see what this means? If I can bring him to the Lord's table, others will surely follow. He's influential, people like and respect him. This is the way I see it: I convert him, he'll talk to some of the women, they'll talk to their husbands—"

Swift Doe was grinning.

"There you may run into a stumbling block," said Margaret.

"What do you mean?"

"The men do respect him. The women—"

"Do not like him," said Swift Doe. "He is an *o-gä-ye-ah-wa-da.*"

"An *o-gä*—"

"A roué," said Margaret. "His wife left him because of his carrying on. It's doubtful the women will pay any attention to what he tells them, about Christianity, about anything."

"Oh." Seth pondered this soberly. "But the *men* like him."

"Something else you should know about Sho-non-ses," said Swift Doe. "He likes to please. He agrees and agrees and tells people what they want to hear, to please them so they will like him."

"Oh, but he wasn't trying to please me. He was genuinely interested. It was perfectly plain—"

"Good luck," said Margaret shortly, and Swift Doe nodded.

Seth went out, his shoulders slightly sagging. By now Swift Doe was almost done with the basket, beginning to rim the top, when again the flap lifted.

In came Moon Dancer. As usual, she looked almost comically solemn.

"Last night I was seized by the dancing frenzy. I danced until I collapsed. I slept, I dreamt, I had a vision about our warriors."

Margaret, tending to Benjamin, was only half listening, but at the word *warriors* she turned her eyes toward Moon Dancer.

"All have been killed!"

Swift Doe gasped, and Margaret started slightly as Moon Dancer looked her way for the first time.

"Except one," Moon Dancer said dramatically.

"Who?" both asked at once.

"I cannot *say* which one. In my vision I saw many corpses piled up in the Iron Axes' village. At the end there was much excitement and a fire so high it burned the sky. It swallowed up the whole vison in front of my eyes so that I could not see who the one was who escaped. All I could make out was his darkened shape. But he alone got away."

"Was he tall? Short? What?" asked Swift Doe.

Moon Dancer shook her head. "I told you, I could not see."

Swift Doe persisted. "It could have been Two Eagles."

"*Nyoh,* it could have been any one of the thirty-four."

Margaret flared. "It's all twaddle, a stupid dream!"

Moon Dancer raised a pudgy finger. "It is so. It happened exactly as I saw it in my vision. I know because I had the *go-na-pa-di-a-so-ka* that proves it. A star, a dog baying and this morning a crow flying over the castle. I did not imagine it." She jabbed her temple. "It came into my brain, through my brain. All I am is the means of passage for it, for all my visions."

Having had her say, Moon Dancer left.

"That woman's not only ridiculous," said Margaret, standing outside looking down the passageway after her, "she's dangerous. I'm sure this was her first stop. Now she'll go and spread it all over the castle. Some of the wives are bound to take what she says as gospel, and Lord knows how they'll react. Maybe even commit suicide. Someone ought to shut her up permanently!"

"Kill her?"

Margaret came back inside. "I didn't say that. It's getting terribly stuffy in here. It's such a nice day, let's go out."

"*Nyoh.* Margaret—do not tell anyone else that Moon Dancer is dangerous and should be killed."

"I said I didn't say that!"

"It is just that if something should happen to her everyone will look at you first."

"Nothing will happen to her; if she's threatened she'll see it in a vision and avoid it." They started down the passageway. "Wait—what was that word she used? *Go-na-pa*—"

"*Di-a-so-ka,*" said Swift Doe. "It means the one of the many."

"What was that about the star, a dog baying, the crow?"

"If you experience three such happenings right after a vision your vision cannot possibly be false. But all three must be *one of many.* There are many stars, but last night she saw only one. Many dogs bay at night; she heard only one. *Go-na-pa-di-a-so-ka.*"

"Brilliant," Margaret answered sarcastically. But worry darkened her face.

85

That night sleep eluded Margaret. She listened to the wind, to Benjamin's measured breathing close by, and her mind churned. She thought not about Moon Dancer but mainly about Seth and Two Eagles. Seth had not even begun to recover from his illness when it became clear that he was attracted to her. Was he just lonely, in desperate need of someone? Was he finding intolerable the distance between him and all that was dear and familiar?

Or had he fallen in love with her? She hoped he only

imagined he was in love. He knew how deeply she and Two Eagles loved each other. He even commented on it. And he wasn't the sort to set his cap for another man's wife, even the white wife of a red man.

Margaret knew she wasn't in love with him. She was fond of him, she enjoyed his company, his wit, his warmth and personality; most of all she admired his dedication. And his wistfulness was endearing. There was something sad about him; he'd survived so much only to face certain failure attempting to convert the Oneida. She recalled the way the enthusiasm drained from his face when they told him the truth about His Longhouse, the way it came back when he resolved to work on only the men of the tribe.

In another place, in another time perhaps, the two of them would have met and become more than friends. Pierre came onto the screen of her mind; she recalled how he had so heartlessly deceived her. The perfect gentleman: gracious, attentive, kindly, caring. And when she accepted his proposal of marriage, he seemed devoted, loving, raising her onto a pedestal. It wasn't until they were reunited in Quebec that his true character had revealed itself.

Seth was no Pierre. There was nothing false or hidden about Seth. He was honest, sweet, likable.

But why dwell on him with Two Eagles so far away and undoubtedly in danger? *Why hadn't they come back?* It was going on three weeks. The raid couldn't have turned into a prolonged battle.

All the wives were asking what could be holding the men up. No one could understand it. His Longhouse's explanation was that after massacring the Montagnais they were taking their time returning, taking the trail that runs down the eastern shore of Lake Ontario, stopping off at Massowaganine. Or they may have stopped off at Tenotoge to brag to the Mohawks about doing their dirty work for them, for it was they who had slain the original Montagnais hunting party.

Finally she slept, but fitfully, dreaming in snatches about Two Eagles, happy episodes out of the past: swim-

ming in the lake, canoeing, taking Benjamin to pick berries. The sun was spilling across the horizon when she got
out of bed, washed, dressed, changed and fed Benjamin
and, taking him with her, climbed to the platform to scan
the trail north.

Half an hour later she gave up.

Long shadows were carpeting the untilled fields and
the sun was painting the low-lying clouds the colors of the
loosestrife assembling in the meadows when a lone warrior approached the open rear gate to be besieged by the
excited Oneidas.

86

Margaret and Swift Doe pushed through the crowd to
where Red Paint sat on the ground, ragged and filthy,
looking as though he'd crawled through a thorn bush, but
otherwise fit. Everyone was questioning him at once.

"Let him speak," said His Longhouse.

After downing a gourdful of water Red Paint told about
the raider's capture, the executions, Fox and Anger Maker's torture. Moon Dancer was standing before him nodding her head with his every disclosure, triumphing in the
confirmation of her vision.

Red Paint paused to drink a second gourdful of water.
"Two Eagles killed Blue Creek," he told Moon Dancer.

"Ahhhh, and gave you his head? Where is it?"

"He would not cut his head off."

"Never mind about that," Margaret interrupted. "Where
is Two Eagles?"

Red Paint fixed her with troubled eyes. "Dead."

"No!"

He nodded. "He, Splitting Moon and I got free; we left

Blue Creek dead and were sneaking off into the woods
when we ran into Iron Axes. Two Eagles yelled run, I ran.
We all did. One of the seal fuckers chased me, but something happened—I think he ran into a bush and it jabbed
his eye. I heard him yelling and when I turned to look he
was down on his knees pawing at his eye."

"What about Two Eagles?"

"I got almost to the river. I could hear rapids. I circled
around and went back to see. I picked my way from tree
to tree. I came around the far side of the village. Somebody had started a great fire. It reached to the treetops; it
was the Windigo."

"A monster as tall as a tree," His Longhouse explained
to Margaret. "The Iron Axes make them."

"Somebody must have thrown a torch at it," said Red
Paint.

"What about Two Eagles!"

"The Iron Axes caught them both," Red Paint continued. "It was hard to see because of the flames and all the
smoke; like seeing shadows moving. But I could make out
Two Eagles and Splitting Moon. They were lying on the
ground at their feet. They were dead, Mar-gar-et. I—could
do nothing."

"But you didn't actually see Two Eagles killed!" rasped
Margaret.

"I tell you, I saw both dead. I am sorry."

"You just finished saying you couldn't see either of
their faces. How can you be so certain it was them lying
there?"

"Would I say it if I was not sure?"

"I told you and Swift Doe before," said Moon Dancer.
"All were killed except one. This one: O-kwen-cha."

The crowd nodded in unison.

Margaret persisted. "Still you never saw their faces."

"Dead!" Red Paint shouted.

"How? Axes? Knives? Strangled? What?"

"I do not know. I told you, it was done before I got
back there. Let me ask you a question: *Who would the*

*Iron Axes have killed but Two Eagles and Splitting Moon?
The only ones left.* I am sorry, Mar-gar-et, so sorry."

She turned and walked off; Swift Doe hurried after her.
Seth, who had been standing on the fringe of the crowd,
caught up with them and set a consoling hand on Margaret's shoulder.

A full moon tinged the woodlands blue-white; the three of
them walked outside the castle. Margaret still rejected Red
Paint's version of the events.

"He saw what he saw," said Swift Doe.

"There are just too many holes in his story. He admitted
everything happened before he got back there. He claims
he saw two bodies on the ground, but all he could make
out were shadows. How can you identify someone lying
down when you can't even see his physique?

"*Neh,* he got away, so did they. They must have. They
just ran off in different directions."

Swift Doe considered this. "Buy why were the Iron
Axes still standing near the burning thing where he left
them? And who else could the two bodies be? They would
not kill their own men. And, as O-kwen-cha said, Two Eagles and Splitting Moon were the only Oneidas left."

"The fact remains, he couldn't positively identify the
two on the ground! Couldn't even describe their builds.
Because the three of them were so badly outnumbered,
he's assuming they couldn't possibly get away. Only he
managed to, didn't he? He makes it sound as if Two Eagles and Splitting Moon never budged from that spot. And
yet it was Two Eagles who yelled, 'Run!' It makes no
sense, it's all too sketchy, too vague."

"Maybe when he's rested a bit and eaten something,
he'll be more specific," said Seth. "Everybody was flinging questions. He was very excited."

"Regardless of what he says he saw, the key is *he ran
off and didn't get back for who knows how long.* Long
enough for anything to happen."

"I still wonder who the two bodies could have been if

they were not Two Eagles and Splitting Moon," murmured Swift Doe.

Margaret spun toward her. "*You're* saying they're dead!"

Swift Doe shrugged.

"And you?" Margaret asked Seth.

"I think we should just hang on. Look how long it took Red Paint to get back. Give them a few more days; if they got away—and I'm sure they must have—they could have taken a different way back. A more circuitous route to evade pursuit. So it'll take longer to get home."

"Yes, yes," murmured Margaret. "That could be it exactly."

"I say we just be patient," said Seth.

Margaret looked to Swift Doe for agreement. Her expression said she didn't agree at all.

 87

A week slipped by and four days of the week following; hope deserted Margaret abruptly. She needed neither Moon Dancer nor Red Paint to confirm her blackest fear. If he were alive, Two Eagles would crawl through fire to get home to her and Benjamin. Unable to crawl, he'd drag himself. It was now eleven days since Red Paint's return. He continued to insist to everyone that he was the sole survivor.

Like a man falling off a cliff grabbing for branches on the way down, Margaret snatched for every explanation as to why Two Eagles and Splitting Moon failed to return. And discarded them all. Logic had always been the mainstay of her thinking. Now, like a snake rising in the path, it rose, cold, indisputable, to destroy her optimism. Two Eagles was dead, it insisted; clinging to hope was absurd.

She dreamt of the pile of decapitated corpses described by Red Paint and the pile of heads, among them Two Eagles', his face bruised and bloodied, the whites of his eyes staring blindly.

Into her heart grief poured. Swift Doe and Seth were convinced he was dead, even though neither was so heartless as to say so. Their expressions gave them away. In between attacks of bereavement so intense they caused her to shake, she took stock of her situation. Her life was suddenly drastically changed. Without Two Eagles and their relationship, she saw herself again as an outsider. It did not matter that she had become fluent in the language, familiar with the ways and customs of the Oneida, that she was a bona fide adoptee. It did not matter that her son was the son of a Pine Tree chief, that she and Two Eagles had been properly married in the eyes of the chiefs, elders and matrons of the tribe. All of that had come to an abrupt end.

She began to feel as Seth felt, that like him she was just another English whiteskin with no right to be there—a transient in the longhouse, an intruder.

During the third week since Red Paint's return, Margaret sat with Seth in his chamber. He continued groping for optimism.

"He could have been stricken with amnesia."

"He's dead," she murmured.

"Margaret—" Seth protested.

"It's going on six weeks since they left there. Had they been successful they would have been back in a week. They left with snow on the ground. Now we're into April. I've thought and thought about it, Seth, and I've accepted it, kicking and screaming in protest. But I have. Why can't you?"

He made a gesture of helplessness.

"I've decided to leave," she murmured.

"But this is your home."

"Please. It *was* my home as long as he was here. Not now. Now I'm reduced to pretending it is, and it doesn't work. I get up in the morning, and my first thought is I'm in the wrong place." She brushed away tears. "I'm going home, back to Daddy and Mother. God only knows how I'll get there."

"I'm going back."

"When?"

"Right away. What's to keep me here?" He looked bleak. "I've failed utterly, and with all that's been happening nobody's even in the mood to listen. By the way, you were right about His Longhouse. He was never interested.

"What puzzles me is how missionaries like Obadiah Hedgepath do it. He's reputedly enormously successful among the Senecas. Jesuits have walked into villages and come out with whole tribes attached to their robes. I can't convert a one. I must say, I came an awfully long way to prove that I never should have left home."

She shook her head. "That makes two of us."

88

It was now a month since Red Paint's return. News of the disaster had taken a heavy toll—both emotional and in numbers of warriors. One third of the Oneidas' fighting strength had been massacred or tortured to death by the Montagnais.

Still, life went on at Onneyuttahage. The hardwood spades were brought out and the fields prepared. Three or four kernels of corn were heaped over with soil, and to each hill four beans of different colors were added. Like the pumpkin and squash that would be planted shortly, they would grow to interlace with the cornstalks.

When Margaret disclosed that she intended to leave, Swift Doe was extremely upset.

"You are my best friend, you go, and I will never see you again. How can you do this?"

"I can't stay here a widow, dear."

"I am a widow."

"You're also an Oneida."

"So are you, flesh of our flesh, bone of our bone." Margaret covered her hand with her own. "I dress like one and talk like one and do everything the rest of you do. I even believed I was one. But not now. Now I'm back to where I was when the *Aventurier* ran aground on the Shaw-na-taw-ty, the Mohawks attacked and I ran for my life.

"I must leave, Swift Doe. This place is crushing me. Everything I see reminds me of him: the empty side of the bed that he never even got to sleep in, Red Paint, His Longhouse, the woods outside, the stream. I'll be living the rest of my days with his ghost. That's inevitable. But not here, I can't stay. Try and understand."

"I do not understand. You are young, you will meet a new husband. Look at the twisting trail of my life: first Long Feather, then Bone, now my bed is empty. You are beautiful, Margaret. All the men look at you. You will find a husband. One will find you. Please stay."

"I can't. Will you walk with us to the gate?"

"I hate this. I will never see you again. Who will take my knife away from me?"

"You've not picked it up in ages."

"I might—" Swift Doe tried to look threatening.

"You won't. You're back to where you should be," Margaret said. "Your resiliency is astounding. Would that a little rubs off on me." She kissed her and held her. "You're my one regret, Swift Doe. I wish I could take you with me."

"Across the O-jik'-ha-dä-gé-ga, the Wide Water? Never!"

"*Neh*, you're right. You'd feel as out of place in England as I've come to feel here. Think of it like that, and you'll understand."

Seth waited outside, his tumpline pack in place, holding hers. He helped her on with it. The three of them walked to the gate. At the gate Red Paint came up to them. He was fully restored, his scratches and bruises healed, his facial stripes freshly painted.

"You are leaving," he murmured. "I am sorry to see you go. You were a good wife to Tékni-ska-je-a-nah, for a whiteskin. Now you will go back to your people, *nyoh*?"

"*Nyoh.*"

"Take with you good memories of Onneyuttahage, Margaret."

"All of them, O-kwen-cha."

He touched Benjamin's cheek. "He has everything of his father except your eyes, *neh?* He will grow up to be the image of him; as tall, as strong, as brave and wise. He is Oneida. You, too, Mar-gar-et, forever. Flesh of our flesh, bone of our bone."

Most of the Oneidas had gathered at the gate. All said solemn good-byes, even the women who had rejected her as an intruder. When she led Seth and Swift Doe out the gate she could see the path heading to the main trail only dimly.

A few steps more and she stopped to kiss Swift Doe good-bye. She, too, looked misty-eyed.

"I love you, Margaret."

"I love you, dear. Think of me sometimes."

"*Nyoh*, all that we had together, all we are losing now."

"Not losing, never. We can never be apart in our thoughts. Good-bye, Swift Doe. Kiss the boys good-bye for me."

Swift Doe walked away quickly without looking back. Margaret too one last look at the castle, the palisade, poking the sky, embracing the longhouses, the people, enclosing a thousand sweet memories.

"Let's go."

89

It was a lovely April day. The earth had come alive with a thousand pleasures for the senses. It was a day too beautiful to be dimmed through tear-scrimmed eyes. But Margaret's melancholy lingered. They walked in silence. A redstart found and followed them, flitting from tree to tree overhead, warbling its *chewy-chewy-chewy-chew-chew-chew.* It helped to distract her; the sight of pink and pure white trillium and deep, purple-red wake-robin helped further. They reached the main trail and started down it toward the distant Hudson.

"We should get off this onto the old trail before too long," she said. "That way we'll avoid any Mohawk hunting parties. They seldom use it, but the south trail below the old trail would be even safer. It runs through the lands of the Munsee basket weavers, who wouldn't harm a fly."

"You're the guide, you decide. How many days to the Hudson?"

"How many *sleeps,* the Iroquois say. Six without pushing ourselves too hard. We should conserve our stamina for the Taconic Mountains on the opposite side. Just cross your fingers we don't run into rain so hard we'll have to seek shelter and be delayed."

The redstart had deserted them; Margaret gazed overhead at the cloudless azure sky. They went on for close to three leagues before Margaret called a halt, and they rested by the side of the path that led from the main trail to the old trail. Margaret hung Benjamin's cradleboard from a branch; they removed their tumpline packs before sitting on a deadfall. She leaned over and pulled a handful of mushrooms from a decayed stump, putting them in her mouth.

"What's that?" Seth asked.

"The Oneida call them *onsĕⁿ' sǎ'*. They're the only mushrooms that survive thawing and freezing, so they're the first ones available come spring. Try some."

He tasted one hesitantly and began chewing. "Not a very definite flavor. You know, I think I saw these on my way to Onneyuttahage when I was so hungry I was reduced to eating bark."

"There are all kinds of edible fungi in these woods. You just have to know the poisonous ones, like the death cap, the destroying angel and others that can kill you in minutes. We'd better go on. We still have three or four hours till nightfall. How are your feet?"

"Fine. These corn-husk moccasins are very comfortable."

"You'll wear out all five pairs before we get to Boston," she said.

They reached the narrow, twisting old trail and stopped a second time to eat a bit of cranberry cornbread. They sat on boulders on either side of the trail opposite each other. Seth held Benjamin. Margaret sighed softly as her pensive mood returned.

"Have you thought about what you want to do when you get home?" he asked.

"Do?"

"It may not have occurred to you, but you'll be the only woman in all of England fluent in Iroquois."

"Only Oneida. And not exactly fluent."

"Come now, you speak it flawlessly. You know, you could teach it. Better yet, go around lecturing on the tribes, recounting your experiences, and dressed as you are in authentic deerskins, why you'd be a positive sensation. You could make a fortune."

"I—don't think so. I wouldn't feel right. Better I put it all behind me."

"But you could make enough in a year or so to live on

the rest of your life." He was rapidly warming to the idea. "People would flock to hear you. You could write a book. An Oneida dictionary, too. People know practically nothing about the Indians, yet they're fascinated by them."

"No thank you. I not only don't find the idea attractive, it repels me."

"Oh. Sorry. I guess I was being insensitive. Margaret . . ."

"Mmmmmm?"

"I just wanted to say it's time I told you."

"What?"

"I—I'm no missionary."

"I know. You proved that. I guess it takes a combination of dedication, old-fashioned brass and an instinct for dealing with the primitive mind. You just don't have it. Neither would I."

He was looking at her strangely. "That's not what I mean. I mean, I'm really not a missionary. Never was. It was all a masquerade. I had a faked letter of introduction to Reverend Allbright in Boston; my services were badly needed—they'll take any warm body—and he couldn't check my letter with London as to its authenticity.

"Margaret, this may shock you, but your father hired me to come over, find you, bring you home."

90

You despicable swine!"

"Margaret . . ."

"Swine, swine, swine!"

"Let me explain."

"You just did! Of all the contemptible—how much is he paying you?"

"Must we go into that?"

"How much?"

Seth's cheeks were reddening, his eyes darted about. "Twenty-five hundred guineas to start, an additional twenty-five hundred if I succeed in bringing you back. Plus expenses."

"And do you get a bonus for Benjamin?"

"Please, I had no idea it would turn out like this."

"Like what?"

"You wrote and told them you were married, but for me Benjamin was a surprise."

"He forced a change in plans, right? No chance for persuasion. You'd have to abduct me."

"Did I do either one? It was your idea to leave—I didn't suggest a thing."

She glared. "You want credit for that? Of all the disgusting—"

"Whether you realize it or not, your father and mother are very worried."

"Please, I don't want to hear. I didn't do this to hurt anybody. I wrote and explained as best I could."

"Your father gave me a copy of your letter. Margaret, I know I've been outrageously deceitful in this. But think about it, what choice was there?"

"A missionary!"

"I had to come to you in—disguise."

"Of course, you needed time to ingratiate yourself with me, become friendly, win me over."

"That was my hope." His candor surprised her. "I hope you don't think I faked my illness. Margaret, it *did* all turn out for the best. You didn't want to stay, you came to hate it there."

"I didn't hate it. It just got too painful."

"There you are."

"That's still no excuse for what you did."

"What *did* I do? Not once did I suggest you leave Two Eagles. Even hint. I saw from the first how you felt about each other."

"You did your best to make me homesick."

It sounded ridiculous, even to her.

"Hold on. *You* were the one who wanted to talk about England and home. You pumped me and pumped me."

"You let me."

"I certainly didn't encourage you."

"Oh, to bloody hell with it, I'm going home. I've no choice but to. And when we dock you'll get another twenty-five hundred guineas for me. Plus expenses. What will you do with all that money, invest it in shares in the latest quack medicine? Start a business selling swampland for real estate?"

"You really think me a cad, don't you?"

"I can think of stronger words than *cad*. You should be thoroughly ashamed!"

"On the contrary, I was actually quite proud of myself, at least starting out. It promised the great adventure of my life: invading the woods of North America to rescue you. It never occurred to me you'd actually be married and with a baby, no less."

"You wretched man," she snapped. "What in God's name ails Englishmen? And Frenchmen? Why so devious? Why can't you be straightforward with women? What, is honesty a sign of weakness? It wasn't to Two Eagles or any of his friends. He was exactly what he presented himself as being, chinks in his armor and all. But you—"

"I—did confess."

"Because your conscience finally got the better of you, now that's it's over. Assuming you have a conscience."

"You'll be pleased to hear it's been thrashing me mercilessly since I first saw you. And Benjamin. And Two Eagles. I felt like Judas Iscariot."

"Which didn't prevent you from going through with it."

"With what? It turned out all events were beyond my control. Or yours, for that matter."

"Which was just dumb luck. If Two Eagles never left, what would you have down, abduct me?"

"And risk his breaking every bone in my body when he came back? Eventually, I would have just—left."

"Mmmmm."

"You don't believe me?"

"Why should I believe anything out of your mouth? You really are a blackguard! I feel so . . . so used."

"I did it for the money, I've admitted that. That's my only crime that I can see. Yes, I posed as a missionary; obviously I needed a cover. I think I've paid in hard coin for my transgressions: I went through a great deal. I left three men dead behind me and kept on with no idea what I'd find when I got to Onneyuttahage. If I even got there. It could have turned out worse than Onekahoncka.

"Your father made me a generous and, as it happened, very timely offer. I was down on my luck. I'd been in partnership in a small ribbon business in Bedworth; we were doing reasonably well until Lloyd ran off with all the money, leaving me with all the debts. I went to work clerking in the office of the Stanhope Mining Company, paid off every farthing, ended up destitute. Five thousand guineas looked like five million. I had no wife, no family, I could pack a bag and go anywhere in the world, as long as somebody else paid. I didn't take the job, I jumped at it."

"Bully for you!"

"You've a right to be annoyed."

"I'm not 'annoyed,' I'm disgusted."

"I know you despise me. So what are we to do, walk all the way to Boston with you seething and scowling? Cross the Atlantic not speaking to each other? Or put the whole mess behind us and behave like civilized human beings?"

"I've said all I'm going to on the subject."

"Good. That's a start."

They resumed walking. Almost at once something fell in front of her, barely missing her head. He bent to examine it. In the swiftly gathering gloom he made out a small creature, its head severed.

"What is it?" he asked.

"A weasel."

"It's head—"

There was a soft flurry of wings above them.

"Don't move."

The owl settled on a branch directly above their heads about seven feet away from the ground.

"Stay absolutely still," she warned.

It peered down, fierce-looking, the V pattern of its face extending from its feathered ear tufts down to its beak, as sharp as the finest Sheffield steel blade. Its face split to curl halfway around dark-rimmed, round yellow eyes.

They eyed them balefully. She eyed its talons gripping the branch like grappling hooks. In the next instant they could relax, release, down it would swoop in absolute eerie silence, its downy plumage muffling all sound.

"Get ready," she murmured.

"Margaret—"

"Shhhh. When I say run—"

The word snapped out. They ran, she clutching Benjamin to her, stumbling over roots and stones in the path, away from that hideous beak that could tear flesh from bone as easily as stripping the skin from an apple. They ran until Seth fell. She helped him to his feet. The pathway behind them twisted so she could no longer see the tree where the owl had perched. Then they heard it *hoo-hoohoo-hoo-hoo*, the sound gradually dying as it flew off toward the main trail.

Seth brushed himself off, looking gray. "If you hadn't been here, I would have run straightaway," he murmured. "When I think of that weasel—"

"You have to wait until it settles on its perch before you run. It just ate, so it was relaxed. And once settled it can't turn about easily, so chances are it'll just let you go."

"And it eats weasel heads?"

"Only the brain. Let's go back and get our things."

91

By Margaret's rough calculation they were now about three days from the Hudson. Crossing the river would take them out of Iroquois Territory, away from any Mohawks from Onekahoncka. The old trail had proven itself safer than the main trail, but even so, detouring farther south down to the Munsee trail appeared a sensible strategy.

It was nearing the end of April. They came upon intermittent showers but no storms of any great severity or duration. The wasps came out of their winter hiding, the snakes were out of the ground, insect hatches were spreading, the tiny creatures' emergence timed perfectly with the return of the swallows. Every day the sun grew brighter, exciting the green fly and humpbacked black fly colonies.

Margaret and Seth were tiring earlier in the day now, Margaret not having walked such a distance in two years. It did not help that the old trail was rougher underfoot than the main trail, which over the years had been beaten flat by the traffic of the tribes.

It was noon, the day the hottest of the year so far; they sat in the shade on deadfalls.

"I think it's time we turned south for the Munsee trail," said Margaret.

"How far is it?" Seth massaged his feet, his expression testifying to his discomfort.

"Never having been on it, I'm not sure. Perhaps five or six leagues. Munsee Territory cuts through the northeast corner of Pennsylvania."

He sighed. "It's probably ten leagues."

"Not that far. Main trails generally cut through the center of a tribe's territory."

"Even a couple of leagues is out of the way. And we're so close to the Hudson—"

"That's true, but Onekahoncka is less than a league north of us, and the Mohawks wander all over their lands. The ones that attacked our ship on the Hudson two years ago came from Onekahoncka. And they were a couple of days from home."

"Isn't it early in the year for hunting parties to be out?"

"Hunting goes on year-round. Shall we keep on and run the risk of meeting one?"

He set his bare feet down gingerly, winced and grinned. "Yes, and save what's left of my feet for up and down the Taconic mountains. They're not that high, but they're not easy climbing. The path we followed coming over was even more rugged than this trail. If we did turn south, we'd just have to come back north to cross the mountains where the four of us crossed, or somewhere near there. And wandering so far afield, couldn't we get lost?"

"You prefer to gamble."

"I wish you wouldn't use that word."

She removed Benjamin from his cradleboard and bounced him on her knee. He responded with happy gurgling and a smile.

"Lucky little prince," said Seth, "carried every step of the way. Let me carry him for a while."

He was gazing at her. She averted her eyes; she wished he wouldn't look at her so wistfully. He must realize he couldn't thrust himself into her affections. It just wasn't the time. Would he try before they got to Boston? She hoped not, and knowing how sensitive he was, she felt he wouldn't take rejection well.

She still resented his deceiving her, and yet, as he pointed out, he'd had no choice. Originally, he hadn't known her from Adam's off ox, so it wasn't as if he harbored mixed feelings about his mission. Then, too, what could he do or even say when he arrived to discover she was married and with a baby? He could hardly admit why he'd come. Two Eagles would have thrown him out the way Night Song's husband threw out Blue Creek.

Were she Seth, she conceded, she'd have likely handled the whole distasteful affair the same way.

Putting aside his mission and his disguise, he had much to recommend him, as much raw courage and tenacity as Two Eagles. Unlike Two Eagles, however, he was no leader. But he was inherently decent and gave liberally of himself to others. He was sweet, too; warm, engaging and always with a smile.

She'd liked him from the first, not just because he was English, but because each of them readily opened up to the other. She liked him more and more as time went on. He grew on her.

Was it because she was lonely and needed a friendly ear, especially now? He was wonderful with Benjamin. Someday he'd make a splendid father. And some woman, one who valued character over wealth and position, would find him an excellent husband.

A pity about Hannah Keaton. She could see how smitten Seth had been with her. Poor woman.

They bedded down that night on a hillock in a small glade, after thoroughly checking the immediate area for snakes and vermin. He noticed that Margaret was edgy.

"Are you worried about the Mohawks?"

"Yes. I think starting tonight, we should take turns on guard. I'll take the first four hours, and you relieve me. Tomorrow night we'll switch."

"Fair enough, only promise you won't let me sleep past your four hours."

She covered a yawn. "If I manage to stay awake I won't." She laughed.

"What's funny?"

"Us. Two white people in Indian deerskins with a blue-eyed Indian baby. Can't you see us walking down the

street in Boston? We're going to have to explain our way
to the docks. Good night, Seth, and thank you."

"What for?"

"Coming into my life when I most needed you."

"My pleasure."

Again she laughed. "It's been anything but."

"Good night, Margaret. Ah—" he paused. "If you don't
mind my saying so, it's as if you've turned a corner. Now
you're convinced you're doing the right thing: going
home."

"I'm convinced it's the only thing I can do. Still, since
we left there hasn't been one night I haven't laid down to
thoughts of Onneyuttahage. Strange. The farther we get
from there the more insistently it calls me back. I grew
very fond of the Oneida, but I could never honestly say
they were my people. It was Two Eagles I belonged with,
not them. I loved Eight Minks and Swift Doe—others,
too—but I never stopped being the square peg.

"Eight Minks told me once after Two Eagles and I were
married that he had told her he thought we shared one
heart. I liked that, I always remembered it.

"He did have his romantic side. Not much to say, but he
spoke volumes.

"He could have been a Tibetan living in a tent or a no-
mad wandering about the desert. It wouldn't have mattered
where he was, who his people were, it was all him, my
Two Eagles. He made me happy, I was content. How
many women can say the same about their marriage? Only
it was so short: Less than two years. I loved him so Seth,
oh I loved him—"

He came over and put his arm around her, patting her
comfortingly. "Look ahead, Margaret, not back. Your father and mother are waiting. They'll be overjoyed to see
you. You'll be happy again."

"Who knows?" She yawned.

"You go to sleep," he said. "I'll take the first watch."

He let her sleep through the night. The sun had just

cleared the horizon when she awoke. She was furious with
him for not waking her. They ate and started out.

Three days later, early in the afternoon, they stopped to
rest and eat. They had come through a drenching
downpour that lasted from early in the morning to almost
noon. Margaret's concern brought lines to her face.

"Getting across the river won't be easy. If there were
just the two of us we could swim, pushing our packs
ahead, but—"

"When the four of us came across we piled everything
on two deadfalls lashed together with our clothing."

"That's an idea. Only we'd use rope."

"Where on earth would we find rope?"

"Make it. Find a fallen slippery elm, strip off lengths of
bark with our knives, cut it into strips."

"Would it be strong enough?"

"Let me finish. We make an elm bark bucket, boil water
from the river mixed with ashes. The strips'll dry quickly
in the sun, then, thanks to the ash water, separate easily
into their filaments. We bind the filaments together in
skeins, twist three strands as tightly as possible and make
a rope up to sixty feet long. Strong as a ship's hawser."

"It sounds as if it'd take us two days," Seth said.

"Only overnight. If we find a slippery elm right off and
get started, we should be all set by sunup."

His hand went up suddenly, "Listen—"

"What?"

"I think I hear water! Stay here."

He ran on ahead, broke through a stand of bushes and
there, idling gently along, was the Hudson. Downstream

and upstream he looked for the rude cross left to mark
Fisk Drummond's grave but he could not see it. He looked
down. His heart leapt; below were four canoes half in the
water and turned over. Back he ran to where she was sitting feeding Benjamin.

"Never mind the rope, come see what I've found!"

They stood looking down at the canoes. To his surprise,
she reacted fearfully.

"Let's get out of here!"

They turned. Mohawks blocked the way.

93

Margaret recognized Hole Face from the harrowing
days she had spent as captive of his chief, Burnt Eye.
At that time Hole Face and Burnt Eye had greeted Two
Eagles, his friends and her when they stopped by
Onekahoncka while searching for Two Eagles' brother
Long Feather. Hole Face was easy to remember: his face
was deeply pitted from smallpox, his long hair was as
white as cotton, his stare was spellbinding. Seth, who also
recognized him, swallowed hard.

"Joshú-we-agoochsa," Margaret murmured. Hole Face
looked surprised that she knew his name. "Remember me?
I am Margaret," she continued.

He recognized her, his black eyes brightened. "Tékni-
ska-je-a-nah's *cannawarori*."

"Not his whore!" she snapped. "His wife."

"Tékni-ska-je-a-nah, who murdered our chief, Ho-ka-
ah-ta-ken."

"It wasn't murder. It was a fair fight. You were there,
you saw, all of you did."

He grunted and turned his eyes on Seth. "I know you,

too, even without your black cloak. You, too, are a murderer; you killed two of our men."

"You tortured one of ours to death and a second died of exposure on the trail."

If Seth presumed this would even matters, Hole Face wasn't about to concede it. Then Margaret noticed that he and his men had a prisoner with the scalp lock of a Mohican. His wrists were bound in front of him, a stick was thrust through the inside of his elbows across the small of his back. He was trembling, terror-stricken.

"You will come with us to our castle," said Hole Face, pointing North.

"*Neh,*" snapped Margaret. "Impossible. We must get across the river. The white chiefs expect us in Massachusetts in the city by the O-jik'-ha-dä-gé-ga. We're late already, held up by the weather. If we are delayed further they will come over the mountains looking for us. They will come into Mohawk Territory."

"We will be here," he said with a grim smile. "So will you. Come along."

"*Neh*. My husband, Tékni-ska-je-a-nah, sent me to escort this man to the waiting white chiefs. In his head he carries a very important secret message."

Curiosity furrowed Hole Face's pitted features. Then his stern look returned.

"Both of you come with us. He killed two of our warriors. He will show our people his blood."

"He killed them while escaping. Be thankful he got away." She moved closer to Hole Face, her tone grim. "If he died while he was your prisoner, Onekahoncka would be burned in reprisal by now, and your people destroyed."

He confronted Seth. "You said nothing about any message."

"It's a secret," she snapped. "I told you. *I-da-o-ta.*"

"Tell me the secret."

"You listen: he must reach the white chiefs as fast as possible." She held her eyes, injecting menace into her tone. "Governor Richard Coote in Albany is party to this mission. If we fail to cross the river and join the white chiefs, he will send up troops to find out the reason for the delay. When he learns that you, Joshú-we-agoochsa, are the cause, his anger will be great." She jabbed his chest with a finger. "His soldiers will seize you and put you in an iron cage."

He licked his lips and stared and held his hand up. "Do not move."

He consulted in low tones with two of the other Mohawks and turned back to her. A worried glint had crept into his eyes.

"He is a murderer. Our chiefs will be angry if we do not bring him in. They will punish us."

"Your chiefs will not know you ran into us, if you do not tell them."

Again he talked to the other two.

"What part has Tékni-ska-je-a-nah in all this?" he asked.

"Governor Coote asked him to see that this man has safe passage from Onneyuttahage to Boston. I agreed to escort him. So you see, if you harm him or even delay him, you will incur Two Eagles' anger along with the anger of the white chiefs and His Excellency, the governor. Do you see now what you are getting into here? A hornet's nest, Joshú-we-agoochsa. You and your whole tribe. How will your chiefs feel about that?"

His face clouded, he bit his lower lip.

"Tell him I have powerful friends in Boston—" began Seth.

"He doesn't care," she muttered between clenched teeth. To Hole Face she said: "Your chiefs' anger will be as great as the governor's and the white chiefs', *neh*? Is that what you want? Listen to me, there is a way out for you all: you have not seen us here, you've seen no one. You will give us two men to paddle us across. You and the rest go on home with your prisoner. Two men." She indicated. "You and you."

He consulted a third time with his friends. All three eyed her with visible apprehension.

"Tell him—" began Seth.

"Shut up." She folded her arms, thrusting her jaw out defiantly. "I'm waiting, Joshú-we-agoochsa."

He was seething with frustration. "Go!" he burst. "Now! I order you. You did not meet us, we did not meet you. Tell Lord Coote, tell the whiteskin chiefs."

"You are a wise man."

"Tell Tékni-ska-je-a-nah. Promise now."

"I promise."

It was all so childish she could scarcely contain her laughter. She, Seth, and Benjamin were transported across the river. The two paddlers swung about to return; Margaret and Seth reached the top of the bank and turned to look. Hole Face and the others had vanished, taking the remaining three canoes. Seth pursed his lips and let a breath out slowly; he looked completely drained.

"You were magnificent," he murmured.

"That poor Mohican. I wonder what he did?"

"Inspired!"

"I should have bullied Hole Face into handing him over, only that would have been pushing it."

"I daresay. Amazing, I've never seen anybody so bamboozled."

"It's like whist, Seth. Bluffing, is all. You just can't show fear. He did; that's when I knew I had him."

"Let's go."

"Not yet. Let me sit for a few minutes and let my heart slow down." She scanned the heavens. "And look, I do believe it's going to rain again."

94

Red Paint listened to His Longhouse just inside the main gate. "I know how Ossivendi Oÿoghi felt about Tékni-ska-je-a-nah and Margaret, but I still cannot believe his turning traitor to the tribe of his family's blood. His brain must have been upside down in his head."

Through the open gate, two dogs came bounding in barking, forcing His Longhouse to move his legs. A knot of shouting boys followed.

"Here, here," snapped His Longhouse. "Quiet down. You will wake the dead in their graves."

"They are coming," shrilled Dawn Maker, Swift Doe's older son.

"Who?" asked Red Paint.

"Tékni-ska-je-a-nah and Tyagohuens!"

The boys ran back out, the dogs scurrying after them, barking even louder. Red Paint and His Longhouse stared at each other.

"It cannot be," murmured Red Paint. "I do not believe it."

Hearing the boys others began converging on the front entrance, among them Swift Doe and Moon Dancer, who looked skeptical.

"They are alive," Red Paint whispered to her. "Alive!" She shook her head. *"Neh."*

"I do not understand, I saw with my own eyes," he babbled.

In dragged Two Eagles, followed by Splitting Moon, both looking consumed with exhaustion. They had lost so much weight, their dirty and ragged buckskins hung on them. Splitting Moon came in six steps and sat down hard

on the ground. Two Eagles knelt beside him and looked
from face to face.

"Where is Margaret? Where is my son? Somebody get
them!"

Swift Doe and Moon Dancer looked anxiously at each
other; Red Paint looked as if he wished he were half the
world away. He examined the tips of his moccasins, then
studied the tops of the palisade.

"They . . . are gone," he mumbled.

"What?"

"Gone," said Swift Doe, then began quietly explaining.
The gawking Oneidas, now drawn up around the two arrivals, stiffened in anticipation of an angry outburst. His
mouth agape, Two Eagles listened, then interrupted, glar-
ing savagely at Red Paint.

"You told them we were dead!" he roared.

"I thought—I mean—I ran, got away from the Iron Ax
chasing me, I circled back, I saw you both lying on the
ground. I saw you! I did!"

"Oeuda," growled Splitting Moon. "What you saw was
two Iron Axes, milk brain. I knocked them out, one, two.
I did not kill either. You saw nobody dead." He nodded toward Two Eagles. "His quick thinking saved both our
skins. When that bunch came up to us and he yelled 'Run'
and you ran, he snatched up two torches and threw them
at the Windigo. It went up like dry leaves. The Iron Axes
froze where they stood, just for breath, just long enough
for us to get moving. Four of them chased us, but we
made it to the river, swam across. They followed us but
we shook them off."

"Only to discover other Iron Axes camped on the north
bank," said Two Eagles. *"They* chased us the rest of that
night. Just before sunrise we lost them. We found a leaky
canoe with no paddles—"

"We broke saplings for poles and started out," Splitting
Moon went on, "heading downstream toward Hochelaga."

"Never mind the rest," said Two Eagles. "We made it,
here we are. Not dead on the ground by the Windigo.

O-kwen-cha—" He leveled a finger at Red Paint. "In my chamber. I want to know all about Margaret and Benjamin and that sickly-faced black cloak who does not know when to stop smiling. Him I never trusted."

In Two Eagles' chamber Splitting Moon and Red Paint sat with Swift Doe. Entering, Two Eagles went to the bunk. They watched as he laid a hand on it then straightened, looked about, spied a cradleboard in the corner, studied it and sent it crashing against the wall. Red Paint's worry was rapidly changing to fear.

Two Eagles whirled on him. "Well?" he barked.

"It has been weeks," interrupted Swift Doe, "*augustuske* into *tegenhonid*. All of us thought that when you did not return you must have been killed with the others."

"All of you were stupid," snapped Splitting Moon.

He was busily rubbing his feet with *okases*, a salve made from a decoction of the dried small twigs and leaves of rosemary.

"Then we were stupid," she murmured. "But it had been so long, we would have thought it even if O-kwencha did not tell us what he saw."

"He saw wrong!" snarled Splitting Moon.

Two Eagles looked devastated. Swift Doe shook her head sympathetically.

"When did they leave?" he asked.

"And for where?" asked Splitting Moon.

"Boston," snapped Two Eagles. "Where he came from. To get on a wooden island and cross the O-jik'-ha-dä-gé-ga. Swift Doe, *when* did they leave!"

"Six sleeps ago," said Red Paint.

Two Eagles' eyes brightened. "Only six? Ahhhh, if we leave now, today, we can catch up with them!"

Splitting Moon groaned. "I cannot walk from here to the front gate."

"Take me with you," said Red Paint.

He shrank from Two Eagles' scowl, then thrust out his chin defiantly.

"*Nyoh*, you must. I made a terrible mistake. You must give me the chance to make up for it. I *am* going."

Swift Doe was staring appealingly on his behalf at Two Eagles.

"All right," he agreed.

"I will come, too," said Splitting Moon in a martyred tone.

"You who cannot make it to the front gate?" Two Eagles laughed brittely.

Splitting Moon bristled. "I will. Give me till after I eat something, and my feet will be stronger than yours."

"Swift Doe," said Two Eagles, "get Sho-non-ses for me. There is something I must tell him."

"I did not say anything about *tite-ti*," said Red Paint as she started through the flap, causing her to hesitate before going out.

"*Ogechta!*" growled splitting Moon.

Swift Doe returned at once with His Longhouse, so quickly one would have thought he was listening outside.

"There is something you must know," said Two Eagles. "I was responsible for the death of our warriors."

He explained about using the signal call of the yellow-billed cuckoo out of season, alerting the Montagnais to their presence. Splitting Moon scoffed and repeatedly dismissed this with waves of both hands.

"Do not listen to him. He is no more guilty than any of us. We all agreed it would be a good signal. We use it often, *neh*?"

"But it was I who suggested it," said Two Eagles.

"So? We could have rejected it. We did not, not one. You have been beating it to death ever since the ambush. I am sick of hearing about it. O-kwen-cha?"

"*Nyoh?*"

"Did you know that *tite-ti* leaves those woods when Gâ'-oh blows? You did not, none of us did. So *ogechta*, my friend. Swift Doe, can you bring us food? We are so sick of mushrooms and rabbit. Just thinking of them my stomach turns over. Have you any hot *onoṅdäät* in your kettle?"

"I have *o' ni' yu stäğe'*."

"Samp! I have not tasted good samp since my wife died! Bring it, bring it, I will eat every drop!"

"Have you any *aque*?" Two Eagles asked her. "Any part except the ribs; ribs are for dogs."

"I have salted venison, the buck you yourself shot. I will fill you both with good hot food."

She went out.

"Tyagohuens makes sense," said His Longhouse. "You should not take the blame for so many dead because of a wrong signal."

"Listen to him," said Splitting Moon.

"*Nyoh,*" added Red Paint.

Two Eagles shook his head. "I do not care what any of you thinks. It sticks in my conscience like a sharp piece of flint and will until I sleep with dirt in my mouth."

His Longhouse shrugged. "As you wish. You are as stubborn as ever, Tékni-ska-je-a-nah, but then is that something you do not know? When will you leave?"

"After we eat," said Splitting Moon. "Do not worry, my friend. We will catch up with them before the mountains on the far side of the Shaw-na-taw-ty."

Two Eagles shook his head. "Maybe. But in the meantime what about the Maquens from Onekahoncka? Margaret is smart; she would not take the main trail, but the old one that is seldom used. Still, they could run into roving hunters. And it would warm the Maquens' stomachs like soup to get their hands on that black cloak. Which puts her in danger. Even if they get safely across the Shawna-taw-ty, there are the Mohicans, the Pocumtucks, Nipmucs—so many tribes that are our enemies between the mountains and the Wide Water. Two whiteskins dressed as Oneidas? That is begging for trouble. Are they armed?" he asked Swift Doe, who had returned with the food.

"Each has a knife."

"You worry too much," said Red Paint. "We will catch up before they even get close to Onekahoncka."

Splitting Moon paused in gorging himself to massage his feet. He sighed. Two Eagles grunted.

"Tonight on the trail, when we are so tired we cannot go another step, I will consult my óyaron and maybe learn something. We must catch up with them. I cannot lose her, I cannot lose Benjamin. I cannot! Swift Doe—"

Taking her by the arm, he steered her outside. "Tell me about her when she left."

"She was very sad. Crying. She did not want to go."

"He talked her into it!"

"*Neh*, she could not stay; she said so. She could not live here without you. *Could not live*, Tékni-ska-je-a-nah."

"It is the same for me."

"What if they get to the O-jik'-ha-dä-gé-ga and leave on a wooden island before you reach there?"

"I will follow."

"How?"

"I will. Somehow. I cannot lose her. Never, never."

IX

LOVE IS THE SPUR

95

The rain fell in torrents as they loped along the main trail. They had passed Tenotoge. Schandisse, the second Mohawk castle, would be next.

"Can I ask a question?" Red Paint asked, running alongside Two Eagles. "What took you so long to get home after you escaped the Iron Axes on the north side of the Kanuwage?"

"We ran into a storm that makes this look like a rain shower," said Splitting Moon, pulling up beside them. "We wrecked our canoe against the rocks. I—was hurt."

"He cracked a bone in his foot and could not walk," explained Two Eagles. "By then, luckily, we were out of Iron Ax Territory into Sokoki Abnaki lands. When the storm let up, we swam back across the river and holed up in a cave until he could walk again. It was almost a whole moon before he could put weight on the bone. We made our way toward Onondaga Territory to the trail that runs north from Massowaganine and on past it down to the white caves."

"I told him and told him," growled Splitting Moon. "Go on without me, I said, leave me, I can make it back myself when my bone heals. Stubborn as the stump in the cornfield that you have to plant around, that one. He refused to go."

"I do not leave crippled friends in the woods of our enemies," snarled Two Eagles.

"You would have gotten home. *She* would not have given up on you and left with him—"

"No more talk about it, my ear pans are too full. Faster!"

They went on without speaking. The storm was abating.

"I, too, have a question," said Splitting Moon. "And do not fire up your mouth at me. I have always been curious: What is this thing you say you have for Mar-gar-et?"

"You mean love?"

"That is the word," said Red Paint. "What does it mean?"

"It is her word for how we feel for each other, so I use it."

"But what does it mean?" persisted Splitting Moon.

"It is hard to say. It is not something you make words about, but something you feel. And we share."

"Like as if both of you have aching heads at the same time?"

"*Neh.*"

"What then? A burning sensation? A churning in the gut? A sharp pain?"

"*Neh*, none of those. I told you, I cannot describe what is it. Only that when two people have it, it is the same feeling for both and they understand without words. Margaret says it is like we both see the same flower that is not there." His two companions looked utterly baffled. "You do not understand, and I cannot explain. But that is 'love.' You need no words."

Red Paint snickered. "*Nyoh.* I have seen you two stare at each other like two frogs on a lily pad; not moving, not making a sound, all eyes."

"That is funny to you? If you knew what it was, if you felt it, you would know it is beautiful. It is the sun rising in your soul, it is all the singing birds bunched in your heart. It is why she is my life and I cannot lose my life. Faster!"

"If we do not catch up to them before Boston we could walk into many guns," muttered Splitting Moon. "The tribes that are there hate us as much as the whiteskins do."

"I cannot worry about that," said Two Eagles. "If we have to walk into that place we will not speak to anyone, keep our eyes over their heads and keep moving."

The rain persisted. Margaret and Seth had reached the crest and started down the eastern slope of the mountain. They found a dilapidated hunter's lean-to. She had just finished washing out Benjamin's extra doeskin. She wrung it out.

"If it's the least bit wet it chafes him," she said.

Placing the skin inside the top of her dress against the warmth of her breasts helped to dry it. They sat surrounded by puddles, with water dripping around them, staring down the slope into the wind-roiled rain.

"Are you all right?" he asked.

"Just brooding. I'm getting good at it. I've been thinking about Ossivendi Oÿoghi."

"Ahhh—"

"Blue Creek. It's uncanny. Everything bad that's happened can be traced back to him." She smiled grimly. "He even afflicts us from the grave. Red Paint told me it was Blue Creek who told the Montagnais the Oneidas were the ones who ambushed them for poaching; that's why they attacked Onneyuttahage. Amazing how one man can exert such a powerful influence. And in the end he got what he wanted most: Two Eagles dead."

" 'They that hate you shall reign over you,' " said Seth.

"The Bible. You're something of a scholar on it, aren't you?"

"I've read it, every word. Hypocrite I may be, but I'm no atheist."

"I've been thinking about something else besides Blue Creek, something that's beginning to nettle my conscience." She cuddled Benjamin and kissed his forehead.

"I can't help thinking it's wrong for me to take him away from his people like this."

"You're his mother, you do what you think best. Particularly since his father—"

"I know, but now, instead of growing up back there, becoming an Oneida, he'll grow up a proper English schoolboy. The point is, England doesn't need every man that's born into the tribe. The Indians do, desperately. The whole race is slowly dying."

"Not the Iroquois."

"Especially the Iroquois. They fought in a war they were forced into, had absolutely nothing to gain from. The Five Nations lost nearly a third of their warriors, the flower of their manhood. At one time there were eight Mohawk castles and three Oneida. Now all we have left is Onneyuttahage and barely seventy warriors to protect it. If the Hurons ever got wind of what happened they'd come swooping down on us."

"*Us?*"

"Us!"

"Sorry, I thought we'd settled all that."

"That I'd 'turned the corner,' " she murmured. "I know, maybe I haven't. My steps may be heading in the 'right' direction, my heart . . . sometimes I think I've left it behind. I know one thing, it will never be the same."

"Cheer up," he said. "You'll feel differently when you get home, when you're settled, back to being English."

"Will I? You seem very sure."

Silence, weighty and uncomfortable, settled between them.

Both sat without speaking, pretending interest in the progress of the storm. It showed no signs of letting up. Seth spoke.

"Margaret, I do not understand how you feel about the tribe's losing Benjamin, so to speak. But think of him, his future. Back home he'll grow up in a loving atmosphere, in luxury, free from danger, from the wilds, doted on by his grandparents, never having to contend with what Hare

did. He'll go to school, to university, become whatever he
fancies. He'll have every chance in life; isn't that what
you want for him?"

"You think he wouldn't have every chance at Onneyuttahage? He'd grow up learning everything about his
world, as limited as it may be in your estimation; he'd get
himself an education to rival Oxford or Cambridge. He'd
be a credit to his people, a provider and protector. By the
time he's thirty, he could be chief of the bear clan.

"He and his peers are the Oneidas' last hope for the future. He could grow up resenting mightily missing out on
that challenge and blame me!"

"Is it so important for him to know all about the tribe?"
Seth asked.

She held Benjamin up at eye level, kissed him, regarded
him at arm's length.

"Absolutely! Not to tell him would be shameful of me.
He'll know everything about his people, about his father;
how brave he was, how good, how respected, how his
friends idolized him . . ."

She began to cry.

96

Three days later Margaret and Seth sought refuge from
the intermittent drizzle in a barn, crawling into an in-
vitingly warm haystack and falling asleep almost instantaneously. At dawn Seth woke to a sight that jolted his
heart: the black eye of a musket muzzle inches from his
face.

"Don'cha' move a muscle, Injun."

The only light came from a candle set on the dirt floor
near the closed door. The man behind the gun was white-

bearded, raw-boned, very nervous—the black metal eye trembled slightly—and in no mood for explanation. Staring down at Seth, he squinted hard then released one hand to rub his eyes.

"I swan. You're no Injun." He lowered the weapon.

Seth got up slowly, very carefully. Margaret was awake.

"Sir, my name is Seth Wilson, this is Margaret Addison. I can explain this if you'll please just put that thing down."

The farmer had turned his rheumy eyes on Margaret. "I swan, you two 'scaped from savages?"

"Ah—" began Seth.

"Exactly," Margaret cut in. "We apologize for trespassing, but we couldn't take any more of the rain."

"How'dja' 'scape? From which tribe?"

"The Mohawks," replied Seth. "We got across the Hudson and came over the mountains."

"I swan. You look beat to the bone. This be your little one? And looky at them straw shoes, they're worn to shreds. Be ya' hungry?"

"Famished," said Margaret.

"Well, folly me, my missus'll fill ya' fulla warm vittles. Oh, my name be Zachariah Judith. My missis is Edwina. Come, bring your packs."

Two Eagles, Splitting Moon and Red Paint swam the turbulent Shaw-na-taw-ty, found the mountain trail and rested briefly before attempting it. These were the lands of the peaceful Mohicans, a tribe that the Iroquois had not fought against in years. Still, the three warriors agreed that after they descended the eastern slope they would get off the trail and paralled it at a distance. Curiously, up to this point they had not encountered a single soul. Two Eagles could only hope their good fortune would hold; there must be no delay. Splitting Moon was right. If they did not catch up with Margaret and the black cloak before Boston, they would endanger themselves marching boldly into town. As well, in such a populous area, it would be hard finding Margaret and Seth.

They decided to avoid all towns, settlements, even isolated farms as they went on. They had little sleep since starting out, and all three were exhausted. Although he didn't complain, it was obvious that Splitting Moon's foot was beginning to hurt him. Red Paint found comfrey; using two stones, he ground a few leaves into powder and made a poultice to reduce the swelling. This he tied to Splitting Moon's foot.

"I am all right, there is no pain," insisted Splitting Moon, hobbling after them as they started up the trail.

"Onewachten," grumbled Two Eagles.

"I am no liar!"

"No pain," muttered Red Paint. "And I have no hole in my arse."

"We will stop here," said Two Eagles. "Sit, tie the *chegasa* tighter and we will give it time to draw the pain."

"Neh, we cannot delay."

"I say we stop, we stop!"

"Neh, you two go on. Leave me."

"I have an idea," murmured Red Paint. "We could make a litter and carry him over the mountain. By the time we get to level ground again the pain should be gone, *neh?"*

"Neh, neh, neh!" boomed Splitting Moon. "I am no cripple, you do not carry me like a dead *aque!"*

He went on ranting, oblivious of Two Eagles sneaking behind him, raising his knife handle forward and knocking him out cold.

97

They carried Splitting Moon up the mountain—securely bound to his litter and gagged. Resting his foot and the comfrey poultice chased his pain, and he was able to resume walking. But carrying him up to the crest had been hard work; by now, Two Eagles and Red Paint needed sleep, more desperately than ever.

They found a hunter's lean-to that got them out of the wind. It had finally stopped raining. They slept until the sun cleared Wachuett Mountain in the east. Two Eagles awoke in a foul mood.

"Ísene! Tesashlíh!"

"We are hurrying!" protested Red Paint. "Let a man have his morning shit. You two did."

"Do it!" snapped Two Eagles. "I have changed my mind: when we get to the bottom we will stick to the main trail. We cannot waste precious time stumbling along in the woods."

"I told you carrying me would slow you down," rasped Splitting Moon.

"Ogechta. Can you walk?"

"As good as last night, see?" He demonstrated.

"He hides his pain well," said Red Paint, grinning as he squatted.

"I have no pain, milk brain! Take your shit and make it fast."

"If we run into trouble, we fight," warned Two Eagles.

"All because of me, because of me," groused Splitting Moon.

"Ogechta!"

"You shut up!"

"Stop it, stop it, stop it," said Red Paint. "Save your anger for the black cloak. I am done, let us go."

98

The holly and the hobblebush were in bloom with tiny flowers and berries as Margaret and Seth reached the summit of Beacon Hill, passed the tall, gibbet-shaped beacon and started down the slope. To the south, on the narrow, tide-washed Neck, which connected Boston to the mainland, early-bird farmers and peddlers were already approaching the town with their wares. In the small wooden houses jammed between Copp's Hill in the North End, Fort Hill in the South End and Beacon Hill in the west, in the mansions of the wealthy on and around Beacon Street and down by the shore between Fort Hill and the Neck, the residents awoke to light the cooking fires and prepare for the day's business.

Below them a thick forest of masts crowded the wharves, and workers and seamen loaded and unloaded cargo.

They had enjoyed their first and last hot meal of the journey in Zachariah Judith's kitchen. The kindhearted farmer had offered Seth a pair of boots in woeful condition, which Seth politely declined, telling him that he planned to "walk his corn-husk moccasins off his feet." By now, Seth and Margaret had discarded their last pair of moccasins and their tumpline packs and walked barefoot down the hill toward the town. They had covered more than eighty leagues in just under three weeks, if anything increasing their pace in the final quarter of the distance. Benjamin still rode his cradleboard; his mother and Seth still wore their buckskins. All they lacked to complete the ensemble was feathers in their hair. Passersby gawked at them.

"Get used to it," muttered Seth. "By noon, we'll be the talk of the town. Look at you!"

"Look at you!"

"Not your clothes, your stride. You look like you could walk clear to Bedworth," he said.

"Imagine if I'd attempted this at Miss Slocumb's School for Young Ladies in Bedworth," she laughed. "Those were the soft days of my life. What's our first stop?"

"Abner Keaton's bookstore on Cornhill Street. Let's see if I can remember: Beacon leads down into School Street, School directly into Cornhill. There's School Street right in front of us."

"Pity your friend doesn't deal in women's clothing. I suppose I can walk around town like this, but traveling clear across the ocean would be embarrassing."

"For us both. But here's the good news: Abner is holding my money, more than twelve hundred guineas."

"Your half-pay?"

"As a matter of fact, yes. We'll be needing clothes, food, rooms, money for the return passage."

"All of which comes under expenses, doesn't it?"

"You could say."

She grinned. "Very well. Just let's not be too free with Daddy's money."

All eyes stayed on them as they walked along, ignoring the attention. Even Indians paused to stare and comment to each other. One overweight young man, who looked as if he'd been up drinking all night, sidled by and emitted a war whoop.

"*Ogechta!*" snapped Margaret, causing him to back away and wide-eye her.

"Remember my telling you that Leonora Keaton wasn't quite right in the head the day we left?" Seth shook his head. "God only knows how the poor soul's doing. I hope and pray Abner hasn't had to put her away."

They got onto Cornhill Street. Every street was a quagmire, mobbed with pedestrians and carts. Boston was noisy, with people yelling at each other out of doorways and windows, across the narrow streets. The clock in the steeple of the First Church struck seven. Like Hanover, King and Ship Streets, Cornhill was given mainly to retail shops. They passed general shops stocked with carpeting, window glass—which was indecently expensive—pewter ware, boots and shoes, Russian leather chairs, fowling pieces, pistols, fishing gear.

Margaret eyed silks, fine cottons and satins longingly. Seth was drawn to silver and silk buttons, stomachers and wigs, crimson britches, enameled French snuff boxes, Waterford long-stemmed clay pipes, Bristol crown glass decanters.

A sign creaking in the gentle breeze read A. KEATON— BOOKSELLER. The window reflected Hurley's Galway Bay Tavern across the street. The outside of the ship boasted a new coat of white paint. The shelves inside Keaton's appeared filled, and another sign on the door said OPEN 8:00 A.M. When Seth jangled the bell, Abner appeared in his shirtsleeves; he gaped, staring at their clothes.

"Seth! Lee, look who's here!" he called back through the curtain separating the shop from their home.

"This Abner, is my friend Margaret Addison and her son, Benjamin."

"Delighted to meet you. Lee!"

"Coming!"

"How is she?" Seth asked, lowering his voice.

"Tip-top, couldn't be better."

"That's a relief."

"Yes. But what are we standing here for? Come in, come in."

Flipping the door sign around to CLOSED, Abner herded them toward the rear. When Leonora came through the curtain, she gasped.

"Couple of visiting Indians, Lee," said Abner.

"Seth Wilson!"

He introduced Margaret, and Leonora set chairs for

them and asked to hold Benjamin. Business appeared good. The Keatons had acquired a wainscot chair, an oak-and-pine press cupboard, a Cromwellian up-and-down stretcher-base table and four expensive-looking maple and oak chairs.

Seth and Margaret explained their clothing and detailed the highlights of their journey. But Margaret lost her smile when she told them the circumstances of Two Eagles' death.

"And, Seth, did you have any success in converting the Indians?" Leonora asked, refilling his cup of tea.

He cleared his throat, glanced Margaret's way and sat up straight, his hands capping his knees. "I'm afraid I've been guilty of deceiving you good people. I—never was a missionary. I only posed as one because it was the best means I could think of for getting to Margaret."

He went on to sketch his true mission and how it came about. Though Abner listened dumbfounded, Leonora did not look at all surprised.

"So it was all playacting," murmured Abner. "With the three of us. Rehearsal for the people you had to contact in Boston."

"I'm not proud of myself, Abner, but I had a most unusual assignment, and to do it—"

"Hannah didn't think you were a missionary from the first," said Leonora, cutting in. "I wasn't altogether convinced myself."

"You mean I was that bad an actor?"

"Pretty bad," said Margaret.

"Come now, I convinced you ..."

"*Fooled* me."

"I could have disguised myself as a trader or trapper, but posing as a missionary seemed, I don't know, more respectable."

"More hypocritical, too," said Margaret, grinning.

"Well you certainly fooled me," said Abner glumly.

"Oh come now, dear," said Leonora, "don't take it so personally. And he's right, playing a missionary does make

sense. Even though you weren't exactly roaringly successful."

Margaret got up to check on Benjamin sleeping in the
wainscot chair. "Seth," she said, "tell me something: What
would you have done if your three companions made it to
Onneyuttahage? All of you showed up?"

"That did worry me a bit starting out; I decided I'd
work at the converting and when I got the chance, slip off
and talk to you. Of course, Benjamin complicated her
leaving," he said, looking at Leonora. "Or would have, if
Two Eagles hadn't been killed."

The coldness of this observation was not lost on Margaret.

"You may have worn false colors," said Leonora, "but
you weren't short on courage or resolve."

"My father advanced him twenty-five hundred guineas
to come and fetch me home," said Margaret, "with twenty-
five hundred more due on delivery. It took courage and resolve, all right, and no small amount of avarice."

"It was an offer too tempting to turn down," said Seth
stiffly. "And need I remind you, it wasn't my idea. He
came to me."

"I've been wondering about that, too; how ever did he
find you? And decide on you?"

"We made contact through a mutual friend. Your father
needed somebody honest and trustworthy, and not overly
ethical."

"Amen," said Abner, Leonora tittered; Margaret showed
no reaction.

"Abner," said Seth, "I left an envelope with you. You
remember, the day I came for tea I gave it to you just before I said good-bye? Gray . . ." He gestured. "So big.
Thick."

"I'll get it." He went into the bedroom and seconds later
reappeared in the doorway, looking confused. "It's not in
the bottom drawer where I put it."

"Oh?"

"Have you seen it, my dear?" Abner asked.

Margaret watched Seth look Leonora's way.

"It must be with your papers, Abner. He keeps bringing papers from the shop into the bedroom. I bring them back out again, a never-ending cycle."

Seth's anxiety was obviously rising by the moment.

After Abner retreated into the shop, they could hear him rummaging about and mumbling. He emerged, grinning, holding up the envelope.

"Amazing," he said. "I don't believe it."

"That you found it?" Seth asked.

"No. That you, my dear, didn't open it."

Seth laughed too heartily. Leonora threatened Abner playfully, wagging her finger.

Margaret stared at Benjamin in the chair. In the envelope was her father's money, his desperate investment.

She suddenly felt like chattel being bought as well as brought back to England.

99

They walked back up Cornhill, gawked at on all sides. Margaret stopped when an outfit caught her eye in a window: a baby's crimson brocade robe with white lace collar, decorated with intricate needlework.

"Buy it," insisted Seth.

"I don't know," she murmured. "I hate to take him out of his doeskins and cradleboard. He's so used to them."

"He's starting a new life."

"I'm sure he already realizes it. All he needs do is look around him. Let's go on."

They entered a ladieswear shop at the corner of Cornhill and Water Streets. The two clerks and four patrons regarded them with exaggerated uneasiness.

"As you may have already gathered," said Seth brusquely to the clerk, "this lady needs a dress. Price no object."

He fanned money across the counter and helped Margaret select a gown of rich silk trimmed with fancy gimp. The bodice was pointed front and back over a full-gathered skirt, cut low at the neck with a falling collar of lace. Under the short full upper sleeves were long white puffed undersleeves. Silken shoes tied with ribbon on the instep matched the lawn green color and texture of the gown. To complete her ensemble Margaret selected a hooded cloak and fur tippet.

In the dressing room she thought of Quebec and shopping with Jeanette Boulanger, the beautiful, life-size china doll married to Major Hertel Boulanger, Pierre's best friend.

Jeanette had turned out to be her true friend two days later, wisely advising her to follow her heart.

The Saturday before, they had made the rounds of Quebec's few shops. Jeanette steered her to Madame Tourette's Fashions of Paris, where she'd made a number of purchases, and when she paid for them Madame Tourette brought out her neatly folded buckskins, suggesting she leave them with her to be burned.

Margaret had asked her instead to wrap them and took them with her. Which turned out surprisingly prescient of her, as if her heart were well ahead of her convictions. Later, on the wharf where she'd gone with Jeanette to say good-bye to Two Eagles and his friends, she had an abrupt change of heart, realizing then and there that it was he she loved. And so she'd left with the Oneidas. Only moments before changing her mind she'd handed Two Eagles her buckskins to give to Eight Minks. But when she crossed the river with them, she'd sneaked into the woods to put her buckskins back on.

Exchanging civilization for the primitive. Changing back now. Again she would save her buckskins as she'd

done at Madame Tourette's—if only to be able to take
them out every so often to remind herself of the idyllic life
she'd had and lost.

When she emerged from the dressing room clerks and patrons alike looked so impressed she could feel her cheeks
glow. Seth had set Benjamin down on the counter; he ap-
plauded, further embarrassing her.

"Extraordinary! What a change! Magic! Sir, would you
mind disposing of these buckskins for us? Burn them, if
you don't mind."

"No," Margaret protested. "Please, just wrap them for
me."

The clerk looked at Seth, who shrugged.

Then, picking up Seth's money, the clerk moved off to
add up the charges. Seth's hand impulsively found Margaret's resting on the counter. She tensed slightly but did not
pull away, instead easing it out from under his, without
look or comment.

"It's all right," he said, "we've plenty of time."

"For what?"

"Nothing, not a thing. Would you mind if we go back
up Cornhill and cross over? I saw a men's clothing store.
After, we'll go find a rooming house, preferably down by
the water, so we can nip out and check on sailings."

Outside the store, as he carried her bundles, she paused
to look up the street. Suddenly she seemed miles distant,
but snapped back and looked in his eyes.

"I miss him so much," she whispered. "It hurts so."

═══ **100** ═══

As Two Eagles and his companions approached the western slope of Beacon Hill, the clock in the First Church finished tolling 5 P.M., the Oneidas were discussing Ataentsic, the woman who fell from the sky, whom Red Pain, Fox, Thrown Bear, Splitting Moon and Anger Maker assumed Margaret to be when they discovered her huddled in a hollow tree with her dead dog in her lap.

According to legend, Ataentsic, in heaven, out gathering medicine leaves for her sick husband, saw her dog fall through a hole and plunge toward the earth, which, at that time, was covered with water. Reaching to catch him, Ataentsic also fell. Down below, the beaver, the turtle and other animals saw her falling and met in council. The turtle called upon the other animals to dive, bring up mud and place it on his back to form a floating island, which became the earth on which Ataentsic landed.

Most Iroquois and most Oneidas—although not Two Eagles—accepted this explanation for the founding of the world.

Ataentsic ruled with her grandson Jouskeha over the world's destinies. He is the Sun, she is the Moon. He is good, she is evil. Together they live in a longhouse at the end of the world. When Margaret first arrived at Onneyuttahage, many of the people believed her to be Ataentsic's incarnation, an opinion she was in no hurry to disavow, perceiving it as defensive strength, badly needed, for one reason because the majority of the women of the tribe did not welcome her.

* * *

Now Red Paint appeared puzzled. "If Two Eagles is married to Ataentsic," he asked Splitting Moon, "why is she now returning to the sky?"

"She is not, she is crossing the O-jik'-ha-dä-gé-ga with the smiling black cloak," muttered Two Eagles.

"*Neh*, not so. She is returning to the sky. The black cloak with her came from there. Was he not always talking about his god and spirits in the sky? He is going back," Red Paint went on. "So is she."

Two Eagles scoffed. "If Margaret is Ataentsic, what does that make our son?"

Splitting Moon, who was still struggling with the notion that Margaret was not Ataentsic but Two Eagles' mortal wife, shook his head resolutely.

"A half-spirit," said Red Paint.

"There is no such thing," rasped Splitting Moon. "Sometimes you talk such *oeuda*."

Red Paint snorted. "What makes you so sure? There could be half-spirits up there." He pointed heavenward.

"Half-spirits," growled Splitting Moon. "Half-brained."

They started up the slope.

"Do you think when we get there we should split up to look for her?" asked Splitting Moon.

"That is a good idea," said Red Paint.

"A bad idea," murmured Two Eagles. "We would stick out like the Windigo on fire in the village of the Iron Axes. If we stay together maybe no one will provoke us."

"You think we will be attacked?" Red Paint asked, his hand straying to his tomahawk in his belt.

"Stay together is what I think. This Boston cannot be as big as Stadacona, Quebec. And maybe we will be lucky and find her right away. Just remember what I said before: Do not talk to anyone. Look over everyone's heads."

"If we do not talk to anyone," said Splitting Moon, "how do we ask about Mar-gar-et?"

"We do not," said Two Eagles. "Look at us: Oneida warriors asking about a whiteskin woman? Would any whiteskin tell us if they knew? *Neh*, they would think we want to find her to kill her or kidnap her. No one would believe she is my wife. No asking, no talking."

Reaching the summit of Beacon Hill, crossing the shadow of the beacon, they got their first glimpse of Boston down to the vessel-cluttered harbor.

"The houses are on top of each other," asserted Red Paint.

"You saw such houses in Stadacona," said Splitting Moon. "Sometimes two houses on top of one. This is bigger than I thought, though. And something else, Tékni-ska-je-a-nah, what if they have already gotten on a ship? Look, they are as many as flies on a dead *aque*."

"*You* look. Most of them are to fish from, not to cross the Wide Water. They have not left yet. I know it, I feel it!"

Two Eagles nevertheless hurried his step. "We will go up and down the streets. We will find her. We will not leave this place until we do."

"With that hair of hers like cornsilk, *nyoh*," said Red Paint, "we will find her."

"It looks to me like many whiteskin women have such hair," said Splitting Moon. "Maybe even more; so many are wearing hats."

"Never mind," said Two Eagles. "Hurry, we do not have much time before it gets dark. When it comes she is certain to go inside someplace and we will have to give up until morning. Hurry!"

⊏⊐ 101 ⊏⊐

Seth kept his distance from both the Colonial Missionary Society building on the corner of Marlborough and Summer Streets and Mrs. Tweed's rooming house on Short

Street, where he'd stayed earlier on the recommendation of
Reverend Albright. He found separate rooms for himself
and Margaret in a house on Ann Street overlooking the
harbor.

Before locating the rooming house, Seth visited the
men's shop on Cornhill Street and invested in a dark red
broadcloth knee-length coat trimmed with gold braid and
gold buttons. He also bought two cravats of fine linen with
lace ends, a three-cornered hat and two pairs of shoes with
small buckles rather high on the instep. It was the clerk
there who recommended Mrs. Whitcomb's rooming house
on Ann Street.

Mrs. Whitcomb turned out to be a stout, motherly sort.
She greeted them warmly, exuding friendliness, asking a
week's rent in advance, with the unused days' rent to be
refunded when they left.

After Margaret fed Benjamin, they went out for supper.
They were walking up Ann Street, about to enter Union,
when Seth suddenly turned sharp right toward a shop window, whipped off his hat and covered his face.

"What on earth?" Margaret gaped at him.

"Shhhh . . ."

Two men walked by, paying no attention to them, engrossed in what sounded like a mild difference of opinion.
Seth restored his hat; they went on.

"Reverends Albright and Frame," he explained. "I
would have introduced you, but—you understand."

They selected a small restaurant, Bixby's, on Cornhill.
Margaret sat at their table with her back to the window. The
waiter eyed Benjamin when he took their order, fetched a
chair for Margaret to set his cradleboard on, and glided off.

"I told you we ought to get him out of his Indian
things," hissed Seth.

"Seth, if it doesn't worry me, you shouldn't let it worry
you."

The restaurant had only a dozen tables, most of them
occupied. Both Margaret and Seth ordered the New England boiled dinner with fish chowder and lobster salad.

"Mind you don't make yourself ill now," warned Seth as the chowder arrived.

"I wasn't planning to wolf down my food."

"So, what's your impression of Boston?"

"It's Bristol," she said, "only not nearly as sooty. A bit rougher around the edges. And loud. And the streets are mud sloughs. Can you imagine if we'd walked all this distance down one of them? May I ask a question?"

He nodded.

"It's none of my business, but I can't help thinking about your three companions. Shouldn't Reverend Albright be told what happened to them? He and his friends must be sitting in their office on pins and needles waiting for word."

Seth looked uncomfortable. "I—don't think I should be the bearer of the bad news."

"Who them? Who else?"

"I'd have to tell them the truth about me; I see no way around that. I would honestly hate to do that."

"You could write them a letter," she said. "Have it hand-delivered the day we leave. Not explain anything about yourself, just say—say you've resigned and are going home. And tell them what happened to your three companions."

"Maybe I'll do that." But his tone said he had no intention of writing anyone.

He didn't. At the moment he was thinking the quicker he got down to the wharves the better his luck might turn out. One thing favored a quick departure: Boston was a busy port; ships docked and sailed daily, except on the Sabbath.

Margaret was attacking her lobster salad, savoring every morsel, when Seth started slightly. Two Eagles! Passing outside with Splitting Moon and Red Paint. No mistaking any of them!

"What is it?" she asked, looking up from her plate. She turned to the window just as they passed out of sight. "Did you see something?"

"Nothing. Something just occurred to me—" He tried not to stammer. "We've more shopping to do before we leave. First thing in the morning."

"We can wait until a few hours before we leave."

"I hate to rush your dinner, but we ought to get back as soon as possible. I'll need all the time I can get to make the rounds of the ships' captains."

"Will they be around at this hour?"

"It's not that late. I'm sure I'll find some." He seemed suddenly restless and uncomfortable.

"Are you all right?" she asked.

"Tip-top."

"You seem nervous."

"Not at all. Say, would you like another glass of port? I would. Waiter, waiter!"

102

By the time Seth and Margaret got back to the rooming house, it was growing dark and the town watch was making the rounds. "You go on up," he said. "I shan't be more than a couple of hours. I feel lucky. Stay in your room. This part of town especially isn't safe for a woman roaming about after dark."

"Benjamin'll protect me, won't you, darling?"

"Seriously, Margaret."

"I'll sit by the window and watch for you. I guess I should wish you good luck."

" 'Guess'?"

"I know it's right, the only thing I can do. But my heart's just not in it. What if he survived? And he's off somewhere hurt and can't get word to me?"

"I'm sorry, Margaret." Seth shook his head. "I know it's

hard for your heart to accept it, but isn't that to be expected? He's dead, it's over and you're going home."

"So why do I feel him inside me sharing my skin? I can't get him out of my system; I wouldn't dream of trying. If you don't see me in the upstairs window when you get back it'll mean I've gone to bed, not out."

A desperate feeling had begun gnawing at Two Eagles' stomach; he'd expected he would find Margaret soon after arriving in town. He was coming to hate Boston. It was too crowded, too loud, too many whiteskins, too many Indians trying to be white: wearing their clothes, assuming their gestures, their loudness. His optimism diminishing stirred him impatience. They were heading up Cornhill Street.

"We have covered this street too many times already," he muttered.

At dusk, Cornhill was even more crowded with pedestrians and wheeled traffic than during the day.

"We should stop now and start up again when the sun rises," suggested Splitting Moon.

"*Neh*, it is still early. I did not come all this way to let her get away because I was off sleeping somewhere."

"But you said yourself that when it gets dark they will go inside, especially with Benjamin."

"Just keep looking," Two Eagles growled.

They were approaching the end of the block, finding it even more congested than the rest of the street. A tight crowd blocked the way in front of the double door to Hurley's Galway Bay Tavern, across the street from Keaton's bookshop.

Hurley's window was imposing: Twelve feet by seven, imported from Pinna de la Vidriera in Spain at prodigious expense and lettered in gold Gothic with white highlighting HURLEY'S GALWAY BAY TAVERN. A magnificent window in the proud eye of proprietor Jeremiah Hurley; not glass but a single faceted jewel to dwarf the biggest diamond ever unearthed.

The Oneidas had to push through the crowd packing the front of the tavern; walking out into the street was impossible, so heavy was the cart and pedestrian traffic. The crowd parted a few inches to give them a path.

Men gawked at Two Eagles' six feet seven inches. Then a short, pudgy young man, redolent of liquor, wearing a coat of frieze under which was a woolen jerkin, on his head a wide-brimmed hat of coarse felt, deliberately stepped in front of Red Paint, blocking his way. Two paces ahead, Two Eagles turned to look back.

"Hey, boyo, what you got them red slashes on your face for?"

Red Paint grunted and tried to step around him, but again the Irishman blocked his way.

"Speak up, ya' red bastard!"

They were squarely in front of Hurley's. Onlookers began shouting encouragement to the pest. He shoved his hat back at a rakish angle and leered at Red Paint.

"Are you deef?"

Buttressed with confidence by the watching crowd, he shouted another insult, set his hands against Red Paint's chest and pushed hard. Red Paint maintained his balance, brushing by him, but the man followed, grabbing his shoulder.

"Where you going? I'm talking to you, ya' red scum!"

He tried to spin him around but wasn't strong enough. Bystanders laughed. Snarling, his hand shot under his jerkin, grabbing his pistol, firing it at Red Paint's back.

The explosion was deafening; blue smoke rose, the crowd—silenced or the moment—began roaring. Pandemonium broke out. Two Eagles and Splitting Moon watched dumfounded as Red Paint sank to the ground, the whites of his eyes rolling up. The crowd was stunned. Then a few men began laughing and pointing at Red Paint. Up came Two Eagles' hands, grabbing the murderer by the throat. He struggled to pull free, his red face turning purple. With a blood-curdling scream that froze everyone around him, Two Eagles released his hold, grabbed him by the crotch and by the front of his coat, lifted him high and sent him crashing through Hurley's window.

The crowd roared; whistles shrilled. Constables came running from all directions. Ignoring everyone, as Splitting Moon—astonished—stood stock-still watching him, Two Eagles climbed through the window to retrieve the offender. Chairs and tables went flying. It took seven patrons to subdue Two Eagles while Red Paint's murderer rolled about the floor, screaming.

Shortly, the law arrived. The two Oneidas were shackled and led away to the hooting and jeering of onlookers.

103

Seth returned to Mrs. Whitcomb's rooming house after a little over an hour. He could find only two captains, and neither was preparing to cross the Atlantic; both commanded coasters. He refused to be discouraged.

"Tomorrow bright and early I'll cover every single wharf. If I get word out, those interested will contact us. Do you think I ought to offer a bonus if we can get a ship, say, within the next thirty-six hours? I do. It'll be well worth it to get out of here."

Margaret sat on the bed while he stood in the doorway. As he spoke, she reflected on his character flaws; his reluctance to contact Reverend Allbright, though as she had reminded herself, that was none of her business; his sometimes insensitive observations. The night before he'd bluntly reminded her Two Eagles was dead. That hurt.

Still, overall, he'd conducted himself as a gentleman, except when touching her hand in the ladies' wear shop. And wasn't that more an impulsive show of affection than boldness?

"I want you to come with me when I make the rounds tomorrow," he said.

"You don't need me."

He frowned. "I wish you'd come, Margaret. We're together in this and I could use your moral support."

Could he? She was beginning to suspect that he did not want her out of his sight. He definitely didn't want her wandering about town on her own.

"Leonora and Abner were so gracious, Leonora especially, I really should stop in and say good-bye."

"There's no need. They don't expect you."

"I want to."

He shrugged. "Then why not wait for me? When I get done we can go together. I don't like you roaming the streets by yourself."

"No even in broad daylight? There's no crime here, these people are much too religious."

"Aren't you being a trifle naive? A beautiful woman like yourself, vulnerable . . ."

Suddenly he was striking her as overbearing. She forced a smile. "I took good care of myself before and during my time with the Oneidas. I took good care of you on the way here."

"You did."

"Trust me. And good luck tomorrow. Good night." She turned away. He closed the door.

104

The Boston constables were not uniformed professional policemen but private citizens elected annually, entrusted with other duties besides bringing in lawbreakers. They found it impossible to get Two Eagles and Splitting

Moon from Cornhill Street to the jail without knocking them unconscious.

Thrust bodily into the cell, Two Eagles went wild, smashing his shoulder against the door, shouting threats. Splitting Moon dropped into a corner. He sat looking up at him.

"What good will that do?"

"Guard!"

The single constable on duty came to the slot in the door and peered in. After one fearful look, he backed off, standing clear of the slot a good three feet.

"What have you done with O-kwen-cha's body?" Two Eagles demanded.

"Who?"

"Red Paint. Our friend that drunken *oueda* murdered!"

"Wouldja' mind lowering your voice? Calm yourself; you've no cause to worry about your friend. He'll be getting himself a Christian burial."

Splitting Moon jumped up. "He is no Christian! He must be buried like all Iroquois, in our territory."

"You two are Iroquois? I never seed an Iroquois. What in thunderation are ya' doing here?"

"We want his body," snapped Two Eagles. "Bring it to us."

"Ya' speak good English."

"Now!"

"I can't do that, it's outta my hands. Sorry." He closed the slot cover. Two Eagles flew at it, hammering it.

"That is iron," said Splitting Moon, "You will break your hand."

"We must get out. Margaret will be leaving. This is wrong, I will kill them all! Help me with this door!" He threw his shoulder against it, rattling it on its hinges.

The slot slid open. "Quiet down, they can hear ya' clear up the block."

"Open this door!" yelled Two Eagles.

"Not a chance, so ya' might as well simmer down. Oh, ya' might be interested in hearing that fella ya' throwed through Hurley's window was Hurley's kid brother, Seamus. Ya' give him concussion of the head and busted his kneecap. You've bought yourself a peck o' trouble, Mr. Iroquois. Now shut up!"

He whipped the cover closed.

Abner Keaton opened the book shop, turning around the CLOSED sign. Leonora came through the curtain, looking exhausted and deeply troubled.

"That fracas last night still gnawing at you, dear?"

"It grates me to the bone! It's so flagrantly unfair. Those three Indians were just walking along minding their own business. That loudmouth pipsqueak Seamus Hurley started the whole thing. He is the biggest troublemaker in town. Everytime there's a to-do at Hurley's he's at the bottom of it.

"Tell me again, what actually did you see?"

"Enough. Rachel and Leah Tuttle were here looking at that Morocco collection of Virgil's works again. They saw what I saw: three Indians trying to get through the crowd, Seamus Hurley taunting one, provoking him, and when he refused to be provoked, shooting the poor creature in the back, the contemptible coward!"

"You saw Hurley provoke him?"

"All three of us did. When he shot the Indian, everybody fell back, and there Hurley stood, the gun smoking in his hand and a grin on him to make your blood boil. Then one of the dead man's friends picked up Seamus and threw him through the window. The three of us cheered to the rafters."

"That window cost a fortune. Jeremiah Hurley must be beside himself."

"He can blame Seamus. Anyway, the constables showed up and took away both Indians, leaving the third one's body lying there, nobody paying the least attention to it. I've never seen such goings-on, and we call ourselves Christians!"

"The body's not there now."

"Of course it's not. It's an absolute outrage. Those two'll hang and Seamus Hurley'll get off with a tap on the wrist!"

"You surprise me, dear. I've never known you to be such an ardent defender of the underdog."

"Make light of it if you please, Abner Keaton!" She started for the door.

"Where are you going?"

"Where do you think? To the jail. Somebody has to be told what really happened; as long as there's a breath in my body those two Indians will never see a rope!"

"Lee, Lee, please don't get involved."

"Very good, Abner, admirable. Those two are lucky *you* weren't the one watching!"

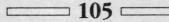

105

Seth dropped in on Margaret before leaving to look for a ship; she had awakened moments before and was sitting up, feeding Benjamin.

"Wish me luck," he said.

"I—wish I could."

"What is it now, Margaret?"

"Two Eagles is here."

"Is he really? Where did you see him, walking down Cornhill Street in a dream?"

"It happened just now. I woke up abruptly, which I never do. I sat up and said it out loud. 'He's alive, he's here.' "

"A dream—"

"It wasn't a dream, I tell you. What if it's so? What if he really is here trying to find us? What am I saying? He is, he is!"

"He's dead, Margaret. For your peace of mind, your sanity, isn't it time you accepted it? In here and here?" He tapped his head and his heart.

"He's here. I feel it, I just know it. It came to me like— like a voice whispering in my ear. It's what woke me. I never wake up like that, suddenly, sitting bolt upright."

"He's dead and buried somewhere up by the St. Lawrence. You've said it in those very words dozens of times, and believed it. Because it's true. Red Paint saw—"

"Does he know what he saw? Have you ever heard a recounting of anything so confusing? And he admitted he had no idea what happened in the few minutes before he circled back. They could have fled right after he did."

"I must go. Will you be all right?"

"Why shouldn't I be?"

"I'm sure this won't take long; the bay's crammed with ships that have come in. Wait for me. We can go together to see Abner and Leonora."

"I can't wait, Seth. I can't sit here talking to the walls. And you could be hours and hours."

"All right, all right!"

He closed the door. He was upset. She'd never seen him so before.

Leonora bustled up to the jail street door, still seething. The constable on duty the night before had been relieved by the late-hour man, who in turn gave over his duties to the day constable, who looked to be in his seventies. Herbert Lansdowne was a handsome, silver-haired, portly man with a magisterial air. He greeted her warmly and ushered her into his cubbyhole office, offering her a stool while he stood leaning against the desk.

"And what can we do for you this lovely morning, Mrs. Keaton?"

"Release the prisoners. They're as guiltless as warm eggs. I saw the whole sorry business. So did Rachel and Leah Tuttle. They were in the shop looking over the Morocco edition of Virgil's works again. I can give you their address."

She recounted in detail exactly what she'd seen. He listened, his lips sealed and curving downward, his dark eyes slowly developing a gleam.

"Interesting," he murmured.

"It's the unvarnished truth!"

"I'm sure, I'm sure, Mrs. Keaton. I'm grateful you've come forward, that you've recognized your responsibility as a citizen."

"Will you let them out or won't you?"

"Please understand, I'm not empowered to just open the door. I haven't the authority."

"Who does?"

"That would be Chief Magistrate Macomber. Do you know him?"

"I know his wife; she's in the shop every week. She's very fond of Congreve's works."

"There you are, you see? You can get to him through her."

"What do I need with her? Let's go see *him*, now. Come along."

"I can't leave here until my relief comes on; that won't be until four this afternoon."

"This is beginning to get under my skin. I'll be back. You be ready to march! I want those two out of this pesthole before sundown. Four sharp, be ready."

Mrs. Whitcomb offered to take care of Benjamin. Margaret made her way up and down the tapered and crooked streets to Cornhill Street and the book shop. Two customers were browsing. Abner stood in the far corner poring over figures in a cumbersome ledger; Leonora was dusting books, casting an occasional eye at one customer, then the other.

"Margaret!" she burst.

"I wanted to thank you for your gracious hospitality and say good-bye. Seth's out now arranging our passage."

"So soon? We've scarcely gotten to know each other. Come on back. Do you have a few minutes?"

"Of course."

"Where's that handsome little prince of yours?"

Margaret told her how Mrs. Whitcomb was caring for Benjamin. As the water simmered in the kettle, they sat at the table for tea.

"Out of the wilderness back to civilization, is it? A drastic change."

"It will be."

Leonora eyes her as she poured from the pot. "I envy you. I'd love to go back home. Just a visit, of course, but that's out of the question right now."

"I noticed the window's broken across the street," Margaret observed.

"Last night. I saw the whole thing like a play on the stage. Three sav—Indians were trying to make their way through the crowd in front; Narragansetts, I think they were. I'm not sure, they all look alike to me." She described the incident. "Then one picked up little Hurley and threw him through the window. What a sight! We don't get such excitement around here.

"First thing this morning I went over to the jail, told the constable what I saw, how Hurley caused it all. I demanded he release the Indians. But they won't get out until at least four this afternoon. I just felt so sorry for them, Margaret, the way you'd feel for anyone suffering such an injustice. It was so grossly unfair. The bullies in this town love to pick on Indians."

"One would think the Indians would give Boston a wide berth."

"Oh, but they can get their liquor here and pick up the odd penny and squander it on trinkets."

Margaret set down her empty cup, looking regretful. "I'd love to stay longer, but I'd better get back. Seth may get lucky. We could leave as early as tonight."

"Forgive me, my dear, but you don't look exactly wild with anticipation."

"I only wish I could be. I've got a rein on my feelings. Deep down I've this nagging suspicion I could be making the mistake of my life, that Two Eagles is alive and here in Boston."

"I can understand that, because it's what you want to believe with all your heart."

"I do. I hadn't thought of that, or maybe I've been deliberately avoiding it."

"And yet it was weeks and weeks and he never came back, never sent word. And his friend said he saw—"

"All that's true, I know, and I'm being stupid, obstinate, but this remnant of doubt refuses to let me go."

"It will, it will, once you're on your way. Home and your loved ones will pull you across. But getting back to last night, *you* should have seen those poor Indians, so out of place, so bewildered."

"They're lucky they've got you for their champion."

"I wouldn't be able to sleep a wink tonight if I didn't speak up. I know—I didn't sleep last night. If all goes as it should, Macomber will free them and order them out of town for their own safety. Maybe they weren't Narragansetts, maybe they were Wampanoags or Niantics—"

They said their good-byes and Margaret was on her way out. By now the two customers had left, and Abner was still poring over his books. He waved good-bye, and she stood outside for a moment, looking about. A dray was passing, piled too high with crates. One jiggled loose, fell off and had to be retrieved. Across the street two men were removing the glass shards from Hurley's window. A third man wearing an apron stood watching them, his back to her, hands on hips, bald head gleaming in the sunlight. She started to cross the street. He turned, weeping. Margaret did not realize that he was Hurley, mourning the loss of his magnificent window.

Leonora called out behind her. Margaret, reaching the opposite side, paused to let her catch up.

"It just occurred to me," murmured Leonora. "Why should I twiddle my thumbs till four waiting for Herbert

Lansdowne? What do I need with him? I'll go straight
over to Macomber, tell him what happened, get him to free
them right away. March him over to the jail, unlock the
door himself. This should be fun. Do you want to come
along?"

"I'd better get back, Leonora. It's the first time I've
ever left Benjamin with a stranger. He may give Mrs.
Whitcomb a hard time."

"Yes, good luck to you both. And Benjamin." She
hugged her again. "Good luck to me. I'm off on my good
deed for the day!"

106

Two Eagles, calmer and quieter but still simmering, refused the stew the constable brought for their dinner.

Splitting Moon emptied both bowls. "It is not bad, you
should try some."

"I will not eat their food. I will take nothing from
them." Two Eagles glared and made fists. "She is leaving
Boston, I feel it. It is a tingling in my bones." He moved
to the little barred rear window, which revealed the back
alley. "We have to get out of here!"

"Not through there, it is too small."

Two Eagles stiffened, shot across the cell, slamming his
shoulder against the door.

"Keep it up," muttered Splitting Moon. "Until you
break your shoulder."

Two Eagles leaned against the door with his forearm,
his forehead against it, hammering the door gently, his
mind whirling. "I had a feeling when we reached the top
of that hill and looked down that this place would be bad
for us, dangerous. Somehow we must get out, find Marga-

ret and get O-kwen-cha's body. What do you think they have done with him?"

"I think I know. Remember the red days? The English buried their dead in boxes like those new muskets come in. They will put him in such a box and bury him."

"Where?"

"They have their burial grounds the same as we. We passed one beside one of those big houses with a bell on top. Maybe in that very one."

Two Eagles looked full circle around him. "I hate this room. Every hour that goes by it shrinks a little. Soon I will have to bow my head to stand up. I am slowly suffocating."

"Stand near the window."

Two Eagles ignored him. Again he leaned against the door with his forearm and slowly, softly pounded it, his frustration mounting, compressing like the steam and gases in a volcano.

Dorcas Macomber, a fluttery, martyred and melodramatic woman, was on her way out when Leonora approached her front door on Beacon Street. Holding her wrist, Leonora poured out her story.

"Dear me," Mrs. Macomber murmured. "That is serious. But I'm afraid Otis isn't here. He had business in Roxbury today. He took the morning coach over bright and early."

"When will he be back?"

"He said around sundown. Is that a problem?"

"It is for the savages. Dorcas, tell him exactly what I've told you, word for word."

"Oh, I'll remember. I'm very good at memorizing. It's my dramatic talent, you know.

"Mmmmm. I'll be back at sundown."

"I'm dreadfully sorry, Leonora."

"So am I."

* * *

Having parted with Leonora, Margaret walked up Cornhill and a little way down King Street looking in shop windows before crossing over, returning to Cornhill and starting for the rooming house. She knew she needed to buy a few more clothes and saw a number of things she liked but didn't have a farthing on her. When Seth got back and their passage was all arranged, the two of them would have to whirlwind shop.

At the rooming house she collected Benjamin and sat with him in the upstairs front window. A nearby church bell was tolling twelve when she spied Seth coming up Ann Street. The spring in his step and his smile attested to his success.

He saw her and waved and did a little jig, tripping over his feet slightly. She came downstairs and met him at the door.

"Success! Success! The *Resolute*, a fine three-master, practically new out of the blocks. Brace yourself: luxury of luxuries, we'll have our very own cabin. With a screen to give us privacy. Not as big as your room upstairs, but better than being buried in the hold like two casks of Xeres sherry, wouldn't you say?"

"You're getting all red, calm down."

"I can't. What heaven-sent luck! The captain's name is Hosea Ready. We sail at seven in the morning tomorrow; destination, Liverpool. Barely thirty leagues from Bedworth by coach. Estimated time of crossing forty-six days!"

"You paid him?"

"I did." He showed a receipt.

"Gave him a bonus?"

"A paltry five guineas." Seth grinned broadly. "Hungry? Let's celebrate by stuffing ourselves. I'm starving."

"We should shop for clothes."

"Absolutely. Let's try King and Shop Streets for a change. I'm told there are some decent men's shops in both." He offered her his arm.

"Seven o'clock tomorrow," she murmured wistfully.

"We should be there at least an hour before. Will there be other passengers?"

"There are two other cabins. I assume they're booked; I didn't ask."

"Seven A.M., nineteen hours from now . . ."

"Don't look so, Margaret. Cheer up, you're going home. Isn't that a marvelous word, *home*? Forty-six days—add one and a half for the southbound coach—and home you'll be, safe and sound. Going home, going home!"

"As you keep saying. So why is it I feel like I'm *leaving* home?"

107

Shadows spilled into the alley. Night was coming on; Two Eagles had reached his limit. Splitting Moon had never seen him so angry, purple and raging, pounding about the little cell. The constable who had taken over for Lansdowne wisely kept his distance from the door. Splitting Moon sat with knees drawn up, his head between his hands.

"Let us out!" Two Eagles roared.

"Shhhh," murmured his friend, "you are giving me an aching head. No one is listening. The next time they come will be when they take us out to hang us."

The slot cover slid across, eyes peered in. They heard a key thrust into the lock, the door slowly opened. Two Eagles, standing by the barred window, threw himself toward it. Another man, bulky and powerful, gun in hand, stopped Two Eagles and held him back. On his feet, Splitting Moon helped, fearful that Two Eagles might strangle the constable who timidly followed the armed man.

A third man—tall, saturnine and middle aged—came in

behind the constable. He seemed unaffected by the sudden tension.

"Calm down," he commanded. "I'm here to help you. Do either of you speak English?"

"Yes," snapped Splitting Moon.

"I am Chief Magistrate Macomber. I've been told by a witness I consider reliable that neither of you was responsible for the disturbance at Hurley's last night. Therefore, I'm going to release you."

"Ahhhh!" sang Splitting Moon. Both started for the door. The constable, who had restored his weapon to his belt, blocked their way, his hand going to the grip of his gun.

"Wait," said Macomber. "You realize there's damage involved. Jeremiah Hurley's window was imported and cost him nearly four hundred guineas. And you broke it. Still, I've decided his brother, not either of you, is responsible for all of this. But I suggest that you two, for your own well being, had best turn around and go back where you came from."

"We will, we will!" burst Splitting Moon.

Two Eagles frowned. "We want our friend's body," he said. "We are Oneida. He must be buried in ground in our territory. If he is not his spirit will be barred from entering the Village of the Dead."

The chief magistrate ran a hand over his mouth and assumed a thoughtful expression, with a suggestion of sympathy.

"I'm sorry. I checked on him, and I'm afraid you're too late. In situations like this, where the deceased is without family or indigent—poor, unable to afford a proper funeral—the body is wrapped, taken out near Bird Island and dropped into the sea. I'm sorry."

Splitting Moon threw a quick look at Two Eagles, who once more appeared on the verge of losing his temper. "Where is this Bird Island?"

"Out in the bay near Nix's Mate Island, where they used

to hang pirates. But see here, you're not thinking of going out there to look for the body? I can't permit that."

"The sea has him," said Splitting Moon to Two Eagles. "If we searched or a hundred moons we could not find him."

So intently was Two Eagles starting at the chief magistrate, Macomber was becoming nervous.

"Very well," he said, "you may go."

"Where are our weapons?" Two Eagles demanded.

"I—think it better for you if they remain with us."

"Give us our weapons," he rasped. "Now. We are free, we have a right to them."

"Let me explain—"

"It is all right," said Splitting Moon nervously. "Come along." Gripping his friend's arm, he steered him through the door.

Outside, they stopped to survey the traffic that had been building since sundown.

"Why did you do that?" snarled Two Eagles, "telling him they could keep our knives and tomahawks?"

"They are not worth starting a fight over. We are out of there. That is all that is important. We can get knives. Where do you want to start looking for Mar-gar-et?"

"They had no right to bury O-kwen-cha in the sea; why do the English always do as they please without asking anyone? I hate the English. Hate them!"

"Shhhh, not here," Splitting Moon cautioned. "Let us go."

"We will search down by the water."

"Splitting Moon's brow crinkled. "But—"

"It is from there she will leave, neh? We will go from ship to ship, to the ones that look like they will be leaving, where the wharves in front of them are empty or have few boxes. We will ask whoever we can find."

"There are so many ships—"

"Only a few leave at any one time."

"But will anyone be around to ask at this hour? And it is such a big area to cover."

"There you go again, throwing fireweed into the stew!"
Two Eagles snorted. "Are you coming or not? Don't! Who
needs you? I can search for her by myself."

"And what will I do, wait for you here? Go, I am coming."

108

Around midnight, clouds like black sheep came rolling
in over the bay. Margaret woke up at five, at the tolling
of the church bells. She dozed for a few minutes and got
up to face her last day in North America, her last day
within reach of Onneyuttahage and the longhouse and their
chamber, her final day as an Oneida. Oddly enough, she
felt more like a member of the tribe at that moment than
she could ever recall feeling before. She chuckled mirth-
lessly; how long would it take her to become once again
completely English? She felt no desire to drop her tribal
identity. Even wearing civilized clothing did not make her
feel less Oneida.

She looked down at Benjamin in the cradle Seth had insisted on buying him. Benjamin would be abandoning his
people as well. Yet Seth and Leonora were not wrong.
What was the point in clinging to Two Eagles's ghost?
Why deliberately court misery? Why give it room in one's
heart?

"It's over, go home."

Mrs. Whitcomb fixed them breakfast of tea and johnny-
cake and refunded Seth's money for the unspent days
under her roof. Day was struggling to dawn when they set
out for Clark's Wharf and the *Resolute*, her holds
crammed with dry Dunfish cod, salt mackerel and lumber
transshipped from Maine.

It had been raining fairly heavily since shortly after midnight; the wharves gleamed. Margaret gazed out over the rumpled black water. Beyond the indistinct horizon lay Liverpool. In less than seven weeks they would land and take the stagecoach down to bedworth in Warwickshire. Home. And the past would be swept away into nostalgia, to be brought back in daydreams.

But she knew that every time she looked at Benjamin visions of Two Eagles would rise in her mind, evoking memories of their times together, their love, and the life that was no more.

She felt Seth staring at her but did not acknowledge it. He knew what she was thinking. Discussing it would only invite a resurgence of the pain.

The workers were almost done loading by the time they reached the gangplank and prepared to start up it. It was raining very heavily now, pocking the sea, leveling it.

Captain Ready, his sou'wester hat his only protection against the downpour, waved greeting as they started to board. She preceded Seth, who carried most of their belongings. Halfway up to the deck she paused for a look back. The gangplank did not provide nearly as lofty a vista of Boston as she'd enjoyed from the summit of Beacon Hill. Now, what she saw looked dreary, unwashed by the rain, a haven of commerce, Christianity and almost no beauty.

The sky was brightening. Gulls shrieked and wheeled above the ship. The feeble light from its lanterns gave it a special look and for a moment she imagined that it wasn't sailing for Liverpool but for some uncharted netherworld where a life as empty as a pauper's purse awaited her.

"Let's get to our cabin and out of these wet things," Seth urged. Seth introduced her to Captain Hosea Ready. His eyes were friendly above his scraggly beard. He tickled Benjamin under the chin with a stumpy finger.

"Are we the only passengers?" she asked.

"No, mum. There be another young couple in Cabin B

and a professor of butterflies and such in C. You've the most spacious accommodations."

Out over the water the sun was threatening to break through and ruin a perfectly good cheerless day. She glanced overhead; the mainmast was a paladin's lance challenging the sky. Much of the canvas was already in place and flapping slightly, the sound like the clapping of hands. Ratlines and spars gleamed in the beginning sunshine. Again she looked shoreward; Boston seemed to whisper, "Go, go."

A cheap, worn chinoiserie screen divided the cabin in equal halves. When she and Seth had dried off and changed their clothes she chanced a look outside. The sun was shining gloriously, drying the vessel, the wharves and Boston. The town's departure from sight would take with it her last chance of ever seeing him again. Was there even a last chance? Why even hope?

She hadn't liked or disliked Boston, had formed no opinion. It was the stone you stepped on crossing a brook.

A whistle shrilled, a horn blasted, men scurried nimbly aloft to release the remaining sails. They would be leaving shortly.

109

Two Eagles and Splitting Moon had searched the port of Boston from Hill's Wharf to Baker's Wharf, where the dockage gave way to shipyards. Few men stayed there after nightfall; most had already filtered into town. Wharf after wharf was stacked with boxes, crates, and casks, and making their way across the waterfront, although they passed ships large enough to cross the Atlantic, with no one about they could not tell which were loading, which unloading.

Seeing no ships anchored beyond Baker's Wharf they retraced their steps. Splitting Moon found a discarded piece of canvas. They stretched it over pilings and took refuge from the rain. Hours later, the crashing of thunder awoke them. They sat watching as lightning stabbed the horizon and turned the waters of the bay an eerie green before the thunder renewed its assault.

Discouragement sat heavily on Two Eagles' heart as they waited for daylight. Gradually, yawning, bleary-eyed men came straggling back from town and went to work. As the Oneidas walked by, the workers stopped to gawk. Splitting Moon pointed out a captain standing at the railing of his ship shouting orders, and Two Eagles got his attention.

"Have you seen a man and woman who are sailing across the Wide Water? She is tall, beautiful, her hair is the color of the sun, she has a baby with her—"

"Get outta here, Injun, before you start trouble. Go back into town and do your begging."

"We are not beggars," shouted Splitting Moon.

The captain eased the flap of his jacket to one side and set his hand on the grip of a pistol. "Git!"

They went on past Clark's Shipyard and Scarlett's Wharf. Ahead, halfway along Clark's Wharf, which jutted well out into the bay, a nearly fully-rigged bark was docked. Her bowsprit pointed seaward so that the ship itself blocked sight of any activity on the wharf. Two Eagles caught Splitting Moon's arm.

"Come!" He broke into a run.

"What is it?"

"Run!"

Onboard the *Resolute* deckhands had removed the gang-plank and were loosing the fore and aft lines from their cleats. Seth stood at the railing with Captain Ready and the other passengers. Margaret stood holding Benjamin in the shadow of the fo'c'sle. She stared into space, thoroughly, utterly depressed by her helplessness, her irrevocable decision to leave.

Far up the wharf where it met the mainland two figures running toward them caught her eye. Now the *Resolute* was drifting away from the pilings. Her sails bellied, tautened; Captain Ready, having taken the wheel, was shouting orders to the men aloft. On the offshore breeze wafting toward Margaret came a faint voice.

Her name! She ran to the railing, shading her eyes, squinting, gasping, crying out. Clutching Benjamin tightly, she climbed onto the railing. The passengers stared. Seth started for her. She sat teetering with her feet over the side, looking down into the murky water. And jumped.

The water hammered the soles of her feet as down she plunged. Kicking vigorously, joy giving her strength, she came up gasping, holding Benjamin high. Above them, Two Eagles came running up. She screamed joyfully. He dove, surfacing beside her, got his arm around her; she held Benjamin up. Kicking and stroking with his free arm, Two Eagles moved them to the barnacle-studded pilings just below the kneeling Splitting Moon. He took Benjamin in his arms and helped Margaret up. Two Eagles followed.

They turned to look at the departing *Resolute* now under full sail. The passengers, shocked, stood motionless. Seth stood where she'd last seen him, frozen to the railing.

Up came his arm slowly. She waved back. Two Eagles spun her about and embraced her. They stood sopping wet. Neither spoke. They could only stare at each other. Then with her fingers she began exploring his face. He stroked her hair. Still not a word was said. Splitting Moon, given Benjamin to hold, stood watching them, utterly rapt. Two Eagles held her face between his huge hands and kissed her. The *Resolute* headed into the sun, a lone figure still at the railing.

She kissed Two Eagles' eyes. "Take us home."

For oh! so wildly do I love him
That paradise itself were dim
And joyless, if not shared with him.

—Thomas Moore

AUTHOR'S NOTE

The spelling of virtually all Iroquoian words is open to dispute. Few scholarly sources agree on the spelling of place names in particular.

This is the case because tribal languages were exclusively oral and only written when transcribed by white men.

This story is a work of fiction based on the history of northeastern American before and during the turn of the eighteenth century. In point of actual fact it was not, for example, until 1704 that the first Protestant mission was established to counteract the influence of the Jesuits. Thoroughgood Moore was the first Anglican missionary to the Iroquois, sent by the Society for the Propagation of the Gospel.

I am deeply indebted to my husband, Alan, without whose superb research this book would not have been possible.

—Barbara Riefe
Stamford, Connecticut

**COMING SOON FROM
BARBARA RIEFE**

Her new novel

Mohawk Woman

in January 1996

0-312-85704-7
$23.95/$34.95 Canada

THE BEST OF TOR/FORGE HISTORICALS

☐ 50747-9 *PEOPLE OF THE LAKES* $6.99
           Kathleen O'Neal & W. Michael Gear $7.99 Canada

☐ 53536-7 *FIRE ALONG THE SKY* $5.99
           Robert Moss $6.99 Canada

☐ 52377-6 *THE WOMAN WHO FELL FROM THE SKY* $5.99
           Barbara Riefe $6.99 Canada

☐ 52293-1 *DEATH COMES AS EPIPHANY* $4.99
           Sharan Newman $5.99 Canada

☐ 53013-6 *NOT OF WAR ONLY* $5.99
           Norman Zollinger $6.99 Canada

Call toll-free 1-800-288-2131 to use your major credit card, buy them at your local bookstore, or
clip and mail this page to order by mail.

Publishers Book and Audio Mailing Service
P.O. Box 120159, Staten Island, NY 10312-0004

Please send me the book(s) I have checked above. I am enclosing $ _____
(Please add $1.50 for the first book, and $.50 for each additional book to cover postage and
handling. Send check or money order only—no CODs.)

Name_____

Address _____

City _____ State / Zip_____

Please allow six weeks for delivery. Prices subject to change without notice.